The characters and events portrayed in this book are fictitious. Any similarity to real persons, living or dead, is coincidental and not intended by the author.
The author acknowledges the trademark status and trademark owners of various products referenced in this work. The publication/use of these trademarks is not associated with or sponsored by the trademark owners.

ISBN-9798322122487

Cover design by: Gregory Armstrong
Contributing Cover image likeness by: Rebecca Armstrong
Printed in the United States of America

ACKNOWLEDGMENTS

This book would not be possible without the people closest to me, the ones who stuck by me, who believed in my potential and, in many ways, encouraged me to find a way of bringing the ideas ever-present in my head out and onto the page.

First and foremost, I want to thank Diane, my wife of over twenty years. Despite my many failures and flaws along the way, she continues to make me a better person. I could not have finished this book without her understanding, friendship, companionship and love. Thank you.

Thank you to my mother who, over the years, never let me forget there was a writer inside of me who was capable of finishing what I started so long ago.

Thank you to my father, gone but never forgotten, who instilled a work ethic that kept me stubbornly trying time after time, no matter what.

Thank you to my daughters, who now and then brought up the subject of my writing and questioned me about my progress and when this book was going to be done. I see the creative and artistic talents in you both, and it makes me want to prove you can accomplish anything you set your minds to.

To the author, Wally Lamb. I thank you for welcoming me into your writing center in high school. Allowing me to share my work and gather valuable feedback at an impressionable time in my life meant so much.

To other friends and family who played a role in my writing inspirations and efforts: Katie McComiskey, a kindhearted classmate growing up and one of my beta readers for this project. To Donna Barriga, former coworker, friend, and other beta reader. Thank you both for your willingness to participate and for your valuable input. To John Bickel and Mark Koch, your friendship and welcoming me as a visitor to Block Island, into your home all those years ago was instrumental in the inspirational setting location for this book. Your insight into the island, its people and how they live helped bring this story to life, and is immensely appreciated.

To my editor, Danielle Lange. As someone with a passion for writing, and as subjects go, spelling was once a better-than-average, stronger suit of mine back in the day, and grammar was never a contender. Thank you for putting up with and working through all of the many mistakes this manuscript provided. Thank you for your patience with all of my emails, questions, and concerns about the writing, editing, and publishing process, and for your contributions to making this book the best it can be.

AUTHOR'S NOTE

This book is the culmination of a dream I have held on to since I was a child. While the desire and passion were always there, the confidence and required ability did not come so easy. Experiences from my life, including the lack thereof, and those people who left an impression helped me become the writer I am today. As a teenager, I had an idea for a story that I can't completely recall today. Over the years and decades—through getting married, starting and raising a family, the many jobs I've held—the urge to write never faded. The inspiration for stories materialized and played like movies in the back of my mind always, and that initial idea morphed and changed, becoming *Mad Season*. I also found a lifelong love of music as a teenager, one that spans most genres and encompasses countless bands and artists. Songs became an important inspirational aspect of my fictional writing imagination. Without the love of music, good movies, and an unrelenting dream, this book would not be possible.

DEDICATION

I found a deep interest and excitement in genealogy in the interim of finishing this book. An appreciation of where I came from and the lives and stories of my ancestors gave me a way to implement that characteristic into my writing. Coming up with character names is not a part of this process that I particularly excel at or overly enjoy. Shuffling through the thousands of first and last names in my family tree has given me a resource for this need as well as a way to honor and pay tribute to loved ones we have lost and those we never got to know.

To my family, this book is filled with familiar names and dedicated in memory of all, most notably, relatives we lost, some tragically and some way too soon– Walter McKinley Armstrong, Nellie Ellen Armstrong, Cody Seymour & Frank Halstead; among many more.

Mad Season

by

Gregory Armstrong

Prologue

"Elly! Elly, come here, before Daddy and I have to go!"

I hated that nickname, but my mother adored it. To me, it brought images of a circus elephant to mind I. My name is Elles, pronounced like the island—Elles Grace Garity.

"Grr, this stupid button!" I growled, whisking into the living room, trying to finish getting dressed.

"Here, let me see it," Mom said, squatting down in front of me.

"Hurry! I'm gonna be late, and I don't want to run!" I huffed as she fixed the top of my very purposely worn, least favorite button-down shirt.

"Well, give me a . . . Honestly, why do you love wearing something that irritates you so much?"

"I don't love this ugly thing!" I shot back. Her hands dropped as she made a puzzled face. "Thomas hates it."

She sighed, rubbing her forehead with both hands—her way of frowning, almost amusingly, at the mind-numbing things I did. "You know very well his name isn't Thomas. It's—"

"I know it's not. He hates that, too. That's the point. He always complains about the colors and pattern on this shirt hurting his eyes and making his head split. That's the only reason why I love *wearing* this butt-ugly shirt. Now, forget the stupid button. I gotta go, or I'll have to run to school!"

—

"Grace . . ."

—

My mother rested her elbow on her bended knee, dropped her head in her hand, and mumbled through a grin she tried to hide. This was her habit as she never quite understood my foolishness—and that included the social goings-on of the one sparsely populated school in town. I guess she figured her best bet was to laugh it all off unless she suspected more sinister behavior than the average "kids being kids."

"Now listen to me," she said, neatening my attire. "Daddy and I will be leaving soon. You have a—"

"While you're gone, are you gonna see about the—"

"You have a good day at school. Don't cause too much trouble, and try not to give Thoma—Tom any seizures, please. We should be back on the afternoon ferry. Don't forget to pack your lunch, and lock up when you leave."

"Okay, but—"

"Love you!"

She was out the door before I could further plead my case. My best friend, Ginny, and I had been scheming for a weekend trip, and since negotiating with our parents hadn't worked, we resorted to plain old-fashioned, outright begging. Our parents were taking the torturous approach of *maybe one day.* We agreed it was time to retaliate with a full-blown, annoy-them-until-they-cave assault.

—

"Grace . . ."

—

That is the day that has been forever burned into my memory. That is where I keep it, covered with a black veil of heartbreak and buried beneath the heaping baggage of feelings I've refused to unpack for all these years.

—

"Grace . . . ?"

—

My life was never bad, none of it, until . . . Hey, I was perfectly happy and content to live my life as it was, no major changes other than growing up and being there, in that place, surrounded by that small community of people who genuinely cared about everyone else. I won't say I had it all. I had enough. I had all I needed which, as I look back now, was better than having it all, despite any of the faults that came with calling a secluded location home. Pardon me for babbling like that energetic fireball of a child I was then, but none of us—

especially me—deserved that day.

—

"Grace—"

"Huh?"

—

I mean, one minute the talk of the town was which one of the locals was spotted flipping off tourists with our five-fingered bird bouquet upon arrivals and departures. I don't know who came up with that little coded gesture, but it was cleverly disguised in the form of a friendly fed-up-with-outsiders, "eff-you" wave. Us kids weren't oblivious. We knew what it meant. Don't blame me for corrupting young minds. I just lived there. Residents in the vicinity of the ferry landing would cast a sly hello or goodbye with that time-honored salute.

Where was I? Oh, yeah. The next minute was a horrible mix of chaotic, gut-wrenching terror of which I was suddenly the centerpiece of attention-swarming concern. Fast forward and I'm doing fine—just fine, all this time. I moved on and separated myself from that day. I pushed it all away faster than they could negotiate how to react, and I left, on my own accord, to deal on my own terms.

When I say I left it all behind, that includes the part of me formerly known as Elles. In a desperate-minded, identity-altering attempt to cope, I started using my middle name.

—

"Grace!"

"Yeah?"

—

So why now? Why in the hell is this all coming back to me, now? That damn day that I have avoided reminding myself of since—

—

"Grace Garity!"

"What?"

—

"I'm sorry, what?"

"Grace, what is going on with you? You have been acting weird and spacing out all week."

"Huh? Nothing. I'm fine. I'm just a little tired, that's all."

And that, for the record, was the second time in as many days that I had been caught daydreaming—a pastime I hadn't allowed myself since childhood.

Chapter 1

When I was a little girl, sometimes I would sit alone in my room watching the outside world and window dreaming. It was never about what was around me or what I could plainly see. My imagination stretched above the trees and rooftops, beyond the horizon. It was only an occasional hobby. I would fill this spare time indulging my curiosity and reveling in the intrigue of the people and places out there. I wondered who they were, where they came from, what their worlds were like.When the moment struck, I would envision what life was like wherever it was my mind wanted to travel to. I only bring it up and reflect on it now because that is obviously when my own life was easier, gentler. Those were the innocent times, when I privately mused about what fate had in store for me, what I had in store for it.

It only took one single moment, like the flick of a switch, to make me stop caring about such frivolous things. That is how long it took for a singular event to cut me so deeply that it turned me inside out with pain. The same little girl gazing out her window, ready to take on the world, grew up in an instant —and without warning.

But enough about me for now. This is not a tale solely focused on tragedy—although it *was* the catalyst to my internal meltdown. This is a story bigger than me. I just got lost for a while and unwittingly proceeded to make it *all* about me. This is about looking cruel reality in its coldhearted face—nearly a decade and a half too late, for everyone involved. What you've got to understand is what happened did not just affect me. The shock waves of that incident spread through a small community, with a smaller circle of loved ones at its center. However, I was the only one who turned away. Torn from the innocent, inquisitive days of my childhood, I was forced to deal with death ripping me to scattered shreds.

* * *

The beckoning voice from before was that of my *newer* best friend, Loyal.

Where or when our friendship officially began is difficult to pinpoint. You can't really classify our relationship as a smash hit from the start. The two of us spent years exhibiting a comfortable communicative distance. Our primitive, pre-explosive-modern-technology-age interactions started exclusively in school. We met in junior high and mainly coexisted as . . . how do I explain? Within the ever-changing and peer-driven social ranks of teenage maturation, we had a uniquely limited affection for one another. We passed occasional notes in class and had each other's backs. Eventually, we transitioned to hanging out in public and taking turns showing up at the other's house, mostly unannounced. The fact was, given our separate and very private backgrounds, we were good for one another but both too disenchanted with the concept of a good thing to accept it at first. There was also, I can safely assume, a healthy amount of fear involved all around. I can only speak from my own point of view at the time, but I had been through enough to make me somewhat standoffish and introverted.

Whether we chose to acknowledge it or not, the seeds were sown, the bond too strong to break. From two mounds of traumatic ashes a friendship arose. Everything I grew to be, the young woman I became, was because of her—of us. Loyal filled a wrecking ball–sized void when I needed it the most. She kept me distracted from the misery I imposed upon myself.

We succeeded through the last two years of high school solidly being one another's rocks. As for our futures —college, career—we encouraged and expected nothing less than total commitment to achievement. It sounds corny, but I guess when you're searching for life's answers, fighting for someone else's cause can almost be as rewarding as fighting for your own. Neither my past nor hers was ever the subject of enlightening conversation. I guess that was a mutually unspoken condition of our relationship. At the time, Loyal was one of three people in my life who was everything to me. I loved her—for more than just the superficial and beneficial reasons. That was a big part of the larger problem. Our friendship, our constant willingness and need to be there for one another, to see each other survive and thrive *for* one another, was the enabling force that allowed me to ignore whom I had been before.

You see, in a dark moment of unraveling weakness, I had left the island—my home—behind. I went numb for a while then damn near tried to sever every part of my past I had once held dear. After my parents died, most of me died with them. I wasn't the same person anymore, and I left more than just people and places in the dust. I stripped myself of my very name! I mean, who does that? It was a deliberate casualty of the newly invented me. And, yes . . . yes, I realize I said the words, *enough about me for now*, but . . . For over fifteen years, my own stupid, narrow-minded, leave-me-alone, knee-jerk reaction has been my downfall. The all-about-me attitude and this thing that happened to me have been my struggle, the silent focus, leading me to a vital crossroads.

I had moved to the mainland with my Uncle John and Aunt Nellie after my parents died. I give my elected guardians a lot of credit for all they did and everything they tried to do. It wasn't easy for them, either. I hadn't given them a choice. They were my only ticket out, short of running away by myself. In my eyes, they were the only ones in the running. They were visiting at the time, which meant they would be leaving soon. They had sympathy. It made perfect sense to a kid who wasn't at all interested in making any of her own in this matter. Essentially, they had all the qualifications I was looking for. The job was theirs. I had taken the keys and locked myself in the waiting car. They played along. *They* packed my bags. I hadn't even thought that far ahead. The consensus was that this would blow over. *She's hurting. She's rebelling. A few days away, a few weeks at best, may do her good.* I guess I showed them. And I am aware of how that sounds. I didn't aspire to prove that. It's just what I did.

The more they tried to comfort me, the harder I pushed back. As far as I was concerned, the past was simply that. No amount of crying or mourning was going to bring them back or change a thing. So I settled in, grew up, went to school, graduated, and became the teacher I always knew I would be.

Career aspirations were all that I had left. I was so intensely driven to move up professionally, that I never really took stock of where I was headed romantically or if it was even the direction I wanted to go. Then I met Jack. To make a doomed love story short, he fell in love, and I . . . had fallen out of touch. Before I could completely wrap my brain around what was happening, an *I do* quickly spiraled into a sobering *What the hell did I just do?*

Poor Jack, he never saw the U-turn coming, and he never stood a chance. It wasn't that I didn't love him. I mean, I'm pretty sure I did, at least as a . . . Okay, truth—I was broken. Deep down I knew it. At first, I didn't want that to get in the way and ruin what we might have had. It wasn't fair to either of us that I went through with it. It wasn't fair to either of us that I was hardly invested in anything that was happening to me unless it involved work or hanging out with Loyal. I was just rolling with the motions, taking whatever life was willing to give me. Jack was a friend first and has always remained one. It wasn't long before we knew it wouldn't work. I think he realized there was too much of me that needed to be fixed—more than I was willing to admit, that's for sure.

Splitting up when we did brought us closer together instead of gradually tearing our marriage apart. So there's that. He and Loyal were there for me when Aunt Nellie passed away. Together, they helped and supported me when Uncle John's health began to fade shortly after, and he needed around-the-clock care. Besides, I couldn't go through that all over again, not by myself. I chose to do it alone the first time, and I left half of me behind in the aftermath. One more twist and what would remain but a nameless empty shell of a human being? I was racked with backed-up emotion and all out of false identities. That's when the uncomfortable and unexpected opportunity to confront my past came along at the expense of career and family—or what was left of both.

The inconceivable idea of going back had never once crossed my mind until events within my life again called for drastic change.

Chapter 2

"Miss Garity! Miss Garity!" One of my former students, a fourth grader now, called to me, sprinting through the open gym doors.

"Woah, slow down! What is it, Carolyn?" I asked, stopping her in her tracks. She caught her breath and swallowed hard.

"It's Abby again," she began as I tilted my head and sighed.

"There's a substitute driver today. I tried to help her get on, but he asked me to find a responsible adult."

I found Abby outside, standing on the sidewalk beside the line of boarding buses. Her arms were crossed firmly over her backpack, gripping it tightly to her chest. She was staring at her bus with frozen angst. I touched her shoulder softly as I passed in front of her and got down to her level. As we locked eyes, I took a slow deep breath and a relaxed smile washed over Abby's face, concentrated on me.

"Hey, what's going on kiddo?"

Her eyes shifted toward the waiting bus, and her bottom lip twitched. I motioned to the driver to hold tight while I remedied the situation. Abby took a deep breath, held it in, and closed her eyes briefly. She opened them and exhaled.

"Now, see there?" I smiled at her for being one step ahead of me. "You already know. Remember what we've practiced all year long, right? You can do this. Ready? Focus, breathe, eyes on me . . . and here we go. Count it down. Ten, nine, eight, seven . . ." We continued on in sync, our voices getting softer with every digit until only our lips moved in silence. "Okay, you got your watch, right?" Abby lifted her arm with a more confident grin. "Good girl. Now, how long?"

"Ten minutes—give or take," she replied, mocking me from our routine.

"Perfect! Find your focus. Count the minutes off and breathe. You can do this."

"Thanks, Miss Garity." She turned and boarded the bus slowly, keeping a watchful eye on me all the way to her seat.

"Get that homework done for Mrs. Barrett's class!" I added while waving.

An impressed voice chimed in. "Well now, looks like maybe I overlooked a candidate for that school counselor position we've been trying to fill."

I laughed off Principal Tunney's assessment before I could stand up straight. I folded my arms and stayed to watch the bus roll away, as per the plan. "She started having these little anxious episodes at the beginning of the year. It's been months. So we'd hoped it was under control by now. I'll give her mother a call before I leave just to— "

"Speaking of which, would you stop in my office before you leave? This whole district review board thing, restructuring—whatever they're calling it this week—is getting a little dicey. It's a fluid situation. So trying to keep the staff informed is touchy. I've been checking in with everyone individually. Nothing serious."

* * *

"So that's it?" I shrieked, standing there in front of his desk. I snapped a hand on my hip and turned away, at a frustrated loss.

"No, that's not *it*, Grace. Don't go blowing things out of proportion before I can fully explain—"

"Please, do explain," I interrupted as I turned back, composed myself, and clasped my hands together in a display of calming reprieve. "I mean, what am I supposed to think when I'm basically told that my job is—"

"You haven't been told anything of the sort. Your position at this school remains intact. As of right now, nothing's chan—"

"As of now?"

"Look, Grace, I understand your concern. I do."

"Do you? Do you though, Frank? Because we hear the rumblings, okay? We're the ones who are left waiting, sorting through the rumors. And *right now*, listening to you, it's sure as hell starting to sound like this little review board has got you wrapped around their little finger."

"Watch yourself, Grace." He raised his hand and pointed a finger at me. "You're one of my best teachers. But you haven't been here long enough to come at me like that." I flopped down in the corner chair, crossed my legs, rested an elbow on my knee, my cheek on my hand, and heard him out. "You've got to trust me. I'm doing everything I can here. You know how these things work. I can't make promises that others aren't prepared to let me keep. The district *is* making changes. The school board's on my ass. I'm in and out of meetings every day, all day, just to get a handle on all this myself. Now, one thing they are pushing hard for is larger classes. None of this is set in stone. I probably shouldn't even be telling you this, but I am because I can see you're getting all worked up over . . ." I adjusted to push up onto my feet, and he held me off with a pausing hand. "The fact is, budget cuts will be coming down, left and right and—"

"Ah, that's it then. See, there ya go. That's all I need to know, Frank, is which unemployment line do I stand in, the left or right—"

"Calm your—"

I got back up and paced the middle of the room. "Four years. Almost four years of my career here. Four years of built-up seniority, Frank. That means nothing anymore?"

"Four years, *including* student teaching ain't nothin', Grace. I have got people that have been here for ten, twenty, who may very well wind up in the same boat as you by week's end for all I know."

Something about this whole thing incensed me from the start. I swear I could have hurdled that desk then and there, snapped the head off his shoulders and— Fortunately for him, he sensed that rage and caught his tongue before I could act.

"Let's just . . . I didn't ask you in here to start a fight, okay?" I dropped my arm off my hip in dismay and looked away from him again. "You know as well as I do, they rarely factor in seniority in these matters, anyway. I'm not saying it's fair, but it is the truth," he argued. "Regardless, they're tying my hands with all this sh—stuff, Grace. I'm just as angry and confused as you are. I can't even end the year peacefully now. I'm gonna have to start shuffling teachers around for next year, probably handing out furloughs or, God help us, layoffs, hoping for the best. The main thing is nothing is for sure right now. It's all a big mess, and I'm just trying to get ahead of it before all those rumors you're talking about get out of—"

"Gimme a break. What is this, your consolation disclaimer?"

"Grace, come on."

I started raising my voice. "Oh, spare me, Frank! I've heard enough double-talk. You keep saying things like 'right now,' 'as of now,' as if there's a—"

"Like there's other opportunities, Grace. Ways to keep you on the inside if it comes to that. There are other positions to fill. I'm telling you there may be options, Grace. Nothing's been decided yet. This is all worst-case scenario, that's all I'm saying. Hey, remember what I said before, outside, right? Now listen, it's just a thought, like I said, a way to keep your foot in the door in case—"

"Oh, my God! You—" I wagged a warning finger at him with a grit in my tone. "Don't even think about finishing that sentence!"

Grace, I—"

"No, I'll tell you what, Frank! In fact, here, let me make this *fluid situation* a little easier for you. Ya know, so you have a little less *shuffling* to do."

"Don't—"

"I quit!" I snapped at him, marching toward the door.

"—say anything you'll regret," he muttered.

"And screw you, too!" I added, slamming the door shut behind me.

First my wandering mind, and now . . . I didn't know why I went off on him the way I did. He—or something—lit a fuse, and I couldn't stop it. That was pretty much how that summer started off—with a bang. The rumors were already out and circulating. It was a hot-topic issue from the start that snowballed into a vengeful, hasty decision on the spot. I mean, I guess for a long time I'd been wrapped up pretty tight while managing to hold all the excess in, pretending I was someone somewhat adept at handling adversity.

So when he asked to see me in his office, I obliged, blinders on. I never saw it coming. I don't recall ever flying off the handle like that before—okay, verbally. They say never burn your bridges but oh, man, and trust me, when I burn them—*poof*! Right down to the smoldering ground. This much was obvious, though, I didn't deal well with horrible, blind-sided disasters, even if they doubled as reminders of what I could have done differently or better. Considering what was on tap, that little ugly incident was one of many to come and the first chip to fall in a harsher wake-up call.

Chapter 3

I dragged my feet to Loyal's bedroom door, tapped it open with a foot, and stood there leaning against the frame with a yawn. I waited patiently for signs of life with no response, digging the sleep out of my eyes. Finally, I reached in and flipped the light switch on. Instantly, a lazy arm forged upward from under the covers, grabbed at the bedside lamp, and switched it off. I promptly countered by parting the room-darkening curtains and raising the window shade. The room flooded with unrelenting sunlight as I left, crossing the hall into the bathroom.

"Oh, my God! You're so annoying!" she grumbled in a raspy voice. "Some of us still have jobs, ya know, and—"

"Loyal, it's Sunday," I informed. "And you do realize the act of looking for work does not, in itself, qualify as having an actual job?"

In the mirror, I spotted Loyal's head pop up from under a mangled mound of pillows and sheets. She rolled over haphazardly. Attempting to sit up out of bed, she lost her footing and went back down fast with a groan.

"Where's . . . What happened to Saturday?" She questioned in a sleepy, confused haze.

I stopped brushing to spit and stepped partway out into the hall. "Well, wherever yesterday went for ya, I'm guessing it didn't make any stops at the grocery store!" I razzed back at her. "Just because we're a couple of cash-strapped bachelorettes, doesn't mean we have to eat like teenage bachelors." Loyal blew the hair out of her face and willed herself to an upright position at the edge of the bed. I disappeared out of sight, this time into my room.

"I mean, who does that anyway?" I continued in a rant.

"Who manages to lose an entire day by sacrificing basic human needs in favor of Friday night power hour at some sleezy bar?"

"Hey!" she shouted back, taking exception. I heard and felt the vibrating thud of her feet hitting the floor as she bounded out of bed. I peaked in just as she took one unsteady step forward with a dizzying "whoa." She stopped to balance herself, proceeding to argue a point while fishing from her overflowing, half-washed hamper of clothes. "For your information, getting all dolled up and plastering a *please hire me* smile on my face all day, for one interview after another, is totally work!" She leaned in closer to the mirror over her dresser studying the skin on her face. "I think it's giving me wrinkles," she remarked aloud.

"They're called bags, Loyal, from not enough sleep. Maybe next time you stop for lunch while you're *working the streets*, ask for a slice of lemon with your water so you can use it to rub on your face. Meanwhile, I would like to beat the breakfast rush."

I emerged from my room, brushing my hair, and there she was, giving me the sad, offended leer. "Working the streets? Jesus . . ."

"I'm sorry. All right? You know what I meant to say. I'm a little—"

"Hurtfully bitchy?"

"On edge. I think they call it being disgruntled these days, right?"

"Yeah . . . bitchy. Hey, I don't blame you. I'm just jealous you kicked Tunney in the proverbial nuts, and I went out quietly compared to—"

"I didn't kick him in the . . . proverbial or not. I— Can we just go eat? Fix yourself up. Put on sunglasses or something. I'll be in the car."

Loyal shouted after me, intrigued. "Hold on! But what about the lemons? Does that really work? Wait, it's Sunday, for real? No bullshit?"

* * *

We shared a corner booth at one of our favorite cafés. As usual, I was halfway to a clean plate while Loyal was still procrastinating on what to order and polishing off her first cup of coffee while snatching strips of bacon from my plate. I slapped her hand away and gobbled the last piece, washing it down with a chug of orange juice. Loyal rolled her eyes.

"Geez, someone's all gung ho for a day of rest."

"Excuse me? Rest?"

"Isn't that like a Bible commandment? One of those tablet rules or something? On Sunday, thou shalt . . . ?" asked the woman whose one and only brush with holiness was once plagiarizing a random parable passage for a social studies class in junior high.

"Oh, very nice, Loyal. I'm no religious savant, but I'm pretty sure God rested for a reason and not because he ordered himself to. Besides, I have plenty to do today and so do you. So have something more than side dishes for once. He rested because he was tired, ya know, from creating the universe, not hungover after toasting himself for doing it. Crap, I gotta run."

"Ha! Who elected you pope? So you're just leaving me?"

"I told you I have to pick up Uncle John's prescription this morning. Jack's out of town for the weekend, remember?"

"Mm." Loyal took a sip of coffee. "He's quite the handy helper, isn't he?" She winked. "Maybe you two should give it another—"

I raised my hand to squash what was coming, displaying my index finger. "Don't with me right now—just don't." I tried, unsuccessfully, to stave off a tight-lipped upward frown. "I'm running on a pretty short fuse lately. Didn't ya hear?" I cautioned.

"He had it coming. You of all people on staff. You could have rocked any position at that school. Frank's just too much of a coward to put his ass on the line for anyone."

"Yeah, but I didn't want *any* job. I wanted the job that I

paid for an education to get."

"*You* paid?"

"Be quiet. My point is, I shouldn't have to count my blessings and settle for being a damn guidance—"

Loyal's eyes widened, and her jaw dropped as I caught myself in mid-unintentional insult. "No! He did not! He had the ballsy nerve to offer you that shitty job?"

"He referenced the option to take— I don't wanna talk about it."

"Guidance counselor, my ass!" Loyal scoffed. "Do you know, more kids came to my office last year in a panic over their precious electronic gizmo batteries dying, and they left their charger at home? The only guidance they needed was to the friggin' supply closet, which I might as well have been the clerk of—"

"Loyal!" I laughed. "You were overqualified and underpaid for that job, anyway. Damn, now I'm really late. I promised Jack I'd walk the dog, too."

"My, my." She hummed.

"Oh, shut up!"

"Ya share a dog together—"

"We don't . . . I didn't even want a dog. And I said, shut—"

"A best friend—"

"Get over yourself. He has other—"

"Subletting the apartment, I'm sorry, former love nest you now share with said best friend—"

"Okay, first of all, love nest? That's a little—"

"Which, if I'm not mistaken, is still technically in both your names."

I scavenged some money from my wallet and laid it on the table in front of her. "Here. Get the full plate special, my treat. Now, shut up." I dashed for the door. In my hurry, I caught a glimpse of the smirk forming on her smug little face.

"You two are the cutest divorced couple I've ever seen," she joked as I exited the café, displaying a choice finger behind my back.

* * *

She was right, of course. Loyal knew this version of me better than I probably wanted or expected anyone to. Her friendship was exactly what I didn't want to need, at a time when I never needed something or someone so much. At some point, something would have to give, though. Jack sacrificed some aspects of his life to be there for me, despite everything that happened between us. The time was coming for me to account for my mistakes and answer to Elles, the part of me I buried with my parents' memory a long time ago.

For some of us, life has that inevitable way of coming full circle. Usually, it happens when we're not paying attention or exactly counting on it, like some wonderful, hauntingly reflective afterthought. Others, the really special cases like me, get sort of stuck halfway around and need a good, hard shot of divine intervention to move us along. My initial plan was to possibly take the summer off, consider my options, dip into my savings, and scout out some new career opportunities.

Because of how it always tended to materialize, change was never on my to-do list. Therefore, nobody was more surprised that I was actually looking forward to this than I. Okay, let's be totally honest. I didn't *do* to-do lists, and I didn't plan anything out much past tomorrow—an odd characteristic for a teacher, I realize. I made it work most of the time. Depending on how her job search was going, Loyal and I had even toyed with the idea of a little vacation, a sort of bestie's getaway while we contemplated our professional futures.

Every one of those plans changed, in a flash, that Sunday. I ran my errands, picked up Uncle John's pills, and brought them to the house. When I arrived, he was mustering up what precious strength he had, rummaging through dresser drawers for something. We never got into what exactly he so urgently needed to find. I was distracted by this glow he had about him that I noticed right away and couldn't get over.

He was in a playfully happy mood, moving around without a struggle, and busier than I'd seen him in months.

His sudden behavior was mysterious, to say the least. On top of everything else, he was turning the house upside down searching for something he'd kept stashed away for so long that it eluded him now. He was cleaning, putting things away, and sorting through a wardrobe of dust-collecting clothes hanging in his closet. He wanted me to stay for lunch and "maybe a game of cards?" that he charmingly suggested in his best guilt-trip-deploying way. He did so, hinting at the not-so-subtle incentive of letting me win if I did. That was a promise he and I both knew he was ill-equipped to keep. Especially since he was most likely about to blurt out the name of some ancient game I'd never heard of in my life. That's how he got you. That was the trick, and I knew better than to test my skills against his when it came to cards. But I stayed.

The afternoon trailed off into early evening. Uncle John was all abuzz with stories of the olden days on and off the island. These were stories, mind you, that he'd amused himself by telling me hundreds of times over the years, and yet, he told them with the same zest every single time. Usually, I wasn't inclined to indulge in a repeat trip down memory lane, but it was different today. It was nice to see him like this, like he was before Aunt Nellie died, before letting that heartbreak wear him down.

I always suspected he drove himself ill after she was gone, and maybe that was part of it. They were rarely apart. The one thing Uncle John had made abundantly clear was that he never wanted to be a burden. Oh, he had laid out the ground rules the day he decided it was time for me to move out on my own and *snap out of it* as he so eloquently put it. I came home, and there he was, waiting in the living room with everything I owned. My clothes were all packed, bedroom stripped to bare walls and floors, contents contained in stacks of boxes. Subtlety was *not* his game, that's for sure.

He had a no-nonsense, resolute look all over his face

and a head-start offering in his hands. This was before my first real job out of college, so he took great pride in gifting me the keys to an apartment, with security deposit and first year's rent paid in full. The objective here: to make sure I would have the worry-free time to find more sufficient means of supporting myself. You never saw someone so deeply moved and appreciative to be thrown out on the spot as me.

It was the first time in my adult life that I openly, and without restraint, started to cry. But wait, there was more. As for the ground rules of *not* living under his roof, I was allowed, unless otherwise requested or necessitated on the grounds of medical emergency, to visit no more than three days a week, never consecutively. The stipulations had as much to do with keeping us close and in touch regularly as they did for keeping me focused on myself more than obsessing over his well-being.

Still, I guess I should have sensed something was wrong when the time came for me to leave. He thanked me for coming over and for staying, something he never did. Not that he didn't want me there or wasn't ever grateful. He was just . . . I don't think he wanted me to sit around and watch him dying inside—or out. Once again, it was at his insistence that I leave, excusing himself to the comfort of his recliner. He dimmed the lights, lay back, put his feet up, a blanket over his lap, and only asked that I get him a beer, some chips, and put on his favorite movie before I left.

Something told me to go back and check in on him after I had run some overdue errands that evening. He was how I left him. But he was gone. The house felt cold and empty, and he was just . . . gone. I stood there numb, and I knew. Next to him on the end table, beside the empty beer bottle and wadded-up bag of chips was a wooden box. I'd never seen it before. The thought did eerily cross my mind that it may have been what he was looking for that morning. Naturally, I assumed he had prepared to leave it for me, knowing full well that I would want no part in hanging around to wrap up the loose ends of his life —to put it morbidly. It does pain me to say, he would have been right. I called 911, waited around to lock the door when they took him away, and went home. When I finally harnessed the nerve to open that box, my entire outlook changed.

Chapter 4

The night of Uncle John's funeral, I sat alone atop the arched bridge at the pond in the park near our apartment. The sky was aglow with a million twinkling stars and the moonlight sparkling on the water. I gazed across at the tiny island in the middle and the little house that took up most of it, lost in my own thoughts. I didn't flinch an ounce when Loyal appeared out of nowhere and sat down beside me. She glimpsed up into the heavens then bowed her head.

"I was hoping you would change your mind," she commented softly.

I hesitated. "I wanted to. I just . . . I couldn't do it."

"I get it, Grace. No explanation needed. You know that. This is me. This is us." We shared a moment of somber silence, broken only by Loyal's uncanny way of attempting to lighten a tense mood. "It was a nice funeral. Not that any are supposed to be good, I mean, or that I've ever been to a bad . . . um . . . Do you know the man wrote his own freakin' eulogy? Did you know that? I've never seen so many people laugh and cry at the same time before."

A laugh of my own escaped through my arduous attempts to hold back those same pent-up emotions I'd trained myself to ignore. "Sounds about right."

That's about the time Loyal noticed it, the distant look, the lost shell of a woman, which was, as of late, becoming increasingly more difficult to mask. I was finally ready to crumble under the weight of being somebody whom I wasn't. I felt my neck and shoulders tighten and tremble, arms crossed, hugging myself. She saw me struggling. Those were unfamiliar avenues for us to travel side by side. For whatever reasons, we just didn't go to those sensitive places. We could handle the supportive, hard stuff. We just never talked about the details or needled around at the root of what was going on with the skeletons in our respective closets.

"Grace . . . Hey, it's okay."

Except, it wasn't.

Loyal wrapped her arm around me and pulled me in close, shoulder to shoulder, in a loving effort to do what we always did for each other in times like these. This time I tensed up. There was no sinking my head into her warm, consoling frame and getting past it in a timely manner this time. As much as I appreciated her being there, the usual methods weren't taking. No girl talk moment of *We'll get through this, together*. I wouldn't even look at her. I was so . . . I wasn't altogether sure what I was exactly—upset, angry, crushed. But that's when she loosened her grip and backed off a bit.

"Grace?" She gulped.

The simple act of sitting there on the edge of that bridge suddenly started to feel like a cruel but appropriate metaphor for my entire life from this point forward. And not just because that tiny island in the middle of the pond seemed to be glaring back at me, trying to tell me something, impart some stupid wisdom on me that I was missing. Until now, I hadn't questioned a single thing I had done, not one disillusioned decision or spontaneous reaction. Apart from the roof over my head, clothes on my back, and meals that Uncle John and Aunt Nellie unconditionally provided, I took personal refuge in raising myself, finishing the job that was meant for. . . It was a choice motivated by self-preservation and made for the sake of my own sanity. Now, I was questioning all of it. *I* didn't deal with things well. *I* didn't allow anyone to help me deal with things. My life, the road I was on, the lane I had shifted into when I took the wheel, to put it quite figuratively, looked dark and dismal. I was solely responsible for switching my life into cruise control before ever giving myself a chance to learn to drive the damn car.

All these things ran through my head. I didn't speak to Loyal about any of it. Where would I start? How could she possibly understand my position? Not that I gave her a fighting chance. Time sort of stood still as I sat there frozen, empty. I started this. I made this mess. I had no fucking clue how to fix it. I closed my eyes for a while, and when I opened them, it hit me like a slap to the head. The answer was staring me in the face. Where it all went wrong is where it needed to begin again.

"Grace, I'm worried about you."

She had never said those words to me before. Ironic, though, how it came across, how I took it—*her* spotting the wreckage and expressing concern to the very person who was entangled in the heap. Out of upheaval, I took solace in a clouded idea to uproot myself once more. I emerged partially from my funk, oddly enough, with a wayward smile and slightly brighter outlook. I turned to Loyal, sincere. "Everyone must think I'm horrible."

"Well, I can't speak for everyone. I mean, *I* do. Yeah, you um . . . you take off, disappear, made me walk all the way down here to find you in my most formal pair of toe-crushing shoes. Christ, think about someone else for a change. My feet are killing me. What the hell's the matter with you anyway?"

I sucked up my tears and chuckled. "You are so stupid. I love you."

"We all say goodbye in our own way." Loyal kissed the top of my head. "You'll find yours. You just gotta give it time, ya know? You'll get there." I spun around and sprung to my feet, heading off into the night. "Hey! Hello! Where are you . . . ?"

"Getting there!" I called out.

"Getting . . . what? Grace, wait up! Getting where? What the hell are you doing now?"

I stopped and turned back to her with a determination I had only felt so strongly about one other time. "Crashing the car."

"Crashing the . . . What the . . . Grace wait! I can't . . . These goddamn . . ." I heard her hopping on the pavement to pluck the shoes off her feet followed by two small distinct splashes in order to give chase. Thus, my mission of self-redemption was born of an enlightened whim. In retrospect, I regret hurrying off the way I did, leaving Loyal confused and clumsily chasing me down after feeding her footwear to the snapping turtles. "Grace! Would you . . . Oh, that's great. Yeah, leave me out here to die, that's nice. Grace!"

* * *

Late that night, I sat cross-legged on my bed. The old wooden cigar box rested in front of me. I stared at it intently, wavering on if I should peak inside or let it be. Eventually, I reached for the latch and slowly lifted the top. There before me, stuffed inside the compact space, were the paper remnants of Uncle John's life: his will, an insurance policy, and other personal documents. This wasn't so bad. What was I afraid would pop out?

As I shuffled through the contents, down to the bottom, my relieved expression turned ghostly pale. I'm almost sure my complexion went as pure white as the piece of paper hidden underneath—a property deed. In my fog of astonishment, a faint knock at the front door barely registered. Shortly thereafter, a louder one at my bedroom door jolted me to my senses. I looked up and smiled with an air of welcomed distraction. Jack came to my bedside and leaned over, embracing me with a warm hug.

"I didn't mean to scare you. Sorry to stop in so late, but I wanted to come by and check on you. What's this?"

I packed up the loose contents of the box in a disorderly clump and shoved it back inside. "Um, just some of Uncle John's things. The usual, nothing exciting."

Jack swiped the chair from my desk, moved it over beside me, and straddled it backwards. He rested his arms over the back and shook his head. "I'm sure Loyal told you about his little prewritten comedy sketch. Good material, you should read it. I think he missed his calling of writing for late-night television."

"I heard, I heard. I haven't seen it yet, but . . ." I wiped my face and threw in a yawn for effect, trying to appear fully composed and in no way shaken in front of him. He watched me as I reached for a glass of water and took a long drink to soothe my dry throat.

Jack shook his head again with more of a confounded nod. "My God, all this time I've known you and I still barely have a clue what's going on in that pretty little head of yours."

I looked away, hiding a blush. When I turned back, Jack gazed into my eyes as if trying to read my mind. I stared back with an innocent, content facade then said, "Join the club."

"You okay, Grace?"

I pondered a moment longer and sat up straight, stretching. Lifting my head back with a big breath in and out, I looked at him again and moved the cigar box to the nightstand. I didn't bother to answer his question. I just placed my hand on his arm. "Thank you for everything you've done, Jack. Really. I mean, for me, for Uncle John. I mean it. Thank you."

In an unfortunately inopportune flash, Loyal passed by my room, stopping at the door. She grinned at the mere sight of us sitting there together, affectionately. "I'm off to bed." She pointed at Jack. "You know the rules here, mister. No sleepovers." My hand pinched the corner of a small throw pillow that was wedged behind my back. Loyal moved past the door and peeked back in. "Don't you two kids go doing anything unmarried couples shouldn't be doing anymore," she taunted.

With a lunge, I winged the pillow at her, missing by an inch as she ducked out of sight.

Jack started to laugh and cleared his throat with a stern look from me. "Don't be too hard on her. Mentally stable roommates are just hard to come by these days!" he joked.

"I heard that Jackson!" Loyal barked back from her room.

Jack spread his arms and turned his head toward the

dividing wall. "Not my name! You know I hate that. How many times . . . That is *not* my name!"

"Wow!" I exclaimed at their foolish banter. I scooted back against the headboard and pillow and slipped under the covers. "You two bicker like a married couple more than *we* ever did."

Jack rolled his eyes with a snarky laugh, struggling for a witty retort. "Just for that"—he wagged his finger at me—"no sympathy booty call for you."

"Eew!!" Loyal and I let out collectively.

"What, too much?" he asked.

"Too much, too soon, too nauseating. No offense," I offered as politely as possible. I took another drink of water and adjusted myself more comfortably. "Thank you, Abbott and Costello."

"Who?" Jack asked.

"Seriously, what would I do without you guys? You really know how to make a grieving girl feel special." I immersed myself fully under the sheets and rolled onto my side facing the wall. "Or at least cheap and easy."

"God, see you always get the last jab in." He turned toward the wall again. "She always gets—" He turned back, and I felt his eyes burning on me as I lay there all tucked in and snug. "Really, an old married couple?" He leaned his head back and called out to Loyal, "She's onto us, babe! Should I just come in there and—"

"Go home, Jackson!" she hollered.

That deed had my wheels spinning half the night. In the process of contemplating what it meant for my future, I scatterbrained through a gamut of emotions. How the hell could I have ever known or imagined anyone in the family still owned the house I grew up in? How could . . . Why would I care, or even pretend to think about things like that? No, no, I was too busy forgetting anything that was worth remembering in the first place. So who was I mad at here? I was angry with myself for not knowing, mad at him for keeping it secret—keeping it, period. For what? I didn't want it. How could he, for one second, think that I would? Yet this false voice of reason inside my head, which eventually lulled me to sleep, kept telling me, *Jesus, it's just a house, Grace. Get a grip.* But it wasn't *just* a house, and I wasn't just overreacting. I was overwhelmed, ultimately, by a strangely confusing sense of . . . gratitude.

Chapter 5

It took one stupid, goddamned piece of paper to bring me to a deep, dark place that made me feel eleven years old again. That house belonged to me now, along with anything and everything inside it. I shuttered to even entertain the possibilities. I started considering all viable options, and upon further review of his will, they were mounting by the second. Pending probate, I was soon to be the lone beneficiary of an eye-popping monetary inheritance. Even so, and surprisingly enough, career and financial stability were the least of my worries. I wrestled with that fact for weeks. I didn't dare tell Loyal or Jack and risk complicating the whole matter with any sort of calm, sensible approach. Hell, I was doing fine on my own by not inviting in objective outsider opinions and maybe injecting a hint of rationality into this—thank you very much.

So after many sleepless nights of anguish and deliberation, I had narrowed it down to two courses of action. Plan A was to contact a real estate agent ASAP and put the old house on the market—as is and unseen by me. Out of sight, out of mind, as far as I was concerned. Sell it to anyone remotely interested, at a buyer's bargain, and be done with it. If I may be facetious for a moment, apparently the *A* in this scenario stood for *Absolutely not going to happen*. Plan B, on the other hand, clearly meant *But why take the easy way out when I can let the guilt of never having the guts to have said goodbye get the better of me?* Or—and this one's really out there—I could air my grievances out loud in a cemetery, arguing with a dead man like a crazy lady over my disastrous life choices. Which, unfortunately, was exactly what I tried to do.

The one-sided conversation started in the car on the way there. It continued as I arrived and sat in the car like a discontented teenager, mad at her parents for something trivial. Oh, I rehearsed it all in my head, every perfectly scripted word. It was a truly beautiful piece of inspired and noteworthy tongue-lashing. When I was finished working myself into a fired-up frenzy, I got out of the car and marched directly to his grave and recited . . . none of it, not one syllable. I don't know if I was more afraid that he would hear me or that I might hear myself saying it. There was a chance I might, in a way, start to hear his side of things. Most of all, when it came right down to it, I was ashamed of everything I intended to say.

To Loyal's point at the park, my way of saying goodbye took the form of reevaluation and deep reflection. Instead of remembering Uncle John and Aunt Nellie for all the good times we had, I was dissecting the reasons why they did every single thing from the time they took me in. I was analyzing their comings and goings, financial decisions, parenting techniques, anything I could think of that I had never paid close attention to in the past. They never had kids of their own, the extravagant couple who preferred a freer, self-employed life of traveling. They had given that lifestyle up because of me. They gave it up because I couldn't cope. Scratch that—I had refused to cope, and I took them in. They didn't even make that call. I didn't let them. So, maybe, just maybe, keeping this house was Uncle John's way of saying *Elles Grace Garity, no more excuses. We're gone now, too. You get back to the life you ran away from*! Because I did run away, and suddenly I found a small part of me that wished it was as easy as all of that. By the end of that summer, my mind was made up. I was going to do the one thing I didn't want to do. The thing that scared me the most.

* * *

The town was decorated for the annual Salute to Summer celebration, two weeks' worth of festivities, ending with the Labor Day parade. Loyal was manning the drunk—pardon me —dunk tank, which was a long-standing tradition, ever since a group of college kids built one for a frat party and filled it with beer. That ended so well that the town seized it for authorized community functions only. Although several fun and weird suggestions poured in for this occasion, including Loyal's to swap beer for wine, standard water won out. I volunteered for the more civilized, and family oriented, face-painting booth. Jack took charge of his usual role of all-purpose floater when and where help was needed. He never let that interfere with fulfilling the unsolicited duties as general good-time troublemaker and instigator. I completed the final touches to one little boy's mug and reached for a mirror, presenting my work for final approval.

"There you go. What do you think?"

"Cool!" he exclaimed and took off in a flash, calling out to his father.

I put the mirror down and dropped the paintbrush into a cup for cleaning. When I turned around, I found Abby standing at the front of the line. We smiled at each other. "Abby, hello! Well, look at you. All ready for third grade?"

"I missed you at school," Abby said, melting my heartstrings.

I sighed and took her hand, then looked up at her mother behind her. "She spotted you over here and couldn't get in line fast enough. She was looking forward to finally having you as her teacher. So after you were let go, well, she was counting on at least seeing you here, anyway."

"Aw, I'm so sorry Abby," I groaned and felt so guilty, doubly so for not clarifying my misconstrued departure.

Her mother spoke softly above Abby's head. "She was a little heartbroken." I touched my hand to the side of Abby's face, brushing her hair gently. "But what did you want to tell Miss Garity, Abby?"

Abby looked at me with the proudest smile. "I rode the bus to and from school every single day for the rest of the year. I remembered everything you taught me."

My jaw dropped with excitement for her. "Abby, that's so awesome! Good stuff, high-five." I raised my hand up in front of

Abby, who leaped and slapped it hard. I picked up a new brush and the pallet. "So what are we transforming this adorable little face into?"

Abby sat down in the chair. "A ferocious lady lion that's not scared of anything!" she replied, confidently.

As she spoke, I spotted Frank Tunney off in the distance. "Oh wow! Well, you know, that's going to require a more talented artist than myself, and my assistant Kim here happens to be the van Gogh of jungle faces." I stood up, to yield to my replacement. "Tell you what, though, I have to go talk to someone while she turns you into a menacing beast. How about I meet you and your mom over at the food pavilion for some lunch after you're done? My treat."

I rubbed the top of her head, and I called out to Frank, catching up to him near the dunk tank. I accompanied him to the nearest picnic table where he sat down to eat. I also caught Loyal's attention across the way. Frank didn't exactly appear enthusiastic to see me and perhaps deservedly so.

"Grace," he said, acknowledging my presence and nothing more. Not the most flattering exchange, but it was a start.

"Relax, Frank, I was just hoping we could clear the air. You know, bury the ol' hatchet gracefully." I offered that last word with a wink, pun always intended when and wherever applicable. For this particular occasion I advantageously threw it in to help extend my sincerest effort to make amends.

Frank sat there taking in the atmosphere of the day, paying me little mind. He pulled a napkin from his pocket, dabbed the sweat from his forehead and replaced it. In a deliberate, time-consuming, procrastinating fashion, he casually took a bite of his chili dog, chewed thoroughly, swallowed, then washed it down with a drink, all before answering. "I'm sorry, you'll have to forgive me. In my nightmares I've imagined if we ever crossed paths again, I'd be on the business end of a Sherman tank while you were laughing maniacally and loading the gun."

I was as impressed as I was insulted. I'm not going to lie, we shared a vision, he and I, or something similar to his thing—a satisfying, post-embarrassing-tantrum dream that I probably had once or twice. Someone caught his eye. He waved to his wife and kids. "Well, ya gotta have military clearance, and try hijacking an armored vehicle from a soldier, it's not . . . Hey, look, I'm not sure where that side of me came from, myself. Well, I mean, I have a good idea, but . . . Anyway, I'm not proud of how I acted, and it's a long sad, boring story why I did. Come on, Frank, that was my first teaching job, ya know? My first *real* career job out of school. You caught me off guard."

He took another bite, still not engaging in eye contact with me. I waited for any indication of interest on his part in continuing the conversation. He just sat there with his back to the table, resting his elbows on it, and squinting into the sun with one leg propped up on his knee.

"Okay, I tried." I started to get up and excuse myself. "I'll get out of your—"

"I fought for you," he finally said before I could get far. "For the record, that is. Even after all the venom you spewed all over me. Suit's still at the cleaners."

I was humbled. I felt Loyal still watching and turned to her.

"I meant what I said. You're one of the best teachers we had, Grace. There's no denying that. Sometimes I'm just the middleman in a cesspool of bureaucracy. Believe me, I hate it as much as you do. But what can I do? Hell, if I put my own career in jeopardy or even thought for one second about quitting over every boneheaded decision the board makes . . ."

"You don't have to keep explaining, Frank. And for the record, I appreciate everything you ever did for me. It's been a rough couple of weeks. First, I lose . . . okay, quit my job in overly dramatic fashion. Then my uncle dies. On top of that, I've been living a lie for a long time, and now it seems like everything else in my life is going to hell. So the least I can do is apologize for the way I treated you."

"Grace, I heard about your loss, and I am sorry. That's from the heart. Whatever else you're going through, I wish you well. Although I can't take full responsibility for your career choices today. This ain't even a paying gig," he joked. "Damn, I tell you what . . ." He wiped his forehead again and stood up, loosening his jacket, trying to cool himself. "It's too hot out here today." Frank walked over toward the dunk tank, removing his blazer. He rolled it up in a ball, pitched it back to me, and unbuttoned the sleeves of his shirt, rolling them halfway up his forearms. "Consider this my olive branch to you, Grace."

Loyal's eyes lit up like last week's opening fireworks. She shook her head and flaunted the go-ahead signal in the form of a cackling expression, while shooing people back from the front of the line.

"I'll give you one shot, and one shot only. You get one ball. The proceeds go to the enrichment and benefit of our little town, and you collect the satisfaction of knowing you got the last laugh on me. Either way, we both walk away and put this whole mess behind us. You get to let off a little steam, and if you're really lucky, I get laughed at by a bunch of children who would just love to see me go under." He positioned himself up on the seat and spread his arms wide, challenging me.

Seeing him perched up there, ready and willing to take the plunge, Loyal grabbed a ball and, all to eagerly, rushed it over to me. "This is no time to throw like a girl now, Grace," she asserted encouraged.

Initially, I shrugged off the opportunity. "I can't do this, Loyal." I laughed. "We talked it out, no hard feelings. Besides, he wants me to. It's not the same."

"Grace Garity, you listen to me. Either you dunk that man, or I will. And I won't even throw the ball. I'll just run over there and punch the friggin' button," she warned, planting the ball firmly in my grasp and wrapping her fingers around mine. "This is a win-win for everyone. You heard him. Wait, wait!" Blocking Frank's view of me, she forced a second ball into my free hand. "In case you miss. I run this attraction, not him."

"I'm not in any jeopardy sittin' up here, you understand. I'm doing you a favor. You get to say you had your shot. Much as I like a cold refreshing swim on a hot day like this, I'm not takin' any dips today. Hell, I've seen you on field day airmail a Wiffle ball a foot over a five-year-old's head."

Even Loyal was stunned and speechless. My hand had a mind of its own, squeezing the ball tighter with every mouthful of slander.

"Then again, I'm a fair man. I don't want to embarrass you, so we can call this off. You can, uh, tuck tail and come on back to work. Art director maybe. Your résumé's plastered all over this field. And that counseling position's still open if you —"

The words narrowly escaped his lips, and I spun around, reared back, and fired. I hit the bull's-eye dead-on with all the aggression-filled force I could muster. Frank crashed down into the waiting tank below with a splashing thud and priceless shock on his face. It's funny how one seemingly meaningless, spontaneous moment can inspire a person to greater heights. When I launched that ball off the palm of my hand, it felt damn good, and not just because of Frank Tunney's antagonizing tongue or his patronizing job offer. I'm pretty sure that was a defining moment in the internal tug-of-war over where I was headed. Any lingering doubts I might have had were cast away as mightily as that throw. It was more than a perfect strike. It was the culmination of all those years spent denying who I was, living this runaway train of a life. The truth was, the last person, the last excuse keeping me here was gone, and his last and final responsibility to me was to send me back home.

All I really remember feeling the rest of that day were the whimpering pleas of the little girl inside me named Elles. The one thing we finally agreed on, after all these years, was that we both wanted to go home. I found my own little isolated spot to watch the parade that afternoon, soul searching from the front lawn of town hall, distant from the street-lined onlookers. The cheerful noises—whistles, clapping, and idle chatter—were all a blur of muffled, joyful sound to me. The uneasy sensation of being caught at the crossroads of life and teetering on the brink of implosion has a way of adding an element of oblivion to one's surroundings, however celebratory they may be.

I had no clue how much harder my life was about to get.

Chapter 6

"So how long will you be gone?" Loyal asked, strolling the carnival grounds with me on the eve of the festivities' end.

"I'm not sure, really. However long it takes to sell a house these days, I guess."

"I still can't believe he never told you about that. Are you sure you want to sell? I mean, clearly, he wanted you to have it. Clearly, we need a vacation home by the beach. Maybe he thought if he told you sooner . . ."

"He would have been right, probably. I don't know. It doesn't matter." I stopped and sat on a bench, looking around, stalling. Loyal looked at me for a moment, sitting beside me. I'm sure I looked jittery and anxious. That's how I felt. "I can't do this anymore, Loyal. I can't be someone I'm not," I admitted aloud, a whirlwind of feelings boiling over inside me. My voice trembled. I put my head back and sucked in a deep breath to calm my nerves. What I really wanted was to scream to the heavens, to expel an overabundance of inner chaos.

"You wanna know what I think?" Loyal asked.

To which I sniffled with a half-hearted laugh. "Please don't do the psychoanalysis thing right now, Loyal. I swear I'll slap you."

"As a professional . . ." she began, wary. "I'm worried about your mental state. I am. As your friend . . . I'm still worried. But! I know you. You'll figure things out."

I looked at her with scared eyes, wishing I shared a fraction of her optimism.

"I know we've never been real open about our pasts. So I hate that I can't help you with whatever you're going through. I have a good feeling, though, that the person I know is stronger than she thinks she is. Although, ya know, if you need some kind of sidekick or just a friend along for the ride, I—"

"Loyal, I gotta do this alone. I'm so sorry, I don't know what else to say."

I wanted to throw up. My stomach was in churning knots, and she looked spooked.

"Damn you, Grace. This is about a lot more than getting rid of some ol' house you don't want. You're coming back. I mean, right? You are . . ."

I reached into my back pocket and pulled out a folded envelope and held it up to a look of bewilderment on her face. I choked up and shifted sideways on the bench, bent on turning the conversation into an offering and declaration of moving on. "You listen to me. I'm going off alone, but I can't do this by myself, Loyal. I don't know if I can do this with you and Jack being so far. You just damn well better pick up the phone anytime I call. You hear me? I don't want either of you worried about me."

"Of course, I—"

"I don't care if it's two in the afternoon or two in the morning. You just . . . promise me you'll pick up and that you'll take care of each other while I'm gone . . . and you'll pick up the phone."

"I promise. You know I do, but what's . . ."

I was clenching the envelope to my chest with one hand, probably to make sure my heart wasn't beating out of my chest. Loyal looked at it, then me suspiciously before I could address what it was. "I don't want to worry about you while I'm gone, either."

"So, you're gonna sh-shove me in a big ol' mailbox for safekeeping."

I welcomed the tension-breaking humor, handing it to her gently. She lifted the front flap and nudged a check far enough out to read. Her eyes popped as she rolled them at me. "Oh, how sweet. You've robbed a bank for me." She sneered. "Grace, what the hell is this? Where did you get—"

"Uncle John left me a few other little surprises."

"Little?" she yelped.

"This is only a small portion of it. Your portion."

Her mouth gaped open, but no words fell out. She reexamined and double-checked the numbers repeatedly, trying to comprehend. I explained before she could begin hyperventilating. "I might be kind of busy for a while. You'll have some things to do now."

"Huh, like what? Move to Paris? Italy? Buy a goddamn house at Buckingham Palace?"

"Well, there's just a lot of things wrong with that sentence that I can't—"

"No shit! There's a lot of zeros here, too! I can't think straight. This is . . . there's no . . . it's too much. This is too much. I can't. Here."

I rejected her advances to hand it back, clutching her arm firmly to calm her down. "I won't have to worry about you if I know you're busy living your dream."

"My—"

"Forget all these dead-end jobs, wasting your time and talents. I happen to know that you want your own practice someday. I want you to have your own practice. Besides, I'm not just doing this for you. You'll obviously pay me back with free sessions for life."

She flung herself onto me with full-on, wrap-around, body-grasping, vice-like grips. Clinging to me, she held her chin just above my shoulder and whispered directly into my ear, "I want you to know, I really hate you for this. And if you don't come back, I'm using every dollar to send the president to go get your ass."

Once she eased up enough that I could breathe, and the blood started flowing back though my veins, I replied, "Good. That's good. See, put that in my file, and we can build on that. How does that hate make you feel?"

* * *

I didn't waste any time gathering up suitcases full of clothes and essentials, tying up loose ends in preparation for an extended stay. I figured, why delay the inevitable. The quicker, the better. Jack didn't take the news any better than Loyal. I refused to let our last morning together become a tear-drenched slobber fest of farewells. Now that she had the only thing missing to make more of herself, neither of them had time to dwell on separations or the reality of a long-distance friendship. I hadn't even allowed myself that luxury.

Honestly—and this was not me trying to make myself feel better about the situation—those two had something. It was an often-sarcastic, standoffish, one-waiting-for-the-other-to-crack sort of thing. Jack had dated me first. That is to say, he had made a strategic maneuver in a larger play for whom he really wanted—Loyal. Even I knew that. We hadn't counted on us hitting it off so well, or my making it so easy for him to think we were something more. I had always known the greater intentions. It was up to him to follow through. He looked at her a certain way first. None of this dynamic had been a factor in our eventual ruin. That was all me and leading up to . . . now. I suppose it should have bothered me. It might have, if Loyal and I weren't so close.

Jack wouldn't think of proposing to me until he had proved himself worthy. Right out of college, he had landed a sweet paid-under-the-table internship with a construction and investment firm. After hitting it off with members of the ownership group, he was in—hands and feet on the bottom rungs of the corporate ladder and ready to climb. A week later, to my surprise, I was wearing a ring. It was a weird time. I loved him, but I had never thought he'd let it get that far. Maybe he had lost sight of the objective. Loyal was a sub-romantic, loose cannon. Maybe Jack hadn't seen her as the settling-down type, or maybe he had gotten tired of waiting for her to show a jealous side so he could make his move. Regardless of personal feelings, they had both grown quite comfortable, playfully despising and aggravating each other—quite obnoxiously at times, as previously demonstrated. With me out of the way, well . . . The best I could do was try to put their wheels in motion before mine were.

"Wish you would have at least reconsidered, let us follow you to the boat," Loyal pleaded.

I shrugged. "It's a long drive. Probably just gonna take it slow, clear my head. Ferries run all day so . . ."

"I should go, anyway," Jack said, stepping up first for goodbyes. "Told the crew I'd pick up breakfast. We'll be on site all day. You take care of yourself. Keep in touch. Hey, Grace, I'm sorry about a lot of things, ya know? And—"

"Nothing to be sorry for, Jack."

"Yeah, well, make sure to call this one a lot or she might make me come get you. And, if anyone over there gives you trouble, we'll both come—"

"I know you would. And she's already put the secret service on standby. Thank you, Jack."

Loyal stood there fiddling with her jean pockets, letting the moment drag on while we watched Jack drive off. She managed to spring half a smile with pouty eyes. "What am I going to do without you?" she asked.

"Oh, that won't be a problem. See, Jack said he'd come by every single day, multiple times if you put out."

It was the perfect implicit and explicit tease, not to mention a way to amuse myself if it didn't work out.

"Ouch, you evil bitch," Loyal replied, swiping my shoulder. "In that case you better get back here before I do something foolish like marry the guy. God, I think I might need my own head examined."

"I gotta go," I squeaked. Lord knows I taught myself quite well that the easiest way of dealing was to not let feelings get in the way. There was some of that in Loyal, too. We didn't even hug, not for lack of want. It would have made the moment too real, too serious for both of us. We leaned in, heads tilted down slightly so our foreheads touched gently. No words were exchanged, not an *I love you, I'll miss you.* Those sentiments were a given—felt and understood.

Chapter 7

That car ride was about the longest I'd ever taken in my life, emotionally speaking. I had entirely too much time to conjure up more conflicting voices in my head than one person should subject themselves to. I tried to combat all the noise by blasting the radio most of the way, rolling down the highways and side roads to the beats and the can't-hear-myself-think logic. I didn't bother to notice, but I can imagine the looks on the passing drivers' faces. I must have put on quite the show while performing my most animated, brave-faced, bucket-seat sing-along.

It didn't even occur to me to think about home in any reflective sort of way. In fact, I somehow convinced myself this would be a simple relocation, devoid of any overdue consequences at all.

I should have known better.

The island was a different sort of place, and I hadn't left on preferable terms. I knew that full well going in, but I guess I was hoping for overall forgetfulness, the kind only time and a willing mind can produce. Really, I don't know whom I was kidding. Deep down, in places I hadn't gone to in over a decade, I was scared out of my mind.

My native home was a different world, with a different breed of people. You almost had to be, to want to live in such a faraway place, so beautiful and serene. Of course, any glorified recollections I had may have been slightly skewed, taken from a child's point of view. Of what I knew, last names didn't matter much. We were all extended family there, for better or worse. Most of the time it was nice having everyone look out for one another. Tourism was essential to our way of life, creating a mutually respectful, coexisting mix of humanity, subject to occasional reckless nuisances. A laid-back, easygoing personality was optimal, and a well-maintained and nurtured tolerance was key.

My parents had earned their place as pillars of our remote society. I hate that, at only twenty-six, my memories of them were already fading. I suppose that happens as the years go by. But I also accelerated the process with misguided, mournful disassociation. I take full regretful credit for that. But, losing them was . . . disastrously hard. Life had been perfect back then. We weren't *just* another family, and they weren't *just* my parents. We were extensively active in the social scene, owners of one of the island's oldest, most prominent hotels.

I would sit on the expansive front deck, watching the ferry bring visitors over in massive herds daily, on the hour. Seeing them file off the boat, I would people watch and play guessing games in my head as to names and origins. Usually, Ginny was there, too. We would entertain ourselves by matching the faces to what we thought their names would be. That was about the deepest extent of my curiosity. My general bias toward outsiders was along the lines of, why do all these strangers have to invade *my* island? I had no desire to get to know these people, make temporary friends for a day, a week, weekend, whatever it was. This was my home. Staring out a bedroom window and daydreaming of what else was out there was one thing. But I never really wanted to be anywhere else, until the day I suddenly wanted to be almost anywhere in the world other than there.

"Your ticket, ma'am. Excuse me, ma'am?"

"Huh? Oh, I'm sorry." I snapped out of my daze, the remains of a midmorning fog burning off over the sound.

"May I see your ticket please, ma'am?" the man repeated.

"Yes, sorry."

Long drives made me sleepy. While everyone else vacated their vehicles in favor of the upstairs' scenic ocean views, I saw no need to leave the comfort of mine. I dozed off to talk radio and awoke about forty minutes later in cramping agony. I shimmied out of the car in close quarters, stretching and cracking out the kinks in my back. Joining the crowd above, I stood at the rail with the wind whipping through my hair, arms crossed, and mind adrift like the motion of the ship. I checked my phone for the time and read a text message from the realtor: Running late, sorry for any inconvenience. Arriving on the noon ferry. See you then, Anne.

The island was a sliver on the horizon. That still left plenty of time to dredge up old memories, the special ones, the ones I retained but locked away. Nervous tension started to build. The mulish facade I wore began to slip away the closer we got to shore. The distant sounds of my childhood were creeping in, playing on the beach. Little by little, my subconscious was butting in. I tried to hold it off with my best stone-faced fix. It didn't last for long. As the ferry circled around and came about south-side into the old harbor, there it was. I felt my heart rate quicken at the sight of my family's old inn, perched straight ahead up on the hill.

It stuck out like a sore thumb, a beckoning old ghost from my past, and I wasn't about to hang around long enough to let the its presence stop me from setting foot on solid ground. I turned away and beat the shortest path back to my car. I was angry and grumbling to myself about it. "Way to go, Grace! You knew damn well it was there, just waiting for you." The thing was, I wasn't too sure what I was even angry about or what triggered it. It was *there*. It hadn't gone anywhere. It *was* going to be the first thing I saw. It's not like I was so ignorant to assume that just because my parents were gone, and I had moved on, that material objects that belonged or once belonged to us just dissolved into dust. Or was I? I mean, I did, in a very real sense, convincingly brainwash myself into accepting that my entire world had vanished. That's why finding that property deed for the house was a punch in the gut, and that's why the premise of *out of sight, out of mind* was so appealing. The second I cleared the line of off-loading traffic,

I hurried out of the lot in the opposite direction. I pulled over on a side road and gripped the steering wheel tightly, taking evasive measures to regroup.

I drove steadily through town, disinterested in sightseeing. Winding through the quiet streets out of town was unexpectedly like second nature. I couldn't help but crack a slight smile, noting how it was just like riding a bicycle, which for nearly half my life, was my basic means of transport. And I had spun my wheels over every inch of road, hundreds of times over.

The next thing I knew, I was in front of the house. I parked mere yards from the driveway. I don't know why, other than the thought of occupying that space felt a little too personal. As I exited the car, my eyes panned the familiar view of Settler's Pond a half mile away. I continued slowly up the driveway, growing more nervous with every step. I stopped short of the front steps, fishing a single key from my purse. Anxiety got the better of me. This was too much too fast. A shaky hand fumbled the key out and down to the ground. A tingly, static sensation blanketed me briefly. Suffice it to say, I rekindled an acquaintance with the side porch for the next hour or so until the real estate agent arrived.

"It's such a gorgeous little island. I don't get out here enough to visit, and it's certainly rare to get a call from anyone who's looking to sell. Are you moving very far?"

"Oh, no. Actually, this is . . . was my uncle's place. He passed away a few months ago. I didn't even know he still owned it." Most of that statement was true, the only truth she needed to know. Why give her reason to think my roots in this matter ran any deeper and risk a conversation that I didn't want to have?

"Oh, I'm so sorry." She sighed, offering condolences. "It's such a lovely home. I can't imagine it would take long to sell at all. In the meantime, I'm sure no one would blame you if you changed your mind and decided to keep it in the family." I responded with only a polite smile and nod. She stood up and gathered her things. "Well then, I've got all I need. I'll get out of your way. It's such a nice day. I'm sure you have better things to do." She noticed the time, to her delight. "I think I'll grab some lunch and poke around in some of the shops before I head back. Any suggestions?"

The question stoned me for a second, and I had to think fast. "Oh, um, it's been a while since I've been here myself. I'm not sure I'm the best person to ask. Thank you, though, for coming out on such short notice." I stood to see her off, shaking her hand.

"No trouble at all. It was a pleasure meeting you. I'll be in touch early next week."

I wanted to follow her out. The thought of her leaving and my having to be there alone turned my stomach sideways. I was always, and I do mean always, a headstrong person, straight from the womb. That is the one embedded trait that never changed. That's the one that set me on this path to begin with. Now look at me. Frightened of my own beginnings, pacing a ten-by-ten-foot porch because I can't bring myself to go inside. I was brave enough to blow a fuse on my boss, tough enough to hurl the most accurate speedball I had ever thrown and dunk his ass for sparking an inner rage that had nothing to do with him in the first place. Yet this was holding me back. *Just go in the frickin' house, you chickenshit.* What if . . . what if I went in there and I was eleven years old again? The last time I had walked out of this house, everything was fine. And then I came home and . . . I had sent Anne in on her own to do her realtor thing, inspections, take pictures, while I waited like a coward. And now I was pep-talking myself into a strung out bundle of pathetic nerves.

Hell, that eleven-year-old had been trapped in me for years. I had put her there. I had put her away in exchange for a modified version. So, even worse, what if I went in there and there was nothing? I was afraid of the nothing. I made one floundering effort. I stood at the back door, swallowed hard, and looked at the doorknob. *Don't just stand here all day! Your obligation and ties to this place ended with the decision to sell.* The realtor locks were even on now, enforcing that. So why I did I bother touching my hand to my pant pocket, feeling for a key that wasn't there?

"Looking for this?"

I turned to see a woman about my age at the end of the front walkway, holding it up in the air.

Chapter 8

"Yes, um, thank— Do I know you?"

"Your friendly neighborhood keystone cop. Get it?"

I glared at her strangely.

"Because the . . ."

"What?" I asked, utterly confounded. She smirked and laughed.

"Sorry, Elles. I was just joking. See, I—"

"What?" I repeated, more spooked. She held up my house key again.

"No, see I found your . . . ya know . . . on your sidewalk made of—"

"Nobody's called me that in fifteen years."

"Oh! So, wait, you didn't get the j—"

"It wasn't funny," I blurted out.

"Damn, well don't hold back on my account."

"Who are you?"

"Uh, Kate-ie. I mean Katie. You probably remember me as— Ya know what? You probably find me about as memorable as ya do funny. So I'll just . . ."

"Katie . . . Sheridan, from school."

It wasn't any great lightbulb moment or that I suddenly recognized her when she said the name. She was the only Katie I'd ever known; therefore, by process of singularity . . .

"Yeah, well, I mean, I'm out now. Of school, that is. Not that I've been to prison. Haven't escaped the rock yet, though."

"Is that what they're calling the island these days?"

"No, it's a— You really don't find me funny, do you?"

"Sorry. It's the audience, I'm sure, not you. Um, I'd invite you in, but I haven't been inside myself. Not too sure of the state of the place."

She looked over the house, nodding. "Do you wanna go grab something to eat? You look a little stressed."

While her comedic career was on the rocks, she was spot-on with my body language. The fact that she, of all people, showed up within hours of my arrival was puzzling. I knew Katie well enough growing up. The island has only one small school. We all got along for the most part. Ginny and I were simply a band of two. Not much, or many, came between us. So nothing against Katie. I guess I would have expected someone else in her place. After quick consideration of personal motives, it was obvious I hadn't considered interacting with anyone else at all. Somewhere along the line, prior to all other contingencies, I subconsciously placed the entire onus of this homecoming success on a dead man: Uncle John.

This was his apparent plan. Perhaps Aunt Nellie's, as well. Nevertheless, it surely wasn't mine. I was just the fool who picked up and followed through on his wishes. So what if Katie didn't exactly meet whatever expectations? I was still hungry, and reviving childhood friendships wasn't tops on my impromptu this-was-your-life, property-purging tour of duty. Christ, what was I getting all worked up for then? It was only lunch. After that, I could get back on that ferry and make Loyal the happiest ex-roommate of all-time . . . or stay. My choice, all mine. No pressure. Minor details to mull over while refueling with a former classmate. She took us to The Oar, a place that played a significant role in my upbringing.

"So, I'm confused. Are you here, like, back for good or . . . ?"

Already, this wasn't going well. Mull over as in, a one-woman mulling. My business wasn't supposed to be a picnic-table subject for two, especially on sacred ground. And by the way, why did I seem to be in my own head, talking to myself so much lately, instead of enjoying the natural ambience of the outdoor lawn nestled by the harmonious Salt Pond? Seriously, I was starting to get on my own nerves. Back to her question, for which I had no answer. I choked up and grinned.

"Hey, I'm sorry. It must be weird, being back after all this time. I didn't mean to intrude. I heard you were back. So, I thought I'd stop by and—"

"You heard? From who? It's not like I called ahead. Nobody knew I was—"

"Oh, please, Elles . . ."

"It's Grace, actually, now."

"Oh, well, since when does this island require prior notice? Hell, besides tourists, our main import and export is gossip, internally speaking. You know that. I'll bet someone around here probably knew you were coming back before you did." That was an attention-grabbing statement, one I certainly hadn't thought of. "So, ya gonna stick around or . . . "

So much for apologies, geez. She wasn't the welcoming committee; she was more like a recruitment advocate. I whiffed at the idea. "Staying?" I groaned. "I couldn't even go inside my own house. That doesn't say much for a person who might have been thinking of sticking around."

It was at that moment Katie's eyes widened, and I saw her wheels kick into motion as the waitress was about to deliver our food. Katie stopped her before she set anything down. "Sorry, we've changed our minds. Could we get that to go?" Before I could disagree or question her, she was off her rocker . . . I mean . . . off her bench—Freudian slip—standing over me with a mischievous grin. "Well, you're not going to figure it out sitting here with me then, are you?" She started crossing the grass toward the restaurant service door.

"But we were just about to—"

"Get the car! I'll get the food!"

I got up, stomach growling, and feeling strangely, amusingly irritated. "Is this really necessary? Our food's here! Why are we . . . I'm eating in the car then!"

That turned out to be more of a prediction than a threat, since we both did, sitting in front of the house, parked behind my car.

Katie caught me looking at her intently as she gobbled a

mouthful, catching a bit of lettuce dribbling out of her mouth. “What? I didn’t have breakfast,” she declared.

“You remind me of someone,” I said with Loyal in mind.

“Oh, yeah? Who’s that?”

“Someone I know back home.”

She stopped chewing and glared at me. “I thought you *were* home.”

“No, I meant . . .” I inhaled a deep breath. ”Ya know we could have eaten there? It’s a nice day outside. It was a better view.”

“Damn!” she exclaimed.

“What?”

“Did you get the drink?”

“Um, I got the car, remember? This was your idea genius. You went—”

“Do you have anything in . . . Can I get some water or something?”

Ah! Now it was starting to make sense. And here I thought she was laying all her cards on the table, bringing me back here to figure it out. I thought eating in the car was just some kind of formality before she invited herself in for dessert.

“Wow!” I replied, shaking my head and cackling at her transparent deceit. “I’m guessing this is the part where I’m supposed to—”

“No, seriously, this burger is dry. I just . . . Okay, fine. But if you eat and run now, it’s gonna look like murder. As the vengeful ghost who will then haunt you, I don’t want that on your conscience so . . .”

Katie’s company, whether mildly appreciated, was beginning to stink more of an intervention than a random visit. I peaked at the house from the corner of my eye, tilting back against the headrest. Katie resumed filling her face like she had recently denounced a hunger strike.

“I thought you were thirsty.”

“Yeah, and I thought you were from here.”

“What, are you trying to choke to make a point?” The

amusing bit was turning hostile. "And what the hell is that supposed to mean?"

"People, ya know, *we* people, are neighborly when someone's in need. At least drag the friggin' garden hose down here or something."

I snatched up my mess of wrappers, crumpled everything into a ball and shoved it into the brown paper bag it all came out of. "Fine, if I get you a drink of water, will you leave?"

"That depends. If I stop harassing you, will you?"

"Stop harassing— What are we doing here? Why are you so insistent that I do this, anyway? I mean, what does it matter? I'm selling the place and we were never friends before —"

"We're not friends now," she informed. I threw both hands up in the air, so exhausted by the whole argument that I couldn't even string another full, coherent response together.

"Yeah, well . . . So . . . What . . ."

"You should stay," Katie said proudly, nodding at me.

"You're nuts. Why?"

"Because— Wait, why am I nuts or—"

"I don't care why you're nuts. Please enlighten me as to why I should stay."

"Because I'm really beginning to enjoy busting your ass. Because you need to. Why else would you be here now?"

"Um . . ." I gestured toward the house.

"You could have done that long-distance. You had no intention of going inside. You could have mailed the—"

"Can I ask you something? Why do you care? I mean if we were never friends, still not now, as you pointed out, why do you care?"

She shrugged her shoulders, nonchalantly, adding a mumbling *I-don't-know* grumble. "Eh, I kinda like you. You should stay. We probably could have been good friends, you and I, back in the day—if it wasn't for that meddling Ginny Carrington demanding all your attention."

"Hey, watch it. She was my best friend."

"Was?" she questioned, pulling a bottle of water from her car door and chugging it.

"Oh, my God!" I scowled.

"Relax, okay? Before you go getting all upset at me, just hear me out. Now, you're right. Our desks at school were closer than *we* ever were. What happened to you and your family was . . . horrible. It was all anyone could talk about, and it left a scar on this town as deep as it is wide. Then, for the longest time, *you* were all everyone was talking about. What happened to poor little Elles Garity?"

"Why are you doing this?"

"What you have to understand Elles—"

"I told you, it's Grace."

"Grace, fine. You have got to understand, they had to move on. You did, and we all did. That was fifteen years ago, Grace. They don't know you anymore. So coming back now, if it is just to finish getting rid of us, you have to understand that anything you do now, any decisions you make, don't just affect you." I turned away, refusing to look at her. "For the record, I hope you do stay. But you're not a kid anymore, and if you mess this up this time, you're gonna find staying here a hell of a lot harder than running away was."

"Cool, I should get—"

"Where are you gonna sleep tonight?" she asked, sounding aggravatingly caring and sincere.

"What are you, good cop, bad cop? Trying to be my mother or some—"

"Sure, if you need one. I mean she's not around right now so—"

"She's dead! Like you said, I'm not a kid anymore. I don't need anyone telling—"

"You're right, you're right. She is dead, dead tired of—"

"What the hell is the matter with you?" I snapped, enraged. "Ya know what, Katie? Forget it!" I got out of her car and into mine, slamming both doors closed.

Katie circled around and stopped alongside me facing the other direction. She didn't speak right away, and I had absolutely nothing left to offer. She appeared to be taking the time to choose her words carefully. When she did, it came out like soft-spoken motherly advice, aimed at defusing the situation. "You can't come halfway back, Elles, no matter what you're calling yourself, who you are now or ever were. You left pieces of yourself behind fifteen years ago. Like it or not, you're gonna have to find those missing pieces 'cause if you don't, you'll never truly get back home."

Chapter 9

Our entire interaction left me shaken. It came out of left field, but a lot of what she said was probably true. The toughest question wasn't whether I was staying or not. That ship had literally sailed. And maybe I was getting stubbornly full of myself, but I was of the opinion that I had absolutely nobody to answer to. I didn't know what I was looking for or what I hoped to achieve, whatever these "pieces" Katie spoke of were. Nobody knew me around here anymore? Well, newsflash, I wasn't even sure *I* knew me anymore. I had to start somewhere. The fortune I inherited wasn't buying me any happiness nor did I expect it would. The only thing money was buying me was time—and disapproval, apparently.

I should have called Loyal, or Jack, but I didn't. Too much was happening in my head. I was fully prepared to spend the rest of the evening in the car, sequestered from anyone else who might want to lay into me for . . . what? What did I do? From the driver's seat to the porch swing, back and forth, for ten, fifteen-minute intervals at a time. The more I thought about everything, the more heated I became, at times breathing like a raging bull ready to charge at anything that crossed me. At least I had the sense to find my way to the more comfortable, leg-roomy passenger's seat by nightfall.

Dinner was a sad selection of assorted snacks I had brought along for the ride. Entertainment was channel surfing on the radio. Once my brain got too weary, and eyelids too heavy, I slid the seat back as far as it went, reclined, and fell asleep—but not before reaching the temporary resolution that come tomorrow, nothing and nobody was going to stand in the way of my being whoever the hell I wanted to be. It didn't matter where I was, the mission was the same: I had to figure out what I was going to do with myself—find a job, a passion, a purpose to my life—and to hell with the public's perception of *poor Elles Garity.*

* * *

I got an earlier start than the sun. In addition to grocery shopping and finding a more functional and suitable place to stay, implementing a new morning routine was exactly what I needed to kick-start my days. Running, perfect. I hadn't done that in a while, and it was just the outlet I needed for exercising both my body and troubled mind. Day one and it was already proving to be a useful means of clearing negative thoughts and organizing priorities. Unfortunately, it was also proving that I was a little more out of shape than anticipated.

As if trudging along the beach through soft sand wasn't challenging enough on my lower body, the rest of me was rebelling, and the shortest way back from here was up a daunting stairway cutting through the bluffs to the top. That wasn't even counting the treacherous path to the first stair. I stood there, mentally defeated, hunched over, hands on knees, catching my breath. A rocky terrain equipped with an anchored rope for added stability, in the event of one single misstep, awaited. Surely I'm making it sound more terrifying than the popular landmark that hundreds of visitors per day flock to for the views alone. But when you're sweat-drenched, rubber-legged, and looking up at almost one hundred fifty steps, you tend to overdramatize. I mean, Jesus, things like this are supposed to look bigger when you're a child, not an adult. I paced myself the rest of the way, one muscle-spasming, calf-cramping step at a time. Halfway up I stopped for a sit-down rest on a landing and appreciated the gorgeous sunrise in front of me while rationing the remaining contents of my water bottle. I felt like I'd attained middle-aged status by the time I reached the top. Not even a mocking voice phased me.

"Ya know, attractions like this one, we generally prefer they be enjoyed by more experienced climbers. Rookies just tend to cause traffic jams and annoy the other tourists." I turned my head to see a police officer resting over on the rail of the observation platform beside me, his face in profile, gazing upon the brightening sky. The way he spoke to me suggested he knew me and was giving me a hard time. I tried to study his features, moving in slowly for a better view. He stayed still and quiet, pulling my curiosity in. "You know what the problem is, don'tcha? I got taller, handsomer, added some muscle." He gloated, playing into my temporary cluelessness. He removed his hat to give me a better look.

"Tom?"

"Almost there," he said, turning to face me at last.

"Tom Deiter?"

He cleared his throat and looked away again. "It's, uh, Sheriff Deiter now. And just what makes you any less compliant to the laws around here than anyone else, anyway?"

My eyes diverted to the sign posted beside the platform that read "Stairway access prohibited between 8 p.m. & 8 a.m." I couldn't tell if he was being serious or not, if this was the second character assassination attempt in as many days. The words *Give me a break!* rang through my head and instead I deflected. "Compliant?"

"It means—"

"I know what it means, Tom. It's been a while. But last I remember, the majority of your vocabulary centered almost exclusively around four letter words."

He put his head down and chuckled to himself. "Well, this is upsetting. Yep, you've, uh, you have put me in a very desirable position, ya know that? Let's see, welcome back this town's most notorious runaway and ignore my sworn civil responsibility, or—"

"Really, Tom? For taking the stairs?"

"Or—and forgive me if this is the part that's gettin' me all warm and fuzzy, since your bodyguard ain't around to stop me this time—I can make a personal dream come true right here and now, slap the cuffs on the formerly untouchable Miss

Garity, and lock 'er up for trespassing and failure to *comply* with the proper signage. That the sort of example y'all are teachin' the kids these days or what?" We both assumed a silent, stone-faced stance, waiting for the other to break eye contact first. Mostly I didn't know whether to laugh in his face or punch him in it. *My* position being, if he was truly willing to act on settling some childhood grudge with a blatant, pathetic abuse of power, I might as well legitimize the charge, but I was way too tired to swing. He put his chin up and scratched at it for a moment, thinking with a *hmm*. "I hereby order you to pay restitution by way of community service."

"What?"

"You can start by treating a well-respected member of local law enforcement to breakfast over at the airport." He grinned from ear to ear. "Welcome home, Elles Garity."

Oh, where to start. First of all, the sight of Tom Deiter in uniform was epic. This was the boy who, as a child, made bullying an art form. Well-liked, attention-demanding —in a class clown, egocentric way. Tom was the oldest in our class. His approach to setting a good example was simple: he cared about us, and all he expected in return was the acknowledgment by his peers of his rambunctious-to-the-core superiority. He picked on us, but he cared. He looked out for our overall well-being—most of the time. The bodyguard he referred to was none other than Ginny Carrington herself. In spite of being years younger and significantly outweighed, she held a very peculiar influence over Tom. His often-immature shenanigans stopped when Ginny stepped in and told him they did.

My place within that dynamic, the benefit of being best friends with Tom Deiter's portable, pint-sized conscience, meant I was *off* limits. All it ever took was a death stare from her soul-snatching eyes if he laid a finger on me, crossed the line with a comment, or dared to insult me. This new and, yet to be determined, improved protector of the people gig was a head-spinning role reversal. To be fair, I gave him the benefit of the doubt.

It took the better part of twenty-four hours and a chance meeting to finally be welcomed home . . . from Sheriff Tom Deiter. My, oh, my. It had to be a prank. Those words just didn't belong in the same sentence, or at least not in that order without further context. All of that aside, something he referenced was eating at me. For a town that supposedly let go of me, got over me, I was getting the distinct feeling they were up to speed on everything that concerned me—when and where I went, my career . . . God knows what else.

Lucky for Tom, I worked up quite the appetite unintentionally trying to kill myself from overexertion. I would have hugged him if I wasn't a gross, quivering mound of exhausted, sopping wet flesh and bone. I accepted his backward offer but insisted he meet me there after I had gone home to shower and change. Doing so, on the other hand, presented quite a stumbling block. The house I couldn't bear to enter had its exterior perks, however: the outdoor shower that, to a woman who spent all day running an inn and hadn't the time or energy to play housekeeper at home, was my mother's answer to an often muddied, sandy, or otherwise grungy child. For now, it was my saving grace, pun intended.

I searched through the compartments of my mobile armoire—the suitcases in my trunk—for a fresh set of clothes and a towel. I was washed and letting pulsating, soothing heat soak in when I was startled by what sounded like a metal object striking a concrete floor. I turned the shower off and my ears to the wind with my head on a swivel like skittish, dripping wet, naked prey. I tiptoed out of the stall, dried off, and dressed in the direction of the garage. I crouched down in front of one of the two doors. Keeping my ears peeled and fingers gripped tightly around the door handle, I lifted with all my might, aiming for the element of surprise on what, or whoever, was inside. A dark-skinned man froze like a deer in headlights. The second he laid eyes on me he greeted my scare tactic with an unaffected semi-embarrassed smile. He bent over to retrieve a fallen wrench off the floor and straightened up, winking at me.

"Beg your pardon, I didn't mean to make a racket. I didn't realize anyone was—"

"What, home? As in *my* home, including this very structure you're standing in?"

What struck me the most was his carefree, nonchalant reaction. He didn't try to run, talk his way out of criminal intent, or even come at me in a threatening fashion. He stood there, staring at me, with a gleam in his eyes. It was creepy in a *sorry for the bother, neighbor* sort of way, like he recognized me as someone familiar. I stepped back, reached up and grabbed the door, and yanked it closed. I leaned against it with a hand over my chest to compose myself. At first glance, I was positive I did not know that man on any level. It was weird. The way he looked at me made me question otherwise. The way my heart pounded fast like when your subconscious, for some inexplicable reason, knows a god-awful truth and is safeguarding it from you. I waited, assuming he'd gone the same way he came in—through the back door.

"I'll just be—"

"Oh! Jesus Christ!" I shouted, nearly leaping out of my skin. "What the hell are you doing?!"

"I didn't mean to scare you, honest, I—"

"You did! Who the hell are you?"

"Oh, my name's F—"

"Not . . . who are you, as in what's your name. Who are you as in, who are you to be creeping around other people's property? My—"

He held both hands up flat, palms out to intercede in his own defense. "Uh, may I?"

I tossed my hands up then folded my arms. "Well, it's a little late to say be my guest but . . . sure."

He walked over to the other garage door and opened it, peering inside. "She's a beaut, ain't she? Needs new tires and a good washin' but . . . See, I been workin' on 'er a little at a time, here and there. Uh, that's why I stopped by." He displayed the wrench in his hand, holding it up. "Left one of my tools behind last time. Oh, I got 'er runnin' and everything, just needed a few . . ."

His voice, as he continued to explain himself, faded away. My eyes fixated on that car. I saw right past him, his lips moving, talking with his hands, and carrying on, but all I could concentrate on was my dad's old 1962 AMC Rambler station wagon. That dusty, time-warped relic was the very representation of why I couldn't go inside that house. It symbolized everything that, deep down, I was afraid to see and how it would make me feel. Here was this complete stranger, this man, this ominous figure raving about a material object from my past like he had been granted guardianship or appointed caretaker with freewill access to something that did not belong to him, stored away in a place he had no business intruding upon. For all that and more, I was furious and done hearing him out.

Chapter 10

"Get out," I said, simply.

"I'm . . . I'm sorry if I—"

"Please, go." I gulped. My father bought the wagon just before I was born. It was the only family vehicle I had ever known. I had never found it to be very eye-catching or endearing to look at, personally. He cherished it, and for a classic that managed to sound like a helicopter on wheels on good days, it held up well over the years. For its faults, it didn't stick out like a sore thumb on an island that put functionality above appearance and style. Vanity is of little use on a nine-square-mile stretch of drivable land where the natives use transportation sparingly.

I walked over to it, gently touched it, glided my fingertips across the front of the hood, crossing to the other side. This was the vacation car that never served that purpose because we couldn't break ourselves away from this slice of heaven to go anywhere else. It was the cargo hauler that we used to fill our freezer full of food to cover the winter months. Other than that, it was my father's basic means of travel to work and back. In short, it was just a damn, stupid car. *So, get a hold of yourself Grace!* I balled my fists up and pounded the roof of the car, irritated with myself for feeling such an emotional attachment.

It wasn't the object I was really mad at, in case that's not clear. It was the uselessness of it now. It was the fact that it was still here, that I had to find it, that I had to . . . So this is what it feels like when reality sinks in—the reality that I never faced. Nothing about my parents' deaths ever kicked in because I made the first move and kicked it all away. I left the garage and pulled the door down slow and easy, as if carefully and respectfully restoring the sanctity of a treasured piece of history.

* * *

Tom was on his second cup of coffee when I arrived post-delay. The airport diner was fitting, given the company I was sharing it with. Tom's father was an aviation mechanic. Tom spent so much time here in his father's shadow, he seemed predestined for a career in the clouds, rather than wearing a badge. I claimed the stool beside him at the bar and brushed aside the last forty-five minutes, hoping for a much-needed relaxed atmosphere.

"We were sure sorry to hear about your uncle, Elles. He was a good man."

"Thanks, Tom. It's Grace now, by the way."

"Yeah, I seem to recall hearin' somethin' about that. You know, if I had known when we was kids that your initials spelled—"

"You would have gotten your teeth knocked down your throat by you know who."

He looked up at the ceiling, thought on it for a moment, and shook his head agreeingly, chuckling. "Yeah, sounds about right. Probably better off, save me some dental work. She was a real firecracker back then, wasn't she? Still is."

"Wait, how did you know that's my middle name, anyway?"

"What?"

"Well, I never told anyone, for exactly that reason. My parents never used it much, and they knew I hated it. For all you know, I could have changed my—"

"I just assumed, Grace, that's all."

"Oh . . . So, you mean Ginny's still . . ."

"Oh yeah, oh yeah. Never left. Got a nice little house, oceanfront view, south end."

"So is she . . . I mean has she . . ."

“Married? Nah, not no more.

“Divorced?”

He clammed up, like he didn’t want to reveal any more. He took a slow sip of coffee, swallowed, and bowed his head, dejected. “She’s . . . she’s, uh . . . widowed, El— Grace.”

“Oh, my God.”

“We had a navy ship come through here a while back, some sort of engine, mechanical emergency. I dunno. Anyway, in addition to the regular crowds, we played temporary host to the entire crew for a few weeks while they made the repairs. Our class was about to graduate high school, prom season and all that, ya know. Ginny hadn’t been asked yet. A small town with a limited teen social scene, suddenly overrun with young, handsome, single, lonely sailors, you can imagine how that turned out. She couldn’t stop talkin’ about him. Came back on shore leave, first time, found out he was a father to be. Just like that. They got hitched and you better believe Dina blew her top.”

“What happened to him?”

Tom looked down at his plate, picking at his food with his fork. “Killed overseas . . . On routine patrol, hostile territory, somethin’ like that, ’bout a year later. Wrecked her pretty good for a while. Shame, ya know. Got to be there for the birth of the first one, never met the second.”

”Kids?” I squawked with disbelief.

“Oh, yeah, boy and a—”

“Yeah, I get it. I um . . . Sorry, can we talk about something else, please?”

Tom just glared at me and continued eating. “Well, okay. What about you? What’ve you—”

“Something else?”

Tom sighed, dejected. “You’re not leavin’ me many options here, Grace. You don’t wanna talk about you or—”

“Went to college, became a teacher. Let’s see, married and divorced within a few months . . . That about covers it.”

How's that for a brief summary of highlights? There were few to mention. Why waste time shining light on the fact that I didn't run away to start over. I ran away to recover. I just found things to keep me busy in the interim. That was another hard fact that was beginning to sink in. I'm not sure Tom knew where to go with that rambled-off list since an awkward silence followed. "So, what about you, Tom? Married? You're a little young to be a sheriff, aren't—"

"You really come here to talk about me, Grace?" I could feel his eyes on me as I ate, reading me, judging me, like he knew something. He cleared his throat and shifted gears. "Ya know, your Uncle John and Aunt Nellie used to come out here every now and then for a visit. They stayed at your folks' place."

"I didn't know that."

"They kept it up real nice, too. Even after Nellie passed, John still came around couple times a year. Until he got sick and he couldn't travel like he—"

"I'm selling it, Tom."

His fork dropped to the plate. He sat motionless for about thirty seconds, cleared his throat again, and used a napkin to dab his face.

"I'm guessing you knew that with your little sales pitch. I never wanted it. I wish he would've told me sooner. I would've —"

"You what? You would've what, Grace? We wouldn't be having this conversation because you—"

"Doesn't matter. It's on the market as of—"

"He left you a goddamn way back in, Gr—" He took a moment to compose himself and softened his tone. "Now that you mentioned it, what exactly is it you want, Grace?"

"To eat, Tom. You invited me to breakfast. So call me crazy, I just thought we were gonna eat and catch up a lit—"

He got up from his bar stool, slurping down the last sips of coffee. "I think we're pretty well caught up. Don't you?

"What is that supposed to mean? And why all the

hostility all of a sudden, Tom? This doesn't have anything to do with you. What I do with my family's house is—"

"You're right. It doesn't have anything to do with *me.* I've got to go check some things out, get out on patrol." He stopped short of the door, panning back at me sitting there sulking in mixed feelings. "It's good to see you, Elles, 'scuse me, Grace. Whatever you're lookin' for, I hope you find it."

He left me there to wonder. I got the distinct impression, by the way he said *me*, that there was more to that than he let on. And the tone in his voice on explanation of how he knew my middle name wasn't sitting right, either. I stuck around awhile longer, spaced out, willing my appetite to return after that engagement. It did not. What I needed *right now* was a good night's sleep. One night living like the homeless, allowing this place to get to me was enough. This was not part of the plan. I checked into one of the smaller, out of the way B and B's, brought a change of clothes and some essentials to my room, and confined myself to solitary reflection.

I opened a window for some fresh air and lay on the bed, trying to let my thoughts go blank, warding off the persistent nagging voice in the back of my mind. I repeatedly corrected everyone on my name because, in truth, I severed the emotional connection to that name when I severed all ties to this island. I could get used to playing the mistaken identity card to the outside world until everyone fell in line. Where it got complicated and harder to ignore was the identity crisis brewing inside of me. Starting over was never easy, a fact I was reminding myself of constantly. Starting over where you have history is an entirely different hurdle. What I was embarking on wasn't a "finding myself" expedition. It was turning out to be an undeniable question of which one of me, the person I suppressed or the one I manifested, did I want to be? More honestly, which one *could* I be? Lord knows, I sharpened my coping skills by not letting emotions be a factor in anything I did since I was eleven years old. I swallowed the difficult ones — hurt, regret, fear, and even happiness—as naturally as the air I breathed. What I was starting to realize is, I perfected that trait through total separation and oblivious disconnection in any situation. So much for a comfortable bed relaxing a troubled spirit.

Hours later, the nearby murmur of two voices outside aroused me from a light slumber. The longer I tuned in, one, deeper than the other, caught my attention. I went to the open window and looked down from the second floor. The unknown, unnamed man from my garage was outside with the front desk clerk. I was eavesdropping on a chat about a faulty dishwasher and scheduling an appointment for repairs, nothing of significance except for the stranger offering up his services. They parted ways, and that's when he noticed me watching. We engaged in a passing glance to which he added a kindly wave. I ducked out of sight, retreating to the edge of the bed with the growing unsettling sense that he was someone of preceding consequence.

Chapter 11

Throughout the night, that man, with his tattered carpenter jeans, weathered fedora, and button-down semi casual shirt, loomed large in my head. Whereas he snuck, ironically, in a back door, other thoughts had begun taking up residency in a more prevalent capacity. It was getting increasingly tough to lie to myself and ignore the warning signs. My belief that I could quietly return to the scene of my tragedy and start the living reincarnation of Elles Garity as someone else was narrow-minded, at best.

The next morning I went to the window again, opened the curtains, and cracked it open to let in some fresh air. Low and behold, there he was. He was by himself this time, fighting to move a refrigerator by hand truck. I don't know what could have possibly possessed me to do what I did next except for kind, decent human nature.

"Hey!" He looked up, holding it steady. I disappeared from the window and hurried down to offer some assistance. "Need a hand?" Deservedly, I got an awkward-looking hesitation in return. "Don't worry, I won't let it crush you. Where are we going with it?" He motioned with his head to the awaiting truck at the end of the driveway. I held onto one side as we rolled it down the uneven slope. We set it on the automatic lift that had been retrofitted to his truck's extended tailgate, and he raised it safely onto the bed. "That's pretty ingenious. Never seen one of these contraptions on a pickup before."

"Sometimes ya gotta improvise to make things easier on yourself."

"I thought you were fixing a dishwasher." He looked at me confused. "That's what I heard you . . . ya know, talking about yester . . ."

He shook his head. "Right, right, got a newer model on the way to replace this ol' thing. Time a year around here people start gettin' ready for next year's needs." He stepped down off the truck and flipped the tailgate closed, wrenching his back in the process. He clutched at it with one hand, letting out a yelp, as his body locked up and hunched sideways.

"Are you okay? Can I . . ."

"No, no, it's . . . it's all right. Workin' too hard. Guess I overdid it just a little too much."

"I'm—I'm sorry . . . about yesterday. I didn't mean to . . ." He straightened up and brushed me off before I could finish apologizing. He went around to the driver's side door and eased himself in. "Well, can I at least, I don't know, buy you breakfast? Or I can help you take this to wherever you're—"

"Tell you what, Grace. You find yourself another place, get settled in, I'll be happy to take you up on that and join you for—"

"Hold on, woah, how . . ." I couldn't believe this guy, talking to me like we were old friends. I had freaked out before and maybe laid into him a little too harshly for being where he didn't belong, and I was trying to make up for it by being neighborly, because that's what we do around here for one another, and now . . . I knew we were a friendly bunch, but it was almost laughable how comfortably acquainted he seemed around me. There was no other way to describe it. My mind was spinning. I had to stop for a second to back up and refocus. "How do . . . How you know anything about my arrange—" In fact, I did laugh—an *Is this guy for real? What is happening right now?* kind of laugh—as I stammered to interrogate him. "And how do you know my name? I don't even know—" He gestured to the B and B, grinning like, *duh*. "Oh, yeah, well that doesn't mean that I . . . That still doesn't explain how you know my—"

"I guess word gets around . . . 'bout the story of the Garity family, house that's hardly been used in years, which you're obviously related to since you drew down on me and chased me off like a thief in the—"

"I said I was sorry. Wait, no, no, I didn't . . . A thief in the . . . You were on my property."

"Calm down now. Just relax yourself. I was just givin' ya the business, that's all."

Then I laughed again, embarrassed and blushing from my flying-off-the-handle overreaction. "I'm sorry . . . again. I guess I'm a little paranoid, or on edge, lately. I'm not exactly homecoming queen around here since I've been back."

He closed his door and hung his arm over the window ledge. "Don't feel bad. I wasn't exactly voted newcomer of the year when I first showed up myself." He started the truck, turning the engine over a few times to get it going. "Thank you for . . . I appreciate the help." He started off before I cold get another word in. Then it suddenly occurred to me . . .

"Wait! You never told me your"— he sped off and was too far gone to hear my holler—"name." I went back inside, half-perplexed by our strange conversation and shaking off the whispers of the warning voices summoned back into my head —for what, though, I hadn't a clue. I remained inside, hidden from the population. I called Loyal and selectively shared vague details of the last few days, playing off any mounting conflicts. Mostly, I just wanted a friendly voice to talk to for a change. Like the new cozy quarters, a lengthy dose of casual, stress-free chitchat did wonders to promote a second night's sound sleep.

Chapter 12

I can't say what possessed me to seek out the company of Katie the next morning. She did leave me with the sneaking feeling that she genuinely cared, with a measure of tough-loving honesty. In any event, and moreover, she was an attractively less-involved and factored-in link to my past. The only trouble was that I didn't know where she lived, but I knew who to ask. I set out for the police station hoping to find Tom. What I found was more than I bargained for—the aforementioned purpose that I was seeking found me instead, completely unprepared. Through my side mirror I spotted a slender, gray-haired gentleman exiting the building. As I parked, he changed course and came over to my car, latched both hands on the door ledge, leaned in, and smiled a wide-eyed grin.

"I'll be damned!" He marveled. It took me a minute to recognize him—older, thinning hair, a raspier voice, and in street clothes.

"Coot?"

"Elles, do my eyes deceive me, Garity," he declared. "What'd you do, come to turn yourself in?" He cackled.

"I'm sorry?"

"Throw yourself at the mercy of the judge for causin' a stir? If that's the case then tell me, what name shall we book you under?" He cracked himself up, razzing me with one zinger after the other. "You lookin' for Tom?"

"I am. Is the chief around?"

He laughed again. "Chief, huh? I guess as long as you're dreamin' it, you might as well live it, huh?"

"I thought that . . . So, you're not . . ."

"Currently on active medical leave, but still the active OCC around here. Don't let 'im tell ya any different."

“OCC?”

“Original Colored Chief. Longest tenured, anyhow. My time’s up when I say it is. Until then, young Mr. Deiter’s gonna have to be satisfied with filling the part. Dropped in to check on things myself. He ain’t here, so I imagine he’s out campaigning for my succession.”

“I guess a lot’s changed since I’ve been gone, huh?”

He studied my face longingly, with a grandfatherish gleam. “Lord, I remember you. Yes, I do. Was you kids who gave me this nickname. You were too young to remember those days, though now, ain’t ya?”

“We started that?”

“Oh, yeah. Police Chief Marcus Larrow at your service. ’Til one of y’all little wise asses decided it’d be funnier to start callin’ me an ol’ coot one day for spoilin’ your fun. Caught on and I ain’t got rid of it since.”

“You’re right, I don’t remember that.”

“Come to think of it, I don’t think you or Ginny ever joined in callin’ me that, even after I gave up and warmed up to it. Took ownership, made it mine. Wore it like a badge of honor. Yeah, they stopped laughin’ after I did that. Talkin’ ’bout, *Watch out! Run! Here comes Ol’ Coot!* Musta been a quality of character thing with the two of you, growin’ up to be teachers and all.”

“She’s a teacher? I . . .”

He took his hand off my car and took a step back. “Looks like you got some serious catchin’ up to do.”

“Yeah, I guess I do. Hey, do you know where I can find—”

“You been around to visit the family yet?” He posed the question, and I froze. It was a fair one, at that, but not one I was ready to hear by any means.

It nearly sucked the breath out of me just to hear those words. Answering it was shamefully embarrassing. “Um . . . no . . . I um . . .”

“Been to the cemetery?”

Now he was just tormenting me, repeating the idea of doing something, no doubt, long overdue. I wasn't there yet. It was going to take time. "Coot, you just asked me that. I haven't —"

"I'm aware of what I asked. Ain't lost my mind yet. Come on." He walked away, waving his arm for me to follow.

"Where exactly?"

"You lookin' for Chief Wannabe, ain't ya? I might know where he's at, but don't nobody drive me around. I do the chauffeurin'." He pulled up behind my car and honked his horn, yapping at me insistently. "Come on now. I ain't got all day."

I may not have participated in or contributed to the giving of that nickname, but good grief, he was as ornery as ever. He may have submitted to it at one time, too. That didn't change the fact that his tenacious, no-nonsense approach earned him every bit of that moniker and reputation. He took us to a dirt road and over the hills along Harwood's Farm and I began to suspect foul play.

"Where are we going? Why would Tom be way out—"

"He ain't. Just so happens, it's my anniversary. I got a pit stop to make, and you're along for the ride. So, you get to be my deputized assistant." He kept his head turning from side to side, as he drove slowly like he was casing houses.

"Alrighty then. Would it be possible to get a little more information as to what we're looking for?"

"We lookin' to keep my ass out of the doghouse. May not have lost my mind, but my memory plain sucks. We ain't got no flower shops this side of the sound. So, we get creative. Keep your eyes open." Was this guy serious? Scouring the landscape and properties of well-known, accomplished green thumbs to steal flowers, admittedly, was comically resourceful of Ol' Coot. He reached in front of me and opened the glove compartment. "Get on in there and grab those."

Perhaps more impressive were the stashed clippers and a bag of zip ties for bundling that he kept in there, leading me to strongly believe this was not his first floral caper. I was tempted to wipe the tool clean of my fingerprints before returning the evidence to the *chief of police*, of all people. In the end, we put together a beautifully pirated bouquet of stealth-like thievery that I was accomplice to. The whole ridiculous escapade itself would have made for quite a tale to tell. The mission, however, was not what he claimed it to be. My thoughts strayed from imagining the oblivious look on Mrs. Larrow's face, to feeling sorry for Ol' Coot. Then he made a second unanticipated—this time, thoroughly terrifying—pit stop. This was not foul play, it was an intervention, and I fell for it, hook, line and . . . cemetery. The only thing sinking was my insides. He came to a stop midway down one of the gravel roads and came clean. "Well, Miss Garity, it was a pleasure seeing you again."

"What do you mean? What about your anniversary, the flowers . . ." Clearly, it was all made-up excuses to bring me here, and I was saying anything to get that car moving again.

"For you."

I couldn't speak. I couldn't move. Coot got out of the car and came around to my side, opening the door.

"Like I said, you got catchin' up to do. In more ways than one. Mrs. Larrow passed six years ago. I know a little 'bout how you're feelin'. Don't matter if they're with you eleven years or thirty-seven. Hardest thing, either way. You remember who found you that night, don'tcha?" I looked up at him with both hands on those flowers, squeezing them like a vice. "Nobody *wants* to go to a funeral. It's the final step, signifies where you finally leave 'em to rest. But ya don't just go for you. Ya go for them. The only thing missing at theirs was one devastated little girl, who can only move on by letting them rest. You didn't miss it. You just a little late."

Growing up I never knew Coot, Sheriff Larrow, all that well. I never got into that kind of trouble. He knew all of us, and by all accounts, he knew me well. He didn't bring me to find Tom. He took me to where he knew I needed to go. I'll never forget him for that—though I wasn't too thrilled with him at the time. The whole world went silent as I stood there cold, in the middle of the road, as Coot drove away.

I don't know how long I stood there almost catatonic. Flashbacks of that day started pouring in.

I was in school, first period math class.

A god-awful sound rocked the entire island.

It wasn't long before the teachers started whispering among themselves and assuring us that everything was under control.

It was just supposed to be a short, routine trip to the mainland and back. When I got home later that day, everyone who was anyone to me, including Coot, had gathered in our living room. Somehow, I just knew. I felt it, aided by the bad-news support group that awaited me. They tried to explain. They were on scene and at my disposal to comfort me. I got the gist of it.

And then I ran.

I dropped my things before any one of them could lay a heartwarming hand on me . . . and I ran.

Darkness fell before I was found. I was sitting alone at the south side of the island, emotionless, fully launched into autopilot mode. So much of me died that day, as well, and I did the only thing I could think of to protect my feelings, my utter absolute despair, from tearing me apart. I separated myself from the hurt. I made a commitment to my denial. I started, then and there, making my own grown-up choices. But I was just a kid. I was a child, and in the blink of an eye, I felt so . . . so endlessly alone. Consoling me was out of the question, because I wanted no part of pity or sympathy. I just wanted out. I wanted nothing else but to leave. I don't know, maybe I thought acknowledgment meant acceptance and saying goodbye—made it forever real.

Maybe Coot saw what everybody else did, too—that I never let myself have a moment. I never allowed myself to . . . I laid the flowers on the headstone and stepped back. I could feel it all building, boiling up from the depths of my burdened soul. I knew that if I let one teardrop fall . . .

And then one did.

It escaped and streamed down my cheek like the first crack in a crumbling concrete levee wall. The other eye sprung a leak, and my vision went blurry. Then *I* crumbled in slow motion to the ground, crying so hard at times, I could barely gasp for air, so hard my muscles ached. I think I squeaked out an "I'm so sorry" somewhere in the storm. I purged and exhausted myself of fifteen years of heartbroken, headstrong restraint. As I was in the throes of running my own well dry, the heavens burst open above me, and the pouring rains came. When it was over, I was emotionally drained and physically spent. I was nothing more than a dehydrated, withered, and depleted pile of human goo curled up on the ground.

Chapter 13

I woke up the next morning woozy and disoriented. I lay there on my stomach, eyes shuttering open to glimpses of a room I didn't recognize. I felt like a zombie with no urgency to move a muscle. I heard noises in another room, then footsteps getting louder and closer. In my clouded peripheral I spotted a figure sideways at the edge of the doorway then disappearing. I must have blanked out for a short time longer when someone spoke to wake me.

"Well, I'm guessing you're pretty hungry, or thirsty, or both."

I batted my eyelids trying to clear the cobwebs. "Where am I?" I muttered.

"Metaphorically or physically?"

I pushed up onto all fours and tossed my body over into a slouched sitting position with my back against the pillows. Katie sat on the side of the bed looking down over me. "I saw someone else before, standing at the door."

"Tom was here. He couldn't stay."

I groaned and washed my hand over my face. I sat up more and panned the room in a daze. "How did I get here?"

"Well, let's see. Coot called Tom, gave him a head's up where you were. You were pretty out of it by the time he got there. He was worried about takin' you anywhere and leaving you by yourself. So he called me and brought you here. Then Tom gave me a lift to go pick up your car from the station, and here we are. Are you . . . okay? Do you need anything? Are you hungry? I can—"

"I could use a hot shower first."

"Sure, bathroom is down the hall. I'll get the water running."

My body was sore from the whole ordeal of expelling fifteen years of bottled-up grief. I closed my eyes and melted away, letting the hot water and steam seep into my pores and penetrate every muscle. I stayed there until the entire bathroom resembled a steam room. When I was done and dressed, my breakfast was ready and waiting, plated at the table where Katie had a head start. "Thanks," I said and took a seat at the table.

"So, are you . . . I mean, I've never seen a person sleep an entire day away like that. Is there anything you need? Do you wanna talk or . . ."

"I'm good. My last roommate, Loyal, she's a licensed therapist, always dissecting my every emotion, getting her practice by invading my head."

Katie rested her elbows on the table and folded her hands together very properly. "Oh, man. And how did that make you feel?"

"Cute." I sneered back at her. "Like jumping off a cliff, honestly sometimes. So don't test me. I'm surrounded by opportunity here."

"Noted. I just thought I'd check in. You were in pretty rough shape by the time you got here."

I chewed on that one, literally and figuratively, for a moment. "Well, other than being ambushed and basically forced to— No, I'm . . . I . . . just . . . I am a horrible person, and I should have gone there sooner."

"You're not horrible. You're still hurting. Can I ask you something, Grace? Why did you come back here? I mean, why now, after all this time."

"I don't know . . . I . . . Uncle John passed away and, I don't . . ."

"Ya know, I was thinking about the other day. I think maybe I was too hard on you. See, I think your coming back was, well, I think with the house, you finally had an excuse to do something you've always wanted to do."

"But, why . . . You were the first one to reach out. You put me up last night. Thank you for that, by the way. I just don't get it. Why you? No offense, but we were never— "

"Friends? Yeah, we covered that. That was a long time ago, Grace. I thought you could use one now, that's all. It's gotta be rough doing this all by yourself, not knowing how everyone would react. Your family's legacy up in the air, ya know. I just wanted to—"

"What legacy? What are you talking about?"

"The National, you didn't—"

"What about it?"

"I assumed you knew. I thought that was part of why you . . . It's been on the town agenda for weeks. I'm sorry, Grace. I really thought you knew."

"I gotta go."

"Wait a minute. What about breakfast? Grace! Where are you . . . Let me get dressed and I'll go with—"

I didn't give her time to negotiate. How could I think about eating blintzes with information like this? It sent shockwaves up and down my spine. I had to see it for myself. Damn the house. It paled in comparison to this—this cornerstone, the foundation of the Garity family. I snatched up my car keys in stride, and I was gone. She thought I knew? Until recently, I didn't know I owned a friggin' house. How the hell would I know? *Grace, calm down, you're spiraling.* Yes, yes! Because, here I was, like an idiot, going out of my way to avoid the biggest obstacle on this goddamn island because I couldn't stand to look at it, never mind the thought of it in anyone else's possession. Okay, fine! Those weren't the only reasons but, still!

I was upset, on the fringe of irate. I pulled up across the street from the inn. *Had* I known, I might not have been so quick to pass it by the first time. *If* anyone had bothered to . . . Who was I kidding? I still would have avoided it, but all that mattered was that I was there now, feasting my eyes on it. I saw it with a critical eye, like something to be rescued, cleaned up, and cared for. The paint was peeling, windows caked in dust. The widow's walk appeared to have been torn off at its base, presumably in a storm. I climbed the stairs, paced the entire length of the deck a few times, slowly. It was so surreal. This place was my mother's dream. The story I had been told may have been embellished for romantic, fairy-tale affect, but that is exactly what owning and running it meant to her. She poured her heart and soul into it, together with her handpicked business partner, who also happened to be Ginny's mom.

I was too busy growing up to ever pay attention to or appreciate the importance, but this much I knew: my mother wanted more out of life than an ordinary job. Unlike me in my youth, she had a knack for meeting others, a love for knowing people, the gift of gab. She could strike up a conversation with a total stranger in a gas station checkout line and secure a fast friend for life or simply be enriched by such a moment for all it was worth. I admired her for that. This inn was a natural progression of that infectious personality. Our fathers had their own careers. As her daughter, her only child, I knew she loved me. I came along, and I was her bundle of joy. This business, this outlet of exploration, traveling the globe in reverse, silly as it may sound, where the world came to her, was truly her baby. She aspired to be what I only envisioned when I was bored.

"Hey!" Katie yelled out, ending this little reminiscent phase. "You could have at least finished eating." I couldn't break away from my own emotions to offer an excuse for rudely walking out. "Ya don't just get up and leave without . . . Hey! Hello! You, uh, you okay?" Even then it took a minute to communicate in any way. I just sort of shook my head affirmatively and gave her a sideways glance. She leaned her back against the deck rail beside me and kept silent at first, staring straight ahead with me. "I, uh, I guess this must be kinda hard for you. I didn't mean for you to find out that way or anything. I honestly . . . I thought that—"

"I didn't know," I muttered softly. "It's my own fault. After my parents . . . I stopped caring about anything else that was left."

"Well, all I can tell you is the people who were running it last just sorta disappeared. I don't know the whole story, but if it makes you feel any better, I hear there are a few investors interested so far. So, with a little luck it'll be—"

"It doesn't!" I snapped back, perturbed. "I don't care about any stupid investors. This was property of the Garity family. This was our inn, and it always will be, if I have anything to say about it."

"That's . . . the problem, Grace. It changed hands. I'm sure Dina had to make a decision . . ."

"So my mother dies and she just got rid of it without asking . . ."

Me? What was I going to do at eleven years old? Whip out my piggy bank, smash it to smithereens, and fork over a collection of coins that amounted to bubble gum earnings?

"Like I said, I don't know the whole story. But what does it matter? I get it, the sentimental value, but it's gonna get sold —"

"To me."

"Grace, be serious. What do you know about running a place like this?"

"I'll figure it out."

"Figure it out? Do you hear yourself? You can't just—"

"Why are you fighting me on this? What happened to supporting me? All that talk about how I might need someone, or was that—"

"Because I don't think you're thinking clearly about this and what it's going to take to—"

"I have plenty of money and all the time in the world. In case you haven't noticed."

"What I've noticed is *you,* doing exactly what you did

before. You show up here, unannounced, to—"

"Who was I supposed to announce it to?"

"— sell a house, without even bothering to reach out to anyone about—"

"Well, who the hell reached out to me?" She took an abrupt step forward and stared a hole through me, as I did her. "Don't look at me like that. Don't you dare. So far, the greeting party has been an old classmate and some stranger rooting around in my father's garage. Not exactly a long-lost resident's welcome."

"A stranger rooting . . ."

"A repairman. Some guy. I don't know."

"You mean Floyd?"

"Whoever. Ya know what, Katie? I don't care who wants me here, okay? I don't care who has a problem with anything I —"

She laughed, offended by the outburst. "Oh, get over yourself, Grace. This isn't just about you. You have no idea of the suffering you left behind."

"I was eleven, Katie! Eleven fucking years old! I took all the suffering with me. Don't you get that?"

"Not all of it, baby girl! You would have figured that out if you visited once or twice, written, or called, something, anything. You're an adult now, by the way. You're all grown-up, and you better realize that you can't just waltz back into town, hiding behind an old pain and old excuses, by another name."

"Screw you!"

"There's more to you being back than old memories and disapproval!"

I started to walk away, pissed off. Katie wouldn't let it rest, hollering after me while I stormed off across the deck. "That's great! That's just fine, Grace Garity. You go ahead and do whatever the hell you wanna do, regardless of how anyone else might feel about it! Just because you've been taught to *call* someone Mom and Dad, doesn't make them the only family you've got!"

Chapter 14

Those last words she said haunted me the rest of the day. I didn't know why or . . . I guess maybe I had an idea based on a fleeting *what-if* feeling I had a long time ago. Nothing was ever confirmed or denied because frankly there was no merit to it, and I never brought it up. Right then, all I had were designs tumbling through my head of restoring the Garity name, our heritage, back to its former glory. How much drama could I be expected to handle at one time? Even if it was something I wouldn't be able to run from for very much longer. Our argument festered in my head as I set out on a cathartic run. It started off as an ill-tempered power walk, graduating into a jog, and becoming a run the angrier I grew.

Part of that anger was based on Katie's and my relationship turning into a regular sounding board for things I could never bring myself to say out loud before, feelings I held hostage inside. A recently developing side effect of the move meant having to admit that Loyal was the only one left alive who understood me, who sympathized, who, in the deepest, darkest reality of my being, hardly *knew* me at all. Jack, as well. They knew what little I revealed. The rest was all window dressing for a life I kept on hold. All this time, I was functioning on cruise control with safeguards always in place. So sue me if I was having trouble figuring out who exactly to be mad at around here—them or me.

I ran so hard and unfocused that when I slowed to catch my breath, I found myself in unfamiliar surroundings. I thought I knew every square inch of this island. Perhaps my muddled mind was playing tricks on me, or possibly, I hadn't been the coast-to-coast explorer I took my younger self to be. Or maybe, from what I saw, this is where I was meant to end up. In a salvage-filled yard of tarp-covered heaps of junk and exposed machine parts, there was my stranger. What did Katie call him? Floyd? I watched him from a distance, milling around. Then he shuffled off inside. I eventually wandered to his front door and lightly knocked. I wasn't sure if I was prepared for him to answer or not. When he didn't, I leaned in closer to the screen door. Looking beyond the kitchen, I could see the back of his head, him resting on the couch, and the tips of his feet up on the coffee table.

"Hello?" I announced my presence, entering cautiously, welfare-minded as he was unresponsive. I made a point to have my footsteps heard all the way to the backside corner of the sofa before he spoke.

"Most people just state their business from outside the door.'"

I exhaled with my hand at my chest. He tilted his head upward to see who I was and grinned. "You didn't answer me. I didn't know if you were . . ."

"Takin' a nap?"

"Okay. Well, you weren't moving. So . . ."

"Well, I don't know how you do it, but I generally sleep in the still position."

"With your door wide open? I could have been a—"

"You come to lecture me on my household habits, or you just bored?" I'm sure if I had thought long and hard enough, I could have come up with a witty reply but, as it was, still fresh from the run and cooling down, I had nothing. I went off to raid his refrigerator for a bottle of water and parked myself on the couch next to him. He watched me take a drink, cross-eyed. "Help yourself."

"Thanks," I responded, as though his pointless generosity was sincere.

"You always just walk into people's houses like it's your own personal rest stop?"

I took another long swig. "Only when they owe me one."

"I gotta start lockin' my door." His television was on

and muted, a baseball game in progress. I found the remote on the coffee table and restored the volume, flipping through channels. "What are you doin'?" he asked me confoundedly.

"Sorry, I'm not much of a sports fan. Come to think of it, I'm not much of a television watcher. What kinda stuff do people watch these—"

"This a payback thing?

"No, Floyd. It's not a payback thing. I'm just taking a rest."

"Just . . . takin' a rest."

"That's all, mm-hmm."

"I see. So you know my name now. You been snoopin'."

"Actually, a little birdy named Katie told me."

"Uh-huh, and did it occur to you that *I* myself was tryin' to rest when you came waltzin' in?"

"Hey, don't let me stop you. You want me to turn the sound back down?"

"No, I don't want you to . . ."

Truth be told, I wasn't actively trying to be an intrusive bother. He was easy to talk to. We had our rocky introduction that was behind us now. For whatever reason, I felt comfortable being myself around this Floyd character, regardless of the weird unexplained vibes I was receiving. He may not have felt the same way yet, but unfortunately for him, my popularity status wasn't growing elsewhere. And since he had technically sprung himself on me first, it was only fair. Besides, I was rapidly starting to enjoy his company, trading snappy repartee as an avenue to open a broader, more neighborly dialogue. He had no vast, in-depth knowledge of who I was, all controversial things . . . *me.*

I needed that right now—someone around me who wasn't connected to the person formally known as Elles. I needed the unassuming company of someone who wasn't up to speed on the reputation that preceded me and, therefore, in a position to judge me for it. He had no idea whom he was dealing with. Sharing an apartment with Loyal, I learned firsthand from an expert how to be the annoying one in the room with the proper proportions of irresistible quirkiness and other likable qualities to eventually have the other person warm up to me. And not to be outdone, I matched his trespass and raised him a bulging forehead vein ready to pop any second now as we worked out the kinks.

"Tell you what. You rest. I'll watch the ball game. Both are better enjoyed quietly."

In honor of his request, I rewarded him with the courtesy of my silence for all of ten seconds. "We had a TV when I was growing up."

"Oh, lord."

"We never watched it much then, either. We didn't even have cable. We had those rabbit ear things with an antenna on the roof until the wind blew it down one day. After that it was just a decorative piece. Never even bothered to get rid of it."

"My favorite color's green."

"What?"

"I figured, long as we're sittin' here spoutin' out random thoughts for no particular reason other than to get on my nerves."

"Okay, let's talk about you, then."

"Even better," he snarled.

"What is it you fix, Floyd? What's your niche? Electrician, mechanic . . ."

"All depends on what definition of fixin' you're usin'."

"Wow! That's not exactly a glowing endorsement there, Floyd."

"Why are you here, again?"

We, mostly I, carried on for hours, overstaying my welcome, annoying Floyd, and feigning interest in a sport I clearly knew nothing about, just to continue spending time with someone who hardly knew me for as long as possible. Conversation was kept at a minimum, limited to station breaks and midgame gatherings on the pitcher's mound. It wasn't an entirely one-sided affair. Floyd found convenience in my stay by sending me to the kitchen to scrounge for snacks and drinks, citing an aching back for good measure. I didn't care. I was in no hurry to leave—until I was the only one still awake in the room, that is. I let myself out and locked up. I didn't bother to inquire as to why he was in my garage or wonder why he was so . . . semi-tolerant of my intrusion.

I was too preoccupied with wasting away the afternoon in nonjudgmental peace of mind. I spent the entirety of the walk back to my room, and the rest of the evening, soaking in the little things: birds chirping; the sights, sounds, and smells; the simplicities of nature. I didn't really understand why, but inviting myself to take in a ball game with Floyd, the back-and-forth banter, mutual sarcasm, laid-back atmosphere . . . it put my mind at ease. Whenever the path I was taking brought me within ocean views, I stopped to take them in. Where certain textures underfoot harkened back to my long-gone yesterdays, I basked in them. I used to love the sound of grinding my shoes on crushed stone in spring and summer, the crackle and crunch of brittle leaves on the pavement in autumn. I had forgotten how to appreciate those little nuances of life.

Those past few days had inspired a change in me I was not about to ignore. I went to sleep with a smile on my face, confident in tomorrow, knowing the rough road ahead led to an oasis on the other side that I could ill afford to neglect. I was remembering the seasons from my youth and the little things I liked about each one, even the undesirable ones. To me seasons are the ultimate, unwavering metaphor for life. Pardon me for philosophizing. Spring is the brand-new start, the rebirth of life. Then summer speaks to the wonderous, youthful time for exploration and maturation. Autumn's color-bursting, cool, crisp days offer a disintegrating prelude and promise of harder times—the eventual gloom and frost-covered darkness and death of winter's grip. None of them can remain eternal, and death itself, in many ways, holds a plan and a gateway to new beginnings. So the cycle goes, and the seasons change.

I could feel my own springtime blooming. I spent too

long hibernating in the ice-cold darkness of death. This was my time to reap the life-giving seeds of spring and grow again —if only I could stay out of my own way while doing it.

Chapter 15

"Knock, knock! Hello! Are you home? Hello!" I had been antsy all day, finally resigned to the fact that I could not make this bid alone. I was having trouble standing still, thus combining my nervous persistent knuckling on Katie's door with the vocalization of my actions for hurried effect. "Knock, knock. Katie, are you—"

"Home?" She flung open the door finally, fed up with my repeated attempts. "No, but I'll leave a message that you stopped by."

"Katie, wait! Please, just listen. I need you to go with me. I need you to keep me calm before I throw up."

"You puke on my doorstep, and I'll knock, knock you out. Okay?" She tried to push the door closed with me pinned against it resistant.

"Please! Look, I'm sorry. I forgive you for the other day. Please can—"

"Oh, uh-huh. *You* forgive *me*? Forget it. I tried, okay? Your thickheaded, stubborn ass, I can't."

"I know. I know all that. You're being very repetitive right now, and I don't need a thesaurus. I just need you to go with me."

"Where?"

"Town hall, to the—"

"Oh, my God. This again. You're—"

"Katie, would you shut up for a minute? I don't expect you to agree with me on this. You came to me, remember? You were right. I need someone by my side. I don't need you to understand or approve, but I need this. And I don't have time to stand here and explain it to you. There's a town council meeting in twenty minutes, and like it or not, I'm going.

Please."

She sighed, giving in, and clunked the back of her head against the door. "We're taking my car. I'm low on gas," she said, ducking inside for her shoes and keys.

"Then, why are we—"

"'You want my support so bad, you're fillin' it up, moneybags."

We sat in the back of the room, waiting for . . . I honestly don't know what. I had never been to one of these assemblies before in my life. I didn't count on damn near town-wide turnout, a roomful of eyes and ears hanging on whatever I had to say. I referred to Katie on the specifics of the proceedings.

"How does this work?" I whispered. She paused then leaned sideways.

"I'm pretty sure they talk about town stuff." I snapped my head around at her. "Yeah, I said it. Does it look like I've ever been to one of these things? You were a teacher."

"What the . . . Christ, was there a monthly newsletter sent out about me or something?"

"Or something. Look, don't schools have those PTO meeting things?"

"What does that have to do with this?"

"I don't know! You dragged me here!"

"They must have some kind of open mic . . . forum thing at some point, right?"

"Open . . . This isn't happy hour at the bar. How the hell should I know!"

I had never carried on such a ridiculous whispering-contest argument in my life. There was a very good reason I didn't attend meetings of this nature. They were dull as hell. Once Katie and I ran out of material to bicker about, the rest was all endless, mind-numbing babbling on about minutes, agendas, and tourism-related dribble. By the time the floor opened to public commentary, I was halfway to dreamland. Luckily, my moral support was there to elbow me to consciousness. “Hey! Hey! I think this is where you come in.”

“Yes!” The foreman called on me, and I jumped to my feet and scooted past Katie and up the center aisle to the podium. “I have something to say.”

“Yes, go ahead. The chair recognizes . . .”

“Grace, um, Grace Garity.”

“Very well, Ms. Garity. You have the floor.”

“Well, I would like to enter a bid for the purchase of the National—”

“Ms. Garity—”

“For the National Inn before—”

“Ms. Garity.” The selectman held up his hand, shushing me. “While we appreciate your interest, you understand, this is not the proper forum for—”

“But I thought this was—”

“Proposals of this nature are handled through the appropriate channels. I’m sorry, but whatever requests you have must be submitted in writing to the town clerk for further consideration and approval of discussions on the matter at future meetings. Thank you. Anyone else?”

That was about how short-lived my enthusiasm was. I felt so stupid standing up there, my embarrassment on full display. My back was to them all, but I could feel their collective awe. After my admonishing, his voice faded away. I collected what pride I had left and brought it straight back to my seat, avoiding any eye contact from the crowd. My behind barely rewarmed the chair when I decided to exit unnoticed through a rear door, Katie in tow. I didn’t have much to contribute to her attempts at subject-changing small talk on the ride back. She parked beside my car with the engine idle and waited in silence a moment while I mentally kicked myself and licked my wounds.

“That, um, that didn’t go well, did it?” I couldn’t comprehend a reply or explanation. I stared straight ahead, motionless, reeling from this roller-coaster ride I put myself on. It was a strange sensation, to feel so close to something good, something life-changing—so right and so defeated at the same time. I'm sure she could see I was ready to burst. I heard all the car doors lock at the same time. "Spill it," she demanded. "Talk to me, Elles. I'm sitting here looking at you, and I'm not comfortable with letting you drive off on your own, so . . ."

"Grace." I whimpered.

"Oh, see? That, right there. We can spend all night in this car for all I care. I don't give a shit what your name is or what you wanna call yourself today or tomorrow. Now, what is going on?"

All I wanted to do at that moment was get out of that car. But she was reflecting exactly what I was feeling, what I should have been saying to myself. The hard part was, if she was asking the questions, that meant I had to answer them, out loud. "I don't know. I . . . don't know why I came back here. I don't know who I'm supposed to be. I don't . . . know how to fix everything I screwed up."

"Okay. So why the inn?"

That was the only question I had a definitive answer for. "Because it's a part of me. It's a connection. You mentioned it and . . . it's like, when you know something in your gut, in your soul, that it's meant to be. It was calling to me, and . . . I just knew that this is my way back."

I watched Katie shake her head out of the corner of my eye and scrunch her face at my confession. "Yeah, well congrats. You fucked that one up good, didn't ya?"

"Thank you," I scoffed. I had to hand it to her. Katie and I were treading a rocky-road friendship that I was struggling to understand. One thing was for sure. She could mix a solemn moment with levity, much the same way as someone else I knew. And speaking of . . .

"Hey, your old roommate there. The one who's a psychiatrist. What's her name, uh . . ."

"Loyal."

"Yeah, look I'm no shrink or anything close, all right? I treat cuts and bruises on almost every part of the body, but I don't deal with heads and hearts. It's obvious yours is pretty damn broken. I'm sure this Loyal might have more profound things to say. You say you don't know why you came back, but you did. Maybe the answer is in your actions. Maybe this is your heart trying to mend itself and your thick head just hasn't caught up yet."

"Wow. That's . . . Are you working for Loyal undercover or—"

"All I know, Grace, is that purchasing some old inn and thinking it's going to solve all your problems is probably a reckless way to go. There's no single answer or magic-fix button here, Grace. You're gonna have to work for it. Now get the hell out of my car. Go take a nap or a walk or whatever the hell you do with yourself. Go sort out your friggin' life, will ya? You're a mess."

I did just that—though maybe not to that extent just yet. For the record, I did sleep on it that night. And for the record, I awoke more resolved to make the buy, to get back a large part of what I felt, and had convinced myself, was rightfully mine. Katie may have had a point about buying it, but to me, reclaiming the inn for the Garity family meant the difference between *being* here again and *belonging* here again. As expected, headlines of my antics spread like wind-driven wildfire across a dried-up hayfield and sat uneasily with some. I did not factor in their opinions or approval. I dreamed the night away imagining a life I never thought I would want, honoring our legacy and the woman whose dream started it all. Now all I had to do was fight for it. Standing on the balcony outside my room, it appeared that fight had only begun to come find me.

"Dina?" I gasped, feeling like all the air was sucked out of my lungs. Ginny's mom was walking on the beach below and stopped purposely, peering up at me. She didn't call out to me or signal. She just stared intently, like in a sentimental trance. My fingers curled around the post that my hands were on and tensed up. It wasn't about her presence or her possible intentions. This was much more than that. This was about what I saw when we locked eyes, the once-upon-a-time, silly suspicions that I choked up and swallowed like a sour lump. My one-track mind wouldn't allow me to focus on anything else, certainly not dirty little unverified scandals or unproven lies. Still, she was a sight to behold. I watched her wipe the emotion from her face as we found our way to one another and met in a full-on, no-words-required bear hug on the beach.

Here's where things got hard—real and hard. It had become commonplace for me to repel and remove feelings from intense situations. After my parents died, I ran to the end of the earth and screamed at the world. I never came to grips with it. I never grieved in the conventional heart-torn way. I shut down. In essence, I vowed to never let anyone or anything that close to me to ever again hurt me to that extreme. My marriage, I submit as exhibit A. I committed to never being vulnerable enough for that potential of pain. That is the mindset that tortured me on and after my wedding day, in our short-lived united infancy. I submersed myself in my work, heart and soul, caring more about others. Hell, I went so far as to identify by another name, all to hide from Elles, the innocence I betrayed. All of this, the grand new plan, the living, breathing ties to who I was, the gut-wrenching truths I hadn't yet uncovered . . . This wasn't just a fight for material possessions anymore. This was about to be a fight for salvation, redemption, and reconciliation.

Chapter 16

"You look good." Dina fawned over me. We sat on the beach that morning getting reacquainted, catching up on our separate lives. "You look scared."

A fair judgment call, one that I wasn't about to submit to. "Why do you say that?"

"Just callin' what I see. You don't know how long I've waited for this day to come. Here you are, sitting right here next to me, looking terrified to be here."

"I didn't exactly step off the ferry onto a welcome matt."

Dina laughed disingenuously. "What were you expecting, a hero's parade to sprout up out of thin air?"

Really? She was going to sit there and pretend that I wasn't aware of what everyone else seemed to be clued in to? I threw *Seriously?* eyes at her. "Give me some credit, Dina. You all saw me coming before I boarded the ferry."

"So . . ."

"So! Nobody was there to greet me when I got here. If everybody knew, nobody seemed to care. I . . . I honestly don't know what I expected. So there ya go. Is that what you wanted to hear?"

"Well, how 'bout that? Neither did we."

"But you *knew* I was coming." Dina looked off. "Oh, okay, so this is what we're doing then? We're gonna just pretend that —"

She cleared her throat and redirected. "Missed you at the funeral."

Correction. We were going to flash back fifteen years and start picking my decisions apart one by one and holding everything I did against me, expecting me to, what? Apologize? Beg everyone for forgiveness because I reacted to the horror that befell me? "That's ancient history. Besides, you know why I didn't . . ."

"Is it though? And that's not the one I'm talkin' about." I looked at her, surprised. "What do you think, I'm some sort of cold-hearted monster? You did what you did. I'd hardly call it ancient history, though. After all, history is something that's generally left in the past and largely forgotten about."

"Has it been? Because it doesn't feel that way."

"No, it doesn't, does it?" Dina turned her body, facing the ocean, her arms draped over her knees, breeze whipping through her hair. "I've lost count how many times I've had this conversation with you in my head over the years. Every single time the context changes."

"You were at Uncle John's funeral?"

"Me, Tom, Coot—"

"Ginny?" I asked apprehensively.

"All those imaginary talks, rehearsed, edited. And I tried to convince myself that I wanted you to be there. Truth is, I don't know what I would have said if you were. So who knows. Maybe it was the best thing for the both of us."

"She wasn't there, was she?"

"There's more to it than that. More than you're aware of. I'm not about to sit here and speak on someone else's behalf. You didn't want anything to do with any—"

"So why come looking for me then, Dina?" I watched her snuff back a welling-up with a deep inhale. "I saw the way you were looking at me. So don't try to tell me you were just passing by or—"

"I wanted to see—"

"But you didn't need me for that, right? You had your spies. Who? Uncle John and Aunt Nellie sending back reports, keeping tabs, watching me from a distance all this time? You didn't need me to be physically here with you right now. This whole damn island is a talking microscope of activity. You didn't have any trouble monitoring me from a hundred miles away. While you were busy playing spy games, I was—"

"What? Forgetting about anyone still alive who ever cared about you?" she snarled back. We both turned away, disgusted.

"That's not fair," I grunted in reply. "If everyone cared so much, why didn't Ginny come to the funeral, too?"

"Life's not fair. You haven't figured that out by now? And why don't you ask her yourself?"

Okay, not so much catching up. At least the hug was mutually genuine. Everything that followed was a residual grudge match of wills. I wanted to have a nice civil reunion. I truly wanted that for us. Then selfish instincts got in the way on both sides. It's a confusing and complicated matter, to be at odds with yourself and the world around you at the same time. How does one make amends with the people and place you abandoned and account for the life you've led since, all at the same time? Doing so could mean questioning everything, to a frightening degree. I was set in my reprogrammed ways and still ignorant of the delicate art of humbling myself and being receptive to the other side of the story. I wasn't the only one guilty of that. It didn't help when fate soon stepped in again and presented me with an opportunity to lose myself in high hopes and tunnel-vision ambition. I drifted into an arrogant subconscious whirlwind of *Damn them all, I will succeed no matter what*, clinging to the failing notion that Elles was long gone, and Grace Garity was here to stay.

I used the day to sort out some unfinished business. I had a voice mailbox full of unreturned messages from the realtors. The last few of which I hadn't even listened to. The house was drawing lots of interest and the beginnings of a bidding war. The one detail preventing me from entertaining offers and pulling the trigger on what I had come here to get rid of was guilt. I stood at my parents' graves and cried myself into oblivion, meanwhile selfishly selling off the physical remains of their lives. There's that word again, *selfish*. There was a theme emerging here. Not one I was particularly proud of later, but not one I was particularly owning up to, either. Foolish pride was too powerful of a deterrent.

After a long phone call, my deepest apologies for appearing unreachable, and a few reconsiderations, I agreed to give the matter my full, undivided attention. I drove home for what I knew would be the last time. I put all fears aside and went inside. The plan was to do a quick sweep, collect heirlooms, salvage anything of Garity family sentimental value. Get in, get out. That *was* the plan. I opened the front door and stepped into a residence I hardly recognized. The walls were repainted with different colors I had never known, floors redone, hardwood where carpet once lay. My eyes were drawn to a spot in the living room that conjured a flashing vision in my mind. That was where I had dropped a thermos of juice, along with my bag, as I stood stunned, before I tore away.

The place was pristine, clean like a hospital room, devoid of any real lived-in character or personal touches. This house that I half grew up in, primarily used for sleeping and meals, now resembled a more generic hotel than the one I spent that same majority half in and around. It was spooky in an uncomfortably foreign way until my aimless wandering found me in the master bedroom. It was changed, as well, except for the closet full of clothes. At first glance, I mistook them for my father's things. Then reality struck that those were gone, too, and Mom's, all of it replaced by the rest of Uncle John's worldly possessions. My room was an unfurnished, neatly organized and stacked storage area. Taped closed and individually labeled boxes, ready to move, were all that was left. I stood there against the doorframe, numb, with my arms folded, letting that thought register. I refused to flinch while trying like hell not to let it overwhelm me. Honestly, alone in the haunting silence, I might have cracked, were it not for a knock at the door. I washed my hands over my face, breathed, collected myself, and answered it.

"Floyd! Hi, what . . . What are you doing here?"

He snarked at me for my reaction. "Nice to see you, too. May I?"

"Huh? Oh, sorry. Yeah, um, come on in. I wasn't expecting anyone.

"Ah, nice place ya got here. Could use a little color, a little more style."

"No kidding. First time I've been inside since I arrived. I wasn't expecting to walk into a clean slate."

"Well, what'd you expect to find, last night's supper dishes from fifteen years ago?"

"Maybe. Or at least my room just like it was, like some kind of time-forgotten shrine. What brings you by, anyway, Floyd? I mean, how'd you know I was here?"

"Oh, I was drivin' by, saw the car, on my way to deliver you a care package of homemade fixins. Thought you could use a few good meals. Make sure you're eatin' good. Got 'em out in the truck."

"Thank you, Floyd. That's sweet." From his mouth through my ears and straight down to the empty pit of my stomach, it started to growl on cue. I hadn't even bothered to grab one of my protein bars when I left my room to come here. "Any of them breakfast?"

Floyd winked and backed away toward the door. "Be right back."

Chapter 17

We sat at the kitchen table, a replacement one at that. Floyd watched me wolf down an omelet sandwich while we chatted.

"Can I ask you something, Floyd?"

"Shoot."

"Why the car? I mean, why my father's car? How did you even . . ."

"Full disclosure time?" When he said those words, I braced for the most off-the-wall or curveball thing I wasn't sure I wanted to hear. Maybe whatever he was about to say summed up the funny vibes or, at the very least, would put me a little more at ease. "Your Uncle John let me tinker around with 'er."

I stopped eating. Sandwich to my lips, I swallowed what was in my mouth and put it down. "You . . . You knew Uncle John?"

"Relatively speaking. I helped him 'clean the slate' as you say."

"Wha . . . here? You helped him here? Do the . . ."

"Repaint, clean, refurnish. Yes, I did." He talked like it was a special memory, like helping Uncle John remake this house into something that wouldn't make me cringe to revisit it, was a humble, honored privilege.

"Floyd, why didn't you say something sooner? Why . . . But what does that have to do with the . . ."

"He drove it around when he would visit. Damn thing stalled out on him so many times, and he knew I liked to keep busy. Asked me if I'd be interested in takin' a look. Told me how it was a prized possession of the previous owner, how someday someone else might wanna keep it runnin' for him." I couldn't help myself. I started to crack up at the notion of inheriting that putrid chunk of steel on wheels. "Or maybe not."

"I'm . . . I'm sorry. It's just . . . I loved my father dearly, Floyd, and I'm sure Uncle John meant well but . . . oh . . ." I settled down and caught my breath. "There's no way in hell I'd be caught driving that thing. But I don't get it, Floyd. When I caught you in the garage, why didn't you tell me any of this then? You just let me think that you were some sort of—"

"Thief?"

"Yes! So you've been in this house a hell of a lot more than me in the past fifteen years." He shook his head as I went on. "And there you are, living in that tiny little . . . after you put your hard work and sweat into a house that I'm . . . Jesus, I should just sign it over to you, Floyd. Or sell it to you for a dollar to make it offi—"

"No, Grace. I don't want your house. That ain't why I helped."

"Why the hell wouldn't you want it? I mean, come on, Floyd. There's gotta be more to you than just a single handyman who's too young to be living a hermit's life out—"

"Ain't interested," he affirmed, sincere and with authority.

"Okay. Sorry, Floyd. I just thought that you could use—"

"A better place than my tiny, rundown shack, livin' in squalor?"

"I didn't say that. Floyd, I didn't mean to . . ."

"It's . . . Nah, it's all right. Forgive me. Guess you ain't the only one with things to work out lately."

I continued eating, taking mental note of the quality of his work that I hadn't noticed before when I was too hungry to care what I was shoving down my throat. "Honestly, I don't know why you're wasting your time fixing appliances and things, anyway. I mean, you made this?"

"Not bad for a hermit, huh?"

"There are certainly better, more interesting things you

could be doing with your hands and your time, Floyd. That's for sure."

"Speakin' of doin' things. I heard you been politickin' to fill your time with a project yourself."

Well, if it was up for debate, there was proof positive. My one major accomplishment in my return so far—being the talk of the town once more. "Yeah, the inn. You, uh, heard. I guess everybody has by now."

"For someone who could have a lot to gain by doin' it, don't sound too excited to me."

"Well, how excited would you be if you got yourself all worked up over it then made a complete fool out of yourself in front of basically the entire town trying to make it happen?"

"Suppose I'd feel pretty stupid."

"Thanks, Floyd." Wow! Note to self, hermits aren't very attuned to showing sympathy, are they? "That's exactly how I feel."

"Then again, if I had the reputation you got 'round here from some people, feelin' stupid 'bout this wouldn't be sayin' much."

"Damn, Floyd, honest much? What'd you do, bring me food to butter me up before you break me down?"

"However you heard it, it's on you. Ain't what I meant, and you know it."

"So what? You think I should do it? You think I should buy the inn?"

"Don't matter what me or anyone else thinks. You feel stupid, it's on you for lettin' it be. You feel like anyone around here's against you, that's on you for lettin' it be. People always gonna find a reason to be against you, 'til you give them a better reason to wanna stand behind you."

I considered his advice while I got up to fetch a glass from the cupboard, fill it with water from the tap, and have a drink. I stood at the counter, feet crossed, wheels spinning, and started to talk it out. "The inn was my mother's dream. Floyd, I spent more time there than I did here when I was a kid, ya know? So many memories I've thrown away."

"There's a fine line between thrown away and hurt too much to hold on to."

"But Katie's right. I don't know anything about owning an inn. What business do I have . . . I'd have to learn how to . . . Not to mention, all the work it probably needs to get it up and running again. I don't . . ." Oh, *now* he was speechless? Mr. Deep Thinker, with all his sound advice was allowing me to ramble on like I'd become so accustomed to, more and more, talking myself in and out of this insane idea. If I screwed this one up, I would— He was just staring at me, like he was just waiting for me to come to some . . . "I'm a teacher, Floyd, for God's sake. I want to. I really want to. What if this is more than I can handle? What if Katie's right? What if . . . What if it needs too much work?" He held his arms out as if to say, what about him, without literally saying it. "I'm only one person, Floyd. I —"

"Now you're two."

"You . . . Really, you'd help me with—"

"Say the word."

"I don't know. I just . . . I gotta deal with this house first. I don't know what's in all the boxes in my room. I gotta move those somewhere before I let any buyers look at the place. There's so much to . . ."

He did it again, with more emphasis this time. "You're in luck. I got no place to be 'til I gotta fix the Maciog's water heater after lunch."

"Nice try, Floyd." Katie barked from outside the screen door, letting herself in from the porch.

"Let me guess, just passing by?" I questioned, sarcastically.

"Hardly. I tracked your ass down, and *he* is under strict doctor's orders not to do any strenuous lifting. So if you need a hand—"

"Doctor's orders, my ass," Floyd grumbled.

"What is she, your nurse?" I smirked at him, to which he grunted back.

"Nurse? She's a glorified pain in my ass, is what she is."

"Better than that pain in your back. Listen, Grace, I stopped by town hall and picked up some forms you need to fill out to make a formal bid. So Mr. Gresham here can either sit his crochety butt down and watch the women work, or he can just *wah-wah-wah* all the way home. Either way, you should get this done ASAP so they have time to review it before the next meeting."

"I don't know what to say. Thank you, Katie, I—"

"Think it over, say it later. Let's get packin'. I'm already hungry and trust me, I'm not as charming when I'm hangry."

"You're charming?"

"Oh, I'm frickin' delightful. Shut up, Floyd. Let's move."

Chapter 18

The house sold just as hints of an early autumn were beginning to show in the form of cool, breezy nights and chilly mornings. This is the time when tourism begins to wind down, beaches go bare, and calm tranquility looms around the corner. Soon the inhabitants who stayed year-round would be winterizing, restaurants and shops squeezing out what profits were left to be had before shutting down on another season. I realized I was about to be homeless. The paperwork that held the key to my future had been submitted weeks prior, and the tedious waiting game had begun. How ironic that the house had sold, but around here, an inflated bank account couldn't buy you anything in a speck on the map where everything was either spoken for or closed. The only other, less attractive, option was to pack up the car and head for the mainland until further notice. Even that was time sensitive as ferry services were transitioning to the offseason schedule of twice a day.

I went back to the inn, where dreams were pending and hopes dwindling. I walked the grounds from front to back, inspecting, visualizing—possibly for nothing more than my own torture, I was fully aware. But it didn't stop me from wishing, wondering what I could do with this place. Could I succeed? Restore the Garity tradition, make my mother proud? I won't lie. The prospect of that overwhelmed me the heavier it weighed. I started reasoning, comparing the percentages of my chances to give it a try against the belief I had in myself to make it work. Then I resorted to what had become my habit since returning to the island—talking to myself, debating my inner Elles. Perched on the edge of the back patio, conflicted on so many levels, I wept, fearing it all slipping away. *What the hell, Grace? What are you thinking*? The limited knowledge I had relating to running a business consisted of what I saw my mother and Dina do and not exactly with full attention to the finer points. I couldn't resist throwing it back on Uncle John, the blame for my current predicament, conspiring with who knows whom, to hand my life over to turmoil once more. And for what?

"What do you want me to do, huh? Come crawling back on my hands and knees, begging everyone to forgive me? I lost! Not them!" Suddenly, I wasn't addressing Uncle John anymore. I broke the dam at the cemetery, yet was still suppressing leftover pain. I couldn't contain it any longer. "What the fuck am I supposed to do without you!? I can't . . . I . . . I don't want . . . I don't wanna be here! Do you hear me!? I can't do this!" I broke down hard. Portions of it came out in blubbering, raging whispers, and some stayed in my head. I didn't mean the things I said, it's just . . . the anger and outbursts were summoned from a child. The next thing I knew, I was cuddled in Tom's arms. I didn't even see him come around. One second I was alone, and the next, I latched on and buried my head in the comfort and safety of his chest and vanquished away all the leftover torment I could.

"Here's some more tissues. I raided a supply closet."

"Thank you, Tom. We shouldn't be in here."

"Eh, town owns it. I work for the town. Besides, I stop in from time to time, keep the rats and raccoons from movin' in."

"Wonderful. We have raccoons here?"

"Never seen one. But I'll be ready for the bastards if they come." We shared a laugh. "Ah, lot of memories here, ya know? I mean, course you know." Then he went quiet, He swiped his hat off and scratched his head nervously. "Damn it, ya gotta talk to her, Grace. She ain't been the same since . . . Well, she won't talk to me."

"Who? Are you . . . Tom are you kidding me? Are you and Ginny—"

"No! No. Well, yes and no. Look, that's not the important thing here, Grace."

"The hell it's not, Tom!"

"She's miserable, Grace. She's distant, even with the kids."

"Well, aren't you the great pretender, Tom. Playing chief and stepfather. What else don't I—"

"Goddammit, Grace! Why does everything turn into a fight with you? I don't wanna argue. Me and Ginny's personal life ain't the point."

"Then, what is?"

"Quality of life, Grace! Can't you see that? This ain't about me."

"It is! It's about you, me, all of us, Tom."

He glared directly at me with a stern look. "Well, it's good to finally hear you admit it."

"How long?"

"How long, what?"

"How long have you and Ginny been—"

"We ain't married if that's what you're getting at. Christ sakes, she needed someone, Grace. You fell to pieces first. You weren't here when she did. You ain't the only one that knows about tough times. Widowed, a single mom of two, after losin' you. She didn't have anyone left. What was I supposed to do?"

"Swoop in and be the hero. You did a good thing. You weren't all she had though, Tom. She still had—"

"Dina had her own problems. They been off and on for years."

"They?"

"Yeah, her and Ginny. Once she found out that . . . never mind. Hell, I ain't tryin' to be no hero, and I'm sorry if you were misinformed about my rank. I'm tryin' to—"

"Misinformed? Tom, you introduced *yourself* to me as—"

"I know I did. Coot reamed me out good for it, too."

"You love her . . . don't you, Tom?"

He kept a stone-faced expression and looked around,

standing up. "You're probably right, though. We should, uh, get outta—"

"Tom Deiter, officer of the law or not, you walk out of this building, I swear I'll burn it to the ground."

He chuckled. "No, you won't."

He was right. It was as hollow as a threat could be. I was never effective playing bad cop in the classroom, either. To my point, though, Tom and Ginny were a destined match from the time we were three feet tall. There was a reason he never challenged her aggressiveness or authority over him when it came to crossing behavioral lines. I don't know where they went astray, if ever. I wasn't around for the fabled naval invasion. Ginny had an indelible way of always corralling him back in line. She protected Tom from himself, and despite his impartial antagonizing nature, she was granted a pass every single time. Sure, I was like them, too young to fully understand all of this and what they had. I couldn't have articulated it then, but the blooming of unrefined love is what that was. Either way, learning the details of their lives that I had missed was thankfully distracting me from my discombobulated one.

Damn him for calling my bluff. Deep down, but not as far as before, I wanted to know more. I was afraid to know more, but I wanted to. Tom and I parted ways for the day. He led me out the back and locked up. I thanked him again, repeatedly, for his being there, consoling me. I didn't want to argue, either, but somehow it was hard not to. Anger at myself was manifesting in misguided ways. Internal battles can spill out to claim unintended, innocent victims. On top of everything else, I was attempting to abolish that. I spotted Tom in his car, pulled up alongside Katie in hers. As he peeled away, she waved me over.

"Ready to go?"

"Go where?"

"Well, I don't know what you're up to here, but squatting is usually illegal."

"So he called you again. Well, I don't know what he told you this time, but I don't need someone running to my rescue every time I—"

"Rent-free, an amazing roommate, you can come and go as you please. No more rescue operations. What more can you ask? Or pay me, your call. I'm easy. Five thousand a month sounds fair."

"Katie, you don't have to do this. I'm not—"

"Ya got no place to go, stupid. You're movin' in. Be quiet. Get your ass in the car and follow me."

Again, I didn't fight it. I was growing fond of our Loyal-like, playfully combative, dare I say, friendship. I complied with a simple, surrendering smile, and that was that. When we got there, she showed me to that same hideous spare bedroom. My eyes widened at the sight of all my boxes neatly stacked in the corner. "How did you . . ."

"Yeah, that part's unfortunate. I don't have a lot of storage space here, so . . ."

"Yeah, but how did you . . ."

"I had a little help."

"Floyd? I thought he wasn't supposed to—"

"Geez, Grace, I know other people. Floyd didn't lift a finger. He just hissed at me and drove." She gestured out the bedroom window facing the back of the house. There was dad's car, safe and sound, parked in the corner of her lot.

"Katie, are you sure this is okay? I don't want to impose."

"Can you cook?"

"Can I . . . um . . . yes?" I answered, curiously.

"Cool, it would be helpful if one of us could. You got a room. I got a live-in chef. See, we both win."

"Alrighty then!"

"Unless . . . the rent could cover delivery . . ."

"Delivery? From where? All the restaurants are closed for the—"

She swung her arm high through the air with a

swooshing airplane sound effect and a quirky grin.

"Okay, that's . . ."

"I'm sayin' I know a pilot, and with that kinda rent, he'd —"

"I'm not paying you five thousand dollars a month."

She dropped her arm down to her side with a ridiculous huff. "Fine. He won't do it, anyway. Not for just money."

"Oh, dear God."

"Hey! Just for that, I want something flambéed or . . . I don't know, tartared for dinner," she announced, leaving the room.

"Great," I muttered to myself. "How's a thousand a month sound? Or two? It's only, like, a ten-minute flight from the . . . Hello?"

Chapter 19

We christened the arrangement and kicked off our first official evening as roommates by hauling dinner, blankets, and chairs to the beach. We set up and collected more driftwood and tinder to add to what we brought and sparked up a fire for warmth. From there we wasted away into the late-night, early-morning hours, talking. We lay side by side in our loungers, covered in flannel under the darkest sky, nursing the dying flames that separated us.

"I heard you were pretty upset today." I held my tongue in response, for fear of reliving it. "Tom told me in confidence."

"So, now you're—"

"Repeating it to you in confidence. That's right." She nodded, unashamed. "Also noticed you've been hanging around with Floyd a lot lately."

"So?"

"Do you think that's wise?"

"To have one friend who doesn't know the old me? Why wouldn't that be wise?"

"Well, I didn't want to say anything but—"

"But what? What's wrong with Floyd? He's a nice guy."

Her expression asked the question before it was let out. "You're not . . ."

"No. And so what if we were? He's like twice my age or something. We get along, that's all." And yet, that appeared to be the least of her worries. She clammed up for a second and repositioned herself on the lounge chair. "Katie, what?"

"Grace, it's not just that. I don't care who you date. It's none of my business but he's . . ."

"He's . . . in witness protection? A murder suspect? What?"

"Nothing, just . . . be careful. Floyd is a good guy. I'm just not sure everyone would approve." I let the subject drop, but I got the sense that this topic had nothing to do with the stench of age or race. Another minute passed with only the sound of the waves crashing on the shore. I stoked the dying fire with a few more pieces of wood and covered up again to lie there and stargaze. "Ya know, whatever anybody might have told you, whatever hard feelings might exist, you were missed. The Garitys were missed. Your family was a big part of this town. Two of them we lost and could never get back. The third one we lost and didn't know *how* to get back or if we ever would."

"I'm not sure anyone tried."

"You were young, Grace, and everyone understood. Hey, I was about the same age at the time, and I couldn't have imagined your horror. You made up your mind then. The fact that you're back, the fact that you are here now, only proves the saying that you can run but you can't hide."

"Yeah, I figured that one out."

"So, what if the inn's not in the cards?"

"I don't know. Reshuffle the deck?"

"You could, but you did that once already, remember? At some point you gotta play the hand you're dealt, not just the one you folded for."

"What if I end up losing?"

"You already lost more than anyone should have to in one crappy draw. I'm no card player, Grace, but as long as you stay in the game, the only way you truly lose is if you chicken out and walk away from the table. You gotta give us a chance to play, too, because we were all in it together."

"Okay, okay." I sniffed with a chuckle. "Enough of the dumb analogy. I know what you're saying."

"God, thank you. I was about ready to slap *myself.* I hate giving those sappy lectures, anyway. Where's the food? I'm starving now.

"In the cooler under your chair. Pass me a water when you get in there?"

"I can't wait to see what you made." She sat forward, shifting sideways on her chair and draped her blanket across her shoulders. She propped the cooler in front of her, pulled two water bottles out, and arced one over to me. She opened a container of food and drew it in close under her nose. "Mm, smells . . .What is this?"

"Hodgepodge tartare. I'll do the shopping from now on, 'kay? Just eat."

She slid a forkful into her mouth and chewed slower with every motion as she hummed a deciding vote. "Hmm, it's um . . . it's . . . I'm not gonna lie. This kinda tastes like last week's leftovers." She took another confirming taste, and the verdict was in. "Wow! Oh, this is . . . Can I ask you something?"

"No. And I'm not hungry."

"Me, either, anymore. This is . . . No, this is not . . . You said you could cook! Did I not specifically ask you if you could cook? Was this not my one and only condition of—"

"I can cook," I said with conviction (also without outwardly emitting a guilty giggle on a bold-faced lie).

"Grace, when someone asks another human being if they can cook, they literally mean can you make something that is *ed-i-ble*, sister. Okay?"

"It is edible. It's food. It came out of your refrigerator. Besides, you asked me if I could cook, not if I was good at it. Your phrasing, not mine. The technical definition of cooking is —"

"Oh! No! Hell no. Don't you dare go all teacher on me. I know what I asked for—something exotic, something fancy—not this. This is—"

"Last week's leftovers. And tartare means raw."

"Oh. Ew." And . . . *boom!* It came to her, and she gasped. "Ooh, yeah, right. I also said flambéed, so I'm just gonna toss this in the fire."

"You could. I don't see any delivery planes flying by. Do you?"

"You're hilarious. I oughta leave your ass here and make

ya sleep in the sand."

"Better than that ugly-ass room you stuck me in," I muttered, jabbing back. Katie's jaw dropped, and I couldn't hold back the laughter any longer. "I'm painting that abomination tomorrow, by the way."

She leaned sideways to toss her dinner into the flames and drew it back, giving it a curious glance. "This came out of my fridge?" I just tilted my head and flashed affirming eyes. "You do the shopping from now on."

We carried on that way for hours, laughing, mocking one another's skills—or lack thereof—bonding over mindless chatter. We dragged ourselves home in the early hours of the next morning. Katie didn't make it to her bed. Half asleep already, she lunged onto the couch instead, nearly snoring before her face hit the throw pillows. I staggered to my room and didn't move until almost noon when Katie shook me from my coma, grabbing and jarring my extremities.

"Hey, hey. Get up. We have company." I was still defogging my brain, squinting at the light, and flickering an assemblance of clarity into my vision as I made my way into the living room. I didn't immediately recognize the finely suited man sitting beside her. Katie got up and attempted to fuss with my wrinkled clothes. "Here, lemme just—"

"Stop it. Katie, what are you—"

"I'm sorry, Mr. . . . Mr. Lafave, right?" She addressed him, embarrassed for me. "Just a long, late night. Grace, this is Mr. Lafave."

"Paul, please," he insisted.

"Grace, this is Mr. Paul Lafave. As in Selectman Lafave."

"I got that, thanks. Is this about the paperwork? Did I fill something out wrong or. . ."

"Not at all. Ms. Garity, please have a seat. I wanted to come over and speak to you personally, without all the red tape formalities. I, um, well to be quite honest, Grace, you caused quite a stir after your—"

"I'm so sorry about that, Mr. . . . Paul. I was acting on

impulse and I—"

"No, no, that's not what I mean. Your family, the former proprietors of the National Inn, correct?"

"Yes, that's right."

"Well, listen, Grace, I'm rather new, relatively speaking. Newer, I should say, to some of the history here. Your unexpected interest in this property, let's just say, caused a hell of a debate."

"Okay. I don't understand. What are you saying?"

"It's yours, Grace, if—"

"Woah, hold on. It's mine?"

"That is, if you still want it. You do still—"

"Just like that? How can you just . . . What about the other bids? I thought it . . ."

"Look, I won't go into specifics. I'm not at liberty to. As far as anyone else knows, best if we never even had this conversation. I understand this is a lot to take in and probably sounds a little—"

"Yeah!" I gasped, delirious with shock. "Is this even legal or . . ."

"Oh, trust me. It's completely on the up-and-up. We value the history that you have in this matter, Grace. As leaders we respect the longevity of tradition that families like yours bring to the community. Nothing would make us happier than to see that continue."

My head went blank. I couldn't wrap my head around what was happening. "So what happens now?"

"Inspections, more paperwork, lots of signatures, stuff like that. It's a little bit of a process, so be patient. We're still finalizing a purchase price and we'll have to make it all official through a vote at the next meeting and such."

"I don't know what to say."

"How about *thank you very much for stopping by, and have a wonderful day*, before he changes his mind," Katie murmured, hanging all over me, trying to temper her own excitement. Mr. Lafave stood up and extended a hand to me.

"No need. I'll let you get woken up. Good luck, Grace. We all look forward to your success. Oh, there's been a slight issue locating the keys, but I'm sure that'll get squared away before it's time to hand them o—"

"Tom . . . Officer Deiter has . . . well, they may know something at the station. I'll call over there first thing after breakfast, if that's okay."

"Good enough. Take care."

"I will. Thank you. You . . . you, too."

Chapter 20

To see us both, anyone would have assumed this was Katie's victory. She started jumping up and down the second Mr. Lafave walked out the door—strange for someone who had just been questioning this. I, on the other hand, did not start celebrating—strange for the person who just got handed a future on a silver platter. Make no mistake, I did not take the enormity of the moment for granted. But I hadn't achieved anything yet. I had yet to even come to terms with what just happened and how.

It was surreal.

There were parts of me that wanted to burst with joy and other parts that felt like wedding day déjà vu.

To recap, I left the life that I had left another one for, to come back home where only controversy and skepticism welcomed me with open arms. I sold the only place I had to live and bought a building that still legally wasn't mine. How's that for a whirlwind?

This was developing way too fast. All I did was submit an offer which was supposed to work its way through the city council chain of command. I wasn't done debating my fears and doubts. My God, I'm all for a quick turnaround, but this was crazy. How could they do this to me?

The next few days felt like time had stopped. As usual, I turned to Loyal to talk me down off a panicked, what-do-I-do-now ledge. And, as always, she calmed me down—*after* she intensified my anxiety level by dive-bombing me with congratulations and cheers.

Little by little, as the days passed by, I started to afford myself the right to accept and even relish the event that was unfolding, cautiously leery of the whole deal unraveling.

Tom stopped by Katie's place a few times. The mystery of the missing keys was . . . sorted out, and I was now the proud, unofficial new owner. Armed with an unauthorized set of keys, I could sneak into my own establishment, undetected, at free will. The whole thing sounded ridiculous, but Tom somehow felt the need to extend to me the criminal advantage of a head start. To that, I had to stop and jokingly ask myself if he was trying to help or scare me out of this move. The joke was on me —it was a fifty-fifty.

In the transaction interim, Loyal was the only one I consulted about my innermost reservations, emotions, and thoughts—the only one among the living, that is. After my little mental breakdown, I started frequenting my parents' grave for further therapeutic support. It's an understatement that my mind was a fabulously overflowing cluster of preparations, and with the help of a guiding hand, I made it a more invitingly solitary retreat.

* * *

"I see you've made yourself right at home."

Dina sauntered toward me down a row of headstones and took a seat on the bench beside me. She glanced at me with a wink, tapped the wooden planks with her hand, and grinned.

"Built it myself. Well, Floyd helped a little."

"Mm, you two have gotten pretty close."

"You too, huh?" I cut her off as she opened her mouth to respond. "Look, Dina . . . I don't wanna do this anymore. I don't wanna fight with you. I don't wanna fight with anyone. I just wanna—"

She shut me down, placing her hand over mine, tapping it lightly then holding on. "At last, we agree on something, hmm? It's a start." She demonstrated that sentiment with a joke. "So! Come here often?"

"Why'd they have to go, Dina?"

"I don't know. It was like I lost my better half. There is

such a thing as a soulmate best friend. I believe that. They might be rare, but that's what your mother and I were."

"And you and Stephen are . . ."

"Over. Separated years ago."

"Dina, I'm so sorry. I didn't know you were divorced."

"Oh, please. Don't be sorry. It was a relief."

"What happened?"

"Ha! What happened? He proved what a heartless, uncaring son of a bitch he is. That's what happened."

"How did Ginny take it?"

She peered at me with a sweet, forgiving smile. "Not as well as me."

Then it occurred to me to relay the premature news—if it was even breaking news at all. "I'm buying the inn."

It was hard to get a read of her reaction as there was none. She sat right there and ghosted me on it, trailing off into memories instead. "Do you remember . . ." She stumbled through her own amusement just to spit it out. "Do you remember ringing that bell for the first time? All by yourself."

The bell she was referring to brought back, easily, one of the most nauseatingly embarrassing incidents of my life. The inn's now detached rooftop adornment, once a simple widow's walk, had been upgraded into a working beacon of sound. In my mother's ever-evolving business scheme to be the center of attention, she had hired a company to devise a blueprint for, and install, a working bell. Initially, the bell would ring to signify a fifteen-minute warning that lunch or dinner was about to be served. That way any sightseeing or shopping guests within long-range earshot could hear it far and wide.

She was so pleased with the results that she bumped it up to a breakfast and special occasions alarm as well. It was not a popular addition among the locals, and though I had chalked it up to a weather-related mishap at first, I never found an answer as to the whereabouts of that bell. I had wanted my turn ringing it so badly. The chore was assigned to staff members randomly. When I had finally gotten my chance, it was awful. The piercing vibration, the head-throbbing volume of noise that thing produced when I went for it and yanked down on that rope with all my might was deafening. I let go so fast to cover my ears that Dina had to catch me as I tripped backward into her arms.

We both cracked up, revisiting the unforgettable episode.

"Why? Why would you bring that up? Of all the . . ."

"Mm, because those are the good times I choose to remember. Not separations, failures, or losses."

"I get it. You think I'm in over my head. Don't you, Dina?"

"Well, you're taller than me. So where does that leave me?" She chuckled.

"You know what I mean. And the fact that you don't have anything to say about it . . ."

"Perspective, Grace. Let me ask you this, what happened when you kept nagging us to let you ring that bell, hmm? What happened when your mother and I told you, over and over, that it might not be such a good idea at your age?"

"You let me, anyway."

"Only because we knew you were too bullheaded to let it go. There was a girl I used to know. She lived around here. Think her name was Elles."

"Still is." I smiled at her with a brightness in my eyes.

"She didn't let anything stop her once she had an idea about something. And if you want the truth, I think that's why you left. Something bad happened, something terrible. It was done, and you couldn't fix it, and you couldn't stop it. That's a hard pill to swallow when you're eleven, almost a teenager, and naive enough to think you've got the world in the palm of your hand. Look at you now. You've got your mind made up. It's just one example, but it's who you are, and it's that bell all over again. So why does it matter what I think?"

"Because I respect what you might have to say. Even if I don't want to hear it. Because you've done what I'm about to do."

"Well, who do you think taught me, hmm?" I looked at my mother's headstone, and Dina heard me before I could bother to answer. "Oh, no, no, she only had the dream and the vision. After that, we only had each other to lean on and bounce ideas off of. If you're going to get that place up and running, you're going to need yourself and a small army of others."

"Gee, thanks for the encouragement."

"Well, you wanted my input. It won't be easy. But if you're interested, I know someone who can help." She groaned as she stood up off the bench, pushing off me for leverage. "You let me know when you're ready. I gotta go check in on Mrs. Strowman and that mangy ol' mutt of hers."

"That ol' grouch is still alive?" I called out as Dina strolled away.

"Mrs. Strowman?"

"No, the dog."

"Oh, heavens no. This is mangy mutt number three. Ya know what they say about pets taking on the personality of their owners. That's why I gotta go make sure she's taking her meds and eating regularly so she's behaved and fit to be around other people. Oh, she's a biter, that one."

"We're still talking about the dog, right?"

"Ha! I wish! No, Mrs. Strowman!" Dina squawked back.

Chapter 21

To answer the obvious question, and for those with inquiring minds, I don't know why I didn't ask Dina for her help. Her years of service in the industry, tending to guests, that wealth of knowledge and experience would be invaluable. Maybe I thought she would offer. Maybe I was thinking of how hard that might be, running the operation with me and not the soulmate friend and business partner whom she apparently couldn't go on doing this without.

From that conversation, though, something she said resonated and has stuck with me to this very day: *perspective*.

Shame on me. For a teacher, it was a word I never much applied to my personal life. But once Dina affixed it, like a sticky note on the walls of my head, there it stayed. I wish I could say I immediately put it to applicable and suitable use. News flash, I did not.

I couldn't get past my own self-pity and was still holding on to bitter, self-serving judgment and unrest.

Oh, I suppose any qualified therapist worth their degree might suggest this kind of self-destructive behavioral pattern could be a side effect of a traumatizing experience or something. Well, guilty as charged. Fortunately for me, that educated psychologist's name was Loyal. I had endured her guinea pigging me for years in the name of her studies. That's not fair; endured may be a stretch since I never fought her on it. I knew I was a mess.

I also knew my self-centeredness might be viewed as a means to minimize potential future damage. If I didn't go looking for friendships, if I didn't seek out love, then I couldn't be hurt like before, right? *Bullshit.* After all, that did not stop me from loving Jack. It did not stop me from loving Loyal. It just prevented them from getting to know the person I really was—Elles Garity, traumatized and in disguise.

Here I was, on the verge of endeavoring to be the best version of me, reclaiming who I always wanted to be, and doing it in the only place where, in my heart, I had always imagined I would stay. If only I could get out of my own way.

Consider this a turning point in the road to redemption, if you will. I do not care. When I said to Dina, *I can't do this anymore*, I wasn't talking about petty arguments and unresolved grudges. I hated the constant moral tug-of-war going on inside me. I wanted no more personality conflicts. No more identity crisis. No more hiding behind a transparent mask. If this was going to be a fight then I was going to have to start throwing punches as well and as hard as I ducked and cowered from them. So with all of that in mind, I bowed to the demon slayer inside me that I once tried to destroy.

Elles? It's Grace. You're up. I'm out.

* * *

"Grace? Grace! Where are you!? Anybody—"

"Shh." I emerged from a dusty shadowed corner of the room. "Quiet down, nobody's supposed to know I'm here, remember?"

"Well, where the hell have you been? You didn't come home last night. Your bed wasn't slept in. You scared the—"

"Sorry dear. I wasn't cheating, honest. You're the only one. I swear."

"Very funny, Grace."

"Close the damn door."

"Joke all you want. If you had any of this, you'd have no reason to cheat, let me tell—"

"Hey, foxy lady. Pick up a broom and start dusting or doing something productive, will ya?"

"Fine. So, what were you doing all night?"

"Running."

"Running. In the dark? In the middle of the night? For

how . . . Season's not over. We're not in visitation lockdown yet. Stranger danger is still in effect. There could be murderers roaming out there. What if—"

"Are you done? I thought you didn't like giving lectures."

"Yeah, well, with you around I'm getting pretty good at it. What's gotten into you?"

"I had some stuff to work out, that's all. Don't worry, warden, I wasn't running all night. I hiked out to the north light and camped out under the stars. It was warm last night, and the waves just lulled me to—"

"Oh, great, the furthest reaches, where no one can hear you scream. A real murderer's paradise."

"For your information, the moon was bright last night. It was beautiful out there, so peaceful. We should— Katie, there's someone peeping through the window."

"Where? Oh, relax. He works for me. Be right back." She snuck out the back door momentarily and reemerged with . . . lunch? At 7 a.m.?

"What is that? A pizza?"

"Breakfast pizza. Oh, my God. It looks so good."

"Katie, what part of breaking and entering, don't you—"

"You have a *key*."

"Which I could get in serious trouble for having. I could lose the inn."

"You don't have it yet."

"Thanks, Captain Negative. Would you be serious? Please?"

"I haven't eaten yet, hello. It's totally cool, okay? I know Josh. We had a . . . never mind. He works at Fiddler's. I owed him one. So I called 'im on my way out the door when I got your text. I told him to make sure he wasn't followed, boss," she mocked.

"Cute. *You* owed *him*? How does that even—"

"Well, if you must know, I kinda ended things in the . . . middle of . . ."

"Ick!"

"Oh, shut up. It gets lonely out here sometimes. Don't judge me. He blurted out the L-word and I freaked."

"Still, that doesn't make any . . . Ya know what, go eat your pizza."

"It's so good."

"Fiddler's . . ." I stopped reaching for cobwebs and lowered my broom, reminiscing. "God, I loved hanging out there. We're going there tonight."

"Well, look at you, Grace, all gung ho to socialize and stuff. You sure you didn't fall and hit your head?"

"Ha, ha. No. And it's Elles now, by the way, and you have . . . is that egg on the corner of your mouth?"

"Come on! Have you never had a breakfast pie be— Elles? Really?"

"I figured, if I'm gonna make a comeback, I gotta . . . ya know . . . come back as the real me." It felt good to say it. It felt good to see the expression on Katie's face when I told her. She smiled from ear to ear, and it made me smile.

She walked over and gently wrapped her arms around me and notched her chin on my shoulder, whispering in my ear, "Welcome home, Elles."

Chapter 22

With that, it was official. From that day forward I stopped correcting anyone who called me Elles. It took some getting used to and a lot of biting my tongue to resist the automatic urge. Katie and I stayed for hours, exploring the inn, floor by floor, room by room. I was satisfied just to be inside, if I could do little more than dust, assess conditions, and compile mental renovation notes. What I quickly started to notice was, other than some dated decor and minor upgrades, it looked fully operational—contrary to reports of it being abandoned, run-down, previous owners overwhelmed and fled the scene.

I must have commented on the suspicious nature of those claims a handful of times before Katie spilled the beans. What I couldn't understand was why I was told these tales or why this narrative of the inn's fate was being floated about town for me to hear. It seemed after my parents died prematurely and most suddenly, Dina tried to carry on as principal owner for years. She tried to be the caretaker of my mother's dream long before I reentered the picture. According to the bits and pieces Katie knew, Dina and Stephen took it on together during the breakdown of their marriage. Yes, the inn had been vacant—for a grand total of two years, two seasons.

It didn't make any sense. I had been shot down and put in my place, rightfully so, for going about this the wrong way. Weeks later, I'm informed that upon further review of my "history" that I am the winning contestant based on who I am, by the very same council? As flattering as that was, the whole thing stank of an underlying conspiracy. I was trying to stay and appear positive. I tried not to let it kill the mood, at least for the sake of keeping to the evening plan and only concerning myself with having a good time. Whatever was going on behind my back, the whole undercover occupancy angle—suspect from the start, I might add—was as good as done. My cover was blown by my own doing when I walked out the front door to lock up. I hit the stairs to leave and . . .

"Damn girl! You are a hard woman to track down!"

"Loyal!" I yelped. "What are you doing here?"

"Uh, well, I thought I'd surprise you. I just didn't know you were in exile! Surprise!"

"Loyal, I can't believe you came all the way out here! Did Jack come with you?"

She rolled her eyes. "Yeah, 'cause that's a three-hour car ride I'm dyin' to take. He sends his love and, oddly enough, had my suitcase packed before I did. But here I am!"

"Loyal! Is everything okay with you guys?"

"It's fine. I'm fine. *We* are fine. I think he's, um, got a little crush on me and, ya know, since you're not there, I've had to be the one to talk to him more, so thank you. You suck, and he's, um . . . Did you know he's got the prettiest brown . . . Ahem. So then you called the other day, and I just had to tell him hey, Grace needs me right now. Yeah . . . so, here I am."

"Um . . . wow! Drink any coffee on the way? Okay, well I'm so glad you're here, idiot. This is Katie, by the way. Katie this is my infatuated, I mean, longtime friend, Loyal. We were actually gonna go out tonight, so now it's a threesome."

"And you said I was the only one," Katie remarked with a snarky tone.

"Don't listen to her. She's got boy-toy problems. Come on, I'll ride with you back to Katie's place."

I have to say, spending time with those two for the few spare hours we had before going out was like being caught between twins separated at birth having a field day at my expense. Before long they were gelling famously, trading and comparing stories featuring yours truly. What started innocently as introductory tales of all three of us became a side-splitting tag-team battle of *Can you top this?* It was a retrospective of my life with Katie covering the formative years, and Loyal on Grace. Listening to them go on was a clinic in perspective reflection. It almost sounded like each was talking about two different people and well, I couldn't even get mad or annoyed. I mean, after a while, I found myself mesmerized like an interested and enlightened third party. Of course, we all have our limitations of how much we can stand having our entire lives broadcast in the spotlight—educational or entertainment value notwithstanding.

I guess I was still noticeably affected when Loyal met up with me outside on the porch, waiting for Katie to finish showering and getting ready to go. "Hey, you got pretty quiet this evening. What's up?" she asked, joining me on the swing.

"I don't know, just thinking, I guess."

"Hey, ya know, all that stuff, we were just having fun, ya know. We didn't mean to—"

"I'm not the same person, Loyal."

"Grace—"

"I'm not upset or anything at you guys fooling around. It's just, I changed. I never noticed how much."

"Grace, everybody changes when they grow."

"You know what I mean. You know who I was when you met me, and it wasn't the same girl Katie was telling stories about. Do you know, from the time I moved away until we met in junior high , I was . . ."

"What? Huh? Distraught, devastated, crushed? Let me know when I hit bingo here . . ."

"Lost."

"Goddamn right you were. I don't even know what happened and I could see—"

"It was a plane crash."

"Grace, you don't have to . . ."

"Yeah, I kinda do. Loyal, you were there for me when I wasn't even there for myself. You pulled me out of depression without ever really knowing why. I owe you that much, so just sit there and listen. My, um, my parents made plans to go to the mainland one day. For months, Ginny and I had been wanting to go somewhere. I don't even remember where anymore. One night, they said they'd be leaving in the morning, and they'd be back long before school was out. I wouldn't even have time to miss 'em. They left the house early, before I did, so Mom could stop at the inn on the way. I went off to school and . . . later that morning, we all heard it." The color started draining from Loyal's face as she listened, her expression one of anticipated horror. "We didn't know what the sound was, but the teachers, they all insisted everything was fine and told us not to worry. They had stopped at the gas station. They were at the pump filling up when a small plane came out of nowhere."

"Jesus . . ."

"They never knew what hit 'em. It hit, slammed into the pumps, right where they were."

"My God, Grace."

"The explosion was so big, it felt like the whole island shook. The school staff were all whispering to each other. We saw them. I remember one of them . . . looking directly at me, just for a split second. I thought it was strange. Then I got home, and everyone was there, gathered in the living room, waiting for me, Uncle John, Aunt Nellie, Coot, Dina. As soon as I saw them . . . I knew. I knew and I just dropped my stuff and ran."

"Grace, I'm . . . God, I'm so sorry."

"I never told anyone before. This is the first time I've said all of that out loud." I smirked, sucking back the emotion of the moment. "I *never* said it out loud. I didn't even know how or, exactly, what happened until I saw an update about the crash on the news. Pilot error or something. I turned it off as soon as I saw what it was about."

I'd never seen Loyal so pale white before. In all the years I'd known her, we had never shared so deeply, so personally. Our friendship was built, in large part, on living in and surviving in the here and now. Our pasts were our pasts. It was an unofficial guideline that nothing mattered before *us*.

This one struck her like a deer in headlights, and the only thing other than mortified sympathy she could bring herself to express was lighthearted sarcasm.

"Jerk," she mocked insincerely. "I come all the way here to help you celebrate, and now we're about to go out to have a good time, and you unload all this on me now?"

"Yeah, well, as I recently reminded myself, I've sort of always been your psychological test subject, which made you my live-in, pro bono therapist. You guys call what I just did a breakthrough or something like that, right?"

"Uh-huh."

"So now that I got that off my chest, we can go celebrate, have that good time."

" Uh-huh. Uh, Grace, I'm glad that you feel better, letting go of that, I am. Just so you know, we're gonna talk about this some more, ya know, as your *therapist*. We'll just put a pin in it for now, so we can do our thing, and . . ." She dabbed at the corner of one eye and found a teardrop. She hunched her shoulders and back in a flustered mini tantrum. I raised a hand to cover my mouth. I dared not laugh. "Oh, what are you doing to me here?"

"I'm sorry, I just . . . You're fine. It's . . ."

"I spent an hour on this makeup, you train wreck."

"Okay, that's a little unnece—"

"Grace, so help me, if I have to—"

"Mm . . . maybe just a little touchup . . . around the—"

"Okay, guys! Are we ready?" Katie came out the front door, and Loyal sprung to her feet.

"Yes! Just need to fix my *face*, and we're off to . . . where?"

Fiddler's was the spot. And I do mean *the* spot. Aptly named by, and in tribute to, the Irish American inhabitants of our population who resided here for generations. Our own private oasis from the masses, it was the proud brainchild, owned and operated by the McComiskey family since before the Garitys were ever a household name. The establishment stood as the one year-round, locally reserved hideaway. It was not advertised or publicized. In effect, it did not exist to anyone else but us. There was no outside signage, by design. The *honor thy neighbors' privacy* system allowed for outside admittance limited to family members and occasional close personal friends.

The concept was simple: an all-inclusive, two-story building featuring a bar, full-service kitchen, lounge, and game rooms downstairs. The entire second floor was designated as free-use living quarters. Fiddler's was the hot spot for winter time socialization, eat-in or takeout, dropping by for drinks, the habitual day trippers. Anything to break the monotony of being stuck at home. Everyone coexisted in a social pecking order of age-based authority. In short, the kids played house, apart from the adults, only two doors and an enclosed staircase away. We all shared a common place to gather regularly with restrictions that sometimes went both ways. Upstairs, there was an understood law to our parentless rule. If the chain of rankings was not respected and followed by all, the freedoms we enjoyed would be in serious risk. Due to separate entrances and expected boundaries, I had never set eyes on where kids were not allowed to go, until this night.

Chapter 23

I can't remember what I had imagined the downstairs to be like, except to say, most nights, before soundproofing was installed, the mixture of music and mingling could easily best whatever horseplay we were up to on the second floor. For me, this rite of passage was an overdue, anxiously awaited thrill. I gave Loyal the history lesson on the ride over, working myself into a giddy ball of excitement in the process. I was first out of the car before Katie could put it in park and first in ahead of the budding bosom buddies. They entered on either side of me, as I stood there in awe, taking it all in. Katie nudged me as they passed me by.

"We're gonna go get a table. Care to join us or . . ."

"Easy for you to say, you're used to it. I can't believe I'm finally here. This is so cool. I feel like I just turned eighteen all over again!" I squealed energetically. Eighteen triggered the all-inclusive, three-year benchmark transitional period. Downstairs had their own clearly defined rule, as well. You were allowed in, although the consumption of alcohol was strictly prohibited. You also bore the double-duty responsibility of checking on the upstairs dwellers when prompted. This house was not without its code of conduct. While one enjoyed the more mature liberties of ascension, you were expected to help keep a watchful eye on your authoritative replacement, at least until you turned twenty-one and earned full entitlement.

"Oh, my God! Is that? . . ."

I turned around in my chair and leaned in to study the figure racing toward me from behind the bar. "Mikey?" I beamed with enthusiasm.

"Elles, bloody Garity, would ya look at that. It's true.

You're back, in the flesh!" He grabbed hold and hoisted me out of my chair, draping my arms over his shoulders and lifting me onto his back as he spun around.

"Okay! Okay, okay, down boy!" I begged.

He let me down and turned to look me over with a wide-eyed, goofy gaze. "You've grown up a little bit now, haven't ya?"

"And you've . . . you've grown very . . . authentic."

"Thanks for noticin'. I thought I'd act the part since I took over the joint. Honor the ol' heritage, eh? How am I doin, eh?"

"A little overboard if you ask me," Katie replied in jest.

"Quiet over there! I'll deal with you in a minute." He fired back.

"It's different. I mean it doesn't have the same flair as the original M and—"

"Don't!" he warned, holding up an index finger, trying not to bumble out a laugh.

"What? I was just going to introduce you to—"

"Don't ya dare, Elles . . ."

"Loyal, this is Mikey McComiskey. The leprechaun formerly known to these parts as—"

"Bloody hell."

"M&M."

"I'll getcha for this, Elles Garity. Not now . . . but I'll getcha."

I looked square at him. "What? I left out the peanut part, at least."

"Christ almighty."

"Mikey, you're terrifying. Why don't ya get us some drinks while I hide me lucky charms!" Katie chimed in.

"It's good to see ya, Elles. But I'm afraid you're gonna have to leave your pets outside. What can I get you ladies? I know what that one's havin'—an escort out the door if she don't behave herself."

"Just a Coke for me. Thanks, Mikey."

"Surprise us," Katie added.

"I'll surprise ya all right. How 'bout a restrainin' order on the rocks?" he mumbled, walking away.

"You are popular with the boys around here, aren't you, Katie? Don't tell me you owe him one, too." Loyal appeared intrigued. *Don't ask*, I mouthed to her.

"Uh-oh, the liquor's on the way and the gloves are off, eh? Careful now, I may have to get a little karaoke contest started up. You better bring it with somethin' a little stronger than soda pop there, sweetheart. What about you, Loyal?"

An expression of wild fascination washed over Loyal's face, hearing us trade fun-loving insults. "Guys, I think I live here now," she announced.

At long last, I lay my wandering eyes on Ginny. As the waitress delivered our drinks, I saw her sitting with Tom across the way. The second I spotted her I was on my feet. Though the music was playing and the room had a boisterous buzz, obvious body language suggested they were arguing about me. Ginny stood up, as well, and slowly made her way toward me. I was sure this was it, the sooner-or-later crossing of paths. I felt ready, nerves and apprehension cast away. If anything, I was eager for this to happen, come what may. Then, face-to-face, eye-to-eye, nothing between us but opportunity, she balked.

"I can't do this right now."

She could barely stand to look at me, moving past like I was nothing more than some damn stumbling block. She walked out the front door without another word or courtesy look back. Tom sulked in his seat, appearing disheartened and disappointed. I returned to my company, choosing to brush off the unfortunate encounter as a forgettable glitch in our otherwise joyful evening. I won't deceive even myself by saying it didn't bother me. It simply served no purpose then, to let animosity further fuel a fire in me that was barely sparked and left to simmer.

For that one evening, I had to be selfish. I had to relax,

unwind, and put everything else on hold. I was never one to drink. I never acquired the taste, and thankfully so. I could have handled the loss of my parents in so many self-abusively addictive ways. Instead, I never saw or understood the appeal. This night was no different. I left that indulgence up to Katie and Loyal, and they embraced the role wholeheartedly. The three of us let loose, making careless spectacles of ourselves and playing games. A contested game of pool turned into a cue-wielding sword fight. Darts was, well, inadvisable after Loyal nearly took one in the back of the head by accident. We wrapped up the night by claiming the karaoke stage to perform a concert not fit for human ears.

I remember it vividly, as the only sober one and sole participant with the shrills of those exploits forever burned into my memory. The worst of it was, I sang no better than them in their inebriated states. Their night was over before mine. We closed the place down with one final encore to the McComiskey boys as they cleaned and straightened up the joint. Tom hung out until the end, offering a safe escort home. He helped me wrangle the schnockered sisters inside and to their beds. Conversely, I was tired but not entirely spent, certainly not ready for the night to end. I accompanied Tom out onto the front stoop.

Chapter 24

"You girls put on a hell of a show tonight."

"I needed it. Thank you for bringing us . . . for helping me bring them home."

"Don't mention it. And I mean that. As far as you know, I was out doin' a little night fishin'. I don't need any more trouble than I already—"

"Say no more. Tom, I'm, um . . . I'm sorry for whatever that was earlier. I was going to talk to her. I really was."

He gazed off into the darkness, considering the ramifications. "Yeah, well, uh . . . I tell ya, I'm at my wit's end tryin' to stay neutral. My gut's tellin' me I should be on her side. Hell, she ain't said it to me directly but . . . My heart won't let me choose. I don't know what the hell happened to me. Sometimes I think she'd be happier if I *had* locked ya up in a cell until she was ready to deal with ya. Maybe it'd be quicker and easier if you just tackle 'er next time she tries to get away. She can't not talk to ya if you're on top of her."

"That's some tough-love imagery there, Tom. You sure you're not takin' that a little further in your head? Maybe some mud, a wrestling ring?"

Tom grunted out a laugh. "Whatever you gals gotta do. Just, uh, keep me out of it, and don't expect me to referee any grudge matches. I should get home and—"

"Tom? What's the rush?"

"Elles, I'm 'bout to get my head chewed off. If there's a chance she's still awake when I get home, I just assume get it done and over with."

"You said yourself, as far as anyone knows—"

"You really tryin' to get me reamed or what? Elles, I can't get caught in the middle of this any more than I already am.

What do you want from me?"

"I wanna see the stars."

"Then go home, put your TV on. Call NASA or somethin'." I noticed he didn't say to lie on the ground and look up. He knew what I was talking about. I started sauntering backward to his truck. "No! Now Elles, not tonight. I can't . . ."

"Chill out, Tom. It's not like I'm askin' ya to take me there for what it used to be."

"It still is. It ain't changed. Elles, it's late. Could we just—" I made a run for his truck before he could catch me. "Elles!"

I jumped in the passenger seat and locked myself in. "Why should you get to be the only one she's mad at tonight, Tom? I'm not getting' out of this truck. So ya got a choice. You can take me up the hill, or lead us both to slaughter. What's it gonna be?"

He stuffed his fists into his jacket pockets begrudgingly. He spun around, digging his heels in the dirt and pitching a fit to the wind. When he finished agonizing over a winless situation, he got behind the wheel.

Another one of our closely guarded local secrets was the observation spot. Growing up, the phrase we heard from the older kids on summer nights was just what I said, *going to see the stars*. It was more about the guys going to find heaven. To us, it was code for make-out central. More stunningly, it was notorious for its spectacular view. Atop Tower Hill was the highest point on the island, popular for the three hundred sixty–degree views. Other than the faint lights from distant shores across the sound, it was a pitch black, star-gazer's dream. Tom reluctantly drove us up there with nary a peep. I rolled my window down, catching the cold breeze on my face and through my hair all the way there. I hopped out and boosted myself off his back tire over and onto the truck bed. I lay flat on my back, facing a clear, wide-open sparkling sky. Tom hoisted himself up onto the top of the cab and sat over me.

"If you don't talk to me, I might fall asleep right here," I teased. "I wouldn't have done it, ya know."

"Done what?"

"Made you take me to your place. I'm not trying to make trouble for you and Ginny, Tom."

"What do ya think this is?"

"A hostile takeover, hijacking, you can spin it to her however you want. I'll take the heat. If she really does want me in jail . . ."

"That's great. I'm glad you're having fun with this."

"I used to love this place. Gosh, I still do. Look at it. I really could fall asleep right here."

"Well, please don't." He slid the back window of his truck open and reached in for a bottle of beer stashed behind the seat.

"I may have been gone for a while, but I remember how she is, Tom. She always got more tough than mad at you. Show me a smile. I'll let ya go when you get happy."

I watched him raise the bottle in the air from my upside-down vantage point. "Way ahead of ya."

"Are you gonna marry her, Tom?"

He choked a sip of beer down as he coughed and looked blindsided at me. "It ain't that simple."

"The proposing or the planning?"

"I thought you came up here to see the stars."

"Is it the kids? Are you not ready to be a full-fledged father yet?"

"Elles . . ."

"Tell me, Tom. *She* wouldn't talk to me, so . . ."

"There's . . ." He took a deep breath to settle his temper and spoke softer and more directly. "Elles, there's things you don't understand."

"So help me. Help me understand, Tom. What . . . ?"

"I can't."

"Why? What am I missing here? Say it. Why is everyone so afraid to—"

"We should, uh, we should both get home, it's—"

"Fine." I sat up fast, leaped back out of the bed and into the driver's seat this time before Tom could react. "But I'm driving!"

"Elles, what the hell are you doin'? Get . . . You can't just —"

I started the engine and revved it over and over as a warning. "You riding up there or inside? I'll take ya either way. Let's go, Tom Deiter!" I gunned it one time. The truck lunged forward, and Tom swore as he caught his feet under him landing on the bed. He jumped to the ground beside the passenger door and leaned inside.

"Elles! Goddammit, if this is about—"

"It's not about anything, Tom. You can't talk about it then you can't talk about it. Getting' in?"

"Then let me drive the damn—" I tapped the gas slightly again. Tom snatched open the door and jumped inside. "What the hell, Elles?"

"Damn," I said matter-of-factly.

"What now?"

"This is a stick."

"So?"

"I never learned to drive stick. Oh well, how hard can it be? Hang on."

"Elles, would you please. . ." His pleas became more high pitched and desperate as I stuttered the truck into gear, pushing onward.

"Ya know something, Tom? I lied."

"About what?" he asked, frantically pulling his seatbelt across his lap and buckling it.

"It is . . . it is about something. Ever since I've been back, people have been avoiding me, dancing around subjects in conversations they don't want to finish, acting sorry, telling me there's more going on around here than—"

"And I told you, I didn't want to get in the middle of this."

"That's fine . . . fine, Tom. There is nothing anyone can say to me that's as bad as what I already know. And as far as anyone who's against or on the fence about me being back, well, maybe it's time I let 'em know that Elles Garity is back and she ain't goin' nowhere."

"Christ, Elles, what are you gonna do? Did you forget I'm a damn police officer?" I put the pedal down and let it fly down the hill, grinding the gears as we picked up speed. Tom tossed his head back and held on to anything he could grab. "My truck, Elles!" he whined. I looked over at him scared shitless and smiled, laughing at my own antics and his anguish at the same time. I lay into the horn as we came barreling down the foot of the hill between two properties. I switched the high beams on, blaring a sound and visual disturbance through the peaceful night. I'm not sure what provoked me to such a juvenile stunt. Tom didn't say another word until I peeled off the road and into Katie's driveway.

It was exhilarating, liberating, to blow off steam while Tom sat helpless, cringing over his precious vintage ride. That part was more of an icing-on-the-cake thing rather than revenge for whatever he wouldn't say. He was just an unwilling participant, a friendly carjacked casualty of my night-capping whim. We sat still in the driveway while the trailing dust cloud settled behind us, and I let my heart stop beating out of my chest. I leaned forward, peaking at the dashboard gauges.

"Oh, you're almost out of gas," I stated casually, not at all trying to be as facetious as it probably sounded by that point.

He flung open his door and bailed out, circling around to open mine. "Out!" he growled. I glared at the scowl on his face and stepped out. He wasted no time replacing me in the cab and slammed his door shut. "You're the most defiant undrunk I ever saw in my life, ya know 'at, Grace?"

"Oh, come on, Tom. I was just having a little fun. I was kidding about driving stick."

"No you weren't."

"No," I admitted, giggling. "You're right, I wasn't, but I did pretty good."

"Pretty . . . pretty good! That's— I'll be sure to tell my mechanic where to send the bill."

"Lighten up, Tom, I—"

"You listen to me, Elles. I was on your side."

"On my . . . About what?"

"Don't matter!"

"Damn it, Tom, spill it. If you've got something to say . . ."

"Be careful. Just be careful, Elles." He started to back up and stopped. "I'm tellin' ya this for your own good. Until you figure everything out for yourself, be real careful who you step on and piss off. Goodnight, Elles."

Chapter 25

I was up before the sun the next morning and, I only assume, hours before Katie and Loyal made a stir. I set out for an extended running-think session along the beach and outskirts of town. I wound up conveniently passing by the school as the day was getting started. From out of sight, I observed the morning traffic until I saw Ginny arrive. I followed her inside from a distance until she entered her classroom. I purposely made no noise, keeping my presence stealth, holding steady just outside the doorway as she pretended not to notice me at first. She sat at her desk, attending to morning preparations, drinking her coffee, and reaching into her bag to retrieve a stack of papers. I held firm. She placed them aside and began thumbing through a daily planner.

"Class will be starting soon, and I've got papers to finish grading. So if you don't mind . . ."

I took a few steps inside. I couldn't help but pan around the room, checking out the setup, the personal touches, comparing them to my own former classroom. I took particular interest in a poster titled "Classroom conduct standards and rules," laminated and displayed on the board behind her desk. I smiled inside, reading it, reminiscing about that little girl, the self-appointed playground monitor, the troubleshooting, pint-sized, bad-ass role she had pulled off so naturally—my Tom-proof protector. Only now she was too involved, too jaded by our severed ties to give me the time of day. I walked in a bit farther, to the front row of desks. I sat down at one, remarking in awe on our once-upon-a-time common dream turned realized double paths.

"We always knew what we wanted to be, didn't we?" She didn't respond. She didn't break concentration on her grading.

I got choked up and tried like hell to bury it. My throat went dry, and when I opened my mouth to speak, I could barely do it. "What do you want me to say, Ginny? I don't know what you . . ." And then she lifted her head, in a frozen state of silent judgment. I scrambled for anything, racking my brain for words, clues, an inkling that she didn't want me to just go away, that we could open a dialogue, even if it started as bitter disdain. A death stare, or a lude gesture, would have been . . . something. But she just looked right through me then refocused on her work while I sat there waiting in vain. "Say *something*!" I grunted at her insistently.

She lifted her head only to check her watch, and the morning bell rang. I contemplated walking out, repaying what she had done to me the night before—although I made considerably more effort than she had put forth. We could keep playing this immature game of whatever this was. I could retreat with the hopes of an early, treacherous winter during which we'd hardly run into each other again until the first sprouts of spring. Not likely. So I staged a spontaneous and awkward sit-in instead. It was a less invasive method than Tom's body slam idea, but it served her right. *She* could ignore me. But an entire class, distracted, wondering who the strange woman in sweat-stained attire was and why she was in attendance today . . . ?

The kids started to file in, gawking in my direction, and my one-person Ms. Carrington protest was on. The longer I stayed, the more complicated my demonstration got. Throughout the morning session, I saw Ginny, the unrattled-woman version, remain undaunted. She taught with such exuberance and passion that I lost all sense of why I was there, caught up in Ginny's respect-commanding, good-humored style of relating to the children. I laughed when they laughed at her corny jokes and observations. I had to resist the reflex to raise my hand when she posed an open question up for grabs to anyone with the answer. In all that time, the fact that she and I had strayed was lost on me. Lunchtime came. She wrapped up class and escorted the famished brood to feast. I lost my will to stay. I sat alone a little longer, moved by what I'd seen, then dismissed myself while they were away.

"Where the hell have you been?" I got into Katie's car, which was waiting for me in the parking lot, with Loyal behind the wheel.

"I just went for a run this morning, that's all. Then I came by to talk to Ginny."

"How'd that go?"

"It didn't. Can we just, I don't know, talk about something else?"

"Oh, okay, well how about your road-raging tear across town last night then?"

"Oh, my . . . Come on. There's no way you heard that."

"No, you're right. I was out like a light. But according to Katie, in addition to everyone else hearing you, a few of them saw you. Now it's spreading around town faster than your reckless driving. What's going on with you, Grace? If Ginny didn't talk to you then where—"

"I was here! Okay? She snubbed me last night, and I let it go. I thought I was okay with it. I had to come talk to her."

"Why?"

"She was my best friend, Loyal."

"I meant why do you have to talk to her so badly *now*, all of a sudden? You never talked about her or mentioned her before."

"I never talked about a lot of things before."

"Grace, look at me."

"I never said . . . I moved away . . ." Here it came, another blockbuster confession. I was just as ashamed to admit this, as well, to someone else. "And I never told her goodbye." Loyal looked conflicted, torn between my truth and what it meant in the greater meaning of why I came home to it. I don't know whom she wanted to be disappointed at more—me or them. "I never saw her again."

"What, so . . . Grace, is that what this is all about? What, is everyone here just waiting on your apology tour? You were a kid for God sakes. You supposed to stick around and wait for her to be good and ready for you to explain yourself for reacting to something that happened to you, not her? And the guy she was sitting with, what's his deal?"

"Tom Deiter. We grew up together. He's the acting sheriff and Ginny's . . . I don't know what they are."

"Wonderful. What is this? An extradition, placing you under hometown arrest until you—"

"Loyal, stop. It's not any of that. This is my life, not a movie script that—"

"I care about you. You . . ." She flailed her hands around, at a loss for how to convey the mixed feelings in her head.

"What, Loyal?"

"You . . . you went off to find yourself, ya know? You married Jack, then broke his heart. You go and leave me to finally do something with my life. I'm workin' on that, ya know. And on top of all that, you leave me with the love of my friggin' life, that *you* stole from me, by the way—"

"Loyal."

"I don't know how to be his girlfriend. I'm not good at—"

"Loyal."

"And now I gotta worry about you being vilified by—"

"Loyal!"

She flopped back in her seat and sighed. "What?"

"Jesus, you're supposed to be the voice of reason here, the stable one, the professional. Maybe I should be worried about you."

She turned her head and looked at me with puppy dog eyes and a sad smile. "I guess I didn't come all the way over here just to surprise you."

"Ya think? Loyal, I'm okay. I can handle myself. You know that."

"Yeah, well, where's this Ginny chick live? We're goin' over so I can kick her ass."

"No. I appreciate the offer. I do, killer. But I can't solve my problems by having my therapist kick my childhood friend's or bully's asses."

"You had a—"

"Bad choice of words, okay? Tom's different now, and he wasn't that intimidating, anyway. All bark. Now he's as . . . I don't know, as confused as I am."

"Okay, so what about all of this drama between you guys?"

"Trust me, I'm working on it. You're not gonna like hearing this, but this is why I haven't told you everything. It's complicated and there's more to it."

"Do I wanna know?"

"No, but I do. I'm working on that, too. For now, can we just focus on you being here?"

She started the car and fixed her face and hair, giving in. "Sure, where to?"

"Hey, Loyal, you'll work things out, too. I promise. You just have to take it slow, stop overthinking everything. I didn't break Jack's heart, ya know. I was never the one he was after in the first place."

She blushed and smirked. "Really? He . . . Thanks, Grace."

"Take a right out of here. I need to make a few stops, and we can grab some lunch." I navigated Loyal on an island sightseeing drive. I pointed out landmarks and shared with her the stories I had been told growing up. We parked downtown to get out and walk around, find somewhere to eat. First, I wanted to take a stroll to town hall. I had some questions for Selectman Lafave, and I wanted the truth.

Loyal waited outside while I confronted him in his office.

"Have a seat, Elles. What can I do for you?

"You can drop the act."

"Um . . . I'm sorry?"

"Mr. Lafave . . . Paul, please don't waste my time or yours. I came here to see you because I have a feeling Dina will tell me some altered version of the truth. I won't buy the inn if—"

"Okay, look. It's not what you think. Never mind, I don't have any idea what you think. Didn't make any sense to me, trickin' someone into buying something they already owned anyway."

"What, me? Why would anyone—"

"You really should talk to Dina. I'm just the middleman in all of this, the schmuck who went along with it for some ungodly reason. I got . . . I got real issues to tend to. I gotta tell you, Miss Garity, you showed up, I didn't even know who you were, and suddenly I got prominent residents turnin' my office upside down. Look, here." He snatched a set of keys from his desk drawer and tossed them on the desk in front of me. "I swear on my mama's . . . I don't need this. I didn't serve two tours in the army, land a job here to be some puppet in her . . . I'm glad you came in. Now that the truth's out, no more finaglin' for me. I've got more important things to do around here. I wash my hands of the whole matter."

I sat there watching him crumble, thinking, *Geez, I came here to demand answers and take charge. I barely said a word, and he's cracking faster than a bundle of nerves on a witness stand under intense examination.* "I'm confused, so . . ."

"The sale was never in question, Elles. That's the bottom line."

"So . . . they lied."

"You wanted the truth. There it is. There were no other bidders. There was no inn for sale. I apologize for gettin' snippy with you at the meeting. All part of her stupid little . . . Look, I'm sure you're a very nice woman with very good intentions. Do me one favor, would ya?"

"What's that?"

"When you do talk to Dina, please impress upon her, the next time she wants to use town officials for her own private chicanery, just . . . leave me out of it. In fact, I'd be grateful if she found another town to do it in. The woman needs to get out of my hair once and for all. She drives me up a damn wall."

"I'll be sure to give her the message."

I was beside myself with . . . I don't know. I couldn't even describe my emotions. I went there for answers, and I got — I had to see Dina. I had to find her. I marched straight out, forgetting Loyal was there. She chased me to the car, begging me to slow down, to stop. The only thing that prevented me from speeding off and making a beeline for Dina's place was me. I stuck the key in the ignition and proceeded to slam my hands on the steering wheel in a fit of lashing out. I balled my fists up and punched them, screaming.

"Grace, stop! You're scaring me! What's wrong?"

I sat there shaking my head, calming myself down, calming Loyal down. She had never seen that side of me. I had never seen this side of me—until I came back here. Why didn't anyone tell me? After I made a fool of myself at the town meeting. After Tom gave me the— Scratch that. I didn't want to see Dina. I didn't want to talk to her. I didn't want to talk to Tom, and God help me, I tried with Ginny. Right then I was even questioning any allegiance to Katie. Loyal came to visit me. This was not fair to her. I sat there, Loyal on pins and needles beside me, and I talked myself down. I slapped on a phony smile and felt the adrenaline wearing off, the stinging soreness from beating a steering wheel senseless coming on. I had to chuckle. Loyal turned in her seat with a sigh of relief and her hand on her head.

"You sure you don't need me to kick someone's—"

"Let's get some lunch," I said, starting the car.

Chapter 26

It might be fair to say, I went a little overboard with anger. Although I'm not convinced that was the case. I knew all of this would be hard. I got that nothing worth fighting for came easy, thus the fighting part. I did not expect, nor did I accept, manipulation. Granted, I didn't have all the facts, in part, because nobody seemed willing to give them to me. Understanding the whole two sides to every story, I found it extremely difficult to fathom why it had to be this way. I wanted the inn. That idea was mine, all me, no matter what anyone assumed. All they had to do was ask, that's all. A damn honorable mention, *Hey, Elles, FYI, you own a freakin' inn!*

So, yes, my emotions of late were getting the better of me—making up with people, slowly burying hatchets. And if Ginny would care to exhibit a single ounce of empathy, that would be spectacular. The full blame for this stalemate wasn't on me anymore, if that was ever the perception. Speaking of stale, one step forward, one shove back.

Loyal and I went shopping on Water Street. She was still trying to delve into my issues, but I was all about enjoying this time with her. I was all *damn the torpedoes being launched at my life from every angle.* She came at an opportune time. The busiest section of town was operating at partial capacity for this time of year. There were no crowds of people to weave through, clambering to get in and out of the few remaining open shops. There were few, if any, lines for food service.

We took our lunch to go across the street to eat on the waterfront. I didn't want to dwell on my problems with Loyal. Besides, knowing the relentless type she was, holding her off was a mere matter of time. I wanted to hear about back home—my other home. I wanted to hear more details about her fumbling things with Jack, where things stood on building a self-sufficient career for herself. I didn't want her to worry about me. I was doing well to keep phone calls between us strategically half-informed, misleading, sugar-coated at times when some hard-to-handle truth slipped out. As I fully admitted, I held things back, but for good reason, for our own good. Navigating this new old world of mine, the need to make it on my own, was tough enough without bearing the extra weight of Loyal or Jack worrying about me, too.

"Yeah, things are starting to come together. Actually, I didn't want to say anything and jinx it, but I ran into a college classmate not too long after you left. We met up a few times, had coffee, hung out, whatever. I was telling her about wanting to start my own practice, ya know." I loved every word out of her mouth, the inspired glow emanating from her being as she brought me up to speed. "So, get this, I'm trying to get all my shit together to branch out on my own, right? Most importantly, find a location to do it. It turns out, she's doing the same thing. She's working for a small therapy group that's growing, taking on some extra therapists. In the meantime, we've been talking about it more and more. We're plotting a partnership, nothing huge, just take over the world kinda stuff. You know me."

"Loyal . . ."

"It's so frickin' intense. I mean, I got steady work. I got a plan. We're just waiting until the timing is right."

"Loyal, that's amazing. I told you!"

"All right look, Jesus, I'm getting myself excited just talkin' about it, and I don't wanna—"

"Loyal, it's okay to get a little excited. Just take it easy. Like you said, wait it out. Don't rush anything until you're ready. And what about—"

"So what about you? Shacking up with Katie a permanent plan or . . ."

"I don't know."

"Uh-huh, well, ya sold your house, genius. What are ya gonna do, become a squatter in a lighthouse? Just think of the times the three of us could have there, huh?"

"You don't live here, ya—"

"Well, not now, but down the road . . ."

"You just focus on your future, would you please? I didn't give you that check so you could throw away—"

"Hey, woah! No offense, Debbie-do-good, but my success is not anchored to your generosity. "

"Debbie-do—"

"Shut up. I'm gonna be a kick-ass success with or without your money, and as much as it meant having you bestow a fortune on me out of love . . . I'm payin' every penny back."

"You don't have to do that."

"Well, I'm payin' someone back, sister. I'll get rich on my own. I don't need you," she scoffed.

"You're such an ass." I chuckled back at her.

"It's gonna take some time, don't get me wrong. I'll tell ya right now, soon as Jack hears about everything that's going on with you, he's gonna wanna take me to stay at the finest inn on the island next spring. And it, uh, looks a little pricey. Maybe there'll be some kind of inaugural-season discount, promo deal thing?"

"How does working off your stay sound?"

Loyal sat back and looked at me sideways, pondering the notion and sneering at me. "That sounds awful. Grace, that's a terrible business plan. You can't do that."

"It was a joke, Loyal, I hope. If I do this, I have—"

"*If* you do this?"

"I have renovations to do, business practices to learn, a meal plan to put together, health and building codes to pass probably, not to mention an entire workforce—that I currently don't have—to help with all of that." My God, when I heard myself laying it all out, what the hell was I thinking? Forget being mad at anyone. I didn't have time to be mad at anyone.

I had six months, tops, to get that inn up and running. I could put on all the brave faces I wanted. How the hell was I going to pull this off with just me and Floyd? Winter was coming, which meant limited access on and off this frozen slab. If I was lucky enough to hire some semblance of a crew and . . . "Oh, my God."

"Grace, geez, relax."

"I don't have a staff. There's so much to do. Loyal, what am I gonna do?"

"Well, first it would be helpful to get a grip! Then maybe ask yourself why the hell we are sitting here, when we can be over there, getting started."

"You're here on vacation. I can't ask you to—"

"I'm here ducking a romance that's spookin' the shit out of me right now, dumbass, and it would be super if I had a reason not to think about it. Please, put me to work." She sprung to her feet, collecting our garbage, waving me along.

"Okay, fine, just . . . Here are the keys. Let yourself in. I gotta make a call. I'll be right there." I grabbed my phone quickly while Loyal scurried off. "Hey, Loyal!" I called after her. "In case I forget to say it, thank you!"

"Hurry the hell up!"

Chapter 27

Thus, my quest to own and operate an entire inn was off and running. This was my chance to revive, to live my mother's dream, our heritage, with The Garity House. Sorry, spoiler alert. That was a change I was saving as incentive to make this work, one of many personal touches I intended to implement in order to make this not just about the past. I wanted to add my stamp, shout out to the community, *This is Garity family history, reborn, and Elles Garity's vision for the present and future combined.* I had color schemes to decide on, upgrades to make, furnishings and decor to purchase. We were way past the point of lists. I had a to-do *book* to write.

Good thing someone was there to keep me grounded. We started with the basics, covering every square inch top to bottom, inside and out. Loyal started a spreadsheet on her phone, and we started putting together a detailed, categorized list of chores, random ideas, options. We cleaned out linen closets, rummaged through stocked shelves, checked equipment and appliances. I immersed myself in the possibilities, the opportunity to fill this place, these rooms, my new life, with memories for years to come. Nothing could top the high I was on, until reinforcements of both the expected and uninvited kind arrived.

"Katie," I said, surprised. "What . . . what are you—"

"I invited her." Loyal spoke up. "I made a call, too. You're gonna need all the help you can get, right?" She leaned in over my shoulder and not-so-subtly whispered, "Um, I only made one call. So, I'm not too sure . . . You might have to help me out with who the other—"

"It's Floyd, silly, Floyd Gresham. Floyd, this is my friend, Loyal. She's visiting for the week. And you're absolutely right.

I am going to need a lot of help. So who better than our resident community handyman extraordinaire? That was my call. Anyway, you guys hang out here for a few. I'm going to take Floyd downstairs so he can look at a few things."

The goal was to put temporary distance between Katie and me for as long as possible. Nobody here was above suspicion except for Floyd, the only one who seemed to have no reason to be anything but genuinely open and honest. Upon our inspections, Loyal and I had found some things that needed attention. That was not a total get-out-of-Katie's-vicinity play, just a conveniently timed excuse. It didn't take Katie long to track us down and address the obvious.

"Elles, can I talk to you for a minute?"

"I'll go get my tools from the truck." Floyd excused himself.

"What's up?" I asked, trying to appear oblivious.

"Well, you tell me. You acted like you barely noticed me up there."

"I just have a lot on my mind."

"Straight from the *Leave Me the Hell Alone* handbook."

"What? I thought you were busy today, anyway."

"I'm done. Hey, if you didn't want me here then why did —"

"Loyal called you, like she said. Not me."

Katie folded her arms and huffed, rolling her eyes. "Wow! Do I get like, a hint maybe, of what this is about or . . ."

I mimicked her, folding my arms, too, at a loss for what else to say. Floyd returned and Katie started to leave.

"Fine! I guess I'll see you at—"

"I know about the sale," I finally confessed.

"What are you talking about?"

"I know that the inn was never up for sale."

"Oh, geez."

"I know it was just a big, orchestrated lie."

"Elles . . ."

"And I know it was always mine. What I can't wrap my

head around is—"

"You think I had something to do with this?"

"You don't exactly look shocked, Katie! What should I think?"

"Yes, I knew about it, okay? Happy? I knew. It wasn't up to me. I knew, and I'm sorry. That's all I can say. What does it matter, Elles? You got what you—"

"Right out of the *Everyone's against Elles* handbook."

"Seriously?"

I had nothing more to say, to Katie that is. I stormed off, disgusted with the whole conversation.

"Elles!"

I went to Fiddler's to think and be alone. I found a table in a quiet corner of the bar with my back to the rest of the room and the hope of blending into the shadows. I didn't want to be seen, heard, spoken to. And in case anyone is keeping score, my streak of walking out and not informing people—i.e., Loyal and Floyd—why or where I was going was fully intact and going strong. I don't recall how many hours I was there. In so many ways, it was a dark moment I just assume be erased from my mind. Why is it that our lowest moments tend to stick with us for an eternity? We can't shake them no matter how hard we try or how many good times we're fortunate enough to pile on in the grim hope of canceling out the bad. If I had only been strong enough to give Katie the benefit of the doubt. If I had decided it was better to view ownership of the inn as a victory, no matter how it came to be, this would have been easier.

During my funk of public isolation, I wondered briefly who might be looking for me, what heartfelt pep talks, even what spiteful things, they would have to say. Only two people dared to approach me. One was Mike McComiskey. He never tried to cheer me up, ask what was wrong. I didn't blame him for that, as I'm sure I left no doubt that something was indeed wrong, and I wasn't giving off *let's talk about it* vibes. He brought me a glass of water, which I drank one sulking sip at a time. For every empty glass, he refilled and kept them flowing. The other person was Floyd. He came to tell me Loyal had caught the ferry home. He said she was sorry to leave but something important came up. I felt bad, but I didn't blame her for going and issuing the standard statement as a reason.

Amid my self-loathing me-time, I later learned that several people had dropped by, either in search of or to check on me. I was too deep inside my head to give a damn at the time.

For weeks after that, the air between Katie and me had gone stale. I spent most of my waking time at the inn. Beyond that, we exchanged civil pleasantries if I showed up for bed when she was still up or if we crossed paths in the morning when I left. Floyd was basically the only one I interacted with. Together, we chipped away at small repairs and cleaned. At first, he brought meals prepared at home for us to share. Eventually, for a change of pace, we would sometimes venture to his house to eat, catch a ball game, or split up a long day's work. Once the grills and ovens were deemed ready, Floyd put his kitchen skills on display. Might I add, he rather excelled at flaunting his amateur chef side. He put my best culinary attempts to shame, a compliment that does not do his dishes full justice.

To put any other speculations to rest, there was nothing between Floyd and me but friendship and respect. We maintained an all-business, working chemistry and a refreshingly honest rapport. There was undoubtedly zero room in my life for dating, anyway—to put it bluntly. We got along in easygoing ways, playing off each other's eccentricities. We both kept things truthful, fun, and light. All deeper, personal stuff, my inner demons, my struggles, were left out. Looking back on those days, the night out with the girls had been a release. My time in seclusion, hanging out with Floyd, was a mental reset, a vitally helpful, cathartic relief. How could I have possibly known that my judgment of Floyd should have been any different unless I paid close enough attention to things I didn't want to see.

Chapter 28

My twenty-seventh birthday loomed on the horizon as mid-October came to pass. With everything on my mind, I hadn't given it much thought other than, fingers crossed, nobody would make a big deal of it. That was a preference that Loyal and I had always shared, and if it was up to me, I preferred to continue the tradition. Our way of celebrating the day had never involved cakes and candles, parties, and gifts but instead simply spending it together doing whatever we did. I guess I fell prey to the point of view of *What's the use in celebrating*? There wasn't a box big or real enough to fit in it the only gift I wanted anymore.

While running errands the morning of my birthday, Floyd asked me to stop at his place to pick up some carpentry supplies and more food. I always tried to limit the time I spent in Floyd's kitchen. Cleanliness was not his problem, but organization was. Keeping everyday utensils and other accoutrement stored in weird, one-stop-shop harmony alongside garage tools went against most people's code of housekeeping conduct. The man's twisted idea of organization was a countertop pegboard backsplash, on which hung everything from hammers, screwdrivers, and pliers to handheld mixers, wooden spoons, and frying pans. Canisters of flour and sugar in the same countertop lineup as those filled with nuts and bolts. It was madness. The only saving, and pardon me, grace was the separation between the two oddly paired categories.

I filled two reusable bags, swiped a bottle of water from the refrigerator for the return trip, and headed back. The one slung over my shoulder knocked a small box of random junk off a shelf onto the floor. I squatted down to gather up the contents and a half-crumpled sticky note in the mix caught my eye. It had my parents' names and address scribbled on it. I stood up in wide-eyed bewilderment. I stuffed it in my pants pocket, replaced the wooden box, and locked the door behind me.

When I got back to the inn, I caught Floyd red-handed in the act of dashing my hopes of an uneventful day. A sweet-baked aroma wafting from the kitchen sounded the "busted" alarm.

"I think I got everything you need, Floyd, except for the —"

"What the hell you doin' back so soon? I gave you a long list of tools I needed. You find everythin'?"

The one person I counted on not having a clue as to the significance of this day somehow got wind, and I trumped his question with a better one. "Who told you?" I waited for an answer that didn't come, while emptying the bag of groceries and putting them away.

"Floyd! I brought the frosting you asked for, but I couldn't find any— Oh!" Dina came waltzing in and stopped in her tracks at the sight of me. "I . . . I thought she was—"

"Out getting an absurdly long list of tools to keep me occupied? I'm back, and if it's all the same to you guys, I'd appreciate it if you could just . . . pretend this is any other day and—"

"I beg your pardon. Parades are not that easily canceled. The floats are already on the move."

"Oh, God. Dina, thank you, but I just don't feel—"

"In other words, what is about to happen, it's too late to stop now. We are doing this whether you like it or not."

"We? Who's we? Floyd, who else is we? What's happening?"

"Hello! Where is every— Oh!" Enter Katie, equally caught off guard. "I thought she was—"

"She's right here. I'm *she.* Look, thank you, everybody. I don't know what you guys have cooked up other than a cake but really, I just want this to be a normal day, okay? So can we not—"

"Oh, *we* haven't cooked anything up," Katie replied.

"See, you've hardly said a handful of words to me in weeks. You've been hiding out here, doin' your thing, feeling sorry for yourself, mad at everyone but Floyd. That's fine."

"Katie, let's . . ." Dina tried to intervene.

"No, no. Let me finish. Just exactly what makes you think either one of us would wanna do anything for your ungrateful ass?"

"I don't . . . You're right. I don't know what would make me think that."

"Damn right, I'm right. And you can't get out of my way quick enough lately. So if you don't wanna partake in any birthday lunch or cake that Floyd has slaved over, *for you*, then you can take yourself on home—to *my* home, that is—and be all alone on your birthday 'cause I'm eatin' cake, girly, and I'm stayin' put." Katie's outburst was bold, emotionally charged, and probably one hundred percent deserved. That didn't mean the words didn't hurt to hear. Dina's one meager attempt to soften Katie's verbal assault led me to believe she felt the same way, too.

Katie made herself scarce as Dina took her turn at me, Floyd in quiet observance. "She's right." Unbelievable! Was she for real, right now? I didn't want a party, but I did nothing to warrant a character assignation on, of all days, my birthday. "You should probably go. There's no reason everyone should suffer in your gloom."

I wasn't upset. I'm not sure what I was. I sure as hell didn't need this hostility or ugly sarcasm. I wanted a peaceful day. So I dismissed myself from the celebration equation as politely suggested. I took Katie's advice and left the rest of them to it. I made it as far as out the door and down the first step when their trap was sprung: four cars, fresh off the ferry. They formed a lineup, parking on the side of the road. Twelve people gathered in a group on the sidewalk then came toward me.

"Elles Garity?"

I hesitated, tongue-tied. "Um, yes . . . ? Who are . . ."

"We were hired to help," he announced, arms out wide to his sides and a smile smeared across his bearded face like some sort of proud savior.

"What . . . huh?"

"Where would you like us to start?"

I turned around and Dina, Katie, and Floyd were standing behind me with grins on their faces. I looked both ways, my jaw locked. Dina stepped up and draped her arm across my shoulders. "You'll have to forgive Katie. She gets pissy when she's hangry." Then she looked over at the tall bearded, ponytail-wearing, slender one. "And you all will have to forgive our Elles. *She* gets speechless when she's been bamboozled."

"Dina?"

"Yeah, darlin'?"

"Who are these people, and what the hell is going on?"

"Oh, them. Yeah, Katie was right. We didn't plan a thing. This was someone else's doing."

Mr. Spokesman of the group came up the stairs and introduced himself. "Good morning. My name's Pedro. Everyone calls me Petey, family name. And this is for you." He handed me an envelope and stood by while I opened it. I removed a handwritten letter and unfolded it.

> *"Dear Grace,*
>
> *I'll try to keep this short and sweet. I'm sorry I didn't stay. I guess you have a lot going on and I didn't want to get in the way. In case you're wondering, I'm not mad. Don't worry because nothing you ever say or do will keep me away. I couldn't stand to see you like this. I couldn't stand not being able to help longer than a few days. We've always been there for each other."*

Halfway through, my eyes started welling up. I paused to clear my line of sight, and Katie took up position at my other side. I could feel her reading over my shoulder.

> *"I thought about what I said, about paying you back. I also know you'd never take the money even if I tried. Since I can't be there to help, Jack and I found some people who could. So, the joke's on you. I found a better way to pay you back.*
>
> *Love Loyal and Jack."*

Chapter 29

The letter was stained with teardrops when I was done. I melted into Dina's arms for a moment, overwhelmed.

"Excuse me," Pedro said.

"What? Oh, I'm sorry, hi . . . Petey, right?" I smiled, fixing my face. "Will you . . . Could you all just give us a minute?"

Dina took a step down and addressed the group. "You all must be hungry. Everyone please, make your way around back to the patio. We'll be serving lunch shortly."

"Lunch?" I whispered to Dina. "Floyd, you made that much food? You mean you all knew about this?"

"Loyal reached out before she left."

"But I don't have anywhere . . . Wait, where are they all going to stay? How are . . ." It was a serious, panic-induced question. And for it, I received three very dumbfounded head-shaking, you've-got-to-be-kidding-me reactions as they all turned away in unison and went back inside. Pulling a foot out of my mouth, I tried, unsuccessfully, to save face. "I was . . . I was actually kidding. I think I have a few spare . . . Guys? I have rooms. I have a staff! I have a staff!" I cheered to myself, the only one still standing there, like a tool, raising fists in the air and looking to the skies, elated.

The reality of it took some time to fully set in, but a million thoughts were racing through my head. The patio had been set up with tables and chairs, white table clothes, place settings, and a grilling and serving station. It was immaculate, and I was doing cartwheels inside, fawning over everything. Floyd did the cooking. Dina and Katie made the rounds, taking orders, preparing and dishing out plates. I was ordered to do nothing but mingle, get to know my heaven-sent faction of newfound employees. That is precisely what I did. I hadn't a clue where they came from, how Loyal and Jack pulled this one off, but they were an eagerly chatty bunch.

I bounced from one table to the next, shaking hands, learning names. I felt more like a politician than a boss, campaigning for their votes. I found myself fascinated with getting to know each of them. I was intrigued to find out what they knew of me and why anyone in their right mind would take this job on. Once everyone was served and satisfied for seconds or thirds, Floyd, Dina, and Katie took turns, as well, mixing in among us, relaxing, socializing until dessert. Floyd and Dina started filling a buffet table with a selection of cookies, brownies, platters of assorted fruits. The unquestionable star of the show was a mouthwatering fresh strawberry and whipped cream–topped red velvet and chocolate-frosted sheet cake. Meanwhile, I snuck away inside under the guise of helping Katie clean up.

"I, um, I never expected . . . I mean, I can't believe Loyal and Jack got all these people here."

"They care about you, Elles. We all . . . we all care. Look, I can't stay. I'll help clear some plates and get out of your way."

"Katie, you don't have to . . ."

"I'm meeting someone for drinks. So . . ."

"I'm sorry, ya know, about accusing you of stuff. It's been hard, figuring out who to trust, who's holding secrets back, who can't even stand to look at me."

"Nobody hates you, Elles. You need to believe that. Hating how things went down or hating what you did, it's not the same as hating you."

"I just want things to be normal again."

"Normal how? It's different with me and Floyd. Floyd wasn't here. You and I never hung out much back then. So I hardly knew you at all. Everyone else who did, they don't know you like that anymore. And you don't know some of *them* as well as you think you did. Fifteen years, Elles. That's a long time to be gone. You finished growing up, ya know? You started a new life without us. Well, without them. You moved on while we had to *carry* on."

"So what am I supposed to do? I mean, what am I supposed to say? I can't keep apologizing to everyone for how I reacted to losing my family."

"That's just it, Elles. Your family's still here."

"It's not the same, Katie. I—"

"Yes. It kind of is. Look, Elles, I know not everything is clear for you right now."

"That's the—"

"Just, let me get this out. I haven't been honest with you, either."

"Katie." Dina overheard, standing in the doorway.

"She has to know this much, Dina. I can't keep doing this. Ginny and I . . . we've been close for years. Now, you can hate *me* if you want. Before you go thinking whatever . . . There's a lot you two have to work out."

"You didn't just show up to the house that day on your own, did you?"

"She didn't know how to face you, Elles. She didn't know if she could, what she would say. She was a wreck from the day you got here, Elles. I told . . . I promised her I'd take care of you until—"

"Until what?"

"Until she was ready, I guess. Until you both were ready."

* * *

I offered to finish clearing up from lunch, putting things away by myself. I needed time to sort it all out in my head. The three of them stayed late, helping the crew claim bedrooms, make up beds, and get settled in. They covered for me so I didn't come off like an antisocial hostess or boss on first impression. Katie's confession threw me some . . . a lot, really. I didn't have the energy or will to be mad. What did it really matter, her motives for befriending me? I hadn't exactly made that mission a breeze.

I went home to get some rest, have a nap, shower, and

change. As the sun was setting, I stood outside, leaning up against my father's car and enjoying the evening air, soothed by the rhythmic sounds of nature, the peacefulness, the encroaching moonlight. Tomorrow was going to be a busy, hectic day. All I could think about was tonight. I let myself slip into a meditative-like state of mind and waited for Katie to tell me it was time. Dina and Katie locked up at the inn and met up with me at the house.

"It's all set," Katie confirmed. "You sure about this?"

"Yeah, yeah, I am. Does she . . ."

"I didn't say a thing. I just suggested where and what time. She's expecting me."

"Okay." I got in my car to leave.

Dina walked over to my door. "Elles, good luck."

I hadn't yet visited or seen Dina's new house. She moved after the split. For this occasion, it was unfamiliar but neutral ground. She had a perfect little landscaped gazebo area perched above the bluffs, at the far edge of her picket-fenced yard. It was beautiful, wrapped in plant life and lights, glowing in the darkness. As I drew closer, I saw Ginny at the table, her back to me. Once she heard my footsteps, she turned and immediately started to stand.

"Please . . . please don't go." I urged longingly. It was just her and me, an opened bottle of wine, and glasses. Ginny had already poured herself some, sipping on it. I sat and she let me gaze upon her for a long moment. I swallowed a lump in my throat. I poured myself a glass and took the slightest sip. I tried to kick things off. "I guess you heard, I'm reopening the inn." She replied only with a fleeting glimpse. "Ginny, how long are we gonna keep doing this?"

She swerved her head, agitated, and spoke. "I don't know."

"Please, say . . . something. Yell, scream, curse at me. I don't ca—"

She jerked back tears and looked away. "What do you want to hear?

"Anything. Ginny, I came back here for—"

"Why? Why did you come back? After all this time. What, someone dies and you—"

"No! Because, it took me this long to realize this is where I belong. It took someone else dying for me to realize I should have never left."

"Well, congratulations on your loss. But you did, without thinking of any of us."

"You're right. I was only thinking of myself. But I was eleven years—"

"Oh, spare me, Elles. Does that mean you didn't know how to pick up a phone? Write a letter? Do ya know what I heard? *Give her time. Give her some space. She'll call. She'll come back.* Year after goddamn year! Until I gave up." Ginny stood up and flung her purse over her shoulder. "Here, I'll give you some more time." She started across the lawn into the darkness.

"Ginny! Did *you*?" She stopped flat-footed and stood there with her back to me. "You didn't call me, either."

She turned to me slowly, with that sniveling death stare I, not so long ago, had wished for. And short-lived as it was, this was dialogue, at each other's throats. "How dare you! You . . . How goddamn dare you! That's right, I forgot, um, you weren't around long enough to catch on, were you?" She leaned in, growling her words at me in rage. "Look at me! Can't you see it?"

As she hurried off, my heart started to pound and race. My breaths grew heavy and fast. I *refused* to see. I slumped back just trying to steady myself. What she was goading me to see was . . . unconscionable. It was too much. It would mean mourning a total lie. Fifteen and a half years spent . . . wasted on . . . How could I ever again face a mirror, look into my own eyes and go on, forever knowing I was never the person I thought I was.

Chapter 30

True to that person I no longer wished to be, I stuffed that late-night meeting deep inside. I diverted all my due attention to the larger tasks at hand. I got a good night's rest, lulled to sleep by organizing, prioritizing to-dos at the inn, forming a mental game plan. I had *employees!* I couldn't help it. Saying it, even thinking it, was still like a *rah-rah* excitement. I had employees to get to know, a mammoth amount of business—running things—that I didn't. The alarm clock beside me that I had never once set, blared to shake me out of bed. The house was still and silent. Katie was already up and gone. She left a note on the dining room table telling me to get there soon, breakfast and everyone was waiting.

The kitchen was a flurry of commotion. Floyd, as usual these days, was in his glory, cooking up a delicious-smelling storm. The crew were filtering in, loading their plates, and shuffling outside. Dina was in the thick of helping Floyd, expediting with a masterful pace. It was truly a sight to behold —my kitchen, for the first time, in full-service, working mode. I watched from a distance, brimming with pride.

"Everyone remember, be sure to fill up! Lots to do today!" Dina called out in the middle of the rush. "Anyone who's never been to the island before, you're in for a sightseeing treat!"

"It's about time you got here." Katie snatched my hand from behind, pulling me away. "Come on, the food's going fast. I saved you a plate."

"Katie, look at this. It's like a well-oiled machine. Shouldn't we be serving inside? It's a little chilly out there."

"I know and floors are getting torn up soon. We didn't want to get in the way. You're food's getting cold. Let's go."

"Yeah, but why can't we eat with— My floors? Why are

my floors getting torn up?"

"It's too noisy out here. Come on. Dina has someone for you to meet." Katie led us into a smaller staff dining room near the office, where a woman about Dina's age was having coffee.

"You must be Elles."

"Yes."

"I'm Birdie, a friend of your mother's."

"You knew my—"

"So you're reestablishing the National. I think I speak for the entire island. We can't wait to see it spring back to life."

"You must be who Dina was talking about."

"Here, sit down and eat. I've just been sitting here chatting it up with Katie until you arrived."

"Oh, okay, well, whatever she said about me, unfortunately it's probably all true."

"There's absolutely no shame in being a dedicated, driven young lady. That's the only way you're going to survive operating something of this size. I hope you're ready to learn."

"You're here to . . . help me?"

"Only if you want me to. Dina did say you could really use the help, and I have a little experience. My family has owned and operated the Shoreham House for nearly a hundred years now."

"That's incredible. I'm speechless. Anything you can teach me would be great. This wouldn't be like a conflict or anything?"

"A conflict? Elles, it would be my pleasure. What kind of community would we be if we can't lend a hand to fellow business owners?"

"The kind with less competition?"

"Ah, conflict of interests, yes. Well, there is a certain percentage of guests who make their usual bookings. Everyone has a favorite stay, of course. But there's *no* shortage of interest, that's for sure. Why, the overflow alone, after everything else is booked solid, would be more than enough to keep your rooms filled, as well. What I'm saying is competition is hardly a factor." Her little pep talk made me optimistic. I admit she had me gushing inside at the thought of what could be. There was still so much to be done, so much to learn. "Besides," she added, in fun, "my husband likes to think I automatically revert to being his personal aid during the offseason. The last thing I want to do on my time off is the exact same thing I do the other six months. So as long as you don't get tired of me and send me home." She winked, and I laughed appreciatively.

"I promise."

"Perfect. Let your people get settled in then unwind a little. I'll be over tomorrow morning."

After breakfast I gathered everyone in the lobby to officially welcome them all. I channeled my inner teacher for introductions and had them stand up, one at a time, to tell the rest of us a little something about themselves: names, where they were from, and anything else they wanted to share. After, we embarked on a full-scale tour of the entire building. Along the way, I pointed out things that needed to be done, prompting and encouraging feedback and some interesting proposals for motifs that hadn't crossed my mind. I was anxious to start building teamwork, dialing up contractors for any larger jobs, finding out who among us was three steps ahead of me and why I was due to have my dining room floor ripped out within the hour. Daily life was about to get hectic around here. So in lieu of a family dinner, I sent Dina and Floyd home, invited the crew to make *themselves* at home, and Katie and I went home to unwind with a movie night.

The days and weeks that followed somehow seemed to pass quickly, which wasn't typically the case this time of year. Winter spoils us here. For those who gladly choose to stick it out, this is our ghost-townish refuge. As lifelong residents, now unbothered by outsiders, we are set free to cherish our tiny world in peace, cold and desolate as it can be. That is the unencumbered solitude most of us look forward to, that we prize. If summer is our *come one, come all* natural wonderland, an obligatory clustered crutch that feeds our fragile economy, then winter is our liberator, an introvert's dream, a frosty, treasured godsend. The streets are bare, the chaos of automobiles, cyclists, and mopeds cast away. The scenery, the chilly tranquility, once more, if just for a handful of months, belongs to only us.

I remember my mother used to love to take long walks when the island was at its most dull. I never understood why, until now. All of this was a tangled mess in my mind, thinking about what this island meant to me, to us, who we were as a different kind of people, and trying to figure out where I stood. At the crack of dawn, I walked myself to work and, my God, I swear I felt my mother's spirit. The emptiness, the barren roads, parking lots. The unrelenting silence. It was magical. The island calls to you. I could hear my every waking thought, uninterrupted by the influx of the outside world. I strolled down Water Street, past the harbor and back, and I could feel it. There's such a healing power here, a calmness. It's not the blue sky and sunshine, blooming-life-aura of summer, but what it is, at its core, takes your breath away.

"Nothin' in the world like the first sniffs of mornin' air to cleanse the soul, is there?" It seems the secret was out with Floyd, as well. "Good mornin', Ms. Garity. I see you caught the same train I did."

"Mornin', Floyd. Do me a favor. Stop calling me Ms. Garity? I gave up teaching. Besides that, you make me sound old, which makes you even older."

"Yes, ma—Elles." As he turned to walk beside me, he stopped to stare across the street, down at the inn. "Got quite a future here for yourself. Excited?"

"I am. I must be crazy, trading a whole career for something I don't know much about yet."

"Oh, you'll be fine. It's what you want. All ya need is patience, a few more hands, assuming the ones you got now will wanna stay."

"I could use a head chef."

He bowed his head and watched his feet as we wandered

along. He knew what I was asking. I deliberately phrased it in the form of a general open-ended statement because, as much as I wanted him to accept, my gut told me he wouldn't. "Careful now. Don't go gettin' too far ahead of yourself. Lots to do still and who knows . . ."

I tuned him out after the first few sentences, confirming what I thought. I didn't wait around to hear what he was getting at. So I just came out with it. "Why do people have a problem with us, Floyd?"

"Pardon?"

"Well, Dina, Tom, everyone hints at it." We both came to a halt, eye to eye. "Nobody's really said why. I mean they haven't flat out objected to our getting along, it's not what they are saying, it's what they aren't that makes me . . ."

"What they sayin'?"

There was something about his eyes when I looked deeper. I couldn't decipher what I saw, but whatever was lurking in there gave me more chills than the air around us—harmless, sorrowful, apologetic chills. The way he looked at me, like our friendship was a fraud, formed out of happenstance.

"We should get inside. They'll be up soon. Birdie will be here." I couldn't bring myself to press him more. For reasons I didn't completely understand, I was scared. He said no more, and I think he and I were equally content to let this one slide.

Chapter 31

"Katie, how's he doing? "

"He's fine. He's resting. Aren't you supposed to be working on bookkeeping stuff with Bridie or—"

"We took a break. Is he in there? Can I—"

"Elles, wait. Look, I only told you he was here because—"

"Because you got caught lying about him being at home."

"Yes, because I knew you'd go over there."

"That's right. So what? The reason his back is flaring up is because of all the extra work. The work he's doing for me. I just want to—"

"Elles, he didn't want you to know he was here."

The day had begun with word that Floyd wasn't coming in. "Debilitated and on mandatory bed rest as a result of overexertion," as it read on his chart, was more precise than the vague information I had initially received on his condition. Katie wasn't wrong. Of course I was going to check on him, so she had no other choice but to tell me that he was admitted to the medical center.

"Please, just go back to work and let him rest. He'll be fine."

I briefly considered giving in to her rationality. Then again, consider this. From the very day I had returned, I had been lied to, deceived, kept in the dark, sheltered from some dark, mysterious truth unless, as the expectation went, I could uncover it for myself. One of the few people who didn't judge me, who *accepted* me unconditionally, was lying limp in a hospital bed for doing nothing more than *helping* me. Still, I wasn't ready for what I saw, brushing through Katie's feeble block and barging into that room. His eyes were closed, lying there peacefully, an oxygen mask cupped over his mouth and nose. He looked frail and tired, older than he was. I got choked up.

"What's wrong with him?" I gasped. "Katie, what's wrong with—"

"Relax, just calm down. It's a little complicated. He gets run down once in a while. He has some lung capacity issues that occasionally require oxygen when he gets like this."

"Like what? Damn it, would somebody be honest with me for once!?"

"Elles, when he wakes up and is ready to talk to you—"

"Ready to talk to me?"

"He needs rest, and stress will only make things worse right now. Whatever the two of you need to work out will have to wait."

I had no words for her, simply astonished. I was so deeply disappointed with all of the unnecessary reoccurring drama that I started trembling. "Oh, fine," I snarled and backed away slowly.

"Elles, I'm sorry. It's not my—"

"No, forget it, just . . . forget it. I wouldn't want to ruin the bullshit-fest you all are putting on for my benefit."

I did go back to work, with an emphasis on *work*, doing what I needed to do to get the inn ready for occupancy on opening day. To hell with everyone and ev-ery-thing else. I was fed up with petty distractions, with trying to decode what everyone around me—who supposedly cared about me—was dropping hints about. For sanity's sake, I reverted to full-blown split personality persona. I presented myself as open and perfectly pleasant to the crew, short-spoken with everybody else.

Dina was still there when I got back and was the unfortunate first to bear the brunt of my newly acquired attitude on display. Ever since my last failed encounter with Ginny, she had been hounding me to host Thanksgiving at the inn, as an official groundbreaking of sorts. That was her spin on it. I, on the other hand, saw it as a cleverly devised smokescreen to pair Ginny and me together in the same room. In order to appease her persistent nags and shut her up, I agreed to this little Thanksgiving-day charade, voicing another fed up "fine." Full disclosure, in accordance with my own better judgment, I had absolutely no intention of showing up to this farce of a supper.

Over the course of the next several weeks, I divided my time between soaking up every ounce of knowledge Birdie had to offer and crashing at Floyd's place prior to and beyond his release. I was there at checkout time to swoop in and snatch him from Katie's capable, well-meaning hands to chauffeur him home myself. My approach to dealing with Floyd was, as Katie put it, complicated. I spent a lot of time willingly playing the part of live-in home healthcare worker while he rested and lounged the days away. Privately, I racked my brain for any intelligible reason for the mysterious dark cloud named Floyd Gresham. Outside of sporadic zoned-out spells, I learned all I never wanted to know about the games of collegiate and professional football, while tempering any overly animated play-by-play reactions from Floyd.

I spared us both the unwanted unpleasantry of my cooking by springing for takeout most nights, with leftovers or sandwiches to fill the gaps. I camped out, sleeping on his couch, which served the dual purpose of avoiding Katie and satisfying a guilt-ridden necessity to hover over Floyd's every need. I was making sure he was comfortable and taking his medications. Basically, I was smothering him like an overbearing mother tending to her injured or malnourished young. The fact that he tolerated my all-inclusive intrusion on his daily life strengthened my interest and, no doubt, substantiated the belief that there was something that connected us.

The house was particularly still one night. I sat on the sofa, unable to put the thoughts and question marks running rampant in my head to rest. The silhouette of an old, dusty acoustic guitar that Floyd kept tucked in the corner caught my attention in the darkness. I lifted it gently by the neck and laid it across my lap, face up. I spread the fingers of one hand over the strings while gliding the other hand up along the side of the neck. I plucked a few strings ever so gently, pondering if there was a tune that would sum up my life, as it stood, and what that might sound like. It was all I could think of to pacify my unsettled soul.

"Long as we seem to be in the same boat, we might as well keep each other company." Floyd came straggling out of his bedroom and sat beside me.

"Can't sleep, either?"

"Somethin' like that."

He watched as I tilted the guitar on its side and held it more properly. I pulled my feet up off the floor and sat cross-legged. I plucked more chords, one at a time, evoking fond memories. "My mother used to have one like this. She couldn't play very well, but . . . when she tried, it was like she was strumming it, apologetically like, for the talent she didn't have but wished she did, ya know?"

"Before I get myself real comfortable, this ain't about to be you playin' some ol' life got me down country song that's gonna make me wanna go bury my head under a pillow, is it?"

I giggled. "I miss 'em. I miss 'em, Floyd. I've spent half my life shutting out the fact that they were gone, instead of missing them and moving on."

"Losin' both your folks in a blink . . . shock like that'll rip ya apart."

"Maybe I took too much time, ya know? Maybe everyone's right to be mad at me. Maybe—"

"Maybe *they* should mind their business. There ain't no "how-to" book. There ain't no rules, no Grieving 101."

I didn't bother to ask what he knew, how he knew. I thought about that little piece of paper I had found with their names inscribed on it. It was in my hip pocket. I kept it on me. I kept it close by for some weird, unexplained reason. There would be a time for Floyd and me to sort out our . . . whatever we had. But that time wasn't now—although it wasn't for a lack of curious prying. "What happened to you, Floyd?" To which, I received a shifty-eyed, evasive glance. "I don't mean to be—"

"Young, stupid, and ignorant happened to me. Period. End of story."

"I'm not asking for your life story here, Floyd. Just wanted to—"

"Get to know me better?"

"What's wrong with that? You know more about me than I know about you. What would your bluesy country song say?" I asked, strumming the guitar, trying to look as if I knew how to play.

"I fix things, I cook, eat, shit, sleep, repeat."

Words could never define my facial expression. "Thank you, Floyd. Now I wanna bury my head."

"You asked."

"Don't you want more, though?"

"Like what?

"Family, wife, kids. Unless . . ."

"Unless what?"

"Well, I don't know. Unless you're—"

"I'm not. Say, if you can't play that thing, could you at least swing it? You got my blessin' to blast me over the head. I'd like to get some sleep tonight."

"Why are you so secretive?"

"Why are you so . . . here?" He got up and aimed for the hallway to his bedroom.

"Where you goin'? Come on! We haven't written a song yet!"

"You didn't like my lyrics. And out of respect for my current company, who won't go sleep at her own damn house, which makes my living room, your bedroom, I'm goin' to *my* bedroom."

“Those were not lyrics, Floyd. That was a crudely descriptive—”

“I gotta get me another TV,” he mumbled under his breath, walking away.

“Hey, Floyd? I’m sorry . . . I’ll get out of your hair in the morning. I don’t want things between you and I to get . . . I just wanted to make sure you were gonna be okay. I shouldn’t have overstayed my welcome. I feel like you’re the only person here that I can count on, the only one I can turn to when all of my other relationships are . . . unstable. So thank you for that.”

He stood there and let me get it all out and turned away from me to gather a response. “Elles, you are welcome at my house any time. But I been livin’ by myself too long to put up with anything different, and you ’bout to drive me cuckoo.”

“Fair enough.” I smirked.

“As far as thankin’ me for anything, don’t.”

“But I—”

“You wanna know more about me? Here it is. Here’s all you need to know—I ain’t no saint. Last damn thing I wanna be is reminded of that every time . . . No number of good deeds ever gonna erase one bad . . .” He stopped himself mid-sentence, frozen in place, broken out in a visibly distraught sweat.

“Floyd, what on earth is—”

“You still needin’ a head chef, ain’t ya?”

“Yeah . . . I do.”

“Then that’s the deal. Accept what I’m askin’. Respect my wishes, and I’ll honor yours. You got yourself a chef.” He looked at me, fashioning a partial smile, and true to the enigma that he was, Floyd ended with these parting words, bundled with a stroke of mocking friendly fire. “Gettin’ late. Go on and put that guitar away. You ain’t no more a song writer than me, and you got more important things to work on. You ain’t gonna redeem yourself ’round here fussin’ over me.”

Chapter 32

Thanksgiving arrived with the same anticipation, on my part, of both funerals I neglected to attend. That is not meant as a joke in poor taste or a dig at my own faults, but as a fair comparison. There were several reasons why I didn't want to make this entire holiday season a big deal. I just used my anger and disappointment toward others as the most current and relevant one. What I told Floyd was true. I never allowed myself the opportunity to really heal by missing my parents. It's not that I *didn't* miss them. It's that I *did* and it was easier to bury that heart-wrenching pain and pretend it wasn't there. I knew that if I pretended hard enough, I could trick my mind into believing it.

The first holiday season without them I was numb. I also didn't spend it here. Reopening the inn and what that meant, being around everything I ran away from, this time of year . . . I could only open so many cans of worms at a time.

Dina had such high hopes for the gathering. I could see it in her glow. Worse yet, the silent treatment offensive didn't appear to phase her in the slightest. She spent the morning determined to make sure everything was perfect. She cooked, she told stories of past Thanksgivings. She was in her glory and laughing herself to happy tears. And all I saw and heard was her pouring it on thicker than the gravy she was about to serve. It was what she *didn't* do from the start that didn't sit well.

This whole thing was her conception, her idea, backed by her plans and her guest list for this small family affair. *Family* being the key word that caused my blood to boil more each time I let it cross my mind. Tom was on that list. Katie was on that list. Me, Dina and Ginny, the kids. Two of these people just didn't belong. Okay, fair enough, Tom was a technicality. I wasn't thinking clearly because noticeably excluded was Floyd. No, I did not ask why. I did not want to hear the same old, played out, lame reasoning. No disrespect to her, but Katie was no more a member of this family than Floyd was. I was only a de facto member myself. The one thing they both had in common was that neither of them had plans or a better place to go for the occasion.

I bit my tongue on the matter. Dina's definition of family, in large part, decided where I was spending the rest of this day and it wasn't alone at a restaurant or in our kitchen, anywhere they would dare come for me. After the table was set, I removed myself to change. Ginny and the kids arrived, and I tried to sneak by. I tried to leave, undetected. I prepared myself for the worst possible reaction. I also feel compelled to point out that, while I come off looking like a sneaky, backstabbing, conniving . . . I'm not any of those things. *She said in a last-ditch, moment-of-truth attempt to convince herself otherwise.* They all had each other. Why did they need me? Floyd had nobody, and pigheaded, ignorant, selfish me was willing to fight drama with drama.

I'll have you know I agonized over this decision. I wrestled with that inner child I had put in charge. Why did this have to happen here, anyway? Did Dina think *this* was neutral ground? Did she seriously think she could force two stubborn, hard-headed women together, and abracadabra, all would be well? I was fully aware this would crush her, but all things considered, I just wanted out. There were too many problems at play that one fancy dinner was not going to solve. I'm not a monster. *Keep telling yourself that, Grace, or whoever we are!* The moral war raged on inside my head. The last thing I wanted right then was to be part of a stand-in family Thanksgiving, because that's what it felt like before I understood what it really was.

"Elles?" I wasn't even three steps down and away from making a clean getaway when Dina called to me from the front door. I stopped, hesitant to look back, kicking myself for not running like a thief in broad daylight. "Everyone's here. We're ready to eat. Where are you—"

"I'm spending Thanksgiving with Floyd." There, I said it! And to whom it may concern, it hurt me, too. I hated this! I hated the on-again, off-again getting along. I hated the drama. I didn't come back here for this, for the nonstop ridicule, to be judged for who I could and couldn't, should and shouldn't hang out with. Would I have stayed if Floyd was invited? We shall never know. I couldn't bear to look at her for longer than it took to utter the five words that must have blistered through the air like a dagger. So I pushed on, with fast feet to my car.

"Elles Garity! You—"

"I'm sorry. I have to go."

I could barely say it without sobbing. The details were in the works from the time I finalized my devious surprise plans. I picked up the turkey dinner with all the trimmings I had preordered and paid for weeks ago from The Oar. I showed up, hands full, kicking on Floyd's door. He opened it and rolled his eyes, reluctantly stepping aside with a scowl of disbelief on his face. He wasn't in cahoots. He was as surprised as the rest.

"Don't just stand there. Get some plates. What game's on first?"

"Elles . . ." He began with the tone of a scolding father. "What in the world are—"

"It's called dinner."

"It's called get your ass back where you belong and . . ."

I made my position clear. I walked over and closed and locked the front door for effect and turned to him with my arms folded. "I'm staying. I brought—"

"Damn it, Elles."

"Floyd, this is not a discussion. As people have been reminding me, I'm an adult. And you deserve to spend this day with someone, too. I brought this lovely dinner. We're going to sit down. We're going to . . . God help me, watch football games. We're going to enjoy each other's company. Now start carving."

He sighed and rubbed the side of his head, grumbling.

"Can't wait for Christmas. Whatcha gonna have me help you hijack Santa's sleigh or somethin'?"

That is exactly what we did—enjoyed the evening, that is, not . . . Christmas would be a bigger beast. Whatever was in store, I may have successfully killed two birds with one stone-cold exit regardless. I didn't exactly foresee a tree full of presents headed my way, so be it. I suspect Floyd, knowing better than to put up a fight, kept his dissatisfied opinions to himself; though, there remained an underlying hint of disapproval in his eyes all day long. We claimed our spots in front of the television, turned the coffee table into a buffet, and stuffed ourselves with dinner, desserts, and small talk for hours.

"I guess I should apologize in advance of any backlash for having me over."

"I didn't have you over. You *took* over."

"You let me in." I grinned. "Don't worry, Floyd, I'll cover for you."

"Cover for me? For—"

"I'll testify under oath, I broke in, held you hostage in your own home, forced a fabulous feast down your throat and . . ." Hey, what the hell? I already had a record, having pulled a similar stunt on Tom. With this latest multiple-victims crime I was quite certain I was now the biggest criminal act on this island since the days of the Revolutionary War.

"Ain't me they gonna crucify."

"You're right. You should be the captor. Nobody's aiming for you, and they might go easier on—"

"This funny to you?"

"You still haven't given me an answer."

"To what?"

"Working for me."

"The hell I didn't. I told you I—"

"I am fully aware of what you told me. I don't want you to do this for me as a bargaining stunt or because we struck some deal I don't even understand."

"I don't need you savin' me, Elles."

"I'm not trying to save you, Floyd. Okay, maybe a little. I've seen you in action, Floyd. You're a repairman to get by. You cook because you love to do it."

"And how exactly would that look, huh? Me workin' for —"

"Like a friend helping a friend. It would look like a guy following his passion and his heart and enjoying what he does for a living."

"Why you need to help me out so bad for?"

"Funny, I've been wondering the same thing about you. So I guess my answer is, for the same reason you've been helping me. Because you are my friend. Unless there's something more I should know."

He reached for the remote and notched the volume up a few ticks. "Yeah, there is. You should know halftime's over."

I leaned forward in my seat, took a paper dessert plate in one hand and the pie slicer in the other. I looked over at Floyd, content in his stuffed-gut orneriness. I dropped the slicer and plate and grabbed the entire untouched whipped cream–smothered caramel apple pie and a fork and got comfortable again. "This is my piece," I taunted.

"Eat the damn pie," Floyd groaned, careless.

"Yeah, you watch me."

"Bon appétit. And I ain't washin' no dishes later, either."

As it turned out, launching a vindictive, turkey-stupor assault into the depths of Floyd Gresham's life having anything to do with me failed. My nagging curiosity was met with unwavering resistance. And as for that pie that I hogged out of *take-that-you-old-tight-lipped-grouch* spite? As good as it was for the first few slices, I regretted it about halfway through. Hours later, we both lay passed out in our respective spots. I was awakened to high headlight beams piercing through the window blinds. In the dark, I found my way outside where Tom had just stepped out of his truck. I yawned and held my face in my hands trying to liven up.

"So who sent you, Tom? Or are you here on official police business? Let me guess, felony eluding of a mandatory family function?" I don't know why, unless I was just so tired, I chose to provoke him. Maybe it was that I just didn't care how he would react to anything I said. I expected him to go berserk, lay into me with a long-winded, inspired *How dare you walk out on us that way?* As I recall, I had done that before. This one was just a little more . . . personal. If I'm honest, I think that's *why* I did it. We were all so busy doing this little dance, trying to figure out how to coexist and live with one another again. We forgot how to just be around one another, the way we used to be. Sadly—and I'll say it, I denied it then—I was the biggest culprit. I wasn't the only culprit. And as sure as I was that Tom was going to come at me for what I had done that day, he did something else—something unexpected but befitting a man who was out of answers. Tom Deiter, classroom clown, playground wannabe bully, Tom Deiter the modern-day man, fill-in father, should-be husband, public protector walked over to me with a hard-nosed, gritty exhaustion, sucked me into a bear hug, and wept. Anything and everything he had to say to me, whatever thoughts he couldn't translate into words, came oozing out. It was an ass-kicking of a different kind and of simple heartbroken proportions. Coming from Tom, it was one of the scariest, most eye-opening moments of my life. He had me as tongue-twisted as he was, and I raised both my arms and inched my hands to his sides and padded them gently, lovingly, like I was saying something back. He wouldn't show me his face. When he finally pulled away, he hung his head, a hand over the top of his hat, holding it in place. He turned around and moped back to his truck, got in, and left. Standing there, so vividly stunned, I felt like I could have been knocked over by a single whisp of wind.

Chapter 33

A time and a place. That is what I said about matters between Floyd and me. There is a time to hurt and a time to heal. As the seasons change, so can the roads of life we travel. I turned my life upside down once. I did it recklessly, to survive. I stayed the course, in a way, to absolve myself of the indecency of running away. I turned my world upside down a second time, to thrust myself into the unknown. I did it because the straight and narrow road I was on was coming to an abrupt and timely end, and the warning sign read, "Under construction . . . detour ahead." At some point, the hurt has got to end, so the healing can truly begin. Pardon my monotony, but when the line between hurting and healing is blurred and frayed, the result is what I had become, who I was. Someone once said, *Seasons change, and so do I.* As this mad season of mine did nothing but drag on, this one, too, must change—and so must I.

I went home that night, back to Katie's where I was still making my home. Floyd was already half laid out on the couch when I left him. I eased his legs up to join the rest of his body and covered him with a blanket. I cleared the coffee table, trashed the remnants of dinner, and played the kitchen radio softly while I washed the dishes. I had to crack a smile when it came to me that they weren't even dishes that were dirtied that day. They were merely penance for the quarrel, for the pie, and for sabotaging the now snoring Floyd's day. *Clever, Mr. Gresham, and well played. I'll give you this one,* I thought. I finished them and dragged myself across town and inside to bed.

Where do I go from here? That was my wide-awake inner-voice pillow talk that wouldn't allow me to catch a wink of sleep. The question reverberated in my head like a flashing neon sign lit up over a vacant motel. I was too drained, too done, to forge a single answer.

A crackling frying pan and the sobering scent of scrambled eggs aroused me the following morning. I crept out from under the sheets in a state of what I'll refer to as "limbo hangover." Katie gave me a hushed once-over from in front of the stove as I fastened the bottom buttons of my blouse and took a swig from a bottle of water in the fridge.

Tom wasn't the only one turning out strange new vibes. Although Katie declined to speak, I didn't feel tension or despisement. If I had to put a name to the mood, it would be more empathic understanding, maybe? Whatever it was, it was a twist between her and me.

"I have to, um, get going. The crew is coming back on the ferry today. So . . ."

"Yeah, yeah, go on. Call me, ya know, if you need anything. I'm here."

"Okay, I will. Katie . . ." We stood still, at a distance, back-to-back as I moved for the door. "Yesterday, it . . . I wasn't trying . . . I didn't mean to . . ."

"I know."

A hard purposeful knocking at the front door startled me, mostly because it felt ominously meant for me. I turned and shared a curious blank stare with Katie before she called out to whomever was on the other side, and just as well, because my body wouldn't move. "Come in!"

The knob turned, and the door pushed open with a foot. Ginny stepped inside and stood there holding an old cardboard box. Everything about her, from her intense expression to her stance, felt like all she wanted to do in that moment, with me six feet straight ahead and directly in her path, was to run me over like a bulldozer. I felt so small, and I didn't understand why until after she was gone. She marched forward and shoved the box into me, forcing me to grab it with both arms. After which, she had something to say but, first, could only stand and emote lock-jawed, hard and heavy, flared-nostril breaths so full of fury that I could almost see them billowing out as she collected her thoughts.

"This belongs to you."

"What is—"

"I'll be damned if we're gonna be the keepers of your family heirlooms any—"

"We? Ginny, what are you talking about? What is this?"

"Shut up," she snorted. "I don't even wanna be in the same room with you right now any longer than I have to be."

"Then why did you come—"

"To get rid of something that I've been holding on to by myself for too long." She started back toward the door and stopped halfway out. "Ya know, yesterday may not have meant anything to you. For your information, I didn't want to be there, either. So I didn't do it for you. I did it for . . . my mother." In that hesitation, I sensed something she wanted to say different from what fell off her lips. "What you did was . . ." Suddenly the way she was looking at me, I caught a harsh glimpse of disgusted ridicule. "Don't ever do that to her again."

With that, she left and swung the door closed with a thud in her wake. There I stood with a presumed box of Garity family relics and unease in the pit of my stomach. I turned my head to Katie, at a loss. I cracked a half-hearted, snickering smile. "First Tom, now Ginny. Tom came by last night after . . . He . . . he, um . . ."

"Yeah, well, you should probably . . ."

"Come by later?"

"Yeah, I'll be there."

I couldn't leave it that way. I couldn't just brush that off and walk out that door without making one last bleeding-heart stand. If anyone was going to help point me in the right direction, if another time was now, then I had to know what I should've known, what I was so blind to see. This season hadn't even begun to see its worst days. A storm was on the horizon. I set the box down on the coffee table, and before my hand could touch the doorknob, I spun back around. "Katie, what am I missing here? What . . . what was that? That wasn't just about what happened yesterday, was it? I can't take it anymore. What the hell is going on? What . . . what am I supposed to know about Floyd? I . . ." I could see her eyes pointing to the coffee table, and my words ran out.

"I, uh, I think if you look, I'm sure you'll find the answer to most those questions."

I sat on the couch looking down into the open box, scrounging for those answers. I reached in and pulled out a folded-up newspaper and held it in my trembling hands. It was the headline that captured my attention, and I continued to read on. I can forgive myself for a lot of things. I can forgive for the things I didn't know, didn't see, or refused to either way. I can forgive for the turning away and even for the pushing away. I accept full responsibility for all of that. But just when I thought I had experienced it all, the one thing that may have cut the deepest, of the two facts I had yet to face, was the short-sighted mistake of betraying myself by befriending an unwilling, overburdened bystander, someone selfishly victimized, cast aside by an unforgiving demon, and left alive to wallow in unimaginable shame. I finished the article, my body tingling, and all I could do was look up and faintly exclaim, "Katie?"

* * *

I sat alone at the furthest, most isolated reaches of the island. This was familiar territory. It's a long, uninhabited, flat stretch of land that ends overlooking the ocean and the beach below. It was the first place that came to mind, the place I had gone when my world fell apart. The first time I came here was to lose myself. Here, on this rocky cliffside, I didn't want to be found. I didn't want to be seen imploding. I didn't want anyone to hear my earth-shattering, wailing screams. I wasn't going to let anyone pretend to remotely know my pain. The inner cave of self-preservation that I crawled into that day was my own.

I had something taken away, stolen from me, that was out of my control. The swift and extreme corrective action that I took was meant to ensure it could never happen again. In that ultra vulnerable, naive, and weakened fragile state of mind, I hid. If I could create something—an impenetrable cocoon, a safe haven that could not be breeched—and cut off access, seal the doors, batten down the hatches, this armored fortress I built would be mine alone, and as God as my witness, I would never let anything be taken from me again.

Little did I know, in doing so, the most important person I shut out was me. I couldn't control the heavens and earth, time, fate, today, tomorrow. I came to this sentimental place to think. I came here to—once and for all—escape. I couldn't move forward living in emotional restraint. I couldn't conquer my small world while trying to shun fate. The proof of my reemergence was this, I sat there with wide-open eyes, open ears, and open mind.

I heard the footsteps closing in, and I didn't have to turn to see who was there. This wasn't like confronting spirits with my gripes. The only part of Floyd that was dead was the haunted soul of a man who didn't know how to fly. No cemeteries, no grave sites involved this time. This was a wall I had to crack, made of flesh and bone, who better be prepared to speak on his own behalf. As for me, there was no need to rehearse some irate speech. I was, for a change, mentally collected, and I knew exactly what I had to say. As he bent down, I leaned in an ear. He picked up a piece of paper I had crumpled up and flicked over my shoulder to the ground.

"So now you know." The words came out of his mouth like his worst realized, now exhaustedly relieved fear.

"The basics. I don't know it all."

He sat down on a rock and proceeded to reflect. "I come here a lot, over the years. Closest place to you I could find."

"To talk to me?"

"Yeah," he choked out.

"And when you come here . . . what do you say?"

"Say I'm so sorry . . ." The sentiment came gushing out in gut-wrenching remorseful tears, which he sucked back to go on. "Tell you what I should've done different, how I could have . . . how I should have stopped . . ."

"Stop." I stood up and kept my back to him. I didn't not look at him because I couldn't. How do I explain? We had built a closeness, a friendship that I had come to cherish. The nature of our meeting came from the part he played in my parents' dying. I couldn't look at him so that I could come to terms with all of that. I couldn't look at him, because to do that, I had to temporarily put us, the *him and me*, aside. "I can't . . . imagine what you must have gone through. I can't . . . I won't put myself in your shoes. But . . ."

"Elles, I—"

"I know you're not to blame, Floyd. In my heart I know that, but the person who is isn't here. I hate what he put on you. Please know, I will listen to everything you have to say. But I can't do this right now, Floyd."

"I know."

"So that's what this is all about—your back, your health, your— You're not some wayward loner who just happened to wind up here."

"No."

"Then why wouldn't . . . If what Katie said is true, then why wouldn't you just tell me?"

"It was too hard. Talkin' into thin air and talkin' to you in person ain't the same. I—"

"You knew me this whole time. You've known about me all along."

"I didn't know how to . . . Elles, I will answer any questions you have. I will tell you anything you want to—"

"I want to . . . I *have* to know it all, but not—"

"Then, let me explain."

"I can't. Not now."

"Elles . . ."

"I can't! Floyd, I'm sorry. I have too much to . . . I need

some time. As much as it hurts me to say this, and I know it's not fair, but I need to hate you right now."

Chapter 34

Hate was not the elicited response that Floyd in any way deserved. It was just the strongly worded language I used to overemphasize my need to process what was difficult to believe. For now, I had to let him go, put space between us, and our friendship on indefinite hold. Having a bombshell like this brought to my attention, so too were brand-new questions, hard-hitting ones such as *What if I hadn't left? What if, in hindsight, everything I was running from, all the unknowns, were the very things that would have saved me from fifteen years of . . .* Well, this was a tough pill to swallow, and priorities demanded it take some time. There were more immediate pressing matters to attend to.

"I need updates people! Talk to me. Bri?"

"Flooring will be finished today. Guest rooms are set and ready to be dressed. The linen order is on schedule and should be here this week."

"Awesome. Petey? Where's Petey? Has anyone seen—" A black-gloved hand arose from behind and under the front desk, along with a muffled reply. "Bri? What is my Events and Entertainment Coordinator doing under the front desk, and why?"

"We needed someone to finish getting the new computer systems up and running."

"Is he qualified for that?"

"He's multitalented." Birdie spoke up, walking into the room. "He fixed some glitches at our place yesterday. You better make that title permanently official before I steal him from you."

"Yeah, I've been meaning to meet with anyone

interested in staying on, so I can figure out—"

"Oh, Elles?" Bri interrupted. "I was thinking of . . . Well, I'd like to apply for the assistant manager position, unless . . . you've got someone else . . ."

I looked over at Birdie. We shared a curious pondering stare, and Birdie winked. "It's your call. You've given her that responsibility, and she has taken charge of it."

"Okay, I have some time now. Let's go talk."

I was already well into the process of accepting online applicants and scheduling interview days. Brianna became my first official in-person interview, and after a long in-depth discussion, she also became my first official hire. Of the temporary calvary of hands that was sent, and to whom I was eternally grateful and indebted to, three of them chose to apply for long-term jobs, including two more full-timers: Pedro with Reno under his supervision.

The weeks leading up to Christmas were laborious with a firestorm of decisions, new hires, final touches, and continued training all around. The inn took on a whole new life and look with fresh, vibrant color schemes and a total refurbishment throughout. Guest rooms were refurnished and rejuvenated with new bedding, linens, and curtains. Each one took on its own unique identity, ambience, and flow, sure to attract the interests of repeat patrons for seasons to come.

"Everyone! Can I have everyone's attention please? Stop whatever you're doing. I need all hands outside. We have a delivery truck coming off the ferry any minute with outside seating and tables to be hauled into downstairs storage. If we can get an assembly line going . . ." I was gloriously immersed in a euphoric happy zone of controlled chaos and ever-evolving transformation. My world was overtaken by the daily grind that kept me busy and moving from early morning rises until well into the more quiet hours of the night. I relished every moment— meeting the new faces of my staff, watching them gel, taking the time to appreciate the contributions in the smallest detail. As I commenced a final walk-through of the finished spaces, I reflected upon the group effort in the redesigning of this old inn of which I had encouraged them all to play an active, creative part.

Bri was addressing the group. "Okay, is everyone here? Everyone ready? Today is decorating day! If you're not assigned to the kitchen, you are pulling boxes from storage room C! Please be careful with anything you carry until we go through it all. These are very old precious Garity family decorations. If you break something, you will be uninvited to the Christmas party, and I will personally send you on an extremely cold swim back to the mainland! Everyone clear?"

She was diving into her new role headfirst and with fiery gusto, cracking the whip—with frightful humor of course, verified by the collective gaggle of laughter that followed her announcement. The rest of the town was already leaps and bounds ahead of me on the holiday decorating front. To celebrate the impending inaugural Garity House season, I initiated plans for a blowout celebration that was in the early planning stages. I invited staff members to volunteer ideas, recipes, their helping hand at baking anything they wished if they so desired. An unseasonably warm day in early December ended with everyone spread out in small gatherings among the array of still-cooling treats, stacks of opened and sifted through boxes, and the tired remains of all our festive efforts.

My mother and Dina had always prided themselves and this business on community outreach and worked tirelessly at leading by that example. I wanted to pick up where they left off and carry it along to exciting and expanding heights. The Christmas party was just the tip of the iceberg. Tons of fluttering ideas were accumulating in my head. With every passing day, my motivation was escalating. I could not wait to open these doors to the visiting world. I could not wait to put the Garity name back into the spotlight. A small, egotistical part of me was geared up to show Birdie, friendly or not, this place was indeed competition. I wasn't gunning for the overflow. I was out to attract a fan base of travelers and convince them that they simply *had* to stay at the most talked about, most popular accommodations this island had to offer.

Enormous expectations, absolutely. Go big or go . . . Unfortunately for everyone else in my crosshairs, I was already there. I was eyeing my future through rose-colored glasses. But make no mistake, this was not a brand-new beginning for me. This was a reconquering. This was a re-establishment in the making. As far as I was concerned, I had only taken a fifteen-year hiatus. There was substance to that life I had led. There were experiences and important pieces I would hold on to for the rest of my life. But the story of who I was, the story of my life had barely been written. I still had obstacles to overcome. I still had those incinerated bridges to my past to finish rebuilding. But hear this, Elles Grace Garity, the girl who once left with a broken heart and a whimper, was back—this time, kicking and screaming. Defeat would not chase me down again.

My internal rally cry was in full, unwavering effect as Christmas fast approached. I wasn't too laser focused on the more career-essential tasks to believe for one second that I could leave all personal things aside unconscionably. Like a spiritually well-balanced Buddhist, my method of daily meditation took the form of carefully crafting those crucial plans, as well. In place of reciting hurt-fueled tantrums and speeches to both the living and the dead, I was now entrenched in thoughtful harmony. I was at *can't-wait* peace with people I needed to address, things I needed to say, and questions I had to ask, truths I could no longer dodge.

"Birdie! I'm glad I caught you before you ran off. Does Harwood's Farm still run the winter sleigh rides through town?"

"Not since a few years back when Marc and Ellen started talking about retirement. Their kids took over the stables. So far, they've been focused on the horseback rides. Why do you ask?"

"I was just curious. I'm gonna head out. I'll catch up with

you later."

* * *

Harwood's Farm, one of the most iconic, relaxing attractions in town. As children, Ginny and I would often pack a snack bag of carrots and apples, throw in a banana or two, and stop by to feed and pet horses. Sometimes we would stay and help groom the ponies. I still remember our first unaccompanied trail ride when we were six years old. Today the farm was a key piece of the puzzle in a plot to spend some alone time with Dina on a nostalgic horse-drawn sleigh ride that was always a favorite holiday adventure. There was only one glitch in that master plan.

"Well, there it is." Curtis Harwood opened the barn doors to reveal the tucked away sleigh, hidden behind bales of hay. "Hasn't seen the streets in a couple seasons. We've been lookin' to fix it up a little, get it back in peak condition."

I stared at it for half a minute, sappy-eyed, remembering the many rides our families took on it with a heartwarming fondness of the good times, innocent happy times. "You think it'll run?"

"No reason it shouldn't. Runnin' it's not the problem, though. Jordan and Luke took their wives on vacation to Cancun and Tracey down in—"

I pulled my phone out of my pocket. "How many helpers do we need?"

He turned his nose up a moment and scratched his chin, thinking. "Well, if you can get two or three people to help, I'll start gatherin' up the horses. You think you can start budging a few of those bales out of the way, I'll, uh, go next door, see if I can find Rich to help me hook up the tractor, pull it on outta there."

Chapter 35

The unsuspecting surprise on her face when she poked her head outside at the sound of prancing hoofs on the pavement was worth the effort. I waved from the back seat, looking pleased with myself for pulling this one together. I read her lips asking, "What in the world?" She ducked inside to grab a coat and rushed over. "Elles, what are you up to now? I thought this old thing was decommissioned."

"She's back in service!" Curtis proclaimed. "Temporarily, for one trip only! When did you ever know Elles Garity to take no for an answer?"

Dina climbed aboard and sat down, her rosy-cheeked face beaming with elation while she wrapped herself in a scarf and bundled up tight. Two quick tongue clicks from Curtis sent the horses trotting downhill toward Water Street, and we were off. Neither of us found the need to talk, exhaling frosty puffs of vapors, appreciating the wintery seaside view until we turned inward. I watched a reminiscent smug smile wash over Dina's face. "I haven't done this since . . ."

"Since Ellen introduced the *no peppermint hot chocolate* rule, I'll bet."

"Never mind! You . . . What do you know about it? You were too young to—"

"I was nine. Ginny was ten. And we only knew what everyone else knew. Which was—"

"Elles Garity . . ." Dina turned red with embarrassment, trying to play off the infamous off-season booze cruise incident that had the whole town in stiches weeks removed from what some dubbed as *Dina-gate*. The Harwood sleigh ride doubled as the horse-powered taxi delivery service for the overly inebriated partygoers who lived too far to stumble home safely. Perhaps the fact that Dina had been so obliterated at the time and, in the aftermath, reeling in the sobering reality that her little stunt had become instant legend, was why she was still trying to live it down and defend herself. Of course, none of us kids saw or dared to make light of it in her presence, but the subsequent rumors alone provided enough fodder for playground gossip and role-playing amusement for days until the bit grew outdated.

"You brought it up!" I cackled.

"I . . . I was younger then. And you weren't even there to —"

"From what we heard *you* were barely there." I gloated.

"I was—"

"You tried to mount a horse from the back of a moving sleigh!"

"I had to—"

"While trying to use other drunk people for leverage to catapult yourself—"

"I had to pee! They were going right by my house and tried to tell me there wasn't any more room! What was I supposed to . . ." We just locked serious eyes for a moment and broke out laughing. "I was *not* the reason they banned alcohol on this silly sleigh."

"No, you were just the final straw . . . in the . . . drink, ya know?"

"Oh, Elles." She sighed. "You've been hanging out with Katie too much."

"Oh, God, you're right."

"So! Is that what this is? Did you arrange this so you could take me on a humiliating trip down unmemorable lane?"

"Good one, but no."

"Ah, so . . . while we're on the subject—"

"I did it so when I asked you something, you couldn't get away."

She looked at me curiously, with a hint of *uh-oh* and

turned away.

"The word *woah* ever cross your mind?"

"Oh, I paid him way too much to even slow down. You'll have to jump. Remember to tuck and roll. Careful, though, you don't wanna break the other arm this time."

"Wha— Heaven sakes, it was only a sprain!" She pouted.

"I know about the accident—everything else about the plane crash, that is."

"How . . . ?"

"Ginny, in a roundabout way. She didn't exactly . . . Anyway, I saw the article."

Suddenly it seemed she was finding it difficult to look at me straight on. "Then you only know what's in print."

"I guess so. Katie kinda filled in some of the blanks. She just kept apologizing. But I wish someone would have—"

"How could we? What were we supposed to say?"

"How about the truth, Dina?"

"The truth . . . is precisely what drove you away the first time."

I didn't raise my voice. I didn't let this setback infuriate me. I just wanted a polite, open, and honest conversation. None of this was worth getting angry over anymore. All I wanted was for everyone to see that I was willing, and hopefully able, to deal with whatever else came my way. I couldn't stomach the madness any longer. "But I came *back,* didn't I? Now everyone decides it's better to walk around here on eggshells until clueless Elles miraculously figures out what nobody wants to say? How is that fair to—"

"Fair went out the window the second that plane fell. None of this is fair, none of it. How you respond, how you live on, that is all that matters."

"Guilty, okay? I admit, I responded irrationally. But . . . but I didn't know how to face anyone any more than you all probably knew how to face me. God! Dina, you all saw me and Floyd getting along, knowing the whole time that . . . I feel like such a fool. That could have been avoided if someone would've told me—"

"What, that your friend Floyd isn't what you think? That he was the pilot of that plane but, good news, by some miracle, he escaped! He survived. Bad news, your parents are still—"

"Yes. Yes. Maybe not in those words but— My God, Dina, I've shielded myself from all of this for too long. You know that. I don't need everyone else . . . You're right. I can see how awkwardly hard that would be."

I could feel Dina studying me as I faced forward, gauging my emotions in the matter. "You have to talk to him, Elles. It took me . . . it took all of us a long time to forgive him and accept that whether we wanted him around as a constant reminder or not, he was going to stick around as long as he had to . . . to make this right, especially with you." I turned to her, speechless. "Oh, he knew all about you long before that happened. He worked with Stephen. They were close. He talked about all of us, all the time, at work, on business trips. Only thing Floyd hadn't done yet was meet most of us in person. But he knew of us well. After he recovered from the crash, he couldn't live with himself. While he waited for you, he did all he could to make it up to us."

"Why didn't he . . ."

"Come find you? He played detective. He knew right where you were. He thought about it. Saw him down there at the ferry many times, scared probably, working up the nerve to get on board."

I got choked up. "He's been wasting his life, waiting for me to—"

"Elles Garity, look at me. Everyone knows that accident was not his fault—except him. What I mean by that is, in his head, he knows better. In his heart, he saw it through your eyes, and he never stopped blaming himself."

"So, he won't forgive himself until—"

"He knows that you do."

"I just don't understand how Floyd got mixed up in it to begin wi—"

"And you won't, until you let him explain it for himself. After all, it's his story to tell. Hear him out, Elles. He's exacted enough punishment on himself. You both have. However you feel about him now, at least give him that."

"I, um, I will. I just need some time." I took a deep breath and regrouped my mental faculties. "Actually, that's not the only thing I wanted to talk to you about."

"Well, you have my inescapable attention. Go on. Let's hear it then."

I stopped myself from diving any deeper into harsh enlightenments for the day.

"Well?"

"It, um . . . it can wait. Let's enjoy the rest of the ride."

This thing with Floyd was taking too many dark turns. The desire to uncover any manipulation perpetrated by her or anyone else to force my hand or trick me into purchasing the inn, was secondary to every mixed emotion I was feeling. As she and I got into it on a personal level, I had a better idea brewing. The topic of me reintroducing myself into this fragile community circle based on who did what and why, learning to coexist with heartbreak and mistrust, was getting tiresome.

I was feeling like I had something to prove to them, justifiable or not. I wasn't mad about the property games anymore. If anything, I was bent on proving them all wrong. The nerve Dina had, or whatever part Uncle John played, to resort to deception and hope for the best. It was like a slap-in-the-face underestimation of what I was capable of. I needed Dina, I needed *everyone*, to see what I had done to the place. I was not about to be some charity case who needed things handed to her or have people thinking I couldn't handle— And that's when it hit me. They didn't know because in the biggest, toughest moment of my life, all I did was prove to everyone that whether I could or not wasn't the issue. I had *refused* to handle the situation. Humbling myself to anything never came easy, and comfortable habits are hard to break. So in an ego-boosting stroke of *Look what I can do*, I bided my time to shine, with other elusive fish to fry.

Chapter 36

I decided today was the day this wall between me and Ginny was coming down, and I made up my mind that stalking—not discretion—was the better part of valor. From a carefully scouted spying position behind a shed, I watched her arrive home from school with the kids, waiting patiently to slip inside. She gathered her bags and the children from the back seats and went inside. I made my move to the front of the house, tiptoeing, listening. I heard Ginny's footsteps trail off farther into the house and peeked inside stealth-like. I crept inside without letting the door make a sound and waited there in plain sight. She came around the corner, clothes changed, hair down, into the kitchen and jumped back a step, startled. She didn't say a thing at first. Neither did I. I was happy just to let her deal with the fact that I was there, in her house, on her turf. And I wasn't leaving without progress or a fight, if it came to that, physical or otherwise. By whatever means, this, too, had to end.

She stood there long enough to make that initial decision either way. Then she turned around and marched right back to where she came from. She was only gone long enough for me to pull a chair out from the table to sit, then she returned. She was breathing heavier, a stern, forbidding expression and conflicted eyes. I kept quiet and still, like an immovable, unavoidable force, leaving the next move up to her. She came toward me as though she wanted nothing more than to grab me and throw me out the door. Then she stopped directly in front of me, launched the daggers from her eyes and in one swift motion . . . slapped me across the face. I must have sensed it coming because I absorbed the blow like a statue. I let the sting subside and returned fire with a joust of verbal outright honest intrigue.

"Feel better?"

She took a few steps backward and looked around. "I have to make dinner," she stated. She went to the cabinets and started gathering pots and pans, placing them on the stove, to the freezer for meat to thaw, and commenced Operation: *Act like Elles isn't here.*

I took my seat and settled in. "Great. I'm starved. What are we having?"

"I don't have time for this."

At last, a semblance of a back-and-forth test of stubborn wills was on. Unless she had the audacity to pack the kids back up and run to Dina's house, all I had to do was stand pat and play it casual and cool like a welcome, longtime . . . friend. "Oh, yeah, I can see you're a little busy there. After dessert then?"

"I've got work to do. Tom will be home soon."

On the other hand, I could switch gears and play the obnoxious guest. At this point I was bent on having fun with this, if nothing else. I shrugged her excuses off with a ridiculous suggestion. "Ooh, ya gonna have him arrest me, then? Hmm? Breaking and entering with intent to—"

She slammed the microwave door, then placed one hand on her hip, the other on her forehead. "I brought you your things . . ."

"You did. That was very nice. Thank—"

"Wasn't that enough?" Her back was to me, but I could see her breathing heavier, getting closer, weakening.

"I'm not leaving, Ginny."

"Then we'll go out."

"Okay, but I call shotgun. Oh, should I call Tom and have him meet us there or . . ."

She turned around, latched onto the countertop with both hands and finally looked at me. She was grimacing, emotions failing to be held in. It was harder for her to talk. "What do you want from me, Elles, or Grace, or . . . whoever the hell you wanna be?

"I wanna know what wasn't in the box." *That* was the defining shot. She broke out in a weeping sob. "Okay, I'll start," I offered. And as hard-nosed as I had arrived, I started to feel my own defenses falter. My voice shivered. She didn't move, but I could see the sinking in her tear-drenched eyes. For the first time, I could see the remembrance in her clouded gaze. I could see the girl I grew up with, the one who resorted to treating me the same way I was now treating Floyd, aching, hating, reacting, and lashing out over circumstances beyond our control, missing, reliving that pain all over again. I started to catch my breath. If she wasn't willing to talk, at least she would sit there and listen. I sat there and revisited a pivotal time with her, consumed by an alternate consciousness. Eleven-year-old Elles began to explain. "Ginny, I'm sorry. I screwed up. I admit it, okay? I didn't know what to do. I lost everything, Ginny. I should have been there for you when you lost your husband. I should have been there when your parents —"

"You didn't lose *everything*."

"You're right . . . And I was hurting too much to consider everyone else—"

"You still don't see it, do you?" she asked, almost amusingly astonished, and I rambled past it.

"When I found out that they—"

"You never even called. You never came back to—"

"Nobody ever called me, either."

"You abandoned *us! We* never left."

"I felt so alone."

"You had me."

"I was only—"

"Eleven years old! I know. Well, boo-hoo, Elles. You—"

"I said I'm sorry!" I bellowed, pounding my fist on the table. "What else do you want? This is me, Elles, Elles Garity, remember? Your *best* friend."

"I want you to understand how much *I* lost that day, too. Because—"

"How much *you*—"

"Because I lost—"

"What?"

"—almost as much as you did."

"What? I don't understand how you can say that. How can you compare—"

"That's the problem, Elles! You *don't* understand! Because you weren't—"

"Understand—"

"—here! Nobody else mattered to you anymore."

"What?!"

"And you never got to figure it out, like I did. So, don't sit there and—"

"Then help me understand! What, Ginny? What did you lose?!"

She squinted at me through gut-twisting tears. She hesitated before spitting out the sickening words that I forced her to say. It was what I knew in my heart and the one blow that my head could not sustain. "My sister."

I knew. As soon as she said it, I knew she was not speaking figuratively, referring to the bond we had that transcended friendship. Still, those two words spoken, confirmed . . . I cannot describe the turmoil that erupted inside of me. My heart may have known when I got older, but it was too late. I had checked out, and any suspicions I might have had, the little clues, I had ignored it all. I stood up, and there was nothing left to say—for now. We melted into one another's arms, and together in a scarred and wounded heap, the levees broke.

Chapter 37

"When did you know?"

Ginny and I were sitting on a bench overlooking the ocean. The evening was calm, mild. Tom came home to the aftermath of our explosive altercation and found us cleaning ourselves up and finishing a box of tissues. I was invited to stay for dinner, then Tom insisted we go somewhere and talk while he stayed inside to watch the kids and cook.

"Couple years before the accident. At least, that's when I started getting suspicious. Mom and Dad were fighting a lot. I mean, they didn't yell, more like . . . loud bickering whispers late at night, after I was in bed."

"So you figured it out on your own."

"No, not exactly. I mean, the more the arguing went on, the more I started to lay awake and listen. I don't think either of them ever said the exact words, ya know? It was more the subject matter."

"But you never told me. I don't remember you ever saying anything about—"

"Guess I didn't think it mattered between you and me. We were like sisters, anyway. That wasn't gonna change. And then . . . it did. A few years later, and in the blink of an eye, you were gone. Trust me, I regretted that decision ever since."

"Ginny." I sighed. "I'm so sorry."

"I know you were going through a lot. I even tried to sneak onto the ferry a few times by myself, ya know. Come find you if nobody else would bring you back."

"Aww, you did?"

"Yeah, well, it's not so easy when you live somewhere where everybody knows you. Not to mention right across the street from parental supervision. First time I tried, Mom was at the inn, saw me, and chased me down. Second time, I guess they were on high alert for a curly-haired stowaway. Didn't even make it past the loading platform."

"You were gonna come get me? All by yourself?"

"I needed you. Hell, with Mom and Dad getting into it constantly, nothing was the same. I started resenting them for not telling me, for not telling *us*. I didn't care what they said. I wasn't going to wait around for you to come to your senses. Wasn't long before Katie started being there for me, trying to keep the peace between me and them. Until Daddy moved out, Katie was more of a mother to me than she was. Actually, that's probably not how it really was, but there was a lot going on, a confusing time, and I wasn't exactly being the most understanding daughter, either."

"What about Tom?"

"Tom, yeah . . . he uh . . ." She giggled, recalling. "He was always asking Katie about me afterwards. Ya know, how was I doing? Was I getting my homework done?"

"Tom? Tom Deiter . . . caring about someone else's homework? Caring about homework in general? What, were ya doing his, too?"

"No, no. Although I might have in the rebellious stage I was in, who knows."

"He loves you, Ginny."

She took a moment to let that observation sink in. Her eyes teared up a little. "I've been treating him pretty bad lately."

"Because of me?"

"You, him . . . me and him, a little bit of everything. He's been holding back for years, ever since we both graduated college and moved back for good. Couldn't take his eyes off me the whole time during my wedding. He was all set to take a job at a precinct somewhere else when Cayle died. He did a one-eighty on that idea faster than I could have an opinion on it. Mom and I still weren't getting along great. So he played it off as me and the kids needing a sense of stability and family with Cayle gone, and I guess I just let him step in."

I smirked at her, suggestively.

"What?"

"Please. You? You've never just *let* Tom do anything you didn't approve of." She laughed and dried her eyes, brushing back the hair blowing in her face. "*You* love him, too."

"Well, I guess I do. I haven't kicked his ass out yet. It's not like we're committed to anything, either, though. Damn fool still has half his stuff at his parents' house. It's been a crazy few years. Kinda feels like we're just playing house over here, ya know?" Ginny got up and paced to the fence, changing the subject. "What about you? I heard you had a dip in the marriage pool yourself. Whatcha run away from him, too?" She poked fun at me.

"Oh!" I gawked at her, jaw dropped.

"Don't look at me like that, sister. We may be back to good but we're not all the way there yet. You thought I was gonna let you off that easily?"

"That's fair. And yes, I did get married, for almost one whole month. I didn't know what I was doing or thinking, honestly. What I got myself into or why. He's a good guy and all. I was trying so hard to pretend I'd moved on from here. That was probably part of it. Problem was, I was doing that and not really living. Took all my spare time and energy to make that illusion feel real." I got up and walked over behind her, hands tucked in my pockets, feeling embarrassed, regretful, more so than I felt in . . . forever. "I was lying . . . to myself, Ginny." She turned around, and I looked into my *sister's* eyes for the first time. The next sentence I spoke to her came out shaky, quivering in my admission. "It was too hard, all of it . . . losing them . . . staying here without them . . . being gone without you."

And standing there with nothing but empty years and time lost between us, I had nothing else to say at that moment. I could not apologize enough—to her, to myself. It was time for the healing to start, whatever that meant; however, both of us needed to work on that in our own ways, separately, together, best friends, sisters, family. All I could do was stand there and hold my arms out and wait and invite her to hug me again. As we embraced and I propped my chin upon her shoulder I said into her ear, "I can't believe you slapped me."

We let go, and she looked down at that hand, flexing her fingers, then at me with a guilty grin. "I can't believe I unclenched my fist first."

My jaw dropped again as Tom called out to us that dinner was almost ready. Ginny winked and started walking back. "Aaww!" I remarked, relieved I hadn't peeled myself off her kitchen floor with a busted lip or black eye.

"Well, don't flatter yourself," she called back as she kept walking. "I probably thought I still had my other rings on. Come on. You wanna meet your niece and nephew?"

I repeated softly to myself, *I have a niece and a nephew.* I smiled at the thought, instinctively touching and rubbing the cheek she targeted. *And a sister with a wicked slapshot.* We started slowly reconnecting over dinner and dessert. We reminisced about the old days, about our teenage years, compared similar experiences, recanted the harder times. All the while, I couldn't help but wonder if I had stayed, where we would be, what would be different. The churning guilt got the better of me. The same curiosity seemed to touch her, too. There was an intermittent distance in her eyes that she tried to hide, passing it off as only being tired. In her defense, it was getting late. Tom had put the kids to bed and, an hour later, followed suit, sprawling out in his chair. I didn't want to leave. I wanted to throw sleeping bags on the living room floor and get out the pillows and blankets. I wanted to borrow a pair of Ginny's pajamas, put a movie on, whip out the snacks, and stay up half the night until one of us zonked out—like we used to do.

Those were the sentimental visions that played in my head on the way home that night. That is the scene I came home to, Katie curled up on the couch. The measly remains of a chip and dip platter on the coffee table and the room, like the rest of the house, as dark as a theater at showtime. I switched the light on, and she sat up out of a half sleep, groggy and barely aware. I went to my room to change then found her still there, coming to, and yawning big enough to insinuate that she had been asleep for hours. I warmed the cushion beside her and helped myself to what was left of the chips while sweeping up a scattered crumb mess with my hands.

"What, are ya gonna make me beg?" she groaned.

"Beg for . . . Wait, how do you know where I . . . Ya know what? Never mind. I don't wanna know."

"Yes, but *I* do want to know. You think I stayed up, watching some old, crappy Christmas movie to make sure you got home safe?"

I chewed on that disingenuous query, quite literally for a few seconds. "Gee, thanks for caring, ma."

"Shut up. I'm tired. You know what I mean. "

"It was good. It was . . . It was really good."

"*Really good?* That's all I get? You care to maybe elaborate?"

"Not tonight, honey. I have a headache."

"You tease."

"Katie, you look as exhausted as I feel. You don't exactly appear to be in any condition to retain what's already been said, much less . . . And, you got dip all over the floor."

"Who cares about dip? I wanna know what—"

"*I* do. Ya know, I live here, too, now."

Katie flopped back on the couch in a huff. "Oh, so flip the rug over." She yawned again, her eyelids fighting a losing battle.

"That, is just *not* how—" I felt her fall sideways across the couch behind my back and I got up, mumbling. "Actually, that *is* probably what you would do." I dragged my feet to my bedroom door and looked back before I turned out the lights. Eyes closed, she blindly reached for a throw pillow and swooped it under her head and curled up tight and snug. The fact that she made the effort to wait up for me made me smile as I headed off to bed.

Chapter 38

That evening spent at Ginny's was like the impossible dream I didn't know I had come true. I hadn't smiled so much, laughed so hard in . . . too long. Leaking *happy* tears was a new sensation, a foreign concept and emotion I never wanted to deprive myself of ever again. Granted, once the truth was finally known by all and the initial wave of ecstatic wonderment had ebbed, what followed was this delicate dance of adjusting to an amazing new dynamic. We were all in the first stages of figuring it out, not just me. What may have been old news to them was just that, a fact devoid of any meaningful relevance existing in a physical form until I reemerged. The ramifications of this news meant I was not only a sister, but an aunt, a potential sister-in-law, among . . . other things? Obviously, there were still a couple of follow-up questions and intricate details yet to be addressed, but there was quite enough to take in already without trying to reconfigure my whole family tree at the same time.

To be perfectly sincere, I was already having trouble grasping that notion in the back of my mind. That night was spent tossing and turning, followed by long periods of staring at the ceiling while my brain spun at a maddening pace. I got out of bed in the middle of the night. The silence was more medicinal than I had ever let it be, so long as I was up and moving around. During the time I had burrowed my soul deep in a chamber, guarded from a vicious world, the quiet times had been unbearable. Now, silence frightened me no more. When needed, like then or when called upon, it centers me and gives me clarity. That night it helped remind me to view all things in proper perspective.

I left the house and drove over to the inn. There, I

went to the kitchen and fixed myself a stack of comfort finger food, four slices of warm, crispy, lightly buttered toast. I plated it and carried it along, room-to-room, casually wandering, proudly surveying the changes. After I had my fill of sustenance and interior scenery, I changed into layers of sweats and flannel for a quick run then simmered in a steaming-hot shower. I wasn't letting a lack of sleep derail the joyous burst of adrenaline-spiked energy coursing through my veins. These were the pre-dawn hours of a busy day. I had a Christmas party to host that evening. The open invitation to which had been promoted by old-fashioned word of mouth by way of, without a doubt, the biggest busybodies in town.

Intertwined in what I hoped to be a town-wide turnout, I had a good impression to make and newfound family relations to nurture, a proper send-off for a soon-to-be departing crew to facilitate, and a fractured friendship to eventually contend with. I hadn't forgotten him. I was postponing him. The entire landscape of my life had flipped so dramatically in a matter of weeks. It was nice to wake up these days with a handful of good problems for a desperately needed change. For now, however, I just needed to clear my overstimulated head. To do so, I drove back to the house and woke up Katie to accompany me on a long-standing tradition Loyal and I started in our college days.

"Good mornin', ladies. My name's Andrew. I'll be your server this morning." Mike McComiskey's brother droned out a lethargically polite greeting and capped it off with straight-shooting, uncourteous honesty. "What do you want?"

"Thanks for doing this so early Andrew. I owe you one."

"Yeah, yeah. It's not a problem. Anything for a friend. Now, please, order something so I can cook it and go back to bed."

"Sure, um. Are there menus or . . ."

He glared back at me with a disinterested look on his face. I glanced across at Katie who looked like a zombie. "We got . . . food."

"Oh, okay. Katie, what do you—"

"Coffee, bring me the pot." She blubbered.

"I guess we'll start with some coffee then, and how about two breakfast platters, extra . . . everything."

"Comin' right up."

There we were, alone at Fiddler's, with the whole place to ourselves. Katie hadn't managed to mutter much of anything intelligible since I nagged her out of her bed and dragged her here before the light of day. Andrew returned to deliver the coffee and two mugs to the table. I took the liberty of pouring her a cup and put it down in front of her. She didn't even flinch at the offering. "That's, uh, that's for you. Unless you want me to drink it for you." I tried to infuse a little humor into her catatonic state. "Um . . . Katie? Are you . . . alive?"

"Ah . . . ha." She half smiled. "I'm just waiting for my brain waves to travel down to my spine and tell my arms to move." She cleared her throat and reached for the mug. "I'm not, uh . . . I'm not used to being awake before the *earth* is."

"I'm sorry. I couldn't sleep." She cocked her head to the side and cast an expression at me that screamed *Are you kidding me?* "What I mean is, sorry, see Loyal and I would always do breakfast together at this little café at least three times a week. Well, it started out as an every day thing when we were still in college, but then when we got jobs and—"

"What the hell are you babbling about?"

"We . . . made kind of a pact with it, ya know? We didn't always have time to meet for breakfast. So we decided to commit to at least a few times a week."

"Oh! So, you wanna be committed. Why didn't you just say—"

"I'm serious, Katie."

"Forgive me. I'll lighten up about two more cups from now."

"It was a way for us to, ya know, stay close and . . ."

"And . . ."

"Well, be there for one another if something was bothering one of us."

"What do you mean?"

"See, the once-a-week thing was promised, ya know, like the standard get together. Anything else was, like, to get out, talk, get something off our chest, relax—"

"So, this, right now, what you're doing to me is—"

"Me, being needy."

"Ah, and me . . . being Loyal."

"In more ways than one." I grinned, proud of the wordplay.

"Ha ha, cute. No need to guilt trip me. I'm too friggin' tired to move. So whatever's on your mind, spill it." I closed my eyes lightly and put my head back, hesitant. "Oh, geez, is it that bad?"

"No. I'm just not used to . . . spilling . . . things."

"Ah, so, these, uh, bonus breakfasts with Loyal, they must have been very quiet then."

"No, they were . . . I mean, we talked. It was just . . . Well, it was more about being there together, in a supportive way. Ya know, sharing good food, casual conversation, a cathartic thing."

"So supporting each other and any problems without actually . . . talking about any problems. Can I ask you something?"

"What?"

"Can I kick you in the ass?"

We both smiled at each other in fun. "Neither one of us were ever very good at, or comfortable, sharing personal stuff."

"Weren't you best friends?"

"Yes, the best, but we just kinda knew when the other needed to . . ."

"I get it, Elles. I'm giving you a hard time that's . . . I get it. I do. I gotta tell ya, though, I'm not much of a Loyal fill-in, in that regard. No, see I don't haul ass out of bed this early in the morning for just anyone, unless he's . . . Doesn't matter. The thing is—" Our breakfast platters were served, loaded with a variety of mouthwatering options, two glasses of water, and an orange juice for me. With a polite hand gesture, Andrew was on his way back upstairs and out of our way. "As you know, I've kinda been caught up in the middle of stuff since you sailed back into our lives here. As you once pointed out, we were never very close, you and I, when we were little. But times have changed, ya know? I like you, Elles, I do. I mean that. But I've put up with some shit from you. Safe to say I have a little more . . . um, insight into things than Loyal, right?"

"True."

"And you like me. You would consider us friends?"

"Of course. What, where are—"

"What I'm saying is—" She put a forkful of food in her mouth and held her fingers to her lips, the mouthful puffing out her cheeks. "Mm, Jesus, he's a good goddamn cook. I gotta eat here more often. What I am saying is, the sun has barely started to rise. Luckily for you, my grouchiness is wearing off. But honestly, Elles, whatever's on your mind, it's just us, okay? It's just me, and I only wake up this early for one thing. So either let me finish eating, take me home and have your way with me, or share something friggin' meaningful. 'Cause one way or another, I'm gettin' somethin' more than butt-crack-of-dawn breakfast out of this." I smirked, cleared my throat and took a long swig of orange juice to consider *that* mouthful of delightful candor as only Katie could express it.

Chapter 39

"Well, I mean, you took charge of the situation, ya know? You made the effort. The ball was pretty much in her court. She fumbled it, and you scooped it up and ran it right through her front door. So good for you. Honestly, I love 'er to death, but she's hardheaded as hell. But I'm happy for you, for real. It sounds like you guys are in a better place. Which is why I don't see the problem."

"Yeah, I know all that, but . . . I don't know. The whole time we were talking, getting better, I just couldn't shake the what-ifs."

"What do you mean?"

"Well, obviously, what if I didn't move away? What if we had stayed in contact? What if . . . what if I knew about us and . . ."

"What does any of that even matter? All you can do now is move on."

"I know. But everything is so complicated now. What do I say to Floyd? I mean, what *can* I say? And Ginny and Tom have been in a holding pattern because of everything she's been through, starting with me. Dina . . . It's just everything now. I feel like I caused all of it. I feel like everyone's lives have been on hold because of what I did."

"I'm gonna stop you right there, okay? This is probably not the best time for self-pity bullshit."

"The more I think about it—"

"Exactly!" She snatched a bit of food into her mouth, then pointed the fork at me. "Quit it. It's not good. Stop thinkin' about it."

"It's my life, Katie. It's what I created. How can I just stop —"

"Ah, so, uh . . . So you think beyond the side effects of you leaving, the aftermath, all that, you think everything that's gone on here . . . *here,* where you haven't been, is your fault."

"Well, no, not . . . I guess not everything. I don't know. See, it's—"

"Do you even know the whole story of Dina and Stephen's breakup, or what, if anything, it has to do with any of this?"

"Well, no, I didn't ask."

"Well, maybe you should. You have that right. You're family, I'm not. Did *you* marry a sailor? Hm? Did you fall for the first handsome thing in a uniform you ever saw just to get back at the mother you weren't getting along with?"

"Oh, God. That's why she—"

"I don't know. I'm sure it played into it. She was kinda being a little snot to everyone around that time, including me. My point is, with or without you, she was in charge of her own life. So was Dina, so was Stephen, even Floyd. Give 'em a little credit, Elles. Yes, if you were here, *some* things *might* have been different. Anything that had to do with you, it wasn't because you were away and we couldn't function without you. It was because we lost an entire family, a big part of us, okay? A lot of bad shit happened post you. You have a chance to help repair a lot of that now. You can't fix it like new or turn back time so it never happened because, truthfully, bad shit would have happened if you were here, just in a different way."

"You mean Dina and—"

"And Cayle. Who knows, maybe the Cayle thing never happens, ya know? Maybe she's not basically a single mom. But —and I don't know the whole story—but once the truth came out about you and Ginny, the damage was already done long before that point. Things steadily went south between them, and things might have been messier with your parents still alive."

"Ginny didn't talk to you about it?"

"Not really. It was a family issue. It wasn't my business,

and it was a very touchy subject. The only thing complicated here, Elles, is the crash, adding that into the mix, and Floyd. Look, Floyd was damaged, deeply, rightfully so. You're gonna have to deal with that. I don't mean for this to sound like it's going to, but you didn't wreck anyone's life, Elles. You left. Everyone knew where to find you, including Floyd. If you ask me, you *all* screwed up. You all let this go on for way too long." Katie drew a glass of water to her lips. She eyeballed my orange juice and put the glass down without taking a sip. "Hey, why the hell didn't I get any orange juice? That little . . ."

"Relax, geez. There some kinda feud I don't know about between you and the McComiskey family or something?"

"No feud. Feuds get aggressive and bloody. This is a friendly rivalry. But I'm winning. It's an Irish thing."

"Winning? They're not your biggest fans."

"That's how I know I'm winning. Hey, you got your . . . thing, I got mine. Like I said, it gets boring around here sometimes. Ya gotta liven things up."

"I'll be sure to let Andrew know you raved about his cooking."

"Don't you dare. They'll have the advantage."

"Whatever." I laughed. "I'll go find you some orange juice."

I was halfway across the room when Katie stopped me. "Hey! For what it's worth, the fact that you opened up to me means a lot. I'm flattered. I really am. But your *cooking?* You suck. I mean, especially compared to this."

"Yeah, about that. Ginny mentioned hearing something about that. I don't know who could have—"

She threw her hands up in a declaration of innocence. "Hey, word travels, ya know. Don't shoot the messenger." I continued into the shadows to find the kitchen as she threw more shade my way, talking with her mouth full. "If you wanna feel sorry for someone, I mean, pity me. I'm the one who's been caught in the middle of all this, got dragged out of bed, had to compliment *Andrew* . . . Don't think I won't make ya pay for *that* one later."

Now, before I say more, and not to reevaluate the level of friendship that Loyal and I always had but, maybe, just for argument's sake, this was why we didn't share intimate details of our lives! I'm not saying it's a bad thing. Katie raised some excellent points. And I don't mean to complain, if only in a self-deprecating way. I really don't. I'm not against openness, but Jesus, I'm trying to find answers, and I appreciate all of her advice. It was well-spoken. All I'm saying is, no wonder Loyal and I had unproductive therapeutic meals together! Because maybe they . . . No, they *were* therapeutic, for our needs, our purposes.

We just wanted the small talk, the support system sitting across the table, knowing we had each other. I came along into Katie's simple little world, and now I had this chick graduating with a master's in interrelationship lecturing—God I hope that's not a thing—with a minor in accumulating more questions! I barely got a word in edgewise. What the . . . flipperty jiggers man?! Sorry, as one who used to teach impressionable adolescent minds, it becomes inherently crucial to improvise at the impulse of tongue-biting profanity. Okay, deep breath . . . I feel better now.

It took Katie saying it out loud for me to really recognize the gravity of everyone's role in everything. It took her saying things I had been thinking all along in various forms and degrees. In a bitter attempt to dodge my own guilt and blame, I wasn't seeing everyone else's struggles. I wasn't factoring in their blame based on the consequences of their actions and the decisions they were making, as Katie put it, *post me*. I had boarded a ferry bound for home with a severe lack of preparation and foresight. I had gotten weighed down by misconception and the gnawing pain I thought I had sufficiently packed away in order to become the person I finally realized I could no longer afford to hide behind.

After an eye-opening breakfast and some thought-provoking, well-spoken advice from someone I came to admire for her unique personality as well as her valuable honesty, I started to examine the whole picture. I started to finally look at every situation, all sides, subjectively and without personal bias.

Deceitfully orchestrated or not—and I *would* get to the bottom of that—I found my purpose, my new career, my future. I knew where I belonged for the rest of my life. Today marked a brand-new beginning, a celebration, not of starting over but starting again, picking up where I left off. For the first time in my adult life, I felt empowered to make something more of my life before the trials of life finished getting the better of me.

When Ginny and I were young, we dreamed of being teachers—although, I can't say for certain why that path was appealing to us both. Maybe it was a means of staying put, helping to raise and educate generations of hometown islanders like us, together. Maybe, like our mothers before us, that was our inn, figuratively speaking. The part of the plan that had us sharing a house may have been far-fetched as we hadn't thought through the prospect of having families of our own. We were silly kids with ambitious hopes.

After my parents died, I think I followed that dream because I needed something to fill the void, to replace the agony. It was the one plan I had before my foundation was ripped away, and after that, reaching for any other stars was the last thing I was motivated to do. That's not to say I hadn't loved teaching. But living, by going through the pre-designated motions, defeated by tragedy, isn't really living at all. I want to say that my freshly started teaching career, when put in danger, had triggered that underlying awareness. I want to say that losing Uncle John, grim as it may be, had been the kick in the pants to do something about it.

Over the years, I have looked back on these defining moments and contemplated if, indeed, those were the reasons why. Perhaps all that matters is that *something* pushed me.

Something, or someone, spoke to me and demanded that I owed it to Elles to give this derailed life another try. Therefore, I can say, as I look back and remember this all-important day, I felt with conviction that I was ready for this new chapter of my life. I was up to the challenges that lay ahead.

Come what may, there was a party to be thrown. Screw the unknowns. *Elles, today let all your worries rest. You can't control tomorrow. It does not yet exist. Cherish your recent victories, and let the awarded fun begin.*

Chapter 40

"Okay, attention! Can I have everyone's attention, please? I just wanted to get everyone together and say a few words ahead of the party this evening." Before gathering *them*, I had needed to take some quiet time in the office to gather myself and my thoughts. I wasn't much for public speeches or taking the spotlight, but I was warming up to the responsibility of it, supplied with encouragement and advice from Birdie and Dina, both of whom were now standing right where I needed them, flanking me on either side. "First and foremost, I wanted to thank everyone for all of your hard work. This place looks incredible. I am blown away by what we have done, and I could not have done it without all of you giving it your all, putting up with me, working together, getting along and so on. This party is not just any ol' party to me."

It didn't take long for my voice to crack and shaky emotions to start welling up inside. "I've had the pleasure of getting to know you all, either sitting down together and chatting, or briefly at some point or another. By now, most, if not all of you, know the history of this place we're standing in right now. Um . . . what you may not and probably don't know is what it took for me to get here. Doing this is a dream that I could not have gotten off the ground without the love and support of these two women standing here with me. Birde, you have taught me *so* much. I can't thank you enough. I am indebted to you. I know I'm the new kid in town, business-wise, but if you ever need anything, anything at all . . . except Petey Pedro over there, hands and eyes off. He's mine. Seriously though, I'm here, and this inn is here for you, always. Dina . . ."

The second her name escaped my lips I was sure I was going to lose it. I had to take a deep breath and fortify the levee.

"I wish I knew what to . . . I can't replace the success you and my mother built. I don't have all the knowledge yet. I don't even know how well this is all going to go. I, um . . . I don't . . ."

Dina turned and hugged me with a whisper in my ear. "We'll talk later. It's all right."

She grabbed and squeezed both my shoulders from behind and stepped back. I smiled at her and moved on. "Anyway, this Christmas party is for everyone. You have all meant so much to me and to my family. Some of you are leaving. There's a lot of new faces coming in. The staff is a work in progress, but bear with us. We're coming along. To the ones who are leaving us, you'll always have a place to stay if and/or when you decide to visit. To the three who decided to stay and the new hires, a few you'll meet today, lots of luck working for and dealing with this family." I had to throw in a few jokes. I had to push for some laughs before I cried." No, but I'm thrilled to see that almost all of you showed up. Um, you're all my first hires, my original crew and I can't wait for opening day to see you all in action. Enjoy tonight. Everyone here has earned it. Eat, drink and just . . . fill this place with energy, happiness, laughter, and love. Remember, this is a party and an open house for the whole community. I know you'll represent the inn well. Everyone who is staying here, please take some time before the festivities to make your rooms appear unlived in. Hide your belongings, clean up so everything looks brand new. There'll be surprises for everyone throughout the course of the night. Let's get all the preparations done. Enjoy the day everyone. Bri?"

I pulled her aside as everyone clapped and scattered on my way out the door. "I have to take care of something this afternoon. Dina knows where to find me if you need to reach me. Also, I have two friends, Loyal and Ja— Well, I'm guessing you know Jack, at least. They're coming in on the morning ferry. I need you to treat them like royalty, okay?"

"Sure."

"They'll be here for a few days, so whatever unspoken-for room they want, get them settled in. Show them around if they want."

"No problem. You got it. Where do you want the band to set up?"

"Band?"

"Oh, boy. I guess I spoiled the surprise. But I need to know where to—"

"I have a band?"

"Well, Petey and Reno, one of them anyway, had some connections to a local mainland band who's done some holiday gigs so they were able to get them booked. I'm sorry. I should have—"

"No, no, it's totally fine. That is awesome! I will fake complete surprise."

"So, where sh—"

"But I trust you, completely. This is what I hired you for. You make the call. I know nothing about any band, and I can't wait to not hear them. I've gotta go. Have Petey do a test run on the sound systems and, uh, make sure he stays on top of things 'til later. Assure him he'll have all night long to be spouting or shooting game at the ladies, or whatever the hell he calls it. Oh, I almost forgot. There's one more thing I need you to do for me after I leave."

"Okay, what's that?"

There is a time-honored spot on this island, a large rock that decades ago became a two-ton monumental canvas of artistic expression. Painted and repainted thousands of times over to display messages—everything from marriage proposals, personal and seasonal greetings, and a variety of countless tributes to the simpler, more casual works of art. I had always thought of it as a publicly owned billboard, introduced, so the legend goes, as a prank and adopted ever since, continuously refaced in our own individually creative ways. I had received a surprise birthday gift of sorts that way one year. I remember my father driving that route and slowing down upon approach, commenting with an indiscriminate *Hey, look at that!* A brand-new bike I had been wanting was propped on its kickstand beside the rock, which had been painted in bright vibrant colors with "Happy Birthday" scrolled across. Ginny had a helping hand in it and was part of the display, sitting in wait on her own bike. I don't think the car had come to a full stop yet before my face lit up, and screaming, I went barreling from the backseat.

It was but one of many memories of this town that flashed in my head as I waited by the rock for Dina, with a contribution of my own this time. For the reason I was there, the timing and weather were about six months off, but this was a symbolic gesture, nonetheless. When she drove up, I was perched on top, nicely dressed, holding a bouquet of flowers. Written across the rock just below my dangling feet, it read "Happy belated Mother's Days." Dina was speechless, with tears of surprise and disbelief, as she got out of the car. I came prepared for the cold. I tapped the empty space of blanket I had spread out and was sitting on. It was an emotional exchange of stares I will never forget as she came near, both hands cupped over her mouth and nose.

"Why . . . How did you . . ."

"I figured I owed you a few."

"Oh, my . . . But how . . ."

"Ginny . . . We talked. And I thought you and I should talk."

Once she sat down, I handed over the flowers. "Oh, Elles, they're beautiful."

"I know a, um, freelance florist in town who helped me get a good deal, so . . . Just, don't ask." She gazed deeply and lovingly at me. We both leaned into each other as she stretched out her arm across my shoulders. "What should I call you?"

"Whatever's comfortable for you. I wouldn't want to push."

"I would, if . . . it just feels like I would be . . ."

"Elles Garity, you refer to me as you wish. It's enough

that you're home."

"Tell me, Dina. Tell me why I am, who I am."

"Oh, Elles. I—"

"Please? I want to know."

"We always wanted kids, your mother and I. That was the last piece of our puzzle. They tried for a long time, until she found out it just wasn't in the cards. Doctors told her she would never be able to have children. That was hard on her. Even when she tried to pretend she was over it, I knew. Then I got pregnant again, and I felt . . . so bad for her—and guilty. I dreaded telling her, even though I knew she'd be happy for us. How could I go and have another after that? Felt like I was . . . rubbing it in. So one night I had an idea, and then I talked to Stephen about it."

"You gave me to her."

"Wasn't too hard of a sell at first. Close as your mom and I were, we figured, hell, we'd see you all the time. We'd know you were safe, loved. We were pretty much guaranteed to see you every day. I guess it was lucky for us that you and Ginny got along as well as you did from the start. Good thing you girls didn't come as a combo package. Twins would have been harder to pull off."

"So what went wrong? I mean between you and . . ."

"Your fa— Stephen let it get to him. We made the offer to your mom and dad. Everyone was on board . . . until he decided he wanted us to back out. By that time . . ."

"You didn't have the heart to take me back."

"Oh, please. I never even thought about that. That's not the kind of offer you just reconsider and take back. I refused. I tried to reason with him. The harder I did, the longer I did, the further we drifted apart."

"He was always nice to me from what I remember. He was just a little . . ."

"Distant?"

"Something like that."

"All part of his pathetic show. *Don't get too invested*

in what you can't have. That was his mindset. He was a businessman who, as your biological father, saw you as and treated you like the deal he squandered and could never get redone. I'm sorry. I don't mean to badmouth . . ."

"It's okay, Dina. I told you I wanted to know."

"Maybe I was a fool not to see that all the right reasons were also the wrong ones, for Stephen, anyway. It ate away at him, and it made him bitter, and it made him mean."

"Did he ever—"

"No. He never got physical. The bitter I could have lived with. It was the bottle that elevated it to mean."

"He started drinking."

"He was unreasonable and weak. He never gave it a chance. It wasn't working. He had to go."

"Wait, so you threw him—"

"I never got the chance. I mean I was going to. There were nights the ferry would come after work, and he wasn't on it. I didn't even mind because I knew at least the house would be peaceful. Your father would tell me he either slept at his office or checked into a motel."

"Dina, I'm so sorry he treated you guys that way. But . . . I don't know. I'm also sorry he had to feel that way. I'm sorry if that—"

"Please, you don't have to apologize. You and Ginny are the biggest victims. Neither of you have anything to be sorry for. He agreed to it, then he reneged and made his choices. That's all there is to it."

"Is that why you never . . . I mean, I know I wasn't cooperative, but . . . you could have visited and—"

"Oh, even if I wanted to, after all that? We couldn't even decide if we were going to keep it a secret forever or not. I think we always planned on telling you both at some point when you got older. Ginny just . . . put it all together somehow, on her own."

"And that's why the two of you had trouble getting along."

"It took her a while to understand. And how could I possibly come and tell you, what, that you lost three parents?"

"I get it."

"Anyway, one day I packed up all of his stuff and shipped it to his office. He didn't even have the guts to make it official. I had a lawyer draw up the papers, signed, mailed them off, he signed, and it was over." She took my hand, held it tight, and added with intense conviction, "Don't you ever go thinking any of this was your fault. Do you hear me, Elles? None of it."

A part of me understood both sides. A bigger part *hated* him for everything. Still, I needed more. "Dina?" I didn't want to say it to her, but I did. "I have to see him."

"I know."

I reached my arms around her midsection and squeezed her tight, overloaded with mixed feelings. "Happy Mother's Day," I whispered.

Chapter 41

What does one do with that? What was *I* supposed to do with that, hearing the broken-home story that featured me? I brought that challenge on myself. I had to know everything because this was new territory for me. This was *my* family for better or worse, literally, because it went both ways to brutal extremes. It was hard, very hard, not to feel guilty as Dina had beseeched me. I understood her argument and why, but how could I not feel guilty when everything that had gone wrong seemed to center around me? Dina selflessly gave up a child to help fill that void in someone else's life.

And they had been amazing parents, considering I was not the easiest child to raise. I was impatient, spoiled, and not totally by their doing. This island was my playground. They worked hard, and I assumed free range, Ginny and I both.

I had also been easygoing, laid-back, and I had my father wrapped around my little finger for God's sake. He and I were a lot alike, I thought, for two people genetically linked by only a last name. No wonder I had never questioned those relationships. Why would I? One of my favorite memories was when my father and I spent an entire summer carving an oar out of driftwood and etching *our* family name—the name I was proud to carry—into it, to hang among the hundreds of other family paddles in The Oar restaurant. When we finished it, we were allowed to have a hand in choosing its place, right beside the Carrington's, and the three of us were there to see it hung. My father was the sap; my mother, the enforcer. She put in every ounce of relentless effort to instill their values, their moral beliefs in me. I wasn't just some adopted charity case that they took for granted. None of their parenting was ever phoned in or taken lightly. I felt nothing but loved and wanted, and I gave every bit of that back.

I'm not discounting anyone's feelings in this whole situation. Yes, the Carringtons had been, for all intents and purposes, family—a second family to me, as we were to Ginny. But it was complex. I had lost my parents—the only ones I had ever known, that is. It may not have made the loss any easier at first, but I could have had a safe place to land—ironically in the family that was generous and caring enough to gift my parents one.

Broken or not, I had Dina and Ginny now, and it was a lot to take in. I found myself straddling a fine line between gratefulness and seething to my core. No matter what anyone said or tried to tell me, I was in the middle. I was grieving for two families now, but make no mistake about it, I was not going to internalize it this time. I would not let it ruin me again.

I had things I needed to confront with Stephen, but they could wait. For now, I had better, more pleasant things to do. I had a party to throw, an inn full of people on my side, and a community waiting for me and what I had to offer.

* * *

"Merry Christmas!"

An ambush awaited me upon my arrival back at the inn later that afternoon. Everyone was gathered around the tree, with Brianna and Pedro standing side by side in front, holding a present between the two of them.

"What did you guys do? What is this?"

Pedro took the gift and darted forward with a jubilant bounce in his step while Brianna explained, "The crew all chipped in. We wanted to give you something to remember us by and celebrate all the hard work, and well . . . here!"

"Oh, my God. You guys, you shouldn't have. What is this? It's heavy." I gushed over it first, wondering what it might be, weighing it in my hands and noticing the beautiful wrapping.

I tore the paper from the corner fold and ripped down the center from top to bottom to reveal a gorgeous silver-plated and wood-mounted plaque. I read it and smiled, eyes watering. It was engraved in two parts, "The Garity family-established National Inn" complete with dates. Below it read, "The Garity House" with the established year and finally, a dedication to my parents in memoriam. Pedro slipped his hand underneath to help hold it as I wiped tears from the corners of my eyes."This is, um . . . This is amazing. Thank you so much."

Then it occurred to me as I was speaking. "But, how did you know about the new name? I never . . ." I had never told anyone, except when I let it slip to Floyd one time. I thought I had remedied it by asking him to keep it under his hat until . . . And this is where the next part took a curveball turn that one-upped even the incredible plaque.

"Yeah, there's actually something else . . ." Pedro started to say. "Part two of the surprise that we were asked to present." He held his arms out wide like a game show model highlighting the grand prize. Everyone moved to part the way, gathered in two groups on either side. Resting on the floor behind them was a long, large object hidden under a red velvet covering. Bri at one end and Reno at the other, they lifted the veil on a new building sign marked, "The Garity House." My heart melted, and my face blushed. I couldn't believe what I was seeing. I had only envisioned it in my mind, which wasn't nearly as effective as seeing it right in front of me, in all its glory, ready to take its place where the old sign still resided. My heart was fluttering, trying to catch my breath. I had no words. My mouth opened but . . . "We can't take credit for this one, though. It's not from us. It's from—"

"Floyd." I gushed.

Loyal and Jack came over to me and stood there gazing at it, soaking in the moment with me. Loyal rested her arm on my shoulder to impart her usual dry wit. "So . . . does this mean you're not coming back home or . . ." I laughed and put my arm around her, sucking back the still-escaping tears. "I am home."

I echoed that sentiment in the parade of hugs that followed, to Katie, to Ginny, the rest of the crew, and so on. Everyone who approached me then surrounded and wished me Merry Christmas and good luck with offerings of congratulations. On cue, the band began to play a soft instrumental holiday tune. After the love fest thinned out and I circled back to Loyal and Jack, I lightly backhanded them both, catching them off guard. "What the hell were ya doing, sending a small army? You didn't have to do that."

"Mm, we kinda did." My jaw dropped at her levity. "Please, you were in over your head."

"Yeah, I kinda was, wasn't I? Still, you went through all that trouble . . ."

"No trouble at all," Jack interrupted. "All workers from different branches of my firm. I reached out to a few people, pulled some strings. We start scaling back around the colder months, anyway, when we're not building as much. People still gotta work."

"Well, thank you, both. Really. I know I haven't exactly said it yet. I'm sorry I haven't called. It's just . . ."

"Eh, you've been a little busy, same with me and Jack. No big deal. We're glad we could help. We were treated to lunch and offered a tour of the place, but we held out for *the* grand tour by the *owner*. We demand the VIP package, ya know."

"Okay, but, um . . ."

"What?"

"I'm sorry . . . Sorry, can we hold off a little longer? I have to take care of something first."

"Take care of . . . Hey, you just got here. Where are you—"

"I'm really sorry, Loyal. You guys mingle. I'm pretty sure the party just started. Have a good time, and I'll be right back. I promise."

I couldn't enjoy myself the rest of the day without at least making one thing right between Floyd and me, a ceasefire of sorts from my end. He deserved to be at that party. He deserved better than to be left out, not just because of the gift, but because of his contributions, because of his friendship.

He came to the door, and his immediate expression was proof enough that he had been anticipating this moment. The skin around his eyes spoke to a lack of quality sleep, and his walk was slow and sluggish. I saw fear in him, as well as sorrow for me deep in his soul. Our imposed time off had easily not served him well. We stood there in a haze of dead air as I stomached what I saw, and he stood silent and still like a convicted felon awaiting sentencing. I got ahold of myself and cleared my throat. He took a step back away from the door, and I let myself in, giving his outfit a once-over.

"Well, you can't go out like that." I kept talking, walking a straight line toward his bedroom. "We're gonna have to find you something suitable."

"What are you doin'?" he asked me in a raspy voice.

"Finding you something less wrinkled." I quickly rooted through his bureau drawers for anything appropriate to fit the occasion and returned to him with two options, handing over a small pile of neatly folded shirts and pants. "Here, pick a combination and—"

"Elles, I'm—"

"There's a Christmas party going on, without you there. Now damn it, Floyd, don't argue with me. Just change, clean yourself up, and let's go." In that moment, his only response was a noticeable drop in stress level, a less fateful demeanor. "I want you there. We all want you there."

"What about—"

"Worry about that later. From the looks of you, you've already done enough of that, anyway."

He shook his head slowly with a soft grunt. "You sweet talker, you."

"Get your ass dressed and looking jolly. I'll keep the car warmed up." He raised his hand in salute before I walked out.

Chapter 42

In my absence the party, to which I had only assigned an approximate start-time window, was just getting ramped up. A few folks from town were already there, others straggling in. The sky was beginning to darken, and the strands of thousands of twinkling white lights outside were getting brighter. Inside, the fireplace was crackling, and the allure of the decked-out lobby, adorned with just the right amount of holiday flair against these freshly painted walls, was breathtaking. Of course I'm being partial, but this was mine, and it looked magnificent. From the moment Floyd and I pulled up out front, I was glowing with pride just as bright as those glittery lights. It was a humbling experience, seeing it all come together, the people that teamed up to make it all happen enjoying the spoils of their efforts. The joy I felt at sharing and showing it off to everyone who came out to join us that evening was immeasurable.

Desserts, side dishes, wine, eggnog, hot cocoa—it was a sensory playground of sights and smells. Birdie and Dina brought bottles of champagne that were chilling in a tinsel-lined crystal bowl of crushed ice. I was enchanted, having just as good a time watching it all unfold. The staff, fully into the spirit, had Pedro rocking his own put-together interpretation of St. Nick. Brianna was dressed up as a youthful, classy Mrs. Claus. Others sported reindeer and elf headbands, among other things. My wandering ears detected the jingling of tiny bells. I must admit, taking it all in made it clear that I had lost my passion for this festive time of year. Due in large part to what we had come from in our respective lives, Loyal and I gravitated toward portraying the happily indifferent, pseudojolly scrooge types, for all the confounding sense that makes. This time, even she and Jack were on the ball, showing out in unmatching dueling ugly Christmas sweaters.

"It's beautiful. You outdone yourself, Elles," Floyd noted, seeing a sampling of the finished product himself for the first time accentuated in a variety of warm and inviting seasonal touches.

"Come on, Floyd. You know very well it wasn't just me. I'm still getting the hang of all this. Come over here and find yourself on the tree."

"Find my—"

I took his hand and pulled him along the way to get an up-close view. He panned the scope of it from star to skirt, with no missed branches in between. The overall trimming proved to be exceedingly sentimental. This was the very same artificial tree my parents hauled out and erected every post-Thanksgiving weekend. In addition to the collection of family decorations, it needed something new, something . . . now. After brainstorming for ideas, one had stood out as a way to forever commemorate the initial Garity House holiday celebration and enshrine everyone who had helped bring it to fruition. I waited eagerly for Floyd to locate the handcrafted ornament adorned with his image. "We had a little individual crafting project. The two rules were everyone had to pick someone else's name out of a hat and then incorporate that person's picture into the design. That's why everyone's creation is so different."

"Yeah, I see that."

"I can't tell you who did yours. Oh, third rule, nobody knows who made what. That made it more fun, ya know, totally anonymous and once you were done just sneak in and find a place to hang it, where it could be seen of course."

"Who took my picture?"

I shrugged my shoulders and gave him shifty eyes. "That's part of anonymity, Floyd. Couldn't tell ya even if I knew. You should have seen everybody in the habit of inspecting the tree a few times a day searching for their faces."

As he was turning away from the tree, I stopped him. Facing the sign that was propped up in front of the baseboard along the wall, I laid hand over hand on his shoulder and stared at it with him for a moment. “I don’t know how much that must have cost you but . . .”

“Nowhere near what I owe,” he grumbled.

“How did you know I was going to stick with the name?”

“Stick with it or not, that’s what it is. This your place now, Elles Garity. Own it.”

I kissed him on the cheek and left it at that. “Thank you, Floyd. Now go get yourself something to eat. Have some fun.” From the corner of my eye, I spotted Jack walking past. “Hold on, Jack! This is Floyd Gresham. Floyd this is my . . . ex-husband and close friend.”

“Floyd.” Jack offered his hand to shake.

“Well, it is nice to meet you.” Floyd reciprocated. “Ex-husband, huh? Well, either she held off cookin’ a meal for ya ’til after the weddin’ or you had enough of not being able to catch the end of a good ballgame.”

To that insult, they shared a laugh. Much as I felt the inclination to react in kind, I issued a straight-faced reply. “That hurt, Floyd.”

“I will change the subject, for my own physical well-being,” Jack replied.

“Smart man,” Floyd acknowledged. “I’m gonna follow my nose and stuff my face. I’ll catch you both later.” He excused himself to partake of the refreshments.

“So, I hear you’ve managed to poach some of the part-timers away from the company.”

“Hey, they couldn’t resist. Besides, one of them said I’m prettier than you, and the other two are guys, so . . .”

“Ooh, okay, ya got me. Well done, well done. No hard feelings. Seriously, Elles, I’m happy for you. I know they’ll be happy working for you.”

“Thank you, Jack.”

“And this place is amazing, by the way. I think Loyal is

sufficiently jealous. So thanks for that. Now I have to up my game, put her in a penthouse or something. I mean, how do I compete with fantasy island?"

"Oh, you just . . . ya know, you give her the fantasy that you both have always wanted from the day you met."

I winked at Jack, and he shied away a remorseful guilty grin and looked around to find Loyal across the room, engaged in conversation with Katie. "You knew the whole time? Even when . . ."

"No hard feelings here, either, Jack."

"Elles, you and I . . . I mean, you were never second choice, Elles. I—"

"I know."

"I feel like I owe you an explanation or apolo—"

"It's okay, Jack. I was . . . someone else. We both knew that. I had all of this to figure out, and I just wasn't ready to face it then."

"Yeah, I guess we never really talked about . . ."

"We're talking about it now. And it's all good. We're both where we're supposed to be. That's all that matters, right?"

"It's funny, I was always intimidated by her. I felt like I wasn't good enough for her, and I didn't even try. Luckily, she had a gorgeous best friend who somehow thought the world of me."

"Still do."

"Thanks. She's changed, ya know?"

"How so?"

"She's been different since . . . I don't . . . The connection you two had, it was like . . ."

"Holding her back?"

"That's not what I was gonna say, but yeah, I guess that, too."

"Jack, I love you, and I love Loyal. She and I have been holding each other back for years. You can say it. We were damaged people. We didn't let it define us. We just let it derail us for a while."

"Well, whatever it is or was, she's focused now, that's for sure. I've never seen her this way. She wants a career, a family. She's . . ."

"Aww, look at her, Jack. Our little Loyal's growing up."

"Oh, God! Why'd ya have to . . . I can't, there's no future now. You've ruined it." He kidded.

"Oh, get ahold of yourself, Jackson."

He broke a smile. "She's called me that all of *one* time since the day after you . . . Oh, then you just said that thing and made her sound like our child, and now it's all creepy. I—"

"Jack."

"What?"

"Be good to her. She needs you. Take care of her, and she'll take care of you."

"I will."

I brushed his shoulder and pecked him on the cheek. "I gotta go do hostess things."

Chapter 43

I need a minute to lament. As to the status of our short-lived matrimonial union, I offer this: closure, a year and a half in the making, is what that was. I regret that Jack must have been carrying that weight the whole time, and I had not afforded him the right to have closure when it was due. At the time, I had considered it not a mistake but . . . There is no better way to put it, other than to say it was me being disconnected. It was Jack settling, whether he acknowledged that fact or not. I do not doubt, however, that his feelings for me were real, and I never have. What I *do* doubt is my investment and capability back then of being the wife and love that he had deserved. There are two manifestations of fate, I believe. Either things happen naturally, for reasons we can't explain, or things happen because, if we are lucky enough, sometimes we have the foresight to understand the gravity of our faults.

That was the reason for this journey I was on, after all. The best and worst of both fates. I had to lose in order to regain. At least, that's the perspective I was taking. "Losing" my job, and then Uncle John, had forced me to take notice and take action, even when I didn't know where it would lead. But I had always known it would bring me home. Jack needed that added element of finality in our romantic past before he could move on.

So with that behind us now, let the party resume.

* * *

Business was picking up, so to speak. A steady flow of townspeople was starting to stream in, including Tom and Ginny with the kids, and other longtimers I hadn't had the chance to catch up with yet. The band had segued from warm-up instrumentals to full-throated rocking Christmas numbers. Nothing thrilled me more than to see this old inn overcome with activity again.

Signs that the night had reached an unbridled pitch were illuminated when song requests snowballed into one guest vocalist after another taking their turn entertaining while the cheering crowd egged them on. Need I highlight the instigators by name? I am obligated, then, to mention myself among the all-female quartet of obvious suspects who took part in an improvised, racy version of "I Saw Mommy Kissing Santa Claus." Ad-libs and substitutions for "Mommy" and/or her actions in reference to dirty deeds, have been omitted from this account to protect the innocent—and the intoxicated, of course.

Let's just say, imaginations ran wild with microphone in hand in front of a raucous live audience. Thankfully, no children old enough to understand our salty lyrics were present. On a side note, I must say this reborn classic version of myself never acquired the taste for, nor apparently required the influence of alcohol when throwing inhibition to the wind. I attribute this increasing pattern of bold behavior to the part of me I had banished. Every single act of reinvigorated rebellion, of whimsical release, all that I had done since *I* took charge and *I* set this comeback in motion had Elles Garity of old written all over them.

The reality was starting to hit me that I could let loose. I could face adversity and the unknowns and roar instead of cringe. I could handle the bad with the good and not let one defeat the other. I wasn't all the way *there* yet, but I was still young. God willing and fingers firmly crossed, I had plenty of time. This party provided one more auspicious glimpse into the life I was reclaiming, renewing my roots in this reclusive sanctuary from the rest of the world. This night could drag on for days for all I cared. I was locked in and felt like I was surfing an endless wave of euphoria, not waiting for the next crash of misfortune but *daring* it to come.

Yes, I'm being dramatic. Maybe not so much *daring*. Let's take it down a notch or . . . ten. But hey, at least I'm learning how to take life in stride.

Shortly after midnight, after hours of fun and excitement, gifts exchanged, games played between new faces and old, the frenzy had faded. Platters and glassware were reduced to crumbs and emptiness, leftovers offered up for the taking. The band played themselves out and disbursed to the quiet comforts of any unoccupied bedrooms. Attendance had dwindled to a select few of us, the perfect accompaniment to end a long, eventful day, gathered in and around the intimate setting of the lobby lounge area.

"Think Katie's coming back down?" Loyal yawned.

"Doubtful," Ginny replied, cozied up at the end of one of the sofas. "I've spied her putting my kids to bed before. It's pretty sad. Her eyelids get heavy when she reads, and she ends up passing out before the storybook ends. You're sure it's okay if they stay, Elles? We didn't bring any other clothes. Tom can pick them up in the morning and get them to the daycare if you need—"

"I wouldn't dream of it. They can hang out here all day, just drop off what they need on your way to school."

"Auntie Elles . . ." Loyal sang.

"I'm still trying to get used to it myself," I added and looked over at Ginny with a glow. "Still trying to get used to a lot of things."

"Well, I for one am glad you have a sister. Not just for the obvious reasons, but now I know there's someone here who can keep an eye on your butt so I don't have to worry."

"Oh, *you* worry about *me*?"

"That's right. I'll say it. You need a role model."

"What?"

"Hey, I was always the older one who kept you out of trouble. Now you have a real older sister to take over for—"

"Oh, good lord. You might want to make an appointment

with yourself when you get home. Just . . . I don't know, lay on a couch in front of a mirror or something."

"Well, any trained professional, which I am, knows full well that in life and in nature in general, it's the older siblings' place to set an example for the younger ones. Ginny is older, therefore . . ."

"You're very wise," I admitted.

"Thank you."

"Need I remind you, I am also a trained professional and I think my *real* older sister, who is also, can back me up on the fact that common sense, as well as psychological behavior, plays a big part in which sibling sets the better example regardless of age—."

She may have had the fancier degree, but I had the background and experience with dealing with irrational, argumentative people who were much smaller but, like Loyal, also always thought they were smarter. Did I mention part of what made our friendship so unique was we loved to test each other? Out of nowhere, sometimes we would have these ridiculous little carried-away verbal battles. Every one of them was heated and vicious, like two apex predator offspring in the wild, willfully using each other to practice and sharpen our skills. Neither of us could ever pass up a good opportunity to slug it out with words. Maturity, age, and intellectual prowess had nothing to do with the outcome. One hundred percent of the time, the winner was determined by who cracked up laughing first.

"So bite me. Yeah, that's right. I've read a few of your textbooks . . . when I wasn't teaching an entire class of instigators. I used to deal with younger, immature versions of yourself every day. I could—"

"Do you guys bicker like this all the time, or is it purely for fun?"

We fired off contradicting answers.

"No."

"Yes! She's just— Wait a minute. You barely know Ginny

but you trust her to take care of me more than Katie?"

You could hear a pin drop in the room. I don't know if tiredness was a factor, but it was enough to spark Ginny's confused intrigue. "Sorry, am I in this now, or—"

"No offense," I cautioned. "It's just that the two of them hit it off like gangbusters right away. I would have thought she'd—"

"Oh, we're kindred, for sure." Loyal nodded smugly.

"Mm, two demented peas in a pod."

"Aww, don't be bitter now, Elles."

"Not at all. I'm glad you have each other, so there's someone watching over my investment."

"Ha! That's a good one. In fact, miss thing, I think I've got her talked into coming up for New Year's in a few weeks. Jack's got a single friend. See, but Ginny's . . . well she's more settled down. She's a mom. She's family oriented. Not that Katie couldn't keep you in line. She just, well she's more of a loose cannon still. Free wheelin', like me."

I watched Ginny roll her eyes and shake her head, exhaustedly entertained by our entire bout, as evidenced by a mumbling comment. "Oy, I've got some catching up to do."

I looked at Loyal much the same with a closing thought. "You do realize you just imploded your whole case with what you just said, right? Wait! New Year's? Katie didn't say anything to me about—"

"I'm stealing your friend," she taunted, just to gloat.

"What the hell's happening?" Ginny asked, befuddled, while Loyal moved on.

"So when's opening day, anyway?" Katie asked. "You throw a hell of a party. I can't wait for the grand opening."

"I'm still working on it. I have to get a photographer in to take pictures for ads, promotions, booking sites. I have to finish putting the meal plans and menus together still, stuff like that. I need to finalize a staff. There's so much to do. I already hired Bri, and if she can't afford a closer place to live then I might have to go with someone—"

"Why doesn't she just stay with Katie?" Ginny suggested.

"We don't have enough space. It's only a two bed—"

"You can stay with us or, better yet, move in with Mom. She would *love* that."

I looked around. "Where is she, by the way? I didn't see her leave."

Chapter 44

It took some extensive searching, but I found Dina in one of the guest rooms on the third floor. She was sitting in an armchair, in the dark, facing the ocean view out the window, deep in thought. I stood at the entrance studying her. I walked within her line of sight to the side of the bed and sat down.

"You should come downstairs. A few of us are still awake." Another extended moment and finally she flinched. She took a quick peak at me and pulled a tissue from her pocket. She folded it carefully and dabbed the corners of her eyes, sniffling. She took a deep breath and tucked the tissue away. "You wanna talk about it?"

"No, no, I was just . . . the party was loud. So I thought I'd take a break and . . ."

"Ya know, it's okay if . . . if you . . ."

"I'll bet you didn't know that this was her favorite room. I never really asked her why she chose this one except that it's on the top floor."

"I remember. Not this room specifically but . . . I know she liked staying in touch, helping clean rooms, checking them to make sure everything was how it should be."

"Yes, she did do that. She was better at stuff than me. I was always content to stay out of the way, do the office work, make sure the bills were paid, lights stayed on, weekly orders placed. Your mom, she was hands-on all the way, never stopped moving. In fact, the only time she liked being in the office was if it gave her an excuse to work late."

"But I remember her . . . she used to come home complaining about how she had to work late to—"

"All part of the act. Once in a while, she would let this room go empty, unreserved just for one night . . . just so she could enjoy this view before heading home. She would sit right here, in this chair, and just enjoy the peace and quiet at the end of a busy day."

"You still miss her a lot, don't you, Dina?"

"Of course I miss . . . I miss her. I miss your father. I miss the way things used to be. I miss the old days. You also remember the overnight trips they used to take, don't you?"

As soon as she said it, I put two and two together. "I do, yeah. When I slept over at Ginny—at your house because they wanted to get away for a—"

She had a gleam in her eye as it came on me. "Why leave? Why go anywhere else when they had the perfect rent-free staycation option right here? Your father would take the next day off of work or call out sick. They'd get an early start, stay here, and have breakfast in bed served. That was the one luxury they took advantage of, having the kitchen cater to them. Other than that, they blended in like any other guest, like they were John and Jane Daytripper. To them, roughing it meant changing it up now and then and staying down the street at the Shoreham House. After they ate, they would usually head to the beach, bring a picnic basket for lunch."

"Where they knew Ginny and I would never find them."

"Precisely. A needle in a haystack on the most crowded beach. Right where she could whet her appetite for meeting new people and fitting right in, all the while knowing you girls would rather find a less touristy beach to play on. We had the additional bedroom off the office but . . . oh, she loved waking up to this view in the summertime, strolling down the hall, smiling, and saying good morning to the guests just making small talk. *I* think she liked pretending she was one of them. She never ever wanted to take owning this place for granted. She wanted to remind herself to stop and appreciate everything they . . ."

I smiled and grunted out a laugh. "You and Stephen

never wanted to join them and—"

"Hell no! My outgoing kindness started and stopped at check-in and checkout. I loved the work, the location. Your mother was the people person. Why do you think I would track you two down sometimes and come armed with a beach chair, a book, and a bagful of snacks? Honestly, your mother and I were like . . . well separated at birth in some ways and worlds apart in others. Eh, who knows, maybe our differences kept us close."

"How did I not see it?" I scratched my head, running my fingers through my hair.

"See what?"

"Right through you. This . . . us . . . mother, daughter. You hated tourists like I hated—"

"No, now I never said hated. Without them we—"

"Dina . . . Mom." It just came out. Sitting there rambling on with her, starting to see and understand the ways in which we were alike. Getting to know her without prying or playing twenty questions or even trying. Just . . . talking. It was nice. It was unexpected. "You know what I mean."

She stood up out of her chair and neatened her outfit. "I'm sure I don't? You're probably right. We should go downstairs and—"

I put my hand down on the bed beside me and patted the comforter lightly telling her to sit. She hesitated then took the hint. "I, um, I know I'm starting to sound like a broken record but . . ."

"What's on your mind?"

"Why . . . why all of this? Why the smokescreen? Dina, the inn was never a ward of the town. There were never any buyers or bidders. Why? Why didn't you just—"

"I was scared."

"Scared of what? I—"

"Scared it would be too much for you, afraid you'd want no part of it, that you'd run away again. You were so quick to sell the house. I didn't know what your plan was."

"Oh, Dina." I sighed with dismay.

"Elles, I tried to keep it running for years, struggling with Stephen. Nobody could fill your mother's role or shoes around here. She was the face. I was the silent bookkeeper partner."

"You? Silent?" I nearly choked on my laughter.

"I'm sorry. I just . . . I know it was your mother's plan for you, but when I couldn't make it work without her and I tried to bring in a few investors to help run the day to day, they started demanding an ownership stake and . . ."

"Wait, my mother's plan for . . . She wanted me to have it? She wanted me to take over when . . ."

"You girls only ever wanted to teach. You had your minds made up. But she never gave up hoping the business would stay in the family. And then after . . . all the pressure was on me to . . . and I nearly lost it. If you hadn't shown up when you did, I might have sold it. I was so close, and I feel so guilty." This time it was Dina who broke down instead of me for once. I strapped my arm around her shoulder, and she leaned into me and gushed a decade-plus worth of heartache. She brought the tissue back out and it quickly became an oversaturated, useless wet rag. Her tears drew mine, and I had to redirect the questioning to somehow soften the moment.

"So, what if this whole thing went on as planned? You were just gonna let me hand the town a huge check for something I already owned? How was that even going to work?"

"Naturally, the town would have endorsed the check over to me and I would have—"

"Uh-huh . . . I'm waiting. You were going to . . . include a check for fifty thousand dollars in my birthday cards for the next—"

"Okay, detective, so I hadn't thought everything through thoroughly. I would have found a way to get you back the—"

"Stop. It's not about the money, Dina. I . . ." I started laughing thinking about Selectman Lafave's parting request to me in his office. "Paul can't stand you."

She started to laugh hard herself and sat up straight. "Paul . . . Lafave?"

"Oh, no, no, Paul. He insisted I call him Paul. Does he know that we're related yet? Because he is not a Carrington fan. I'm just saying. I run a business here now so . . ."

"Oh, Paul is a horse's ass. I should have known better than to trust him to keep a secret. Wait 'til I see him a—"

"Well, don't worry, I'm still on his good side. He put his trust in me for one thing, anyway, to keep you away from him."

"He—"

"Troublemaker."

Dina looked at me sideways with a wink. "Like mother, like daughter."

Mother and daughter was a phrase I was slowly starting to warm up to and accept little by little. It came at a time in my life when having a parent to lean on and learn from was still very much beneficial, someone to share the ups and downs with, someone just to talk to. It also came at a time when I was finally making peace with and, in some ways, still mourning the loss of the parents who raised me. It was a hard, conflicting period for me. Whenever I felt the stress of guilt or mixed emotions weighing on me, I shut it down by reminding myself how awfully hard this whole ordeal must have been, and still was, for Dina, as well. My parents were gone, and I was over feeling sad for the sake of feeling sad.

Two days later, after heavy consideration of Ginny's proposal and whole-hearted approval from Dina, we moved in together. Katie had a new roommate, and I had the beginning of an excitingly nervous new phase living with my . . . mother. Dina was gathering intel on my favorite foods and meals, even the most insignificant of my likes and dislikes, before all my belongings and family boxes were transported from Katie's place to hers. With Ginny's full support and blessing, the three of us spent a day unpacking, organizing, and unearthing the memories attached to the contents inside those boxes I had yet to dig into. It was like some strange tributary memorial service and promotional ceremony wrapped up in a transitioning from my old life to this fresh new reboot.

That move would mark the last change of address I would ever make. This house that Dina swapped for the one she raised Ginny in, the one her marriage shattered in, would be the one she grew old in. It would be the one she shared with me and my family, enjoying spending time with her four grandchildren. Eventually, it would be the house she spent her final years in, resting eternally, peacefully in the knowledge of her daughters forging a stronger, more unbreakable bond than two best friends could ever make. If there was a stitch of descension to be had it was this: the one dividing, tease-factor line in Ginny's and my relationship was in regards to who was Mom's favorite child. Since living with her wasn't always bright skies and butterflies, naturally I always assumed sacrifice gave me a saintly decisive upper hand in that contest. What fun is a realized sisterhood without a healthy smidgen of good old-fashioned, controversy-based sibling rivalry?

Chapter 45

"Knock, knock! Hello! Anyone home?" I called out, letting myself in through Katie's front door.

"In here!" Katie replied from my old bedroom, also occupied by Loyal and Brianna.

"Oh, it's a party and I wasn't invited." I cackled at them all.

"No, just giving Bri a little preview of the place, gotta conduct an in-person screening of new candidates, make sure potential replacements meet my strict expectations and standards of what an acceptable roommate should be, all that kinda—"

"Katie?"

"Hmm?"

"Please, drop the act. Really, you should probably just stop talking now before Bri changes her mind and I lose an employee."

"Hey, I *just* got used to sharing my house with someone, okay? I surprised myself when I brought you in. I liked having the companionship. Besides, I, uh . . . I wanna make sure I get a good one this time."

"Oh, uh-huh, okay. Well, I'm sure it will work out fine for everyone. And Bri, just remember, the couch in my office is a pull-out, just in case."

"Good to know. But I'm sure this will do. Seriously, I know you guys are just messing with each other, I think. But anyway, thank you both for helping me out. I can't wait to hire some movers and get all my stuff here."

"Hire? No way. It's the offseason. I'm sure we have some suitable muscle around here with nothing else to do, don't we, Elles?"

"Absolutely. I'm paying my people while they stay here and train. You're the boss, round up whoever you want, Reno, Marcus, Pedro—"

"Ahem," Katie interjected. "I said muscle."

"She's right, leave Pedro out. He's more of a looker than a lifter."

"Really? Well, let me get my coat. Speaking of training, I have to head to work, anyway. I'm sorry I'm late. We got caught up talking. Birdie's probably waiting for me to—"

"Don't be silly. You're here. Take the day off. Get better acquainted with your new housemate. I'll cover for ya. I just stopped in to look for Loyal. I thought we could get some brunch, hang out for your last day, just the two of us before you go back."

"Yeah, that'd be great. I might have to track down Jack first and let him know."

"Don't worry about Jack. I'm pretty sure the McComiskey boys offered to show him a good time today."

"Show him a good time?" Katie's initial laughter was a prelude to a more concerned question. "Oh, God. What are they gonna do to him?"

"Should . . . I be worried?" Loyal directed toward me.

"Well, um . . ." I looked past Loyal to Katie. "What do ya think?"

Loyal looked at me, then at Katie with nervous intrigue. Katie shrugged her shoulders at me. "I mean . . ." Katie began, to which I finished.

"Only if they made him sign a waiver, right?"

Loyal and Bri stared down one another, while Katie and I kept perfectly composed straight faces.

"They're not . . . They've gotta be screwing with us." Bri shriveled her face with undecided indifference.

I walked out of the room to complete the hoax while stirring Loyal's curiosity at the same time. "Come on! I know a place that serves a great breakfast platter pizza."

"Wait . . ." I could almost feel Loyal rolling her eyes at the both of us, begging for answers. "You guys *are* screwing with us. Is Jack gonna die? I'm sorry, did you say breakfast platter *pizza*? I'm sure he'll be fine."

I threw it in to prove how easily distracted Loyal's mind worked, especially when it came to something unexperienced or unheard of. I had no intention of taking her there or ordering anything so vile, let alone watching anyone eat it, not again. And honestly, neither I nor Katie had the slightest inkling of what they had in mind for Jack, only that the bit about signing a waiver wasn't the worst idea in the world considering what trouble could be found by those two brothers on a restless winter's day. Although, now that we had conspired to prank it up, suddenly I was picturing a snow-making machine, a sled full of gin and whiskey, unlawful dune diving and . . . I'm sure he'll be okay.

I took Loyal somewhere a little more peaceful and out of the way, to the airport diner instead. It stayed open year-round and, by now, had a more subdued atmosphere than Fiddler's Bar.

"So, you ready for all this?" Loyal asked, digging into her clam chowder starter.

"What? A whole new life, whole new career, change of scenery, not to mention, *surprise!* whole new family?"

"Well, any or all of that, but yeah."

"I'm nervous. Excited nervous, but . . ."

"You're gonna kill it."

"What makes you say that?"

"Look at you. Come on. I've never seen you so . . ."

"What, Loyal?" I blushed.

"Alive. So . . . ambitious." She dropped her spoon into her bowl and grinned with starry eyes. "So happy."

"I guess we both finally climbed out of the gutter, huh?"

"All right, well that's a little harsh but . . ." She nodded her head, iffy at first and then agreeingly. "I'll give you that. We could have done better for ourselves sooner."

"I wish you were doing this with me. I mean living here, right next door."

"Hmm, ya got an island shrink?"

"Nah, a lot of us are normal. The head cases and nutjobs here are harmless, eccentric, well-to-do misers or introverts. All they mostly want is to be left alone."

"Can't blame 'em there. Umm . . ." Loyal's eyes widened, looking through me. "Elles . . ."

"Yes?"

"This is an airport, correct?"

"Yeah. What's the matter?"

"Well, nothing, other than the giraffe strolling down the runway."

I turned to look and sighed. Sure enough. I called out to the help behind the counter. "Rainey! Better call Elam's Farm!"

He leaned across the counter to peek. "Shit! Again? I'm on it."

"What's mildly troubling is neither of you seem overly surprised."

"Also, let them know the McComiskey boys are at it again!"

"What the . . . ?" Loyal squawked.

"Kidding, I'm kidding. It's . . . We have wild nature preserves here, an exotic animal farm. They get bored and escape once in a while."

"I hate you so much. Holy crap. This guy wants to escape back to his motherland."

"You think that's something, wait 'til you see them try to wrangle it."

"Jesus, must be lookin' for one huge goddamn airplane. I can't wait to visit this place in the summer."

Chapter 46

For the next forty-five minutes, Loyal proceeded to munch down her side of fries while watching the capture, calling a play by play of the action like she was at a live sporting event. A team of vehicles arrived on scene and systematically surrounded the escapee. They boxed it in with precise maneuvering, like a well-trained recovery, escorting the docile giant into a caged-off trailer and drove off like business as usual. It was, in fact, another one of our quirky, everyday occurrences we were accustomed to. I must say, though, it was less entertaining than watching volunteers help lasso a stray zebra or llama gone AWOL from Elam's Farm over the years. Our luncheon conversation ran dry while Loyal bore witness to, and was enamored with, the situation at hand.

"Well, ya don't see that every day. What is summer like around here, a three-ringed circus?"

I cleared my throat to that loaded question. "Unfortunately, it has nothing to do with the animals, though. Those animals, anyway."

Loyal glared at me curiously as though a eureka moment flashed in her head. "You're really from here, huh? I mean, you . . . you know this place. That—" She raised her hand toward where the outdoor action had just taken place. "That's normal for you. I just sat here, eating my lunch, watching a damn suburban safari-convoy-cowboy thing, and you didn't blink an eye. This is . . . this is nuts, you're . . . you're not coming back, are you? I mean, I know you said, but I didn't think you were actually going to leave and . . ."

"Loyal . . ."

"I'm gonna miss you." She whimpered, displaying pouty lips and eyes.

"I'm gonna miss you, too."

"Look at this. I've been here for a week, and you've been busy, what, throwing a Christmas bash, building your friggin' family empire, having your staff cater to me and Jack while you're putting your life back together, which doesn't include me anymore, and I've hardly had time to spend with you."

I reached across the table and pinned my hand over hers. "Loyal, Loyal, get a grip." I chuckled. "This has *everything* to do with you. I'm not leaving you behind. You are welcome here any time you want to visit. You're like family to me, and that means you'll be like family to everyone else here the more you show your face and the more they get to know you."

"Really?"

"Yes! Loyal, I don't know what would've become of me if we hadn't met."

"Wow, so . . . so like, I saved your life?"

"Sure!" I fired back quickly and with a hint of sarcasm. Then I smiled with sincerity and love. "We saved each other, didn't we?"

She grinned back at me. "Yeah, we did, didn't we? And now you're trying to steal back your old flame."

"What?"

"Oh, please, Miss Innocent. I saw you kiss Jack at the party, buttering him up, making a move on my—"

"You're ridiculous."

"I want a lifetime, standing reservation."

"You got it."

"At least a week every summer with optional weekend holiday stays. And I don't want any ol' room."

"Play your cards right, I'll book you the honeymoon suite."

"Full room service?"

"Your feet will never touch the floor. I'll have shirtless, oiled-up men in Speedos carry you to and from the beach on a bedazzled surfboard."

"You're ridiculous." She mirrored back.

"I'm sorry we didn't get to hang out much this week."

"It's okay."

"We should go find your better half, so we can all hang out the rest of the day. The boys might have anointed him an honorary Irishman by now. He's around Mikey too long, he may develop a horribly stereotyped, bad accent."

"Hey, Elles?"

"Yeah?"

"What was that thing you said to me after Uncle John died?" I rattled my head, clueless. "Remember, when I found you at the park after his services? You took off, and I asked you where you were going. You said, to crash the car. It just stuck with me. I didn't know what you were trying to—"

"Philosophical."

"Huh?"

"Being on the wrong path of life, being lost, not knowing which exit to take, that kinda stuff."

"Go on."

"Okay, well don't overthink it. It's a metaphorical thing. It's like, all of a sudden, I knew what I had to do. I knew *what*, I just didn't know *how* to get there. I was scared, nervous, and looking for a way back home. That's why I went to the park in the first place, to think. Then you showed up trying to comfort me, and it hit me. The first time my life got wrecked, it was out of my control. So this time, I figured I had a choice. I could dillydally around, figure out the road I needed to be on, change lanes, waste time, procrastinate the whole thing into oblivion, or . . . wreck it myself this time, no excuses, newly paved road . . . leave myself no other option . . . crash the car."

"Wow! Oh, my that . . . that is deep. No that is good shit. That is . . . You *were* reading my textbooks."

"Oh, no, that's all me. I'm deeper than your shoes laying at the bottom of the pond, sweetheart."

"Oh, you're . . . You still owe me for those, by the way!"

"Can't believe you actually did that."

"Hey! I had to chase you down."

"Let's go."

She chased me again, out the diner door, unrelenting. "Seriously, though. I'm writing that shit down and using it. You can't stop me. People pay a lot of money to have their lives fixed by having people like me tell them that kind of . . ."

Chapter 47

Christmas came and went. I don't mean to sound blasé like it was just another day. It was more than that. It was more than I could've asked for given the path that brought me here. But there was no bounty of gifts given or exchanged on that holiest morning. It was talked about, discussed in brief. We all agreed that being together, having each other, as corny as it sounds, were all that any of us wanted. The week passed and Loyal made good on her New Year's plot to lure Katie away for a visit with her and Jack and an unnamed blind date. With the staff on leave to spend time with their families, I made the most of that opportunity myself, inserting and welcoming a displaced Floyd into the Garity-Carrington fold. Like me, he was a complicated victim, who no more deserved his descent into remorseful, bitter hell than I did.

In other, more appealing news, a mild winter had taken hold. The days, as they thankfully tend to do here in the interim of mass influx, were starting to drag. In the collective calm of the offseason, we exhale, we refresh, and we meditate in many ways. There are the smaller gatherings of social circles, the larger get-togethers, and the church parish potluck fundraising dinners. Believe me, I was all in for all of it, popcorn-flowing movie and game nights, Zen-like roaming on the empty nature trails, and reserved do-nothing nights, count me in. The low-key, laid-back, gloomy weather months, don't get me wrong, were amazing in that respect. But the highlight for me during that time was, by far, the anticipation of opening day and watching the reservation numbers take off and start to soar. This was happening. All other side drama issues to be settled were in the works to be dealt with.

My emotions had been trending in a dramatically

different direction for weeks now. I was still learning how to be that way, how to be *happy*, still learning how to not expect disaster. There's such an incredible contrast between being happy in order to survive day by day, robotically, stuck on high alert, and truly embracing the act of putting your heart out there again for the world to see. This whole business of losing a family, but wait, you had more you could have turned to, so now you know, and here they are, is unimaginable. They've been here all along. And by that, I mean my entire life, before tragedy, after, during my self-imposed exile. I've never been on a roller-coaster ride in the literal sense. You can ask me today, as I write these thoughts, about missing out on that experience, and I will tell you this: I *lived* that experience.

There were little ups and downs as a kid, normal stuff, certainly not the typical blueprint beginning of the ride. Then that big fall came, when I was on top of the world. And if you would like me to continue this soliloquy any further, it came down hard and fast and crashed—or I jumped off, I don't know. All I know is, there I was riding it again, in a different light, from horrified to recovered and out of my mind enjoying it. *Look Mom, no hands!* This was me, telling myself it was okay to enjoy it. I was managing my anger. I put that out there because I couldn't do battle with the part of me that wanted someone to pay for who I became. I could blame myself for running away. Others could hate that I left. We could pass that blame back and forth for truths untold, things unknown, all the things by which grudges were fueled, but someone *was* to blame. I get it. It was a delicate multilayered affair. It was tough to stomach *who* was to blame.

With learning to live and learning to love and be loved, all these good things, came learning to have the strength to face the real foe. I don't mean just standing there in his presence. I mean standing there and not letting rage rule the moment.

The question beckoned to me: how to deal with the other person who played a role in damn near obliterating me. In a testament to my mental growth, I didn't keep this bottled up. I went to Dina and Ginny, the other two infinitely involved with this relative dilemma. I understood their disdain for this man. Stephen had left his family. Dina had to let him go. Ginny refused to even speak his name. But the neutral space he had placed between him and me, from what little I remembered of him made him just a man, as good as a stranger to me. Their best advice to me was, don't do this with an angry, vengeful heart. As badly as he hurt those two, they didn't want this to be about *them*. They needed this to be about him and me. From my point of view, though, how could it be just about me? And this may sound cold to say, somewhat ironic, some might even claim hypocritical coming from me—Stephen Carrington betrayed us all.

* * *

"Hey! What the hell?" I yelped. Winter did not relent to spring without first spreading a few accumulating snowstorms along the way. Little did I know, entering the front door of the inn made me a sitting-duck target for a perfectly placed snowball shot, fired off so fast that I never saw it coming.

"Oh! I'm so sorry Miss Garity. I didn't expect you to be here. I thought you were Bri. She said you went off island to—"

"A few things there, Jonathan. First thing is, we're family here. So call me Miss Garity again and you're fired, okay? It's Elles. Second, I'm back and now covered in snow. I'm guessing if you mistook me for Bri, I might find her . . ."

"Around back maybe? I'm not really sure. She's a pretty good hider."

"Ah!"

"We were all a little bored inside so, she, um . . ."

"She did what any good manager would do." He looked at me peculiarly unsure where I was going with this. "She called you all outside for a good old-fashioned"—he started to cautiously nod his head— "teamwork-oriented exercise in . . ."

"S . . . um . . . snow removal?" he stammered

unconvincingly.

"Right!"

I grinned with false transparent ignorance. "Wait here. Don't move while I go find Bri and the others."

I don't know what it was that clicked in that moment. When that snowball hit me, something else did, too. The innocent playfulness of childhood, those days passed me by too quickly. I grew up too fast. The accelerated end of adolescence and my teenage years suffered. I wanted to blow off steam, too. I wanted to play, and the best part was that nobody except one person, Jonathan, knew I was now in the game. I snuck around the side of the building like a cunning cat looking to pounce. I squatted down for handfuls of snow until I packed a tightly rounded, double fist-sized projectile. Keeping my eyes peeled in either direction, I pinned my back flat against the side of the building and waited, listening.

At the first hint of a single step slowly taken, the affirming sound of compacting snow underfoot, I pivoted wildly, kicked back, and leaned into a hurling blind pitch. The dumb luck of my aim had me in stitches as Pedro stood not ten feet away in frozen shock. His ski-cap-wearing forehead took the brunt, the splatted remains covering his face and beard. His expression lent itself to that of a stunned deer. I couldn't take it. Caught up in the magnificence of my own clownery, I let my guard down. That's when hidden attackers sprang out from behind icy bunkers and garden features like stockpiled ammo-wielding ninjas. In all the likewise wintry wars I'd been a part of growing up here, this was without a shred of doubt, the greatest all-out, no-mercy, rapid-fire snowball fight of my freaking life.

When it was over, when we could laugh no harder nor lift an arm and swing any longer, pleas of truce and full surrender rang out. Everyone was soaked through to the skin, a cold-whipped infantry of underdressed, shivering casualties. We formed an exhausted, orderly line, battered and bantering, to the shelter inside. We shed our waterlogged shoes in an unpaired, puddled mess in the entryway and schlepped off to the comforts of warm showers and dry clothes. My entire body, every muscle, ached from a fury of fun. In the aftermath I lay, sprawled across the bed, in the room where Dina and I had our post-party talk. Ginny came in. I could barely lift my sore neck and head.

"What the hell happened to you?"

"Hey, what's up?" I muttered. They were the only words I had the energy to say.

"Uh, well, Mom's downstairs mopping up a small lake under a mountain of shoes, and it's like a ghost town in here."

I dragged myself backward, closer to the headboard, and propped the pillows behind my back. "Everyone's in their rooms. We were just doing a little team bonding, acting like a total bunch of grown-up children and . . . Oh, my God, you should have been here, Ginny."

"A real throwdown, huh?"

"We would have kicked ass, you and I, as a team. Ouch!"

She lay down beside me, grinning at the after effects of the tomfoolery. "Not all that old, yet not as young as you used to be. *Wah-wah.*"

"Oh, my God, it hurts. My back, it hurts so bad."

"Well, I guess I'll let you get some rest. We just dropped by to tell you the landscapers called back. They're on standby whenever the weather starts to cooperate and you're ready to spruce up outside. Birdie left the name and number of the exterior designer they used to use, too."

"That's awesome, thanks. I'll get all over that as soon as I can move. Anything else?"

"Well . . . Nah, you look tired. It's not important."

"Ginny, I'm incapacitated not unconscious—yet. Go ahead. What is it?"

"I just wanted to apologize."

"For what?"

"For when you showed up at the house that day. For slapping you. It's been on my mind for a while. I just haven't said any—"

"Ginny, it's fine. It's over with. I'm not holding it against you or anything. Why is this bothering you?"

"Because of why I did it."

I sat up a little more vertically and twisted my body as much as I could to face her. "Okay . . ."

"I don't know. I don't want to make things awkward between us or . . ."

"Ginny, you and I have been through it enough, haven't we? I think we sufficiently passed the awkward stage a long time ago. Whatever it is, you belted me pretty good, by the way. Matter of fact, maybe it's good you weren't here earlier. I'm either afraid of taking another shot from you or I owe you one."

"Probably the latter. Eh, I'd go with both."

"Oh, goody, something to look forward to. Sleep with one eye open."

"Please, I already do. Obviously, you've never spent a night alone in a house with my children."

"Mm, yes, the children. Revenge will be sweeter with Auntie Elles's little hired soldiers of fortune with me on the dark side."

"Okay, relax, Darth. It was one slap."

I leaned in closer, deepening my voice. "But you enjoyed it. I saw the pleasure in your eyes."

"That wasn't pleasure. It was . . . Oy, I think I'll go see if Mom needs any help."

"Ginny, talk."

"Okay, well, I think I swung at you because of Dad, not so much because of things between us."

"Ginny, you don't have to—"

"No, no, just let me . . . I haven't seen or spoken to him in years. Everything else he did for us, or to us, aside, I always felt like . . ."

"Like what?"

"Like you were his favorite. And I know, I know

that's . . . whatever. That doesn't matter now. He's out of the picture. It was hard back then, ya know, before I knew about me and you. One of the things that started making me suspicious was the way he would look at you. We would all be out on the boat or something, and now and then I would catch this indescribable look on his face when he would look at you. It was like he was somewhere else."

"According to what you guys have told me, I think we know what that was."

"I know but . . . and I didn't think much more of it then. Things got worse after you left."

"God, Ginny, I know I asked Dina this already, but did he ever hit—"

"No, he never laid a hand on me or Mom. He would've had to put the bottle down to do that. He, um, he was just distant, ya know, disengaged. It was like you were all that mattered. I wasn't even there, or just having me wasn't good enough. So maybe I was partly mad at you. Maybe if you were there, he would have loved us both. But I can't blame you either for—"

"Ginny, I'm sorry he did this to you, that he treated you that way. You're gonna make me cry, and I'm too sore to cry."

"I just, I wanted you to know that it wasn't you. You were standing there, and I think all I saw was him—or both of you."

"I mean, there's always hope. He may have felt it. You hit me hard enough for the both of us," I joked, somewhat.

Ginny blushed, embarrassed. She pushed up off the bed and onto her feet. "I don't know. I hate this. It's so stupid. I'm gonna let you get some rest."

"Hey, Ginny, do we, I mean, do you guys still have the boat?"

"Yeah, it's docked in the harbor. We haven't used it in a few years."

"Ginny?"

"Yeah?"

"You want me to"—I made a sweeping open-hand

motion with my hand—"relay the message when I see him?"

"Thanks. I appreciate the offer. You just say whatever you have to say."

Chapter 48

What to say to him indeed. Of all the manufactured scenarios I came up with, I never once imagined all roads converging at this one critical juncture. I sat inside at the airport waiting, making him come to me. The thaw was done, allusions of spring sifting through the air. As I watched the runway, my stomach a ball of anxious energy, exciting things were happening at the inn. A team of professionals was en route, scheduled to refurbish the exterior. Touch-ups were being facilitated by Dina and Birdie, deck refinishing, back garden area replanted, every single window cleaned crystal clear. I brought in the experts for those integral curb-appeal results to top it all off. The sign was the icing on the cake, the final stroke. I was going to be there for that.

Anxious, that I was, because I did and didn't want to do this. No, I'll clarify that. I did not want to be in this position to have the choice to do this. Damn him. Sitting there, alone with my thoughts, don't misconstrue me as predictable, falling on old habits again to get through. There was no ego here, no self-righteous *How could you?* speeches being prepared in my head. There was just a girl, a disappointed daughter, one side of the story in hand, wanting to hear his. I simply wanted to know why. I didn't consider myself his judge, just his lame justification as it would seem.

My God, there it was, a floating speck in the northern sky. This was getting real. My right leg started to involuntarily shake. I wanted to be sick. What would he have to say, the man who had made it unfathomably necessary for me to be here today, holding out for his sorry ass? I was already failing to approach this objectively. That was his cross to bear. I wasn't doing this for him. I was doing it for me and whatever came of it, then c'est la vie. The small plane circled 'round and swooped down for a landing. The hatch opened and a pinstripe-suited male figure emerged. From afar I couldn't even recognize if it was him. He held a cell phone to his ear, finishing a call. Another man stepped out onto the tarmac conferring with him, then climbed back aboard. He walked toward the diner. I didn't like his body language, his businessman-like walk. I was not some loose end he was trying to tie up to broker a deal. "Stay calm, Elles," I said out loud. Some old, nervous habits are here to stay.

It felt like a who'll-flinch-first standoff when he walked through the door. It certainly wasn't me. My back was to him, so I didn't catch his reaction to seeing me. I heard him come in and felt him pause, perhaps to take this moment in.

"Elles." He exhaled. To that I turned my head. He spread his arms. I was tempted. I turned away and stood my ground. He took his seat at the table.

"Um . . ." I cleared my throat and blinked, trying to disestablish a commitment to his gaze. "Thank you for coming, Stephen." I looked up and engaged direct eye contact when I spoke his name, an explicitly tactful work-around for calling him *Dad*. My way of informing him, there were no secrets, no incriminating details left dangling here. I could see the impression of shame woven deep within in his face that he was keeping in poor disguise. He bowed his head and pushed back in his chair, interlaced his fingers, and rested his forearms on the table looking up at me.

"You're so . . . grown-up."

"Twenty-seven." I added just to make the deadbeat-dad reminder exact. He had said a total of five words, and my intuition had him pegged.

"I, um, well, I guess you know that I'm . . . I wanted to call you so many times. I wanted to tell you about—"

"About . . ."

He winced and lowered his head again to take a breath.

Why was I getting the impression that he felt like *I* was the disappointment here? Because I wasn't throwing myself at him, shouting, *Daddy, Daddy!*? "Jesus, Elles, I'm your father. You asked me to come here and I—"

"To tell me about *what*?" I reasserted his unfinished thought. It took something extra in me to exude a modicum of kindness in my attitude and tone toward him.

"Well, about me. That I'm your father."

The strain in his voice swayed little sympathy from me. That said, I'm not completely heartless and my emotions were stronger than me. A single tear trickled down my face, grasping for whatever it was I had to say. His heart appeared to melt at the sight of my pain, at the admission of his. I found myself a hostage to my thoughts and how different this could have been. Then just as quick, I reminded myself of the mindless things he had done. I pulled that same crumpled-up notepaper from Floyd's place and slid it with my fingertips across the table. The mood changed. He looked but did not reach for it. I yanked any residual personal feelings for him back and toughened up. For this, he stumbled for appropriate words, something, anything, a goddamn plausible excuse for which I might have credited him an iota of forgiveness.

"Tell me why." I squealed with bated breath. I swear to the depths of my soul, he was either dismissive or offended that I presented him with it, that I expected him to answer for what that paper represented. The thing about the handwriting that I initially missed was that it was his. Stephen wrote my parents' names and address on that Post-it Note. For whatever reason, it called to me the night I threw it on the ground at Floyd's feet and inexplicably spotted the inconsistency before I retrieved it and left. Otherwise, I would have left it there as food for that evening's prevailing breeze. The longer I waited for sound to protrude from his defiant lips the more disgustedly impatient I grew. "How dare you even think of yourself as my father?"

"Elles, I didn't even know. I could barely think the night

before."

"Don't you try—"

"That's why I waited, to sleep it off."

"You don't get to play the victim." My voice got more stern.

"All I was trying to do was get home to see you, your sister, and your mother. That's all I wanted to—"

"Tell me what you did wrong."

"You've got to believe me. I didn't realize Floyd got on that plane. I was too . . . He should have never taken off without —"

"You're not blaming him for this." I grinded my teeth as I growled.

"It was a *mistake*! No one is to—"

"I don't care! I did not ask you here so that I could absolve you! I need you to explain to me what you did!"

"I got out of the plane! That's all I did. What else can I—"

"You were drunk."

"Yes! I tried to do the right—"

"And you let Floyd—"

"No! You want to hear it, then for God's sake, listen to what I'm trying to tell you. I offered him a lesson, that's all. It was an excuse to get back home."

"You wouldn't have needed excuses if you would have—"

"I didn't do it! I didn't even hear about the crash until the evening news. I got off the plane before Floyd got in. Yes, I was hungover. I got up and staggered out. He must have thought I was still inside."

I exhaled a vile sigh. "All because of me."

"Giving you away was the first mistake."

"No, it wasn't. That was you giving up on us. That's why my parents are dead. That's why Dina's happier in divorce, and that's why Ginny never wants to see you a—"

"*You're* here, though. You—"

"I'm . . . You think I called you here to—" Even if he hadn't cut me off, I doubt I could have repeated whatever putrid words were coming.

"Look, if things aren't working out for you here. I mean, too much history."

"Oh, my God." I wanted to strangle him with his own tie.

"I'd love for you to meet my wife. You can—"

"I don't want to *know* your wife. This . . . You're unbelievable," I moaned.

"Elles, there's still time for you and me."

"You make me sick." I gurgled from every part of my being.

"What do you want me to—"

"I haven't heard you accept responsibility yet."

His mouth dropped open in stumbling defense. "All I ever wanted was—"

"I don't give a shit what you wanted. That's all this has ever been about, isn't it? What *you* wanted. You egotistical son of a bitch. What *I* wanted, what I had, you took away. What I wanted now was for you to come here and give me something, apologize, show an ounce of fucking regret, some remorse."

"I apologize, Elles. Damn it, I apologize, okay? For letting you go, for —"

"God!" I turned away from him with gut-wrenching disbelief at what was transpiring here.

"It doesn't change that I'm your father."

It was quite possibly the most despicable thing he could have said. It infuriated me to no end. I'd already defined and made my distinction known. He burned that bridge. At least I know whom I got that trait from. That's the closest satisfaction he will get from me. I snatched the paper away and held it in his face. "Why did you write this? Hmm? Was it to make Floyd apologize or did you—"

"This is—"

"Shut up. You had your turn. I'm talking now. How many —" I crushed the paper into a ball with my fist and flung it at him hard. "How many people did you affect? Fifteen years of my *life!* You had time. You had all that time and you . . . you put Dina through hell, alienated your firstborn child. You left Floyd to wallow in his misery. And then there's me. You took my parents away. You! You put Floyd Gresham on that plane. I'm done. You can get back on yours." He raised the thumb of his clenched hand to his mouth and jammed his index knuckle in. "Goodbye Stephen. Don't come back here again."

He turned to notice Rainey, absorbedly engrossed behind the counter, and got up to leave without dispute. I stayed there to defuse and watched him go. He stopped at the foot of the hatch stairs and gave a half look back. So help me, I tried to keep my composure. I had gotten a vibe the very second I watched him exit that plane. I'm all for hearing both sides of any story, but there was already so much written in this one. He had a reputation to debunk with me. According to everything I had heard, this was his one shot and he screwed that up, too. I guess I had held out hope that some of what I had been told was far-fetched, at minimum an overreactive-obscured-by-close-personal-perception point of view. I had hoped he might provide more viable insight into why it all went down this way. I didn't come away with any great earth-shattering revelations, at least nothing good or that would ever remotely make me want to think of him as *Dad*. It saddens me to say, this preemptive answer-finding mission, before I settled up with Floyd, was a cruel enlightening bust.

Chapter 49

Dina and Ginny were both at the house when I got home. I would assume it was more for the moral support aspect than anything else since neither of them hounded me for information. The plane had been long gone by the time I left the diner. I stayed there chatting it up with Rainey until I had sufficiently simmered down. I let my "biological father" go that day, which by comparison and given his cavalier attitude, was one of the easiest hard things I've ever done. I'm sure I still showed some lingering signs of the toll it took on me but honestly, I felt liberated. He took something from me that was irreplaceable. He blew up all of our lives, and I shattered whatever impudent self-centered ideas he may have been clinging to where he and I were concerned. That neither brought me satisfaction nor, by any stretch of the imagination, evened up the score. It simply was what it was—over. I freed myself of the evil that had imprisoned Elles and created Grace, and as anyone who encountered me the rest of that day can attest, it propelled me into an emphatically happier place.

"Good morning, everyone!" A friendly chorus of reciprocation greeted me outside the inn. I couldn't wait to get there and see the progress. The three of us arrived, and there were workers everywhere and scaffolding up along the building face. I scooted inside ahead of Dina and Ginny to the front desk—and to Brianna's relief. "Looks like it's going well so far. What's the word?"

"Oh, thank God, you're here. It's a bit of a madhouse around here right now."

"I can see."

"Just give me one second to finish this and I'll get you up

to speed, so—"

"Oh, silly, silly girl, I'm not here to take charge."

"Oh . . ." A disheartened veil fell over her face. "But there's a *lot* going on right now, and I thought that you were—"

"Here with the calvary. Here come the other two troops now, see?"

"O . . . kay. So you're not gonna . . ."

"Help? Absolutely. We are here at your disposal." I relaxed hunched over the desk to put her mind at east. "Honestly, Bri, I had a very . . . mm . . . hostile morning."

"Oh, I'm sorry. I didn't . . ."

"Don't be. What's done is done. And all I wanna do right now is keep busy and unwind, all at the same time. Are ya with me?"

"I . . . guess?"

I smiled at her. "Bri, you look petrified. Relax. It looks like you've got everything under control. I'm here, Ginny, Dina. I'm sure Birdie is floating around here somewhere?"

"She's with the kitchen and wait staff. Floyd and some guy he brought in are working on the menu and recipes."

"Perfect. Ya see, you know more than me already. I'm not trying to be a hard-ass, Bri. I'm feeling great. This place looks great. I'm, *we* are happy to help, but I'm just not in an "in charge" mood right now. You're the boss, right?" I pointed at her proudly.

"Um, right . . ."

"*You* are the manager of the freakin' Garity House Inn, and you're killin' it! And today, we are your humble employees."

I may have been a teeny tiny bit of a hard-ass at first, in a happy-go-lucky, weird way. The residue of dealing with *him* was still fizzling out. I had full faith in Brianna's abilities, however. My fake pep talk became a real one then morphed into a cheerleading demonstration because the more I didn't think about *him* . . . Well, I guess he gave me something after all—a relentless drive. Insinuating that being here might not be working out for me, hinting at— Nope, not going there. While he was off remarrying, forgetting he ever had a past here, I was now doubling down on a future, running this inn, living my re-energized life on this island, and spending every free chance I had with the family *he* rejected—*my* family. I was getting downright giddy tooting Bri's horn and ass-kicking her confidence into gear. And as I hit a high note by reminding her of her position, Dina, Ginny, Bri, everyone within earshot —was pin-drop quiet, staring at me. I did a slow three-sixty with a shit-eating grin scoping out all of them and came back around to Bri.

"Say it with me." And together we did. *"I'm the manager of the freakin' Garity House Inn.* Damn straight you are."

"Are you . . . You sure you're okay?" she asked timidly.

I was better than okay. I felt like a weight had been lifted off my shoulders, and his name was—irrelevant. "Never better." I toned it down a bit. "Consider us under your command. You have three extra sets of hands. Put us to work. What can we do to help?"

"You can . . . Oh! The landscapers showed up short a few guys. You can help in the garden."

"Wow! You really took that power to heart, didn't ya? Stuck it right to me there, giving me the dirty job."

"I didn't mean to—"

"Bri, Bri, lesson number one. If you're gonna work for and with me, you're really gonna have to lighten up. Or, be tougher. Stick to your guns. Either way, I was kidding. Gardening. You want us to go gardening."

"Y-yes."

"Perfect." I started to walk in the other direction with Dina and Ginny in tow. "We'll be in the kitchen if you need us. I can't wait to see what's going on with the menus." I peeked back at the baffled look on Bri's face just to mess with her a little more. "Oh please, where'd ya think I was going? I'm the boss for cryin' out loud."

The three of us sat in a line along a stone wall plant enclosure, work gloves on, tiny shovels and rakes in hand. On our way, we had gone through the kitchen to show our faces and check in. This was a lazy working day for me. I was all too happy to relinquish complete authority into Bri's capable hands. Having been relegated to the nice sit-down task of digging up the old plants and replacing them with the new, we worked and talked at a leisurely sun-bathed pace.

"So, Miss Jubilee, how long do you intend to leave us in suspense?" Dina finally asked.

"What do you mean?"

"Elles Garity!" she scolded. "You came home looking fit to punch a hole through a brick wall, and all you can say is there's nothing much to say?"

"Hm, two names." I grinned at Ginny's observation. "Not really on my level yet. I've been on a three-name basis when she's miffed at me for years."

"She's hot on your heels," Dina warned.

"Punch a hole, hmm. Now see, I wasn't getting that. Were you getting that, Ginny?"

"Well, you certainly looked like you would have enjoyed doing so."

"Look, I understand if you guys are curious, naturally. I just didn't bring it up because I'm over it."

Dina stopped working and rested her arms. "Over it, just like that?"

"No, not just like that, but actually I'm with Ginny on this one. He's scum, not worth our time."

"Went that well, did it?"

"What did you ever see in him?" It was a thought that slipped out of my mouth.

"A different person."

"I just don't get it. Did giving me up for adoption—agreeing to it, I might add—mess him up that bad?"

She pondered that for a moment. "Steph—"

"Please, Dina, I'd rather not hear his name."

"He's a, what's the word . . . narcissistic man."

"You're telling me."

"He wasn't always that bad. It's what attracted me to him at first."

"You're kidding." Ginny sighed.

"It was a more subtle, charming quality then. He came off confident and going places."

"Yeah," I agreed. "He went places. He just neglected to bring the people he pretended to care about with him. How do you do it, Dina? How do you defend him after . . ."

"I don't know. I guess if I don't defend him a little, I feel like the fool for not seeing him for what he was from the beginning." Ginny and I sat up and stared at each other. "But, if you want the God's honest truth, I just can't find it in me to hate the man. We had two beautiful girls together, who have grown up to be amazing young women. I can't very well regret everything. What does that say about having you? And that is where the sentimental bullshit ends. He didn't start out like that. He was a hardworking, self-made, borderline arrogant man. Bottom of the barrel handsome, loving, decent man. I went for quality over looks. What can I say? I struck out."

Ginny and I kept planting while she carried on. "He showed his true colors. You said it best, an awful human being, not worthy of your time. You asked me what messed him up so badly. So here's my theory. I suspect he always had it in him. He was the type to always want what he couldn't have, if only to brag that he had it. He lived an average life, secretly admiring a lavish one. Since we seem to be in good-riddance agreement, don't kid yourself, Elles. In his weakest moment, he proved you were nothing more than a prize that belonged to him. He wanted it back, the shiny new trophy he helped gift away before he got to even open the box, show it off to the world then put it on a shelf."

"Too bad that wasn't half the man I sat down with today. No offense but if you're at all trying to endear him to us, that was a horrendous pitch."

"Amen," Ginny said.

"Now, if you both don't mind, no more about *he who from this day forth shall remain unspoken of*. Back to work. Put a wiggle in it, ladies. There's a garden to finish," Dina directed.

Staying true to that mantra, I don't believe any of us ever did mention *him* with any slight significance again.

Chapter 50

"Five, four, three . . ." At last, the countdown was on for the big reveal, the new sign was bolted into place, and everyone was gathered on the street out front for the unveiling. " . . . two, one!" With a tug of the ropes at either end, the concealing tarp dropped to the deck rooftop. Hoots, hollers, and whistles erupted along with a serenade of clapping hands. Dina on one side of me, Ginny on the other, they both leaned in, squeezing me into an Elles sandwich. *Happy tears* does not begin to describe my emotions. All of us who were there in physical form were joined by the spiritual presence of the ones who couldn't be with us. I could feel them looking on, the Garity name up there in big bold letters for the entire visiting world to see. I was overwhelmed, filled with a bubbling blend of satisfying, grievous, and tender pride. Dina kissed my cheek and gently assisted in drying my eyes as she whispered in my ear, "They would be so proud of you."

The reveal was bittersweet, a formal ceremony of unofficial opening status. The truth was, with Dina's help, we had reached into the inn's virtual vault of records, pulled out, dusted off, and gone through the old guestbooks. We identified and made a contact list of former repeat and annual patrons. From that we had sent out the first wave of discount invitations, enticing them to book their first stay. A few of them had already trickled in. I was looking forward to the results of another idea we brainstormed while I was settling into my new living arrangements.

I wanted to take my mother's connections with her guests to a deeper, more informative and connective level. We spent a day off the island shopping for journals, customized them to the inn and personalized each one further to the individual rooms and distributed them. I wanted to capture the essence of every visit in writing. I wanted to hear any stories they had to tell during their trip to the island, their feedback on accommodations, thoughts, concerns, suggestions, I wanted all of it, whatever they were willing to share, and no better guests to review our services than former frequent ones. Speaking of reviews, my next stop was the kitchen where Floyd had been hibernating for the past week, finalizing and perfecting the menus along with the "guy" I hadn't formally met yet.

"Floyd Gresham!" I called out before I turned the last corner.

"If it ain't Elles Garity, proprietor. 'Bout time you remembered where your bread is buttered. You like that?" They pointed and cackled to each other like they were co-hosting chef comedy jam. I like mine better, by the way.

"Well, I prefer to think of the room rentals as the—"

Floyd took me by the shoulders and led me to a bar stool, shooshing and sitting me down. "Now you just sit right down there and take notice." He held a plate out while his partner served up a sample and placed it in front of me. Floyd grabbed a fork and knife and lay them beside the plate. "You can have the credit for enticing them in the door for an expensive sleepover, but this, this right here is where you get 'em hooked. This is where you got one chance, let 'em take that first bite, watch their taste buds light up as they savor it, swallow, and say out loud, *Hot damn! Book me for the next ten years because this is the place!*

"Well, hell, Floyd, with passion like that, I might have to put your face on all the adver— Oh, my . . ."

"Uh-huh." He clapped his hands together and rubbed them, ecstatic.

"Oh, Floyd. This is amazing. I think you're getting better. Where did you learn to cook like this? And why aren't you head chef of some fancy five-star restaurant that I could never afford to sit at a table in?"

He positioned himself behind the other man and slapped his hands on his shoulders, grinning from ear to ear.

"Hello." I smiled politely, clueless as to his identity.

"Elles Garity, meet Mister Emanuel Sutton."

"You can call me Manny. Please to finally meet you, ma'am."

"Hello Manny. You *cannot* call me ma'am. It makes me feel ancient. Floyd, did we . . . Did I hire another . . ."

"This man right here is the genius. I am merely his extremely gifted, debonair apprentice."

I had to laugh, surprised by his glowing exuberance. "What's gotten into you, Floyd? I've never seen you so excited."

"Excited for you." He winced, propping a hand on the small of his back and trying to stay standing straight.

"Floyd, are—"

"Just a twinge. Never mind me, Elles. This is the man that is gonna have mouths watering from one side of this island to the next. This is *the* chef who can make The Garity House famous."

I polished off the sample and rested my chin on my knuckles for brief consideration. "I mean, how can I disagree? If he can cook like this . . . How do you guys know each other, exactly? You never—"

"We served together."

"Really? Floyd, you served in . . ."

"Oh, yeah, two years. You better believe it. The Dirty Dish Café, Bethesda, Maryland, waitstaff, service with a salute." He turned and split a high five with Manny and tried to pass off another wince.

"Okay, ya got me on that one."

Birdie came in dressed for a formal occasion and eyeballing my attire. "You're not even ready. What . . . Dina forgot to fill you in."

"Well, things have been a little hectic. Fill me in on what?"

"The business owners' assembly."

"The . . . That sounds frightening. I'm supposed to be going to this?"

"Well, unless you intend to oust yourself from the opportunity to take advantage of a wealth of experience and knowledge."

"I just . . . I don't know if I'm ready to—"

"To what, turn this potential into a thriving gold mine? Ready or not, how's it gonna look to the rest of us if you pass this up, and the new kid in town is the only one not there?"

"I see your point."

She took me by the hand and nudged me off my stool. "Well then, let's get a move on. We've got to stop home and get you dressed on the way."

I held off her pull long enough to address the passive elephant in the room and make a deciding stand. "We'll continue this. In fact, spread the word. Let the staff know, and have Bri set it up. Starting with breakfast, tomorrow's a taste-all-buffet day. And Floyd! Manny's hired on one condition—you get that back checked out."

Chapter 51

"So what is this business owners thing, anyway? I'm not gonna have to give a speech or anything . . ."

"Just a short one." I rolled my eyes at Birdie as she drove. "No speeches, it's not an awards banquet. It's a . . . it's more like a collaborative gathering. We get together in the spring and fall, discuss the tourism market, ya know, go over any concerns, strategies, and ideas for better, more effective public relations. We like to keep each other in check, make sure we're all on the same page, on the same team, that sort of stuff."

"Sounds interesting. Good, so I can sit at the back of the room, watch and listen, get a feel for the whole—"

"Oh, heavens, no. You'll be with me, there's no anonymity there. Besides, like I said, you're the new kid in town. There'll be a spotlight on you the minute you walk through the door."

"Excellent, I can hardly wait."

"Anyone that doesn't know you, is gonna want to. And the ones that do know you, well, the open house, that was a good introduction. But nobody's forgotten about the Garity family around here and what your folks meant to this community. Hell, your family will probably be the talk of the room all—"

"Turn around."

"What? We're almost—"

"Turn the car around, please? We have to go back. I can't do this by myself."

"By yourself? You're with—"

"That's not what I mean. Look, no disrespect but this thing sounds too important to leave out people who are as much a part of the history of this inn as I am. Drop me off and go. I'll be there. We'll be a little late, but if the Garitys and/ or Carringtons are gonna be the talk of the room, we might as well make a grand entrance while we're at it, right?"

When Birdie started talking about my family's legacy in this town, I knew what I had to do. This wasn't just about me and salvaging the Garity name anymore. Born a Carrington, adopted a Garity, the business of this inn that was taken on before I was ever conceived, it's all connected, tied together through me. How did it not hit me before now? Instead of asking myself if Dina wanted to be involved, I should have been saying that she earned and deserved every right to equal ownership, as did Ginny. That's why I went back, because if there was to be an owners' function then The Garity House would be a few representatives short.

That first meeting was one I will never forget. I saw a different side of Dina that day. I saw her let go of a lot of pain. I saw in her smiles, her laughter that of a woman reliving the glory days before devastation and years of interpersonal disintegrating discord. Ginny and I sat back and watched with the spotlight fittingly shining on her. She healed in some deep-seated ways before our eyes.

* * *

I took a walk by myself later that day. I drove out to the North Lighthouse lot, shed my shoes, and trekked barefoot down the flat, empty beach to watch the sunset. My mind drifted along the way, reflecting on the seasons of my life so far. I thought about my childhood, gazing out my bedroom window, fearless, untested, and running wild. I thought about Ginny and me playing hide and seek in the maze, a wooded seaside grid of trails a person could voluntarily get lost in for hours without a care. Then there was the time when we were banned from setting foot on Sterns Farm for making a game of setting his chickens free to race them through the field. For that stunt Dina sentenced us to a week's worth of assistant farmhand chores, a worthwhile punishment Ginny did repeatedly admit for selecting the fastest fowl.

As the sun dipped lower over the ocean and the sky faded a little dimmer, so, too, did the memories of the benchmark moments of my early adult life—my first boyfriend, sweet sixteen, learning to drive, graduations. At the time I had placed no greater importance on those accomplishments than on another heartbeat or breath of air. Now I could hear that resounding voice as sure as I heard my own: *You did that, Elles Garity. You survived. You made it through.* I needed to hear that from myself more than from anyone else. A little more, every day, I needed to know it was okay to finally live this life instead of only having it. The walk served my redeemed spirit well. By the time I reached the lighthouse I was drenched in inner peace. And I wasn't alone. Tom was sitting at the edge of the lighthouse's slab, feet in the sand. I hunkered down beside him, scooped up two handfuls of cool, dry sand, and let it sift through my fingers then brushed the rest away.

He peered upward in the sky and droned, "You ain't much of a search party, but I guess you'll have to do."

"Well, I hate to burst your bubble, but the only thing I was searchin' for is tranquility."

"Yeah, ain't we all." He snickered.

"Oh, come on, Tom. What could you possibly have to get away from, huh? Two rowdy, screamin' kids, a girlfriend and sister-in-law, or soon to be, with an exciting new lease on life?"

"Soon to be?"

I reaffirmed the innuendo with a head tilt and gleam in my eyes. It drew a hardy laugh out of Tom. "Oh, hell, Elles. Dina would shoot clear over the moon if that were to ever happen."

"So, what's stoppin' ya?"

"I don't know. I don't . . ." He looked away at the sun beginning to set and exhaled like a deflating balloon.

"What is it, Tom?" He reached into his jacket pocket, pulled out a small jewelry box, and held it out in front of him, staring at it, then looked at me. "Um, I don't wanna be rude, Tom, but this might, uh, this might put a kink in our relationship if you're about to—" He chuckled. "Is that what I think it is?" He nodded his head slowly and flipped the box open with a finger. I took it from his hands gently and studied it. "It's beautiful."

"Yeah, I been holdin' on to it for years. Never felt like the appropriate time." He rose to his feet and swiped the officer's hat off his head, slapping it to the ground. "Hell, Elles, I never wanted this."

"Never wanted . . ."

"This life on hold. This lousy, damn job. It's all right, I guess, but . . ."

"Tom, relax. You make a good living. Why did you become a police officer, then, if you—"

"I did it for her. Elles, you knew the younger me. I had no clue what I wanted to be back then, but lawman sure as hell never crossed my mind."

"I mean, it wouldn't have won you any *most-likely-to* awards in high school, that's for—"

"I'm serious, Elles."

"Well, you did it for Ginny. That's a good thing, right?"

"I did it to . . ."

"To what, Tom?"

He took his seat again to lay out his point. "When she fell for Cayle, it took everyone by surprise, I mean everyone. It was obvious she was just actin' out. And I wanted him to just . . . and then he did and I . . ."

"Thomas Deiter, what happened to him overseas is not your fault."

"I know that. Don't make the guilt go away for wishin' it on 'im, though. Before that, I was gonna go away to school again or somethin', get outta here, find a different place for me and move on. After he was out of the picture, though, I still had a chance, so I—"

"You got yourself a steady job to win her back. Look at

you, the hopeless romantic one."

"Hopeless, maybe."

"It's not hopeless, you fool. You got her. You got the ring. You got everything you—"

"I don't know what I wanna be, Elles. How am I supposed to propose, then lay somethin' on her like that after all this time?"

"You're asking me? Tom, I only ever wanted to be one thing, and I only did that because . . . well, because like you, I guess I put my life on hold. Now look at me. I'm one-third owner of a frickin' inn. Look at us! We're still young. You've got time, Tom. You've got some financial freedom, and you've got time."

"Yeah, I guess so."

"As for Ginny—" I snapped the box shut and handed it back to him. "Some things may not wait forever. A navy ship passes by here right now and you're in trouble, buddy."

"Yeah, you may be right about that."

"She's in a better place. She's happier. Another young stud in uniform, she's ready to rock and roll."

"Got it, Elles! You always enjoyed torturing me, ya know that? Hell, I remember one time you . . ."

Chapter 52

The previous summer had started with a piece-by-piece, unceremonious dismantling and subsequent reconstructing of the assumed life I was barely living. The next summer began, I like to think, before sunrise, with an amateur introduction to yoga on a cliff behind the southeast lighthouse.

"Is the blood supposed to be rushing to my face?" I inquired with slightly humorous concern.

"Ow! I think. What is this demonic position called again?" Katie griped with a strain in her tone.

"Adho Mukha Svanasana," Ginny promptly replied, sounding the most relaxed and tuned-in of the three of us out there on our mats under a purple and orange sky.

"Oh, yeah? What's that, Swahili for dog in heat, ready and waiting?" Katie grumbled while struggling to keep the pose.

"Downward Dog, Miss Nefarious."

"Yeah, well, whatever. What's the difference?"

"Katie, please don't make me laugh," I pleaded. "Both ends of my body are going numb as it is."

"Hey, she's your sister. I suggested lounge chairs and wine on the beach and listening to the waves, remember? Besides, she better come up with something new before this downward thing forces something upward, if you know what I mean."

"Oh, Katie! I specifically told you not to eat breakfast right before we did this," Ginny moaned.

Katie gave in, flopped to her stomach, and rolled onto her back with a huff and panting.

"And . . . relax," Ginny instructed. We both followed

Katie, twisted, and dropped to our mats, laid out.

"See, it's not so bad. What did I tell you guys? It's a nice, gentle—"

"Gentle?" Katie argued.

"It's a nice, *gentle* way to wake up, mind, body, spirit, all that. Good quality time, a positive way to start the day."

"Yeah, well—"

"No, she's right." I agreed. "It's just the first day. We just gotta give it a chance, get used to it. It'll be good for all of us, 'specially once I regain feeling in my arms and legs."

"Hey, Elles." Ginny turned to me, pivoting on her side. "Did you give any more thought to what we talked about last week?"

"About the . . . I don't know, Ginny. I'm still learning the business end of things. I don't wanna put too much on my plate right away."

"Yeah, but that's seasonal, and it only overlaps the less busy months."

"I admit it would be pretty cool, you and I, just like we planned."

"Exactly. And Mrs. Lawson could finally retire just like—"

"Like you always wanted?"

"Well, come on. I mean, what kind of authority-abusing, child hater tries to flunk a third grader?"

"In her defense, your handwriting was—"

"I was seven, okay?"

"Remember when M— Dina—"

"Threatened to quote, *vote her ass off the island* if she went through with it?" I went quiet for a few seconds. "Hey, what's wrong?"

"It's stupid. It's just hard, ya know, referring to her as Mom when talking about the past, us as kids. She was always Dina to me until now. Just makes me feel like I'm forgetting my own—"

"Hey, it's okay. I miss 'em, too. It's just something else ya gotta get used to now, that's all. Would ya look at this?" Ginny pointed across my body to a sound asleep and drooling Katie on my right. Ginny stood up and started folding her mat. "I don't know about you, but I'm starving."

I dashed to my feet as she started to walk away. "Whoa, hold on. Slow down. We can't just leave her here."

Ginny waved me on. "Ah, she already ate. Let the grouch sleep. She'll be fine. Look at her, that figure. She doesn't even try to work out. Meanwhile I'm still trying to lose baby weight. Ugh, she makes me sick."

"You're horrible." I laughed, trailing after her.

"She'll make a sexy backdrop when all the tourists come out and start wandering around. You comin'?"

Ginny raised a good point in that Katie wasn't exactly thrilled with the concept of a crack-of-dawn workout session to begin with. She looked so peaceful and comfortable, and waking her would most definitely have meant spending the next hour or so trying to enjoy our breakfasts while listening to Miss Morning Personality Defect sulk and complain about being talked into doing this with us in the first place. That, however, did not stop the guilt of leaving her behind from catching up with me. By the time we got back to the inn, I had texted her approximately five times, and she had finally replied with: YOU DITCHED ME?!!

By the time she caught up to us, we instead spent the latter half of breakfast subject to her coffee guzzling, stink-eyed, pouty silent treatment. Afterward, I had a quick shower, changed, and dropped the girls off at home. I drove slowly along the eastern edge of the island until I spotted Floyd fishing off his motorboat. I found a place on the shore where he could see me. I raised my arm over my head and signaled his attention with an air horn and a bring-it-in, gesturing wave. I caught up with him at the boat launch.

"If you're houndin' me for the dinner special, I ain't barely had time to cast a line, let alone catch it!" he shouted over the noise of the idling engine.

"I thought you might like some company, if you got an

extra pole."

"Always carry extra equipment, but fishin's about a whole lot of peace and quiet and patience." He raised his eyebrows at me with an insinuating air of accusation to the contrary, to which I just smiled.

"I'll do my best."

He extended a hand and, in true gentlemanly fashion, proceeded to carefully help me climb in. Once firmly aboard on my feet, he traded chivalry for trickery and his own general amusement. Call it a lesson in boating 101. He gunned the engine without warning and watched as I was thrown backward into my seat, grasping at anything to catch my fall.

Chapter 53

"So, this is it? We just sit out here for hours waiting? Wishing and hoping, huh?"

"Well, you could try *here fishy, fishy*, but it very rarely works."

"Good one, Floyd. I didn't really invite myself out here to fish."

"You don't say."

"Yeah, I guess you figured that out already, huh?"

"Can't say it's a shocking development, if that's what you mean."

"I, um, I had a visit with a former employer of yours a few weeks ago." To that he had nothing to say. "It, uh, it went about as well as anyone, including myself, expected." Still, not a peep or break in concentration. I put my pole down and turned in my chair. "I owe you an apology."

"You don't owe me a—"

"I do, and I'm *so* sorry, for what he did to you, what *I* did to you."

Then he looked at me remorsefully. "It's water under the bridge."

"No, no it's not. I appreciate you saying that—"

"Elles—"

"But it's not. There is absolutely no earthly excuse for what he put you through, for not admitting that what happened was his fault, and—"

"I know you ain't mad at me. I always blamed myself, true or not. The only thing that matters to me now is whether or not you—"

"I am." Just then, I realized it. All this time I took to sort it all out, work through my feelings and find where Floyd and

I stood, that one aspect escaped me. He looked as surprised as I when I corrected him on it. "I *am* mad at you, Floyd. Maybe . . . I don't know, maybe that's why it took me this long to bring it up. I've been confused as hell about who to be mad at and why. But you, you knew where I was all along, didn't you?" His eyes sunk back, and his face went flush. I truly felt for this man, but if we were going to get right again, I had to let it all out. "Just like he did. I was gone before you even woke up in recovery. Nobody knew if I'd ever come back. I didn't even know I'd ever come back, Floyd. So here I am, learning how to be the me that I used to be, and I find out that the entire time, all of this, everything I was running from could have been avoided. And you all just let me. And *you* . . . just let me?"

He could barely speak, tripping over his words. "Elles, I . . . I don't know what to say."

The strange thing was Floyd wasn't even family, and I never spoke so passionately about anything, or to anyone, in my life like I was pouring my soul out to him on that boat. He wasn't family in the literal sense, and I don't have the words to describe how he was more than a friend. He was just a victim, like me. Repairing our relationship meant he had to hear, and he had to feel and understand everything that I felt—the good, the bad, the indescribable, the incredible.

"Look at me, Floyd. Please look at me. I didn't understand any of this, none of it, until I confronted him. I hoped I was wrong. God help me, I wanted to be wrong about him. But he sat there, smug and cocky, and confirmed every damn fear that I had. He's a coward, a gutless, pathetic monster who tried to drink away his own inadequacies, stroke his own ego, and ruin the rest of us along the way. I *was* mad at you, Floyd. I was mad that you let him tear you down, mad that you hung around here all these years wasting your life away waiting for someone to return who never intended to, just so you could—"

"Find a way to make it up to you."

I lunged out of my chair and threw my arms around him,

squeezing tight and cried with him. "I *was* mad. I understand why you stayed, and it means the world that you did that for me. But you listen to me, Floyd Gresham. You don't owe me a thing, not a single thing." I pulled back and sat down again, both of us wiping our faces. "Do you hear me? It's *over*. Elles Garity is home. And you're done wasting your life. Do you hear me?"

He shook his head. "No better place I'd rather waste it than here."

"Ya know, until the accident, I never left this island for more than a day. Maybe some things happen for a reason. Maybe I had to leave to really appreciate it. I never would have met Loyal or Jack otherwise. But some people and some acts I can't forgive. I guess all we can really do is be lucky or smart enough to find the good within the bad."

"I'm startin' to wonder why I was ever worried about you. You were gonna find a way back with or without me, Elles Garity. You are deeply wise beyond your years, living proof that adversity builds character."

"Thank you, Floyd. That means a lot."

"Now, is it my damn turn?" I laughed at his honesty. "Scarin' all my fish away and I can't even get a word in edgewise."

"Oh, please. I don't know what more I can take."

"Unless you feelin' like swimmin' you gonna sit there and hear what I gotta say."

"You're right. You're right, Floyd. Let's hear it."

"And you're right . . . about damn near everything. Ya know, to this day, I don't even know how I survived. Some mechanical malfunction, I didn't know what to do. I ain't had enough lessons to that point, not enough for no impromptu solo flight, that's for sure. Comin' in like some out-of-control bat out of hell, panickin'. Looked over my shoulder to wake his ass up in the back and . . . Last thing I remember thinkin' was that son of a bitch chickened out. You know why he wanted to come that day? He scored some big contract, biggest professional accomplishment of his life. All I was, was a low-level intern tryin' to climb that ladder. He and I hit it off, started pallin' around town. He was proud of himself. The whole team was excited, wanted to celebrate, go out, party. Not him. Went into his office, poured himself a glass, and started settin' his sights on more victories before the ink was dry on that one. He loved Dina, of that, and believe me when I say, I have no doubt. He couldn't lose. He just couldn't stand to lose. And one win wasn't enough. He was bent on one more."

"He wanted them back."

"I don't know what the hell he wanted. I don't know what he thought was gonna happen different. I was just foolish enough to ride along with him. I just thought he was in the back, just sleepin' it off. 'Til that engine lost power, it wasn't no ride along no more. It was just me, barrelin'towards the ground faster than I could think."

"So, then how did you . . ."

"Wish I could tell you. Wish I knew myself. Said it yourself, maybe some things are meant to happen. Maybe I was s'posed to make sure you were okay. That's all I got for ya. That's all I ever came up with. What you call wastin' my life, I call bein' sick and tired of being told how lucky I was to still be alive, every minute of every day wonderin' what I coulda done different to stop it, kept everyone alive."

"Like I said, it's over now. No more wondering, no more *what-ifs*. I had a family, and I have one again. Not many people get that chance. I won't let anyone, or anything, screw it up this time. That includes you, Floyd. Consider yourself family."

"I appreciate that."

"So what are we doing sittin' here letting dinner get—" I no sooner turned to reach down for my fishing pole and suddenly the fish weren't the only thing eluding us. For the record, I was the only one who caught a fish—too bad it hooked and dragged the pole with it before I could react. "Away. Oops."

"Oops?"

"I'll buy you a—"

"That was a three-hundred-dollar, handcrafted work of —"

"Three hundred?!"

"Yes!"

"What the hell ya fishin' for, gold-plated bass?"

"Oh, lord! Shoulda left your fumblin' behind on solid ground."

Chapter 54

What more can I say about this life of mine that has endured a marathon of emotional scars, that has run the gamut of love, loss, rebirth, ups and downs before age twenty-eight? I said from the start this was not a comeback story, because it is mine to define. This is, therefore, my chronicle of survival.

"Welcome to The Garity House, checking in?"

"Yes, reservations for two, under Lydon."

"Ryan, 212 is requesting extra pillows. And could you have someone deliver a luggage caddy to the family in 106 for checkout? Thank you."

I spent most of my time that summer tending to and/or overseeing daily activities at the inn while Dina eased back into a semi-involved role to help make our first season go as smoothly as possible. These century-old wooden bones have held up formidably over the decades, but as Dina and Birdie both stressed, it does command a great deal of vigilance and TLC, a fact echoed in the few glitches and inconveniences we navigated.

"Bri! Where's . . . Oh, Bri, can you see if you can get ahold of Oscar to deal with—"

"The backed-up plumbing in 114? All taken care of, Elles. I believe he ran over to Floyd's place to salvage some tools or parts from his stockpile."

"Perfect. You're the best. The Corianos went hiking for the day, so let's make sure that's resolved by the time they get back."

"You got it. Oh, and some guy named Marcus called and left a message earlier about consulting work."

"Yes, he's that publicity and marketing resource through one of Dina's old contacts that she reached out to. Ya know, to help teach Pedro and Reno some of the ins and outs of—"

"Oh, right! I remember now. Sorry, it's been a busy season."

"Not a problem. Give him a call back when you get a chance. See what he's willing and available to do. Offer him the VIP suite, on us of course. Unfortunately, we missed the window for this year's top entertainment, but I want to get a jump on looking into things like concert and other event sponsorships around the island for next season and beyond."

"Okay, um, we have a VIP . . . ?"

"Otherwise known as my room away from home by the office. If we can get him out here this summer, I'll sweeten it up with whatever amenities I can to seal the deal. I'll leave that detective work to you. Be discrete."

Those were the typical learning curves and challenges we pulled together on and sought to overcome. As summer went on, tougher tests and harder situations came up, but they paled in comparison to the unseen complexities of family relations. Sharing the same house with Dina made it easier for us. We stumbled into meaningful little talks over meals, with subject matter that slowly sealed a deeper mother-daughter connection. That didn't mean it wasn't weird at times. It wasn't like with Uncle John and Aunt Nellie. I never thought of them as parents for obvious reasons. On the other hand, biologically speaking, it took a lot of strong-mindedness to keep reminding myself of who Dina was. How I addressed her was key. Even though she left it up to me and whatever I felt comfortable with, I quickly figured out that *Dina* just wasn't going to work. She wasn't that person anymore, the mother of my best friend who was *like* a second mother. Often, I had to squash the internal phony notion that *she* was the adopted mom. I understand why she did what she did. But for the life of me, when I think of the battles she must have fought through in her head, I can't imagine having been in her shoes, resisting natural motherly temptations. The thought of it, that I can't stand to entertain, always gives me goosebumps.

As I said, she and I, that was the easy part, if you want to call it that. Ginny's and my mending was a more strenuous one. Treading lightly and staying aware of potential potholes and the constant threat of land mines and ticking time bombs, the deep-seated issues and hurdles neither of us had overcome yet—those were the dangerous underlying hitches we had to stay mindful of. That was no more true than in mid-July, when Loyal and Jack arrived for a week's vacation. To all outward appearances, Ginny and Loyal got along. In my defense, I was too busy being pulled in seven different directions at once, keeping up with the demands of my world, to give more attention to one or the other or, more importantly, to stop and notice if I was.

One of my fondest memories of that summer, because of how it played out so comically, was spending the day with the three of them, without a clue as to what any of us wanted to do beyond steering clear of the infesting mobs. The perfect outing came to me over drinks and a game of pool at Fiddler's that afternoon.

"Three-ball, side pocket," Jack declared, steadying his stance and locking in on his aim. With the snap of his cue, the ball ripped across the table into the hole. "Bam! I can't be stopped. You all better come up with a new plan for somethin' else to do. Can't be much fun for you, watching me clear this table like a sharpshooter."

"Settle down, Annie Oakley. You made three lucky shots in a row," Loyal moaned.

"You just call me a woman?"

"Whatever, I don't know any famous . . . poolers? I dunno."

Jack stood up straight, looking up in thought. "I don't think that's what they're—"

"I don't care! Come on, Elles. There must be *something*

better we can do than sit around watching Jack play with his —"

"Woah!" Jack bellowed.

"Someone had to say it."

"I've got it!" I jumped up out of my chair at the table. "Harwood's."

"Hey, that would be fun." Ginny spoke up. "I haven't done that since we were kids. But there's no way on such short notice. They're probably booked solid for the next—"

"They don't take all the horses out at once. They do it in smaller groups," I argued.

"Um, horses?" Loyal questioned.

"That's true, and we've ridden enough. It's like riding a bike," Ginny added.

"Are bikes an option? Because . . ." Loyal continued to timidly try and talk us out of it, while Ginny strengthened the plan.

"I mean, they've got those horses trail trained, so we don't even need instructors."

"Jack?" Loyal looked to him for a voice of reason. "Did you want to—"

"Hold, hold on. Okay, you want us all to go horseback riding?" he asked.

"It's perfect. The trails are off the beaten path. Oh, and they go along a rocky beach that can't be used for anything else. So it's nice and quiet." I continued to sell it.

The nervous terror all over Loyal's face was evident. She kept staring at Jack, praying he'd find a way to squirm them both out of the whole idea. "I . . . I don't think this is a good idea, especially without instructors. Neither of us have ever been on a—"

I took the cue stick out of Jack's hands carefully and handed it off behind my back to Ginny who hung it back in the rack on the wall. "You've got us. Don't worry. It'll be fun." Loyal picked up her glass of wine and downed what was left of it, while Jack made one last plea. "Yeah, but . . . but I was about to win, and—"

"Oh, Jack, no . . . No you weren't," I informed him. "Katie's a shark." He looked at her.

"It's true," she confessed.

"She was just waiting to pounce on your first missed shot. See, um, some of us kids used to sneak down here, ya know, after hours, and play. Katie's the pro pooler around here, never lost a game." Katie and I started for the door, flanking Jack as I took him by the arm. "Come on. It'll be fun. I promise." Loyal followed, begging our attention.

"Guys, can we take a vote or . . . Maybe a nice walk?"

Chapter 55

Unlike the McComiskeys, Tom, and some of his friends, the Harwood boys were always easier to sway. After pulling the carriage out of retirement, I was able to sweet-talk our own self-guided trail ride out of them, provided I saw to it the horses we used were groomed, fed, and ready for the next group of riders. We gathered some fruit and veggies from the feed storage boxes so Ginny and I could spend some time warming up Loyal and Jack to the whole idea of their first ride. We let the two of them choose their favorites and, one at a time, brought them out of their stalls into the middle alley of the stable for introductions and brief instructional lessons. I recognized Loyal's horse as one of the senior members of the Harwoods' herd. She was in luck. He was the one who knew these trails the best and hardly required any manual prodding.To help calm her nerves, I let Loyal help me and gave her and Jack both a hands-on, all-points demonstration of how to harness and saddle their respective beasts

"Um, Elles, I think mine is hungry. I think he's about to eat my shoelaces. Ah! Oh . . . my God, he's licking me!"

I tried to hold back my laughter. "Relax, Loyal. Here, give him some celery. His name is Major . . . I think. He looks familiar. And he's not trying to eat you, ya goofball. That's just their way of getting to know you, checking if they know you, or get a feel for who you've been around."

"Oh, wonderful, my reputation with him is already shot."

"Oh!" Ginny stifled Loyal. "We don't say the *s-h-o-t* word around these guys. Especially him. He's getting up there in age and it's almost time to . . ."

"To . . . what?" Loyal's eyes bulged.

Ginny!" I scowled.

"Ya know, the ol' *take 'em behind the woodshed and . . .*"

Suddenly Loyal's fears of riding were back seat to her horse's mortality. I had to stop the horror story before she started to believe Ginny's lies.

"Don't listen to her. What's wrong with you? She's just messing with you. Now, come over here, take this brush, and I'll show you how to get him all prettied up." A brief tutorial on simple commands and we were ready to mount up for a test walk up and down the aisle before heading out. I had Jack stand on the other side of Loyal's horse to assist her in getting both feet secured in place once she was on.

"Okay, nothing to it. You're gonna put your foot in the stirrup, steady yourself, reach up and grab the knob of the saddle, push off, swing your other leg over, and you're on. Got it?"

"Um, yeah. Isn't there like . . . some kind of ladder we can just wheel over, and I can just—"

"Loyal, it's a horse, not a swimming pool."

"Swimming! Now, that's a great idea. We brought suits. We can go back and change—"

"I promise you, Loyal, these guys know the routine. It's what they were bred to do. This is gonna be fun, you'll see. Okay, ready? I'll hold on to you."

She tiptoed cautiously over beside me, whimpering softly. "O-kay, good boy. She's making me do this."

"Okay, Jack, you ready?" I double-checked.

"Ready for . . ."

"When she brings her other leg over, hold the stirrup still so she can slide her foot in nice and snug. Okay, Loyal, foot in. Okay now, that's it, grab the . . . There you go, now on the count of three, ready? She got a little bounce in her step, ready to hoist herself up, and I held my hands on her hips to give her extra leverage. "One"—she started to hum intensely—"two"—her bounce grew quicker and higher—"Three—"

"Hey, wait! Check the—" Ginny started blurting out a

warning cry—a second too late.

For my own peace of mind, I consider this my retroactive verbal waiver. I had no prior knowledge that anything bad was about to transpire. Furthermore, please the conscience court, familiar looking or not, I experienced no other memory-jogging insight that would have allowed me to stop — Oh, forget it. This wasn't my fault! What happened next was a thing of unexpected, laugh-rioting, heart-stopping, it-could-only-happen-to-Loyal calamity. To her credit, and my astonishment, she executed her mount by the book. She propelled herself upward and, in the same motion, lifted and swung her leg over and . . . vanished out of sight, saddle, and all. Good thing Jack was in position and waiting with catlike reflexes on the spot. Loyal's momentum appeared to take her up and over and off, into Jack's unsuspecting arms, breaking her fall to the floor. I stood there with both hands over my mouth, heart nearly thrust out of my chest for that hesitation before Loyal exclaimed.

"Holy shit!"

The saddle wasn't really gone. That is, it hadn't fallen off along with Loyal. It was still attached, sitting sideways. It was at that moment I realized what Ginny was trying to say. This was vintage Major at his finest. I started to laugh hysterically through my fingers, hunched over. Loyal sprung out of Jack's arms onto her feet and stumbled around the front end of the horse, who stood there stout, like nothing had gone wrong, which only made what I knew even funnier.

"What the f—" Loyal gawked at me, looking like she was about to crumble to the ground or pass out. "What the hell was that?"

I looked over at Ginny, who was as red-faced, amused, and scared shitless as I was. Jack barely laid hands on the back of Loyal's shoulders, and she swatted him away in her fractured discomposure. She was just lucky that was all that was fractured. Once I was able to gather myself, catch my breath, and withstand her death stare, I started to explain.

"I'm sorry. I'm . . . That was—"

"What's so goddamn funny?" she squawked.

"It's just . . ." I reeled it in, patting my chest and taking one more deep breath in and out." Loyal, I'm . . . I totally forgot what a prankster Major can be to—"

"Oh, great, ya hooked me up with a horse with a sense of humor."

"No, it's not—You chose him. Look, horses can have a warped sense of—"

"Ya think?"

"No, see, what I mean is—"

"He tricked you," Ginny jumped in.

"What?" Loyal asked.

"Well, what he did was, when Elles put the saddle on, Major held his breath. He waited for her to get the saddle on and all tightened up, and then he exhaled."

"So . . ."

"Well, that made the saddle loose. So when you hoisted yourself on up, you— He used to try to pull the same thing on all the newbies. Or he still does. I—"

"Oh! How lovely, I picked a homicidal, four-legged, hoofed, two-ton psycho, who tried to murder me for his own amusement."

The air fell deafly silent with her statement of conviction, as we all took turns glaring at one another back and forth. Loyal was still catching her own breath, seemingly waiting for some acceptable response from me. All I could offer was to studder another laugh through clenched lips and shake my head.

"He's just a horse."

In a strange way, that little incident shook the jitters loose for Loyal. I guess she figured the worst had happened already—thrown off before the horse left the barn. So what more could go wrong? After she walked off the soreness, she pierced a determined stare through Major's eyes and into his soul, as if to say, *How dare you toss me? You're getting ridden whether you damn well like it or not.*

"Isn't it beautiful Jack?" Loyal shouted out, taking in the beach view as they rode side by side. Then she tilted her head back at me as I brought up the rear. "I would have learned to ride a long time ago if I knew they had self-driving ones!" she joked.

"Yeah, just keep your feet still please.Who knows what else he's got in mind. If he even gets a hint of you digging in with your heels, he may start galloping off—"

"Not a chance! He's had his fun. I'm in charge now!"

"Just pay attention, will ya? We should have switched horses like I—"

"No need! I'm a trained professional! I'm in his head! Don't mind us! We're workin' stuff out!"

"Great! Now she's a horse shrink!" Jack hollered.

"Well, she's not totally wrong! One of them is working stuff out! And I think my horse just stepped in it!" I remarked.

"Ha ha! All part of the cleansing process! I'm friggin' amazing!"

"Oh, for the love of . . . Jack!" I called to him over the steady warm breeze.

"Yeah?"

"When she fell, you caught her clean, right? You sure she didn't crack her head?"

"No! I'm pretty sure it was cracked already!"

Amid the conversation, I noticed Ginny had fallen behind. Upon glancing back, I noticed she was taking a slower pace, and she appeared to be spaced out as we rode. I signaled my horse to stop and take a few steps back, letting Ginny catch up.

"What's wrong, Ginny?"

"Huh? Oh, I don't know, it's—"

"What? You look like you're seeing a ghost."

"Maybe I am."

"Okay, you're gonna have to gimme a little more. Did I . . . do something or . . . ?" There was no reply. She just kept gazing in the distance at Loyal and Jack, chatting it up down the beach, getting farther away. Ginny, you look like you're about to burst into—"

"It's just . . . I'm watching you guys, ya know? You and Loyal, back and forth. And I like her and all. She seems really . . . really . . ." It hadn't even occurred to me before then. I had two best friends, separately, at two very different and distinct points in my life. I hadn't taken into account the hurt that might put on Ginny, the feelings she was having now, until she made it clear. "We used to be that way."

"Ginny, I'm here. What's going on? Where's this coming from? I didn't—"

"I mean, I may not have much right to— I'm a hypocrite. So sue me, okay?"

"What are you talking a—"

"You found a new best friend. Katie and I got closer. I'm no better than you. I get it, but—"

"You're jealous, aren't you?"

"I am not—"

"I didn't mean . . . Ginny, it's okay." I pulled the reins and stopped. She did, too. I got off my horse and heard Loyal yelling back at us. I waved her on and waited for Ginny to dismount. "Come here." I put my arm around her, and we stepped over the rocks to a sandy clearing at the water's edge. "Talk to me."

"I don't know. It's stupid. I feel like I've been replaced. The way you two get along and . . . I just feel like I don't belong or left out of something. I don't know. I hate this. I'm trying not to . . ."

I reached over and dried the dampness under her eyes with the end of my sleeve. "Hey." She looked at me, tremoring with emotion. "I'm sorry. I didn't know this was bothering you. Ginny, you and I have something Loyal and I will never have."

She rested her head on my shoulder and sucked back the feelings. "I'm the one who's sorry."

"No, you don't have to be. Tell you what, week's almost

over, then it's you and me the rest of the summer. And Dina . . . Mom . . . but mostly us." I managed to force a short laugh out of her.

"You don't have to do that. I'm not asking you to—"

"I'm offering. In fact, I insist. All right? We'll go hiking, sailing. Maybe Floyd can teach us how to fish, we—"

"No."

"No? No, never mind. I've tried that. You're right, fishing sucks. Shit, I still owe Floyd three hundred dollars."

"For what?"

"It's nothing, stupid pole. We should probably get a move on for now though before Butch and Sundance up there get away."

Chapter 56

I stayed true to my word. We both made a commitment to spend more time together and stuck with it. Harkening back to our mischievous youths, we sometimes acted like complete lawless children that summer, making up for lost time. We even gave Mom fits a time or two, dropping Ginny's kids off on her doorstep, ringing the bell and running like thieves when Tom was on duty and couldn't watch them. One of those times, we didn't make a clean escape. She caught sight of me, ducked behind a tree, peaking back to make sure she found them. I saw her lips move, grumbling at first for falling for that stunt again. Then we exchanged a guilty smile before I took off after Ginny. More than anything, I think she was just on cloud nine that her girls were getting along, even if it meant we were united in cahoots, giving into, and maybe paying homage to, old immature, irresponsible behaviors for a little while.

Props to the work staff who put up with us, as well. Their understanding while I split my time between Ginny and the grown-up business world that I continued training in under Mom's helpful tutelage, was appreciated and rewarded with well-earned bonuses. It was never a dream to be wildly wealthy, anyway. I was happy striving to live by rich-enough-to-get-by means—stashing away modest savings for a family, kids, retirement down the road, thus enjoying the less extravagant luxuries of life in the meantime. The one major malfunction at the inn came when the mercury started to rise to oppressive levels in late July with electricity usages at a first-time taxing high.

"Candles, what about candles? Do you have any—"

"Let's try to keep fire-making methods out of the equation here, Katie. We've only been open for three months, and I'd like to keep the streak going without human error endangering that."

"Good thinking. I'll take someone with me and have a look through storage, see if we can round up any electric lanterns or . . ."

I ran my fingers through my hair frantically. "This can't be happening. The last thing I need is bad reviews because of a stupid power outage."

"Relax." Pedro grasped my shoulder from behind with a calming tone. "Everything is better now."

"Is it fixed? Are we back on—"

"No, no. I meant relax, my date with that girl who was here with her family last week is back on. She just called."

"Pedro . . ." I rolled my eyes.

"What?" He raised his hands, clowning around with a lit-up face. "You told me to keep you posted, remember? I thought you were interested in my situation."

I couldn't help but chuckle as he started to walk away.

"I swear to God, your situation is going to be downgraded to unemployed if I don't see some lights soon."

He held his hand up, strutting away. "Have no fear m'lady. The problem has been isolated in the depths of ye olde establishment."

"What?"

"The fuse boxes in the basement. Ye shall have light by the eve of . . ."

"Yeah, yeah, King Arthur, just keep me posted."

"Okay, okay, I'm here. Sorry, Gracie started throwing a little tantrum when I tried to leave. What can I do to help out?"

"Nothing, I guess. Looks like the problem's been identified. They're working on it now. So we're just waiting. We should be back up and running before . . . dark? If my medieval-to-modern English translation is accurate."

"Well, I'm here now. You and Katie had plans, right? No reason to hang around here."

"Are you sure, Ginny? I can stay if—"

"No, please, go. I'll let you know when the power's back on. Have a good time. Anything else while you're gone?"

"Yeah, I'd like to comp the guests for the inconvenience. I was thinking we could print up some vouchers for free lunch or dinner somewhere for every room. What do ya think?"

"Better yet, how 'bout I call Brandon over at The Oar? They always have gift certificates on hand."

"That'll work, and maybe if you could do some research on industrial generators so I can avoid any more panic attacks over this in the future? That'd be great."

When I wasn't manning the front desk, building guest relations, or traversing the pleasures and pitfalls of the business, I spent a lot of leisure time on the water. The old sailboat our families purchased together and shared custody of was given a full inspection and sea-worthy bill of health. Sailing wasn't the only long-lost pastime I was dedicating time to. My skin hadn't seen this impressive level of a full-body tan in ages, and while I was busy addressing my mental and physical well-being and enjoying life, rediscovering my youth, Dina and Ginny consistently kept their conspiring heads on a rotating swivel to find me a potential husband number two. I'm pretty sure they had Brianna and Katie on the lookout, as well. I let them have their fun, if for no other reason than to keep Dina's outspoken hopes alive for walking one of us down the aisle and the prospect of more grandchildren. Not that I wasn't looking with mild interest or outwardly declaring myself back on the open dating market. One mishandled love affair gone wrong and everything else under reconstruction or new in my life considered, I wasn't in a fired-up hurry to add romance into the mix just yet.

It had barely been just over a year ago that I was grading tests and doling out gold stars to my third grade students. Now here I was counting stars instead, aka stalking my own social media feeds and online reviews, boosting my confidence with positive feedback and valuable constructive criticisms. I knew I shouldn't get too wrapped up in doing so or put too much stock in such distractions, but I couldn't help myself most times. I find myself fortunate to have been surrounded by family, friends, employees that embodied elements of both, everyone who made that first season special, fun, challenging, and rewarding, but I digress. Nothing in my life has been given or come naturally without sacrifice, especially of the supreme variety.The propensity to be foreboding, having been instilled in me, is a hard way to live. Again, whatever would happen from here, what challenges would arise, how I would react and take it all, would rest on my perspective.

"Elles! Where— Oh, there you are. What are ya doing hanging out in here?"

"Hey sis, I was just—"

"Ick, I'm begging you. Please stop calling me that. Makes me sound like I'm a growth on the back of your neck or something."

"Gross! And with that visual, you've left me no choice."

"Good, now save the office work for later. Come on, everyone's waiting to take this group photo. The staff's outside getting restless. So—"

"I know, I know. I just . . . I needed a quiet minute."

"Why? What's wrong?" Ginny flung the door closed behind her and took a seat with a nervous posture.

"Nothing." I laughed. "Relax, it's been a crazy summer, a crazier year, ya know? I just needed to, I don't know, step back, take a moment to let myself breathe and reflect."

"It has been wild, hasn't it? I mean, look at us, sitting here together like this. And you, you're all Gracie's been talking about all summer. Feels like she just learned to say *mommy* and now it's all *auntie, auntie . . .*"

"I still can't believe you named her after me." I blushed, infatuated.

"Well, truth is, I can't take credit for that."

"What do you mean? It was a sweet gesture—"

"Look, don't flatter yourself too much on my behalf, okay? I mean, Mom did it."

"Wait, so Mom . . ."

"Yeah, well I didn't go running to town hall afterwards to try and change it or anything. Let's just say, first pregnancy, heavily sedated, she definitely pulled an end around on me when I was vulnerable."

"Ginny!"

"They popped her out, the nurse asked what her name was and . . ."

"And . . ."

"Well, what do you want from me? Cayle wasn't about to put up a fight against her, and she had the birth certificate written up before I could even . . . I mean, even if I had wanted to . . ."

"Was it even on your list?"

"Yes, of course you were on . . ." We locked eyes in a momentary, tell-the-truth stare down before we both cracked up. "You were on *a* list, anyway."

"I'll take it. At least I was on your mind. Would you have . . . I mean if you could have . . ."

"Mm, it's a solid sixty-forty. Besides, they put her in my arms, and she looked like a Gracie. How could I take that away from her?"

"Thank you, Ginny."

"Now, can we go take this picture already? I have things to do today."

"Yeah, I'm behind this morning, too. I can't believe Labor Day weekend is here already, and I have to pick up Floyd from the medical center."

"Again?"

"Yeah, his back has been acting up a lot lately, but he insisted he wasn't missing the final season hoorah, and I want him in the picture." I stood up and grabbed my car keys off the desk. "Tell the photographer to hold tight and calm the savages, will ya? I'll bring him back as quick as I can."

Chapter 57

Tom Deiter, the boy I used to love to antagonize, had been the kid who commanded attention by whatever means possible—to a point. Somewhere between my leaving and coming back, he grew into a man stuck in the middle of almost living the life he wanted with the person he wanted to share it with and playing caregiver as runner-up in the wake of someone else's untimely demise. That is an awful, but seemingly accurate, summation of his life. I had been off, not dealing with the loss of my parents. Dina had been dealing with a husband who went off the rails, and Ginny . . . Ginny had been battling all of that and so much more. Poor Tom Deiter had been caught helpless, trapped in the eye of this twisting storm. Through it all, he played his part, waited his turn, and kept his grand plan on hold.

"You guys see anything? What did he say, Elles? Did he say what this was even about?"

"No, just for us to meet him near old harbor. I don't—"

"There's his patrol car." Katie spoke up, pointing out the unoccupied car up ahead on the roadside. We all searched for Tom—me, Ginny, Dina, Katie, and Floyd stuffed into one car, prowling the streets for whatever we were summoned here to see."

"This is ridiculous. I'm not in the mood to play hide-and-seek with this man right now." Ginny rambled. "He's been acting weird all week and—"

"What's that?" Floyd pointed toward the pier, squinting into the rising, blinding sun like the rest of us.

"Is that someone fishing? Ya know what, I don't care. I'm squished. Just park the car so we can get out," Ginny grumbled.

Floyd was the first one out of the back seat. He held his

hand over his eyes like a visor and peered at the silhouette of a figure in the distance. An arm rose high in the air and waved. "I think that's him. Look."

"What is he doing?" Dina snarled.

"What's that stuff all over the pier?" Katie added.

The answers became clearer the closer we got. Tom stood at the far end of a decorated long wooden path; a narrow white carpet stretched from the tips of our toes all the way to the bottom of his soles. All the way down, sprinkled Chrysanthemums aligned either side, creating a gorgeously fashioned, out-of-place aisle. The five of us stood there staring, all of us, including Tom, perfectly still. Ginny took a wary step backward like a skittish cat and turned to us, not knowing what to do with herself.

"Oh, my God," Katie murmured.

"What . . . what is he . . . Elles, what is he doing?" Ginny stuttered.

I grabbed Ginny by both shoulders and aimed her body in the right direction. I nudged her forward a few more steps, with resistance, until her feet touched the carpet, then I slid around behind her. She looked across the pier, down at her feet, then at me with breathless fear. *Walk!* I mouthed with encouragement. "That way." Dina followed up, flicking her hand forward repeatedly.

It must have felt like a mile-long walk for Ginny to think about what was waiting at the other end. We watched in suspense as she walked the length of that pier with trembling reservation, like a bashful schoolgirl crossing a sixth-grade gymnasium floor in the thick of twirling lights syncing to a slow song in a passive attempt to ask her first crush to dance. It was an adorably priceless moment, and Katie and I simultaneously pulled our cell phones from our pockets. While Dina was captivated watching the scene play out, entranced in a teary-eyed, beaming state of supreme glee, as were we, the two of us held our cameras up capturing perfect opportunistic candid shots when Ginny wasn't peeking back.

"Goddammit, I'm gonna cry," Katie choked out. I relaxed my arms, pinning my phone to my chest with both hands. Dina leaned in and glared at me accusingly.

"What?" I squawked. I held my hand out in defense. "I had nothing to do with— Okay, Tom and I were talking, a while back, and the subject was brought up. I might have urged him to move things along, that's all."

"Whether he wanted to or not, that boy never stood a chance."

"Shut up, Floyd!" the three of us proclaimed.

They met, taking each other's hands, and Tom bent down to a knee. We were too far away to catch the words, but nevertheless, witnessing the proposal in silence was purely magical. We waited for the confirming head nod and subsequent binding kiss, and gave them a round of applauding cheers.

* * *

"Hey!" Loyal hollered to me.

"Jesus Christ! You scared the—"

"What the hell are you doing sitting way out here? The wedding's tomorrow and Ginny's freaking out, wondering where you are. By the way, I may not know her well enough yet, but I'm pretty sure she threatened my life if I didn't hunt you down and bring you back."

She had found me alone in my car, lost in the past. "Sounds like her. Sorry, I guess I was just remembering—"

"That there's a bridezilla about to implode if you're not there? Let's go. Get your retrospective ass in gear. I wanna live!"

She pushed off the car door, and I looked away. "Oh, my God, Elles, I'm . . . I'm so stupid. I just realized it's the anniversary of—"

"It's okay. I'm good."

"Are you sure? I'm sorry."

"Loyal, it's fine, really. There's just a lot going on right now. You gonna follow me back or what? We can't have Ginny storming the island in a rage of destruction, can we?"

"Okay, okay. I'm gonna get in my car and you . . . you just rear-end me one time or just give me a tap or something. Back it on in before you drive away. Do what you need to do. I deserve it for being so thoughtlessly insensitive."

"Loyal, I love you, but if you don't get in your car and drive, I'll feed you to Ginny myself. Okay?"

"Okay, okay. I'm going. Ya try to offer a little solace. At least now I know where the menacing gene comes from."

A year had gone by, two summer seasons in the books, and there I was with nothing better to do than find myself back at the scene of the proposal, visualizing the whole thing. Ginny and I were both on the cusp of life-changing landmarks. Hers was a little bigger than mine. This was her wedding day. And it was being held, where else? No, not there, sorry. If it were only possible. The Garity House garden is a bit small and ill-equipped for such events. Not to mention, there are much more aesthetically pleasing locations. A temporary venue had been built, a grand, spacious platform overlooking the beach and Great Salt Pond. Walls of framework-lined lattice were assembled, adorned with the finest lace drapery and string lights from corner to corner and ceiling to floor. A built-in bar was placed opposite the head table, where the water view served as the backdrop through the picture window–sized cutout.

A chandelier hung from the cathedral-high rafters over the centralized dance floor. The entire structure was covered with a thin sky-blue twinkling veil that caught the moonlight when the sun went down. All of that was for the reception, of course. The ceremony itself took place on the beach below. My role as maid of honor came with the unenviable, fought-over and forced-upon duty of giving a speech. To say it was a privilege I did not covet would be an understatement. When my turn to shine came, I took to the stage, mic in hand, with no note cards and shooting blindly from the heartfelt hip. To that end, the one thing I had prepared was to open with a not-so-innocent joke. Palming a full glass of water in my hand, I chugged it down, displaying the index finger of that hand to the bewildered crowd. I set the empty glass on the nearest table and let out an extended, refreshing *ahh*."

"Hello, everyone, and welcome to the official start of a wonderful journey. This is, um . . . this is gonna be emotional for me. And let the record show, I was fully against getting up here in front of all of you this evening and doing this. I assure you, I have prepared. That was my fifth straight glass of water, so I have successfully guaranteed this will be short and sweet. Any willing replacements, please stand by. If all goes according to plan, I'll be tagging out in two minutes." At least it drew a generous smattering of all the quality laughs I had not bargained for. "This is hard, for a lot of reasons, and please forgive me, but there's a story that goes along with this toast. Um, as it turns out, I guess I'm partly to blame and partly to thank for this long overdue union finally coming to fruition."

Ginny and I swapped smiling glances. "When me and Ginny were growing up, we were best friends. We got along like best friends do, played like best friends. We disagreed, fought like best friends do. Most of all, we always made up, had each other's backs, like the best of friends are supposed to do. Unfortunately, as fate is known to do, circumstances beyond our control, and a truth that we didn't know, was the only unbearable force that broke us apart. *That* is where the blame part comes in but this is a wedding, one of the happiest days of her—of our—lives. So this is the part where I move on from grimmer times and talk about happiness and the fact that I deserve all the credit for all of us being here today. Don't worry, Ginny. I'm just kidding. It's a solid seventy-thirty."

This time we traded winks with a side of blushing smiles. "My apologies to everyone. That's an inside joke. As you can all maybe tell, I didn't write any sort of formal speech for this occasion. How could I? There's a significant gap in our friendship that only time can heal. We're on the right track. We missed out on so much together, the tougher trials of teenage years, becoming women, everything that entails, all the messy confusing parts, blah-blah-blah. More important than any of that, we missed out on sharing our lives . . . together. Then, as instantaneously as we were separated, fate brought us back together again. Again by circumstances beyond our control, or maybe"—I cocked my head and appealed to the heavens above—"maybe by spirits, despite our lack of control. What I learned, what I think we both learned, was that Carrington-Garity women are stronger than we gave ourselves credit for. As it turns out, I've only known this beautiful bride over here for less than half my life. What I will always remember, is the girl I grew up with, my best friend, my protector. We've been through an awful lot, together and apart, haven't we? What some of you may not know is that handsome transformation of a man sitting beside her is nothing like the boy I grew up with. That boy I grew up with clearly had eyes for that girl I grew up with ever since we were kids. There's a chance I was the only one who saw it then, or perhaps, of the three of us, the only one who would have ever admitted it then. It's said that adversity makes us stronger. A good friend reminded me of that not long ago. Well, I've never been prouder to share and celebrate a day like this with two people that I've spent less than half my life with, and whom it could be argued, I only barely know. But we're getting there. We're on the right track now."

I reached for my glass of champagne. I raised it high in the air to signify the coming toast and lowered it. "We reunited as friends often do. We are working on knowing each other again. We are working on the making-up part. As for that truth that we once upon a time didn't know, it had everything to do with the bond we always felt and now . . . the things that tore best friends apart will never destroy what we really are. From here on out, we may often get along, play together, and now work together. There will be times when we'll disagree and argue, but we are better than best friends. We are sisters, and nothing and nobody will ever keep us apart again." I raised my glass again and smiled with teardrops down my cheeks. “At long last, to the happy couple. If we’ve learned anything, let nothing or nobody separate us. We are only getting stronger. Cheers.”

Chapter 58

I don't mean to brag, but I would say I hit the nail point-blank and damn hard on the head as far as winging a maid of honor speech off the top of my head, which I initially wanted no part of. I started with a joke that landed and ended with not a dry eye in the room. Not bad for using the spotlight to bundle a tribute to the bride and groom with a backstory summary of our lives that exercised some demons in what amounted to a themed toast of even brighter days to come. Too bad my bladder didn't hold up as well. I couldn't hand the microphone back over to the DJ fast enough, and I saw Ginny curling her finger, motioning me over. I clenched up, shuffling over to the table in front of her. I cut her off before she could speak, acknowledging the pleased approval plastered on her face followed by an excusing plea.

"Thanks, but can this wait? I think I jinxed myself. I really gotta pee." When I exited the bathroom stall at The Oar, I found Ginny leaning over a sink, fixing her face in the mirror.

"All better now?"

"So much better." I let out an exhale of satisfied relief.

"Good." She straightened up and stood before me, embracing me with a loving hug. "Thank you. That was beautiful." She pulled away and hit me with a swift backhanded swipe across my arm. "Jerk."

"Ow!"

"Your stupid speech ruined my makeup job."

"Um, your welcome?"

She leaned in close to the mirror, dabbing at her cheeks and around her eyes. "God, I look like hell, real eye candy for the honeymoon."

"Oh, you'll be fine. What time does your flight leave?"

"6:00 a.m."

"Yikes."

"Tell me about it. By the time this party's over, we'll be doing all our sleeping on the plane. Is Ryan still coming with you to drop us off at the airport?" I bit my lip and rolled my eyes a little, humming softly. "Come on, you know you guys hit it off. Why are you fighting it?"

"I dunno, cautious jitters, I guess. I rushed into where you're at the first time, ya know?"

"Well, whatever, it's your call. All I'm saying is you make a cute couple. Just take it easy. Give it a chance, that's all. He gets too serious too fast, let me know. I'll kick his ass."

"Yeah." I rubbed my arm. "I believe you would. You need to set up a Zoom session with Loyal, by the way. You got a real aggression thing goin' on."

"It's all part of my charm. We better get back out there before my reception becomes a search party. Although we could walk a little slow. I'm dreading the father-daughter dance segment."

"Why? Mom said she'd fill in."

Ginny headed for the restroom door and sneered back at me. "Obviously you've never seen the woman dance. Lift my train, will ya? Watch the door."

"She could start. I could have Coot or someone cut in."

"No thanks. I've seen him dance, too. He could spin me around like a top. He's still surprisingly nimble for his age."

"Then I guess you're stuck with me."

She stopped in her baby footsteps as we negotiated our way through the door. "Yeah, 'cause that won't be weirder. No, ya know what? Let's do it."

"Really?"

"You pick the song. Nothing sappy, something fast and jazzy. If we're doing this, we might as well swing it and show 'em how it's done."

As is typically the case around here, especially in the offseason, the party lasted late into the night. Ginny stayed awake for the charter boat ride across the sound but conked out fast a few miles into the drive on the other side. We said our goodbyes at the curbside check-in, and Ryan and I hopped on a Cessna and landed back on the island by midmorning.

I had met Ryan three months prior. An extravagant, badly matched blind date ended when the girl he was with bailed, pulling a disappearing act after lunch and leaving on the next ferry.

I had felt bad for the guy when I heard him at the front desk jokingly asking for recommendations for a recently ditched bachelor with a day and a half left to fill. I stepped in and offered a few suggestions, along with an afternoon guided tour, on the house, and things took off from there. A week later, he turned up again. Undeterred by the fact that The Garity House had no vacancies, he snuck in on a last-minute bed and breakfast cancellation on the other side of town. This time, the outing was on him. He also posted a glowing five-star review, boasting about the *incredibly attractive guest services ambassador to paradise*—his words, not mine—so how could I resist?

In a somewhat shocking development, that was the summer that Katie, feeling a little left out of finding a steadier situation herself, relationship-wise, started changing her stripes. She spent a considerable amount of time outside of work making herself noticeable within the heavily congested public beach and club scenes. Business at the inn was booming. Year two and the staff had everything running smoothly. I took the opportunity to step back a little myself, find a good balance by broadening my personal life. It is amazing what results can come from hurling your life into a tailspin, even if it's done without one shred of foresight, or if out of necessity, in search of clarity.

The day Ginny and Tom left for their honeymoon happened to be the same day, one year ago, that they were engaged. It sticks with me, and always will, for two very different reasons, because two very conflicting things happened on that day. Ryan and I were engaging in a semi-long-distance relationship. He came down on Fridays after work and stayed with Mom and me on weekends. He was there that day, a Saturday. After a long, eventful night, a tiresome drive, and a short flight of our own, we had brunch and tucked ourselves into bed for a much-needed rest. Within minutes I was zapped like a burned-out light. I had never slept so soundly, unmoving, in all my life. Then again, I had never dreamed so vividly, either. It was so indescribably real, so alive, as though I were there. My mind was wide awake and alert in a weirdly calm physical sense, adrift in another realm, visiting a parallel reminiscent world while my body slept.

* * *

"Engaged! I can't believe it! Let's see it, come on." We huddled around Ginny once she made it back to us. She was almost floating back down the pier with an exuberant bounce of disbelief in her step and an expression etched on her face to match. She presented her shaking, newly bejeweled hand and finger for us to behold.

"Oh, like you ain't seen it before, Elles," Tom taunted. Suddenly three sets of eyes zeroed in on me.

"Hey, I told you the subject was brought up. Besides, I didn't see it in the daylight the first time. It's gorgeous!"

"Well, it's about time," Dina asserted. "You put this all together yourself?"

"Mostly. I may have had a little help with the arrangements." We all turned to Floyd, standing suspiciously quiet behind us with a guilt-ridden smirk, and we moaned in stereo.

"Floyd Gresham, I am impressed," I remarked.

"Well, if you all don't mind, now that the cat's out of the bag, I'm gonna get on back and get a jump on the lunch prep before I go home and take a little nap. Feelin' a bit run down lately."

"Well hold on, Floyd, I'll give you a lift back to—"

"No, no. You already had a carload comin' here. Let the lovebirds ride alone, and I'll walk myself back. Nice cool day anyway." He slid between us and reached out to Tom with an open hand. "Congratulations, Officer, on what will no doubt prove to be the greatest"—he shifted his eyes to Ginny—"and, may I say, finest lookin' capture of your career."

"Thank you, Floyd. Get yourself some rest. And, uh, if you're still offerin', I could use a hand with those building plans for the wedding, I was talkin' about."

"Mrs. soon-to-be Deiter." He pinched the brim of his hat and tipped it to Ginny and started his walk.

"Plans? What . . . ?" Ginny's curiosity spiked.

"Oh, no. I been puttin' this off way too long to give away all my secrets. Only thing you get from me today is that shiny rock you're wearin'. Well, we better get this lady home and out of the cold. I'll, uh, clean up here, if you all don't mind giving Ginny a—"

"Not a chance, Tom Deiter." Dina reprimanded him for even thinking of finishing that thought. "You heard what Floyd said. You lovebirds take a hike. There's a couple kids that might like to hear the news. The girls and I will restore the pier to its former boring glory and drop the flowers off later. Now, go."

It didn't take very long for word to spread. By noon whispers and aspirations for a celebratory, ladies-only dinner party at Katie and Brianna's was already catching fire throughout the inn and gaining momentum. Not to be outdone, the guys conspired to haul Tom off to Fiddler's for an evening of drinks, bar games, overall rowdy behavior, and questionable decision-making—from the scattered reports we were hearing. On this, we decided to take the out of sight, out of mind position and go with: what was good for the geese was their business, so long as they kept their noses out of ours. It's not like we had anything close to saintly intentions of gathering around a table and playing a nice, civilized game of cards or acting like the responsible, more mature adults—far from it.

What we had brewing was a disorganized prelude, an *un*ladylike, language-spewing and undignified bachelorette party warm-up of biblical proportions. A fitting analogy since, if the night had gone on uninterrupted, I have no doubt the bowl-hugging accompanying phrase *Oh, God* would have passed through everyone's lips the next day, among other unmentionable things. Just as well. This dinner stunk of a convenient excuse to throw a season-ending bash, anyway. It was still September.We had plenty of time to divide and conquer the two and give them each the appropriate attention to detail they deserved.

A second bottle of wine had been freshly uncorked and the music notched up a few decimals when the telephone rang. Katie squeezed through the dancing bodies in the living room to answer it. Jamie, the Inn's night-shfit desk clerk shouted out, "If that's about any of the boys, let's just have Coot start checkin' 'em into the steel cage motel, and we'll pick up their hungover asses tomorrow!"

Katie covered the receiver with both hands and cupped it to her ear to hear better. I didn't pay her all that much attention when she belted out over the music, "Elles, it's Floyd!"

"Tell him I'll call him tomorrow!"

"Elles . . ." Her voice cracked with a horrified sense of urgency, and the ghostly look on her face said it all.

The rest of that night was a surreal blur. Just as the reality of what was happening set in, I sat up in my bed, jolted awake by the sheer gravity of the memory. In the dark, I folded the covers over and sat on the edge, brushing the hair out of my face.

"Hey hon, everything okay?" The raspy voice on the other side of me slurred.

"Yeah, go back to sleep. I'm gonna get some air." I felt for a necklace on the nightstand and fastened it around my neck. I put my robe on and waddled my groggy seven-and-a-half-months pregnant self out to the kitchen for a bottle of water from the fridge. I ducked into the living room and reached up on the fireplace mantle for the urn.

"Which spot is it this time?"

"Near North Point, I think."

"Cold outside, should put a jacket on."

I stood there, already shaking off a shiver, while Cody got my coat from the closet and helped me put it on, hitching it up over my shoulders snugly.

"It's not just you we need to keep warm." He planted a soft slow kiss on my forehead and massaged my back. "Hey, it's a long walk out there. You sure you don't want me to go with you this time?"

I thought about it in the time it took me to work my swollen feet into my slide-ons and politely rejected the offer. "No.Thank you, though. The sun'll be up soon."

"You've been waking up to this same nightmare every year for the past five years, even when you were with that, um . . ."

"Ryan."

"Ryan, yeah. Sure wish there was something I could do to help."

I kissed him back on the cheek and touched his shoulder. "It's not a nightmare, just an annual reminder. And you are helping, just by understanding and supporting me. Will you get a hold of Mrs. Lawson for me in a little while, have her get class started for me, call the school and tell them I'll be late?"

"You got it."

I grabbed my car keys off the hook around the corner and started out the door.

"Hey!"

I stopped to look back.

"Don't be having our baby out there on the beach.

Sandy's not on our short list of names."

I smiled and tossed him an appreciative, loving wave as I left.

Chapter 59

Floyd Fremont "Monte" Gresham. I had never known his middle name or that he even had one, not to mention a former nickname. I found his lock box of documents and forms of identification in his closet in accordance with the letter he left behind. Floyd passed away the day Ginny and Tom got engaged. That was the phone call at Katie's. The doctors described it as *due to complications.* In the end, Floyd succumbed to underlying conditions as a result of long-term injuries sustained in the plane crash. That's about all I could stand to hear, anyway. I guess that's fancy medical talk for *He wasn't such a lucky survivor after all.* He just managed to somehow postpone the inevitable until he was satisfied that the collateral damage of Stephen's selfishness, that being mostly me, was going to be okay.

The truth is, I really don't know how okay I was, if at all. His death hit me hard. Maybe down deep, knowing he wasn't quite right physically, I had expected it eventually. Maybe, and it may have been a product of denial and positive thinking clouding my head, I had wanted Floyd to have the same chance at redemption that I had. The damage that was done, the people whose lives were all affected by someone else's actions, none of it that he endorsed, Floyd Gresham was okay with being a simple handyman. He was the happiest of grumps to ever grace our little town, pun fully intended. Hell, he might've had it better than any of us on this island when I think about it, and I still do to this day, even with the husband, kids, and grandchildren. Floyd found a way to not only fit in, but endear himself to us, long before I was back in the picture.

He was in and out of the medical center a lot that summer, and I regret that I didn't give it much thought. I was busy with a new business and fulfilling the destiny that I devoted myself to make happen. I stayed in constant touch with his doctor on his disabling condition. I was aware of the treatments, aware of the so-called possible deteriorating conditions. I'm sure I didn't want to believe they could be as grim as all of that. I spent a lot of time with him the last week he was in, before the engagement. He was immobile at the time, but he otherwise showed no sign of slowing down. He was anxious to get back on his feet and get back to work. He and Dina had collaborated on the menu, and he was excited at the chance to implement it. He brought his old buddy, his mentor, in to do this with, someone to take his place if ever . . . I should have seen it then.

"Here ya go, Floyd, no medical center or hospital-esque food for you today." I cleaned off his bedside tray and set the containers of food on it. I wheeled it over his lap and raised his bed up from the flat position for him to enjoy. He opened the lids, peeked inside, and inspected the contents, sniffing and contemplating. He rolled his eyes at me as if to ask the question I saw coming. "I didn't make it, ya old—"

"I didn't say a damn thing," he grumbled, innocently."

"Yeah, yeah, you didn't have to. I also brought you a newspaper, and some of the flowers are from Katie."

"Flowers," he scoffed, snubbing his nose at them.

"Flowers, yes. When someone brings them to a person, say in your situation, it means *I'm thinking of you, get better soon*. Where do you want me to—" He stopped short of taking the first bite to roll his eyes again. "Never mind, I'll put 'em on the windowsill, where you can't reach them." I made myself at home in the large cushy chair in the corner beside his bed and turned on the television, flipping through channels to find a baseball game.

"How's service goin' over at the inn?" he asked, filling his face.

"You tell me."

He looked down at the spread for a moment and

laughed, shaking his head. “Yeah, makes sense. Damn it, he always could outcook me. You get those new desserts rolled out and—”

“Floyd, they are a hit. Don’t you worry.”

“Just tryin’ to give you my best, is all. I didn’t spend all those days, all those hours, workin’ my tail off to help fix that place up right just to see it flutter or fail.”

“Well, it’s more than fluttering. Guests are flying through the doors, getting a good night’s sleep, and raving about the meals. And you worked your tail to the bone, which is why you need to not worry about what’s going on over there for now and rest.”

“Yes ma’am.” He complied. “Been raining some this week. You—”

“The junkyard is covered and secure, Cap’n Spare Parts. Good lord, Floyd, can we talk about something else other than —”

“Thank you . . . for takin’ care of things, seein’ that my place is kept neat.”

“I wouldn’t go as far as to say neat. But you’re welcome.”

“How’s . . . how’s, uh . . .”

“Ya know, you’re making it almost impossible for me to pay attention to this game here, Floyd. My God, do you ever shut up?” My jabbing humor was half-sincere. Until I met Floyd, I’m not sure I ever knew what a shortstop was, or a can of corn that didn’t come from the grocery store straight into my cupboard, or understood the satisfaction of yelling, *That was outside the box. He didn’t even get the bat off his shoulders! Are you blind?*

Somehow, I had inadvertently become a sports fan when I wasn’t looking to add it to my short list of hobbies. I had watched enough ball with Floyd to know that when a conversation got stale, when he had good intentions but nothing much substantial to say, all I had to do was shift the focus to the field. Floyd wasn’t much of a conversationalist. He had his moments. He preferred to save the talking until there was a skill to teach or DIY self-sustaining lesson to be taught. We shared a lot of those moments bringing the inn up to code and inhabitable again. For a simple blue-collar man, that's where he shined, when the chatter was of a deeper, more meaningful nature. We sat there that day in each other's company for nearly two and a half hours, socializing through trading commentary relevant to the game. Around the start of the seventh inning stretch I noticed him attempting not to stare at me out of the corner of his eye and failing.

"What's on your mind, Floyd?" I asked, as he seemed to be of a rare mind to want to talk.

"Oh, I dunno. Guess I'm just think' 'bout everything we've done. Whatcha made of yourself."

I indulged his sudden need to chat, just for kicks. I picked up the remote, switched the television off, curled my legs up under me in the chair like a gossip girl, and turned toward him. It was all I could do not to crack myself up as he turned his head away to sigh in secret.

"Oh, hell," he mumbled.

I flipped the TV back on and hit mute to humanely end a chunk of his suffering. "You sure that's all you got to say, Floyd?"

When he turned his head back again, I saw the gaze of a proud father, the sincerity in his eyes, mouth slightly gaped in wonderment. "Glad to see you get your life back."

"I never lost it, Floyd. I just . . . stopped really living it for a while."

"I wish I'd had a chance to know your— If they could see you now. They'd be so—"

"I know."

"Do ya?"

"Ya know, it's funny. After I moved away, I didn't think about it much at all, if ever. I didn't let myself. I robbed myself of emotions. Sometimes at night, I would catch my mind going to that place, and I'd put a stop to it. Then other times I would feel guilty about it, try to make myself cry to make up for it.

They weren't gone if I didn't believe it. Even though they were. Stupid, huh?"

"Not any more stupid than me, when I used to see that accident in my head night after night, replay it over and over, tryin' to change it, make it so I did more, makin' it so I never took off to begin with. Wake up and everything be back to the way it was. You ever think about that? Ever dream about that?"

"Not anymore. Got too much good stuff goin' on. You got too much good stuff goin' on, too."

"Yeah, head chef of The Garity House Inn. Who'da thunk it?"

"Well, I hope that's not all you're aiming for."

"Whatcha mean?"

"Oh, come on, Floyd. There's room on this island for one more restaurant if you and Manny ever wanna start something up."

"What and leave you high and dry?"

"It was just a thought. Something down the line to think about. You know I'd hate to lose you, but ya gotta keep your options open."

"Think I'll stay where I'm at, if it's all the same to you."

"Well, whatever you want, Floyd. I guess I'll just have to be content with The Garity House world dominance for the next say . . . thirty, thirty-five years 'til I'm ready to retire. Or until you make that move and put my food service out of business." I got up from the chair, stretching. "But to do that you gotta get yourself better. Doctor said more exercise could do ya some good, too. So, guess what?"

His eyes widened. "Oh, no."

"They're sayin' if you're a good boy, they might release you tomorrow. Long walks on the beach to start, with me, or me and Ginny. Maybe even Katie will—"

"You ain't funny. Get your ass on outta here before I ring for security."

I grabbed the flowers off the windowsill. "She sent you this arrangement and everything." He flashed a dirty look. "I'll just, uh, I'll take these with me."

"Yeah, you go ahead and do that."

"Hey! I said a *good* boy. Night, Floyd."

Chapter 60

He knew something was up. He felt it. I submit that Floyd knew that his *time* was almost up. Something was going on, something lying dormant in his soul until it was time for him to go, that only he was privy to. I should have seen the signs. I could have spent more time with him. Aren't those the after words everyone who has ever lost someone says? It's not just about me. This story, none of this, was ever just about me. That is precisely why I object to the notion that this is a comeback story. This is a come-*together* story that *involves* me. And it is about everyone around me. For Floyd, all I know, all I believe, is that for his role in this mess, he received a stay of eternal absolution. His delay was a stroke of merciful divine intervention.That is how I see it. We are better people for it. He left us, a better person for it. That is how I will remember him.

Floyd had started a salvage business of sorts. Whereas we can be dependent on essential supply reserves to make daily life normal, he made *himself* essential to an assortment of our needs—whether you had a worn fan belt, appliances on the fritz, a porch light inconveniently burned out. If a grounded plane at the airport required a new propeller, I kid you not, I saw a few of those protruding out from under his tarps. Hell, if you tore your rotator cuff while rowing a boat on the pond, he probably had one of those lying around somewhere. That would just be creepy, so I retract that hypothetical with full apologies. My point is this: he wasn't just a man waiting around to die or hoping I would come home so he could repair someone else's major screwup.

I helped fix that when I told Stephen, in no uncertain terms, to go, *insert expletive here,* himself and to stay the hell away from us. Dina helped that cause first when she cut him loose to find another life anywhere else, and Ginny did the same.

We were *all* okay eventually—though it took some delayed reactions and time to get there. Tom and Ginny brought a child of their own into the world, a girl they named Skylar Rose. Tom didn't run for sheriff. Instead, he completed the arduous hours of pilot training and passed his certification. He flies the puddle jumpers to and from the island while also serving on the town council. In addition to her busy working-mother life, Ginny won State Teacher of the Year one time and has never let me forget it. She had a duplicate of her award printed, framed, and hung on one on my walls for the sole purpose of rubbing it in. Always one to keep us on our toes, Katie threw us all for a loop. Funny how an initial living arrangement of unforeseen interest worked out. She and Brianna have been a self-professed common law couple for what feels like forever now.

* * *

"Well, fancy running into you way out here this time of mornin'."

"Three guesses, right? Let's see, Ginny, Dina, or Cody sent you out here. Mornin' Coot."

"Mornin', just doin' my rounds, honest. By no one's sneaking request."

"I might have bought that, too, unless you've forgotten you're retired."

"I do. I am, and I ain't *that* senile yet. This job's about more than law breakers and keepin' the peace, 'specially startin' this time of year. It's about the preservation and welfare of the land and everybody on it, includin' you two."

"So, you're still working, just on a volunteer basis now, that it?"

He caught up to me, stood at my side, and rested both hands on his hips. "Do this job as long as I have, servin' the community and all, it's second nature. Just 'cause I *officially* stopped doin' the job don't mean I can turn off carin', watchin' after that same land, those same people, as easily."

"That's very noble of you, Coot. Now all we need is a whole new young generation of locals just like you."

"Oh, I think we're in good hands."

He lay his hand gently on my belly and rolled his eyes up at me." Looks like you've gotten us off to a good start."

I blushed and started to walk along the beach with my feet ankle deep to the rising tide.

"Hey, you!" a voice called out. I looked over to see Loyal walking down the beach toward me. She broke into a jog to catch up.

"Loyal? Where did you come from? What are you—"

"Flew in last night, crashed at Katie's. I wanted to surprise you."

"Loyal, it's— You came out here this early looking for—"

"I wanted to catch you before you went to work, school, or wherever you . . . You're still a hard person to track down. Cody told me where I could find you. Good morning, Coot."

He tipped his head with a wink and took one last glimpse at the sunrise.

"Well, I got habitual rounds to finish. Gotta keep fit somehow. I'll see the two of you around."

Coot walked away, and Loyal took a few steps back, looking at me from head to toe with the biggest grin.

"Flew in, huh? Loyal, what are you staring at? Like you've never seen a—" Her cheeks got puffier as her smile intensified. "Oh, God, you weirdo. Please tell me you didn't come all the way here just to—"

"Can I touch it? Just one . . ." I stood still while she slipped her hand inside my jacket and touched my belly. She shot me an ecstatic look and gasped. "He kicked, or . . . she."

"Aah, see there, my baby's smart—senses danger."

That's when Loyal spotted the urn in my other hand, partially hidden by the bump.

"Oh, guess I'm not just battling lady hormones here,

huh? Maybe this wasn't such a spur of the moment trip, after all. I didn't realize it was—"

"It's fine, Loyal. Fifth year anniversary . . . could probably use the moral support, anyway. So . . ."

"So . . . what?"

"Loyal, I appreciate the lie, but you don't make last-minute trips for no reason. What's up?"

"Can't a girl just wanna take a walk on the beach, keep her oldest and dearest friend company?"

"Sure, and Jack is . . ."

"Look, this isn't about—" I side-eyed her with a hard bluff-calling stare. "It's not *just* about—"

"What happened?" I sighed.

"Hey, contrary to your newfound motherly instincts, I didn't come here to talk about my personal life, ma, okay? But if you must know—"

"Yeah, well, if it is motherly instincts, you only have yourself to blame. You were always way better at helping solve other people's problems than your own."

"Oh, yeah? Well, you're right, but I've gotten better. I—"

"Besides, Jack was here last week. You're a little late."

"That little shit. He said he was going out with some friends to the bar or—"

"He did, it just wasn't exactly down the street."

"So, I guess you know that—"

"Yeah."

"We're better off as bitter friends. You know what I mean. We just work better that way. Hey, if it makes you feel better, the whole thing was very symbolically ceremonious.

"How's that?"

"Well, we made a weekend of it, flew back to Vegas for the de-loping, had the Elvis impersonator sing "Heartbreak Hotel" while he tore the marriage certificate into bits and pieces. Then we gambled away our celebration budget, headed on down to skid row, and caught a cab back to the airport."

We looked at each other, serious at first, then broke out in a tight-lipped *What can ya do?* kind of laughter.We came to a point near some larger rocks, and I stopped, holding the urn in front of me. I started to take another step and Loyal reached out, put her own hands on the urn, and took it gently from me. "Here! Let me." I stood there and watched as she sprinkled some of Floyd's ashes in the wet sand around the rocks. When she was done, she backed up beside me and took my hand. We shared a silent moment of remembrance with the morning sun casting a blanket of warmth over us. I squeezed her hand first, then she squeezed mine back, as though exchanging a no-words-required message.

"Five years, wow," Loyal noted. "Well, six . . . if you count —"

"I could never have done any of this without you, Loyal." My eyes started to tear up and it spread to her, too. She wiped her eyes and sniffled.

"Well, you can just thank me for all the practice. Ya know, in a few years, when you're the best mom ever."

I turned and leaned in for a hug. As soon as we touched, we both felt quick swift kicks, and Loyal jumped back as I giggled. "Told ya, kid knows trouble."

As the new day dawned, we started the long walk back. Another chapter of my life written, page turned, season changing.

"I talked to my parents the other day," she blurted out of nowhere.

"You— Parents? I don't think I've ever heard you mention—"

"I mean, I am getting older, wiser, ya know? Plus this friend of mine who started getting all in touch with her feelings a few years ago started rubbing off on me or somethin'. So . . ."

"Well, I'm happy for ya, Loyal. I—"

"Hey, what the hell was that reaction, anyway? *Parents?* Of course I have . . . What did ya think, I was hatched from some immaculate egg or somethin'? Oh, I cannot wait for this kid to be born. The stories I'll have to . . ."

Chapter 61

No matter how unplanned it was, Loyal showing up that morning, of all days, was perfect timing. For the record, if it appeared, in the immediate aftermath, or even five years later, that I was taking Floyd's death well, or better than the rest, that is only because of how much I had grown. It is a testament to what I learned. Loyal and I may have been stuck in life's holding pattern for a while, but neither of us would have come through it as strong without the other. I just moved forward first and made sure to pull her along with me, instead of leaving *anyone* behind like before. There was a time that I had lived my life in gloom, a time I had buckled under the weight of tragedy and grief. The load I held on to, the hurt, the wreckage, the void, I had allowed it all to keep me down, to shut Elles down.

My legs had fallen out from under me, and I collapsed to my knees in shock when Katie broke the news to me. *I'm so sorry, Elles. I'm so sorry. There was nothing they could do. He's gone.* She knew what that blow meant to me. You could hear it in her strained, deflated voice. Every loss is different. Everyone holds their own special place in our hearts. Choices, I had them then, at eleven years old. I didn't know how to sort them out. I bailed. I gave in. I had them this time, too, just over an age threshold into my thirties. I chose perspective. Sure, I mourned his loss but mostly by celebrating his life. The Floyd that I knew, unquestionably, would have wanted that. He would have wanted levity and sarcasm, truth in his eulogy, and that is what I gave him. I couldn't do the old ways anymore. It was too much. Perspective lets me believe that he survived for a reason. Perspective says when I saw my teaching job in possible peril and flipped a switch, when I was talking to myself, placing my life in certain upheaval without a solid plan, that somewhere beyond my conscious understanding, there existed the living, breathing embodiment of an angel on my shoulder.

The easy decision I had made was to scatter his ashes around the shores of the island. The hard part was choosing one spot, so I didn't. I dare say, due to that inability to decide, Floyd Gresham is the most well-traveled deceased man on God's green earth. I'm sure I'm not the first to think of it. So, okay, as unlikely as that may be, at least I made that true on this patch of earth. The piece of him that is left, I keep in a memorial locket I wear around my neck, close to my heart. I refuse to let the events of and surrounding my life define who I was, who I am, and, most definitely, who I will and have become, because fate and father time be damned, I, and I alone, write my own story. That gradual philosophical change in how I think about things and how I respond to any given moment, got me back to where I belonged. Season after season, those doors open to the visiting world, and The Garity House lives on and will do so long after I am gone.

* * *

"Liz! Honey, don't forget the ponchos for the boys in case we're still out on the boat if it starts raining later!" She came clomping down the stairs where I waited at the bottom, a handful of gear in one hand, a pint-sized bundle of blond-haired energy and excitement tugging on the other. I had caught him in midair as he bounded into my arms off the second to last stair.

"I think I've got everything. Brent took the cooler and fishing gear when he left with David. Are you sure Grandma's gonna be okay here by herself?"

"I want Gramma Dina to come, too!" Kevin squealed, jumping up and down.

"You just go park your little butt in the car and buckle up, or you'll be swimming to the boat, mister," I warned, teasing. "She'll be fine. She could use a day off without all the noise and commotion."

"Honestly, Mom, I don't know why you insist on rejecting our offer. The place hasn't been rented yet. It's right on the lake. You and Dad could have a nice little retirement place to yourselves, and Grandma could—"

"Make her own decisions, which echoed my own. I told you. It's nothing personal. We appreciate the offer but we—"

"Belong here. I know, I know. I don't need another history lesson, Mom. I just hate having you guys such a long drive and sail away if anything ever happened, that's all."

"Well, I'll just need you to think positively then. Besides, *if* something were to happen, your brother is more than capable of handling things out here until you arrive to give him a hand. In the meantime, that offer does go both ways. You could—"

"Oh, no. No, I told you before, I'm not the welcome-wagon type. I'm not a people person like you are, always into meeting strangers. I wouldn't mind moving out here if we ever had the chance. I just don't know that I could deal with all the damn tourists invading and littering up—"

"My island." I smiled proudly.

"Yes, your island. I don't know how you and Aunt Ginny put up with it your whole lives, quite honestly. You have your things? We better get moving before *Dad* has all four of us swimming for the boat." I started to giggle as we locked up and headed out the door. "Yeah, ha ha, Mother. I was twelve. I'm never falling for that again. Thought you were hilarious. I still can't believe you made us kids all—"

"You mean your father—"

"Give it up, woman. Dad ratted you out years ago."

I gasped at the accusation. "No, he did— He put me up to it! *Everyone's aboard Elly, Let's go!* That's what he—"

"Yeah, right. I've heard the stories, too. Uncle Tom's told me."

"Uncle— Why would you ever listen to a word that man —"

"Troublemakers, Aunt Ginny and you both. That's what he always said, and I have the childhood to prove it, so don't even . . ."

It was a big day, a big gathering on the pond and the open sea. Loyal and Jack were visiting, too. I do wish those two had made it. Still, Loyal put my marriage record with him to shame. They were together for all of four years. Jack is remarried now, with a wife and one son. I don't think Loyal was ever the marrying type, and she made her peace with it. Too much of the addictive freewheeling, answer-to-nobody lifestyle in her, by her own admission. It was another mutual divorce, at least. She did end up building a successful practice with that college classmate of hers. They rent office spaces from Jack's company and operate on a larger scale these days. Loyal's considering early retirement. I've been told she has a lovely, secluded destination in mind.

As for me, well . . . Let me first add this little tidbit of interesting note. Over the years, living with Dina, and with my limited knowledge of Carrington family lineage, certain pieces of information came to light. She had an older sister named Nellie, the black sheep of the family. Yes, it's a very confusing twist on a couple Ginny and I once believed came from my . . . well, adopted father's side. Turns out Uncle John was well-liked on our side, more so than her. Pretty clever, folks. How's that for long-distance undercover observation? It's no wonder my birth family always knew what I was up to, how and where I was.

I am still going strong alongside Ginny in a long-lasting, reinvigorated teaching career. Cody and I will mark our thirtieth anniversary this coming fall. Elizabeth, our firstborn, never had a tolerance for small-town life. She moved to the mainland, into the city for college, got hitched, and never looked back. Her family's on the frequent visitor program, though, thankfully enough. Charlie hung around, sucked in by a calculatedly fostered knack for an ownership stake in the tourism industry. I drop by from time to time, always willing to fill in where extra hands are needed. I clean rooms, cover the front desk. Or, and this is one of my favorite beneficiary parts, if Cody and I just want to sit out on the deck among the guests any time of day, we are free to relax, stay as long as we want, order up and enjoy an on-the-house meal or two, or three.

I don't look back on any of the tribulations and triumphs I have faced and refer to happy endings. Endings infer something is over. Happy is but one of many emotions, those indefinite and interchangeable iterations of life, and those "ever afters" were conceived for storybooks and Hollywood. If I were to dig deeper than that, I would rather divide the defining eras of my life into thirds: the before, limbo, and the after. Of the three, by no means discounting the others, for me the after is the best. Being in the after reminds me to bask in victories, cherish my fortunes, and trample down the demons that feed my fears. Because I've healed the open wounds. I've embraced and repurposed my ugly scars. I have survived. Alive and *living* drives me to not forget where I have been, what I—what we—overcame.

* * *

"Okay, did the final walk-through, inspections. Looks like we are good to go. I'm gonna grab the keys. Do me a favor and just do one final check of the kitchen, make sure everything is off, and we're— Mom! I didn't expect to see you here. What's goin' on? Something wrong?"

"Hey, Charlie. Everything's fine. I just, um . . ."

"What's up? It's been a long day. We were just about to lock up for the season."

"I know. The place looks great. I was . . . well, I was thinking I would like to close up shop this year? Feeling a little nostalgic, ya know?"

"Um, well, yeah. Yeah, of course. I just sent Brandon to the—"

"I heard. I'll send him out. I haven't done a walk-through in so long. I miss it."

"Okay, but don't take too long."

"I won't, I won't. I just want to stroll through, take a little walk down memory lane. You go. Go on home. We're still on for dinner tonight. Dad and I will see you there."

The truth was, that feeling of nostalgia was there at the end of every season and grew stronger every year. I grew up here. My kids grew up here. My grandchildren, some of them, anyway. This old inn was my salvation. Ginny and I, Dina for a spell, even Katie, all the employees who have come and gone, we all had a helping hand in running it like a well-oiled machine. It never felt like work, though it was a grind. And until I needed to walk away, and my son took over, this was a matriarchal affair. I wanted to lock up because now I could do so without it being an official chore. It is simply for the joy. It is for the echoes of the good times. Just like the first time, I went over every inch. I walked the halls. I didn't hear the silence because all the while my mind was reverberating the daily sounds of never-ending activity.

I meandered through every room, until I got to the one Dina was in that night. At first I stood in the doorway, leaning against the frame. I visualized us sitting on the bed, having our talk, her telling me this was my mother's favorite room. Then the smile in my eyes spread to my entire face. I stepped inside and sat in the same armchair they both had before me. I gazed into the moonlight, fondly lost in the horizon, window dreaming the way I did a long time ago. My name is Elles Grace Garity-Sutton. Save the silly acronyms, please. I'll say again, sixty-some-odd years removed. Thanks again, Mom and Dad. I was born and mostly raised here on this island. This is where, as a girl, I looked beyond the trees with curiosity for other people and places I couldn't see. I never wanted to be anywhere else but here. This is home, the place I will never leave again.

THE END

Made in United States
Orlando, FL
21 August 2024

50620555R10198